THE
FALSE
MIRROR

By Alan Dean Foster
Published by Ballantine Books:

The Black Hole
Cachalot
Dark Star
The Metrognome and Other Stories
Midworld
Nor Crystal Tears
Sentenced to Prism
Splinter of the Mind's Eye
Star Trek® Logs One–Ten
Voyage to the City of the Dead
... Who Needs Enemies?
With Friends Like These ...

The Icerigger Trilogy:
Icerigger
Mission to Moulokin
The Deluge Drivers

The Adventures of Flinx of the Commonwealth:
For Love of Mother-Not
The Tar-Aiym Krang
Orphan Star
The End of the Matter
Bloodhype
Flinx in Flux

The Damned
Book One: A Call to Arms
Book Two: The False Mirror

THE FALSE MIRROR

BOOK TWO OF THE DAMNED

ALAN DEAN FOSTER

A DEL REY BOOK · BALLANTINE BOOKS · NEW YORK

A Del Rey Book
Published by Ballantine Books

Copyright © 1992 by Thranx, Inc.

Library of Congress Cataloging-in-Publication Data
Foster, Alan Dean, 1946–
The false mirror : book two of the damned / Alan Dean Foster.—1st ed.
p.   cm.
ISBN 0-345-35856-2
I. Title.
PS3556.0756F3   1992
813'.54—dc20   91-73136
                                                          CIP

Text design by Holly Johnson

Manufactured in the United States of America

First Edition: April 1992
10 9 8 7 6 5 4 3 2 1

For Harry E. Fischer,
Able-bodied seaman and fellow voyager.

THE
FALSE
MIRROR

——— 1 ———

By the time he was twelve years old, Ranji knew he liked to kill. His parents, naturally, encouraged him.

By the time of the Trials he had added four years of experience, education, and maturity to a great deal of additional height, weight, and strength. With these came confidence in his abilities, a soft-spoken assurance much admired and valued by the rest of the soldier-trainees in his age group.

There was no jealousy among them, that being an alien concept shared by the multitude of monsters whose ultimate goal was the destruction of civilization. Why would anyone be jealous of him? Were they not all striving for the same end, seeking enthusiastically the same results? Achievement among friends was to be applauded, not envied. Who would not wish to have a soldier more skilled in the arts of combat than oneself fighting on his flank?

So each trainee strove to outdo his or her competitors while simultaneously urging them to greater achievement.

Until the monsters arrived on the scene, civilization had been advancing steadily across the cosmos, spreading organization where hitherto had been only chaos. The pace had been slow but gratifyingly inexorable. Occasional setbacks were accepted and taken in stride until ground lost could, as it inevitably was, be regained.

Then a thousand or so years ago the alliance of monsters had been encountered, and everything had changed.

Many were unpleasant to contemplate physically as well as intellectually, while others differed little in appearance from Ranji's own kind. The worst were utterly unpredictable, savage and cunning beyond belief, possessed of a feral intelligence that made them awful to encounter on the battlefield.

With such as these in the vanguard, the alliance of monsters had wreaked considerable havoc. But their recent advances had been halted, the situation stabilized. Soon the civilized peoples would begin pushing them back, rescuing as they advanced those poor, benighted populations who had suffered for centuries under the monsters' dominion.

Ranji and his friends knew this to be inevitable. Their own training both as soldiers and civilized citizens proved it so. No matter how strong, the forces of chaos could never overcome and defeat those of civilization. Not as long as determined fighters like Ranji-aar and his companions continued to rise through the ranks to take their place at the forefront of civilization's defense.

While there was no place in true society for jealousy, room was allowed for pardonable pride. In the fifteen-to-seventeen-year-old cluster, he and his trainee squad repeatedly graded out at or near the top of their class. In fact, on all of Cossuut only one other squad regularly posted scores matching those of Ranji's. That was a group from Kizzmat Township, which lay just on the other side of the Massmari mountains, near the junction of the rivers Nerse and Joutoula. Near enough for a friendly rivalry of reputations to have been invented by the media. As graduation exercises progressed, both squads qualified easily for the planetary finals in their age group.

His mother and father took quiet pride in the effortless qualification of their son and his friends, as they had in all his achievements. Their delight was perhaps magnified somewhat by the fact that neither of them had been a soldier. Ranji's father worked in a factory which produced nanotronic components, while his mother was a teacher. Certainly her tutoring abilities contributed to Ranji's success, as well as to that of his younger brother, Saguio, and his baby sister, Cynsa.

Though jealousy was unknown among the trainees, it was still a good thing that Ranji was not the best at everything. His friend Birachii-uun was stronger, Cossinza-iiv much faster. But in Ranji was found the best combination of warrior attributes, a fact which was reflected in his individual scores. Certainly he was the smartest of his companions.

Though only sixteen, he was often nominated to serve as leader during important exercises. This was almost unheard of. Strategy leaders were inevitably chosen from the ranks of seniors: seventeen- and eighteen-year-olds. Fully conscious of such honors, he carried them well. Coupled with exceptional organizational skills, his drive and determination rarely disappointed those who placed their faith in him. His ability was a fact his peers recognized and applauded.

He took pleasure in his accomplishments because he saw how much they pleased his parents. To him, approbation meant little. He was interested only in the job at hand, and in doing it well. For that reason he looked forward eagerly to the coming graduation finals.

Until those were passed there was always the chance of failing, of not being awarded full soldier status. Even accomplished students like Ranji had been known to crack under the pressure. No opprobrium attached to such individuals. They simply served the war effort in some other fashion more suited to their actual skills.

Ranji was calm and ready. He had no intention of failing. He *could* not fail. Not only did he want, like any healthy member of his species, to be a soldier: he *had* to be. He knew, sensed, felt, that he'd been born to it. To kill and chance being killed in the defense of civilization. To fight the enemy for real, not merely in simulations.

He always tried to approach the schooling simulations in that state of mind, striving to convince himself that he was not participating in simple tests but was actually engaging in combat against the monsters; killing for real, destroying them one after another to protect his civilization, his friends, his world.

Not to mention revenging his real mother and father.

Along with the parents of most of his friends, they had perished when the monsters had invaded and destroyed Houcilat. He, his brother, and his sister had been adopted and raised on Cossuut.

He had studied the history of the incident from an early age, and the details had long ago burned themselves into his memory. How the monsters had swept down without warning to ravage and obliterate every structure, every vestige of civilization in their lust for destruction. How they had seared the planet's surface so badly that it could no longer support higher life. And most meritoriously, how a few shuttles had darted gallantly through the withering enemy fire to rescue what survivors they could, including himself and his siblings, and carry them to the safety of waiting starships and an eventual life of comparative peace on Cossuut.

His teachers had put off explaining his history to him until he was old enough to comprehend, if not to understand. Only when he asked for the information was it supplied. As he studied, and learned, he developed the determination which had characterized him throughout his adolescence.

He carried the horrific images of vanished Houcilat with him into every test, every trial. They added resolve to his efforts, enabling him to rise above even those of his mates, whose histories were no less tragic than his own.

There were twenty-five of them, the same number as in an actual commissioned attack squad. They had practiced together, trained together since childhood, defeating one school team after another. Now the culmination of those untiring efforts was at hand. Some of his friends were apprehensive, others uncertain. As for Ranji, he burned with anticipation.

Suddenly there were no more teams to defeat, no more bedazzled opponents to overwhelm and intimidate. Ranji and his friends had reached the summit of achievement: the planetary finals for their age cluster. Of the hundreds of squads that had entered in hopes of being declared undisputed strategic champions, only the team from Kizzmat Township stood in the way of Ranji and his friends. Mysterious, enigmatic Kizzmat, from over the Massmari mountains. Kizzmat, who in defeating one competitor after another had demonstrated skills and swiftness equal to Ranji's own.

He was not worried. No matter their opponents' record, Ranji and his friends never took them lightly. Such caution, along with many other talents, was the legacy of their class-level supervisor.

Instructor Kouuad was shorter than he seemed to be. Extensive combat experience and many honors gave him stature. Indeed, it was unusual for so experienced a soldier to be assigned to teach younger age levels. From the time they were old enough to understand such things, Ranji and his companions were conscious of their great luck in having Kouuad as their teacher.

Kouuad-iel-an's field career had been brought to an early and untimely end by a severe injury which not even the best physicians had been able to completely repair. It was rumored that he had suffered the damage in hand-to-hand combat with one of the most vicious of the monsters themselves. His fellow teachers held him in some awe. The effect of his reputation on his pupils was profound.

It was mentioned that access to such an extraordinary instructor gave the trainees of Ciilpaan an unfair advantage over the others in their age cluster. All such protests were disallowed by the officials. It was the trainees who took the tests, not their teacher. As for Ranji and his friends, they were more than willing to credit Kouuad for much of their success.

"I warn you now," the venerable soldier told them one morning when they had assembled for practice. "Hitherto you have run over, around, and through your opposition. But this is no mere township exercise approaching. These are your cluster's planetary finals. Career success can be guaranteed in a few days. The trainees of Kizzmat know this. You need to ponder it as well.

"Remember that their record is as proud as yours. They will not go down easily. I have seen recordings of them in action. They are tougher and more resourceful than any group you have yet confronted." Kouuad paced back and forth in front of the large-screen simulator.

"Do not let your successes go to your heads. Everything you have achieved in your lives to date is history. All your accomplishments lie in the past. Only this forthcoming confrontation matters. Everything else is dust. That is as true of real combat as of simulated.

"Realize, too, that even as I speak thus to you, they are receiving similar advice, they will be equally well prepared." He stopped and smiled proudly, squinting through aged eyes that had seen too much death.

"You have met every challenge thrown at you. All that remains is your cluster championship for all Cossuut. Bear in mind that beyond this lies actual combat against the monsters. If you can advance that day in your minds and approach this competition as if actual warfare were involved, I think you will do well. Realize that you compete not for pride or prize, but to preserve civilization."

Amusement suffused his expression.

"There is nothing wrong with winning a prize, though. The record of your performance, both individually and as a group, will become a matter of permanence. You want that record to be approving."

"Don't worry, honored teacher," said an enthusiastic Bielon. "We intend to win." Murmurs of agreement rose from those around her.

"What about the Kizzmatis' methods?" came a question from the back row.

"Yes," said another. "How do they differ from what we have encountered so far?"

"Strategically we do not know what to expect," Kouuad explained. "Their tactics are unpredictable. That has been one of their greatest strengths, as it has been one of yours. They are famous improvisers, swift and decisive. Those of you who are squad leaders will therefore accrue additional burdens in the field. The rest of you must obey your leaders' instructions implicitly. There will be no time for animated, lengthy tactical debate in *this* competition. Things will happen quickly. The Kizzmati are fast." He stared hard at them. "I am counting on you to be faster."

He was silent for a long moment. "These are the planetary finals. There will be no opprobrium attached to losing, no disgrace in defeat. To finish second among thousands is the grandest of accomplishments."

"We're not coming in second!" someone shouted from the back. Kouuad tilted his head slightly and smiled anew.

"You have already exceeded the achievements of the majority of your contemporaries. Despite the knowledge that the greatest prize of all is within your grasp, you should not forget that." He checked his chronometer.

"I have nothing more to teach you. I suggest you all go home and try to get a good night's sleep. Tomorrow morning we leave for the competition site in the Joultasik foothills."

A buzz of conversation rose from Ranji's friends. Until then they had not been told where the competition was to be held. Secrecy insured that neither side would be able to spy in advance on the competition matrix and thus gain an unfair advantage over the competition.

Ranji was pleased. The Joultasik would provide variations in terrain, and he usually performed best in multiple environments.

"What do you think our chances are?" he asked his father that night. They sat at the dining table; mother and father at opposite angles, Ranji, his brother, and his baby sister at the foot of the triangle.

"You're gonna kill 'em, wipe 'em out, massacre 'em! Just like you have all the others!" Bereft of weaponry, Saguio waved an eating utensil instead. Ranji gave his younger sibling a tolerant look.

"I want you to fight hard, but also to be careful, dear. I don't want you or any of your friends to get hurt." His mother was refilling their glasses with cold fruit juice. "The Kizzmatis' reputation rivals your own. They're going to be hard to beat."

"I know, Mother."

"You'll kick the crap out of 'em." Saguio tried to speak and shovel food in at the same time.

Ranji regarded his sibling fondly. If anything, Saguio was going to be a little taller, a little stronger than his older brother. But not smarter. Testing had already been extensive enough to show that. Still, he was going to be a credit to his family line.

Not his present family, Ranji reminded himself darkly. The one that had been brutally extinguished by the monsters. They would win tomorrow. All he had to do was picture the Kizzmatis as monsters.

"We will, Saguio."

His father gestured with his glass. "Beware overconfidence, Ranji. Never chance overconfidence. Not because it might cost you tomorrow, but because it will certainly cost you in combat. I don't care if you win tomorrow or not. Just reaching the finals is a supreme achievement. Where I don't want you to lose is on the real battlefield."

"Don't worry, Father. I would never go into battle overconfident against the monsters." He picked at his food. "It's striking how close in appearance they are to us. Many times I've sat studying the files and wondered if I was looking at my own kind, until the differences became apparent."

"Physical similarities mean nothing," his mother said softly. She touched her forehead, then her chest. "Here and here they are radically different from us, programmed to kill, to have no mercy, to destroy civilization wherever they find it. They cannot build; they can only destroy."

"That is why they must be stopped." His father grunted. "If you and your friends can contribute to that, you will gain the gratitude not only of your own kind but of all civilized beings everywhere."

"Tear 'em up tomorrow, Ranj," his brother growled.

"I'll do my best, Sagui."

"You always have." His mother turned to Cynsa, who had begun squealing and pounding on the table. Ranji's baby sister was a terror.

He smiled to himself. When she matured she'd probably be a tougher fighter than either him or his brother. All three of them would do their adoptive parents as well as their original lineage proud.

Trial finals first, he reminded himself. Graduation before combat. He'd been pointing toward tomorrow ever since awareness had claimed him. He and Birachii and Cossinza and all the rest. Now the ultimate goal lay within their grasp. Only one more challenge to turn back, one more group to demoralize and defeat. One more height to scale.

He dug into the remnants of his meal. He wasn't hungry, but he knew he was going to need the fuel.

Everyone knew about the Finals Maze. If you were training to be a soldier, you heard about it at least once a month all your life. Externally its appearance differed little from similar competition mazes. What might be found inside was a different matter entirely.

There would be partitions, of course. Sheer, nonreflective, smooth-sided walls of impenetrable ceramic that would tower over the tallest team member. These divided the Maze into corridors and arenas, passageways and pits. Each partitioned region differed in size and shape from those immediately tangent to it.

The Maze contained differing habitats, each of a type undeclared in advance. Those attempting to pass through might encounter burning desert, frozen tundra, steaming jungle, or temperate forest. The Maze might be filled with water, fresh or salt. In addition to doing battle with their competition, they would have to adapt instantly and successfully to whatever local or alien biota had been programmed into the test field. A squad could defeat its armed opponents only to be wiped out by a mock avalanche or flood.

You took your people and advanced through the Maze with the aim of wiping out your opponents or capturing their headquarters position before they could reach yours. Goals were easy to envision but difficult to achieve.

The sun was out and a few clouds marred the pale blue sky. Not that it made any difference. Local conditions were meaningless inside the Maze, which could generate its own internal weather. Ranji ignored the bustle around him as he ran through a detailed final check of his own equipment. The special competition pistol he carried would register mock injury or death if its beam struck an opponent. In all respects except its nonlethality it was identical to real military hardware.

Though access to the test area was limited, a fair crowd was present. The Finals attracted interested observers and media recorders from all over Cossuut. No family members were allowed to attend. They would have to content themselves with watching the action at home, on visual.

It was much remarked upon that the two final teams lived so close to one another yet had never before met in competition. A quirk of scheduling had started them competing in opposite directions, in effect forcing them to battle through a world's worth of opponents before the time came when they would be allowed to test one another.

As he continued with the necessary preparations Ranji regulated his breathing, trying to keep it slow and steady, using the biocontrol techniques he had learned to moderate his adrenaline level. He could see his companions doing likewise. No one said much. This was the last opportunity any of them would have until the end of the competition to indulge in private thoughts. Once in the Maze, their attention would become focused and they would have to act and think in unison.

They were twenty-five to a team. Fourteen boys, eleven girls. On the far side of the Maze twenty-five young men and women from Kizzmat Township were at this very moment going through the same motions and thinking many of the same thoughts as Ranji and his friends. Afterward there would be a celebration, a party, where victor and loser could meet in an atmosphere of genuine conviviality and friendship. But before that happened they would do their very best to mock-murder each other.

Ecozones occupied Ranji's thoughts. He hoped the Maze wouldn't be full of, say, arctic tundra. Tundra simplified things too much. There was nowhere to hide, not enough variables. Dense jungle would suit him better. Or maybe desiccated granite. Hopefully there wouldn't be a lot of water. He didn't like fighting wet.

Whatever they encountered, he and his friends were prepared. They had trained in all conditions.

He was one of five squad leaders. Birachii was another, Cossinza a third. Pretty blond Gjiann from the outskirts of the township was

a fourth, and Kohmaddu the fifth. Heavyset and slow, she compen-
sated for physical deficiences with a brilliant mind and undisputed
courage and daring. No matter how tough the competition, her squad
rarely suffered a loss.

They were ready for the Kizzmatis, all right. Victory lay on the
far side of the Maze. All they had to do was enter and take it.

2

The pale glow of predawn heralded the incipient appearance of Cossuut's sun as the five squads which comprised the Trials group assembled for Kouuad's final briefing.

"I don't have to tell you how proud I am of what you have already accomplished." Their squat instructor surveyed them in fatherly fashion. "You have surpassed not only my expectations but also those of your parents and learning mates.

"I am especially gratified by the performance of those of you whose origins lie with devastated Houcilat. Your achievements stand out all the more because of the additional burdens that were placed on your maturation. Soon you will be given the opportunity to seek compensation. Keep that in mind as you enter these Trials." He strove to make eye contact with each of them in turn.

"May it go well for you," he said finally. "Let each do their best. Whatever results, I will be there for you when all is over."

They waited in respectful silence until their instructor was out of earshot. It had been a typical Kouuad speech: terse, to the point, and devoid of the flowery exhortations sometimes favored by other instructors. No matter. They did not need fancy words. They had *training.* Ranji knew they would not let the old warrior down.

A certain amount of pomp and ceremony was unavoidable as they were marched to the south entrance of the Maze and subjected to final Trial instructions. Somewhere to the north of their starting position lay the Kizzmati headquarters and twenty-five highly trained opponents as dedicated to winning as themselves. In between were the unscalable ceramic walls that cut the Maze up into multiple twists and terrains.

Ranji paid little attention to the declamatory Trials official. He and his companions knew the rules by heart. They were assembled across from the Maze entrance, already planning and plotting, their

13

eyes alert for potential antagonists even though they knew that the
Trials had yet to begin.

Tense and expectant as he was, he knew this was no more than
a student exercise, a prelude to the real thing, to actual combat. That
would come soon enough. First there was this one final test to get
past. A last chance to accrue artificial glory.

As the official droned on, some of Ranji's friends began running
in place or performing restricted range-of-motion calisthenics to stay
loose. Cossinza's quintet was particularly agitated. As the fastest of
the five squads, they had been given the task of moving out first,
striking quickly for the enemy's headquarters in hopes of bypassing
or catching any defenders off guard. It was a risky strategy but one
they had brought off before. For it to work, Cossinza had to find the
shortest path through the Maze on the initial try.

The rest of the group would advance more deliberately, cautious
but still pressing the attack. Relentlessness was their hallmark, a natural tendency which Kouuad had wisely encouraged. As far as Ranji
was concerned, emphasis on a strong defense was the sign of a battle
already half-lost.

No martial music, no blaring sirens announced the start of the
Trial Finals. An official simply gestured in their direction, and a couple of squad leaders responded in kind. Led by Cossinza's people, the
young representatives of Ciilpaan entered the Maze.

Immediately they separated into their respective squads. Moving
forward at the run, Ranji's quintet passed through a ceramic portal
that opened onto gently rolling desert terrain. His heart sank even as
the temperature rose alarmingly. He didn't favor desert fighting. Automatically he and his colleagues made appropriate adjustments to
their equipment and camouflage.

Small sandstone buttes glazed with the hue of forgotten rust protruded from shifting dunes. To their right a small pool of water
collected at the end of a dry gully. Alien-looking, spiny plants were
the only visible life in the artificial landscape. Ranji reminded his
friends to avoid them. The Maze was as much their opponent as the
Kizzmatis.

Squads Four and Two hugged opposite walls as all three moved
forward, Four taking up positions on slightly higher ground to cover
Two's advance while Ranji's people worked their way up the middle.
While it was unlikely that their opponents had come this far already,

no one from Ciilpaan was taking any chances. The Kizzmatis did not have a reputation as sluggards.

Ranji's squad entered the gully. As they used its cover and then that of a smaller tributary to work their way northward, he wondered how Cossinza's people were faring. They had disappeared into a different branch of the Maze. He glanced at his wrist communicator but did not adjust it. Communication was allowed and possible only within individual Maze partitions. Splitting up offered a testing group more attack options but reduced their ability to coordinate strategy and defend their own headquarters. Radical groups that divided into the maximum five squads were usually overwhelmed, while those in which all twenty-five participants stayed together were almost always outflanked.

It didn't matter to the Ciilpaans. They were prepared for anything. Such tactical flexibility had been a major contributor to their string of successes.

It took them most of the day to cross the desert partition, advancing with a proven mix of care and speed. Evening produced the first of several surprises.

Gleaming walls narrowed to form an intersection. Whiteness glimmered beyond. Not the white of gypsum sand but of ice and snow. Bitter cold leaked through the portal. Ranji's people were forced to make hasty readjustments to their equipment.

The instant they darted through the opening temperature and visibility fell sharply. Snow swirled around them, and the clear desert sky of the partition just traversed was replaced by wind and scudding dark clouds.

Ranji smiled to himself. There had been rumors. Not only would they have to make their way through an infernally uncooperative Maze, avoiding natural difficulties and traps along with their opponents, they would also have to cope with environments that changed with each new partition. That meant altering tactics accordingly. It was challenge enough to tax the most resourceful.

Among other things, it meant they could not predetermine how to allocate their supplies of food and water. Not when they might have to go from spending days in a comparatively benign temperate forest to a week on a barren tundra. It complicated everything. Which was, of course, the intention of the Maze's designers.

The next partition was dominated by higher, damper desert.

Dense succulent vegetation mimicked lusher climes while small creatures scurried through the undergrowth. A sudden downpour caught them unaware, leaving everyone drenched and considerably less buoyant than they had been the previous morning.

And still no sign of the Kizzmatis.

Squad Four was out of range, having decided to explore a different partition, but he was still in communication with Two. Again he found himself wondering at Cossinza's progress, decrying the inability of the communicators to penetrate the ceramic walls of the Maze.

Then the dry air was full of questing beams of colored light and he was too busy shouting orders to worry about the circumstances of distant colleagues.

As he scrambled frantically for the cover of a cluster of thick-leaved bushes, he found himself marveling at the Kizzmatis' speed. He'd repeatedly been told how fast they were, but it was still a shock to encounter them this early in the game. From the volume of fire it was impossible to tell how many of them there were. He guessed more than one full squad but less than three. Lights flickered overhead, hunting responsive targets.

A quick check revealed that his squad had suffered two minor "injuries" and no "deaths." They were still at full strength, which suggested either that the Kizzmatis were very bad shots or else that they had also not expected to run into their opponents quite so soon. A hasty call indicated that Birachii's Squad Two was in equally good shape. He felt better.

"I think we've surprised them." Birachii sounded confident over the communicator.

Ranji kept his lips close to the pickup. "It's mutual. Don't try to move on 'em too fast. We want to be in position to support each other."

"Check. How many you estimate?"

"One to three squads."

"Affirmative. We're behind a little hill. I'll try to work our way around to the west. They'll expect us to come over the top."

"Don't count on it. Don't count on anything with this lot. Watch yourselves."

Birachii responded with a rude noise, which left Ranji and his companions grinning.

"They didn't waste any time." Tourmast-eir used his perception lens to try and peer through the thick brush. "By my ancestors, they're quick."

"Hopefully they're thinking the same of us," said someone else. He held his pistol with both hands. "Maybe they'll run right into our line of fire."

"Wonder if they've crossed more of the Maze than we have?" mused a fourth member of the squad.

This was not how his people should be thinking. "Nobody covers ground faster than the Ciilpaan," Ranji snapped. It didn't matter that he did not believe it, only that his squad believed him.

"Check," murmured Tourmast-eir. Crawling on his belly, he began edging to his right. "Let's try and get behind them."

"No." Ranji put a restraining hand on his friend's leg. "The first thing they'd expect in a situation like this is a flanking move. They'll be setting up for it."

"Won't matter if we move faster than them," observed Weenn-oon.

"If we don't and I'm right, then it's Trial end for this squad. You ready to chance that, Weenn?" The older boy subsided, thoughtful. "What do you have in mind, Ranji?"

"Their reputation's as exalted as ours. I've been thinking ever since we were told that they'd be our final opponents that the same old strategies won't work. This isn't slow-stupid Goriiava from down south. I've believed all along that we'd have to try something new to prevail."

"Maybe so," Weenn agreed, "but we can't sit here waiting for them to flank us, either."

"How about setting up and waiting for them back at the last partition?" Tourmast looked hopeful. "The snow on the other side might blind them temporarily."

"Good idea, except that we don't progress by going backward. I don't want us to get into a protracted firefight. If that's what they want then let them initiate it by retreating to a defensive position. If they do that then we'll respond with countering strategies, but only then."

Off to their left, Birachii's group continued to exchange heavy fire with the enemy. That presented possibilities as well as dangers. He relented enough to allow Tourmast to reconnoiter. His friend returned moments later.

"I can see the fire off to the west. Still no sign of anyone in front of us."

Ranji considered. "So all of them are engaging Squad Two . . . or else there's more of them ahead, waiting for us." He eyed his companions. As usual, they were waiting for him to make the decisions.

"We're moving. Not flanking. Straight ahead and in close-order single file. If they're all on Squad Two, then we'll be able to slip in behind. If not, we offer as small a target as possible and try to sneak past to the next partition. Kinjoww-uiv, you take tail position." The girl nodded. She had wonderful reflexes and would hopefully insure that as they advanced no enemy troops would slip up on their rear.

"No shooting unless you're *positive* you have a target." Letting the sharp-sighted Tourmast lead the way, he rolled onto his belly and followed his colleague into the brush.

His hands were protected by field gloves, but loose gravel scraped his cheeks. He found himself wishing for the soft sands of the desert environment they had traversed two partitions back. Participants, naturally, had no control over the Trial environments. He reminded himself that students who spent time complaining about the harshness of their surroundings rarely did well in competition. It was, of course, irrelevant to actual combat.

Boots paused ahead of him. "I see them," Tourmast whispered back tersely. "Three . . . no, four. They're not looking this way. They're all firing at Squad Two's position."

"Got one, got one!" The soft yell of triumph whispered over the communicator. If Birachii's people were indeed occupying the full attention of the enemy and doing well in the bargain, then it opened up all sorts of strategic possibilities for Ranji's squad. At the least, it meant they were already in position to wipe out a good portion of Squad Two's assailants, at little risk to themselves. They had been presented with a wonderful opportunity.

Too wonderful.

If their reputation was legitimate, and there was no reason to assume it was otherwise, it was hard to believe the Kizzmatis would leave themselves open in such a fashion, much less throw all their resources into an all-out attack on Birachii's well-defended hill position. Ranji made up his mind quickly.

"Keep moving . . . and don't slow down!"

"But . . ."

He hurried to stifle dissent. "I know what you're all thinking. That we should go to Birachii's aid. But if they are trying to flank him, he's in good position to hold them off; if they're not, then this is our best chance to slip past and make progress through the Maze. That's our ultimate objective. So let's move."

The battle of light pistols raged silently on their left as they hurried forward, halting only when the next intersection became visible. Ahead Ranji could make out vegetation denser than any they'd yet encountered. Specific shapes were blurred by a dark curtain of rain. No moisture fell in the partition they currently occupied. A light, cool breeze blew in their faces while a glance behind showed only distant flashes of light.

"Up and left," he ordered curtly. Rising in a body, they headed toward the portal in a crouching run.

Which sent them stumbling into the squad of startled Kizzmatis who were busily occupied in excavating a defensive position just inside the next intersection.

Clearly they expected that any advancing Ciilpaan would be tied down by the firefight behind. So confident were they of having enough time to finish their fortifications that they hadn't even posted a guard. Tools fashioned from locally obtained Maze materials were thrown aside as the Kizzmatis scrambled wildly for their weapons.

In the ensuing close-quarter gunfight Ranji "lost" two of his own people before all five of the enemy could be taken out. Now he found himself regarding the sullen Kizzmati squad leader as he contemplated new options. The youth was even taller and more muscular than Ranji himself.

"You're good." His opponent spoke reluctantly as he sat on the slab of rock where he'd been "killed." "Real good." He grinned unpleasantly, displaying a true warrior's smile. "But it won't matter. The outcome will be the same."

As if on cue, Ranji's communicator suddenly filled the air with shouts and curses. "Birachii!" Ranji yelled into the pickup. "What's happening? What's going on?"

His friend's voice was panicky. "Behind us! They were behind us all the time. They were behind us *before* the shooting started! They just wanted to find out how many of us there were before they attacked. They . . . !"

Communications ceased. "Birachii!" Ranji said tightly. "Birachii, report. Anyone from Squad Two, report." Silence taunted him.

The enemy squad leader looked smug. "Taken out. All of 'em."

Slowly Ranji let his wrist communicator drop, gazed narrowly at his defeated opponent. "We're even, then. Your people have taken Birachii's squad; we've taken yours."

"At the cost of forty percent of your strength," the squad leader reminded him, alluding to the pair of Ranji's companions who'd received fatal "hits" during the unexpected confrontation.

"You don't know how many of your own went down in the fight with Birachii's squad. Our strength in this part of the Maze could still be equal."

"I doubt it." The Kizzmati leader and his companions exchanged amused glances. "You see, we're *all* here." He nodded toward the now distant end of the partition.

"What are you talking about?" Tourmast looked uneasy.

"All twenty-five of us. All five squads. We just blasted through the main entrance and kept moving as fast as we could, figuring you'd split up to try different passages. That way we'd be in shape to overwhelm any opposition."

Tourmast was shaking his head. "That's old, outmoded strategy. Nobody fights like that anymore. It's too predictable, too easy to defend against."

The squad leader's grin widened. "Sure is. That's why we figured it'd be the last thing you'd be expecting."

"A concerted defense could have pinned you down here long enough for one of our squads to take your headquarters," Ranji pointed out.

His opponent nodded. "Sure could. But it hasn't, and now it won't. Your squad can't do a damn thing now. All our remaining forces are between you and *your* headquarters. You're finished."

"In real combat a single burst could have wiped out your entire group," Tourmast observed angrily.

"This isn't real combat. Neither side has access to heavy weapons. All we're given are these." He held up his light pistol, which had automatically deactivated the instant its owner had suffered his fatal "injury." "You modify tactics to adapt to local conditions." He turned his attention back to Ranji.

"I'm estimating from our speed of advance that the body of our group is more than halfway to your headquarters, with nothing between them and it capable of stopping them. You're fast ... faster than any group we've ever fought. But it won't do you any good. Because the rest of your people are advancing in expectation of encountering resistance, and there isn't any. We're all here, in one place."

"That means your headquarters is completely undefended," Ranji observed.

"Unless I'm lying to you." His opponent was clearly enjoying himself. "Are you going to base strategy on the words of a 'dead' opponent? Not that it matters. I was watching your face when I made my guess. We *are* more than halfway to your headquarters. Which means that you're less than halfway to ours. There's no way you can get there first.

"If you've any sense at all you'll have left one squad behind to defend. There'll be at least ten to fifteen of us attacking. The outcome's inevitable. Why not register your surrender now?" The Kizzmati stretched. "The sooner we march out of here and off Trial rations, the more pleasant it'll be for all of us."

"Not a chance," Tourmast growled.

Their opponent looked disappointed. "Oh, well. Prolong it if you must."

Ranji turned to leave, hesitated. "How can you be so sure your group will get to our headquarters before any of our people can reach yours? Maybe this isn't the shortest route through the Maze. Maybe your other squads will wander around for days in search of the right intersection."

The squad leader put his hands behind his head, leaned back. "Oh, this is the shortest route, all right. You see, six days ago we were finally able to bribe the member of the Trials committee we'd been in contact with to provide us with a map." A stunned Ranji noted that this confession was uttered without a hint of embarrassment or regret.

"You can't do that. It will invalidate the results!"

"Think so? The Trials are supposed to simulate real combat conditions. That means you win by any means possible short of inflicting actual physical injury on your opponents. There's nothing in the rules against bribery. At worst we'll have to repeat the Finals in a new Maze. Myself, I think we'll gain merit for innovation.

"The teachers aren't interested in methodology. Their sole concern is turning out winners, survivors. For all you and I know, this is the standard tactic previous Finals winners have employed."

Ranji walked off to confer with his two surviving companions.

"He can't be right . . . can he?" Weenn looked dazed. "Knowing the route through the Maze would give them an unbeatable advantage."

"No wonder they felt safe in keeping their whole strength together," Tourmast muttered. "Surely the judges won't uphold this."

"Unless the Kizzmati is right and they're only interested in who wins, and not by what means." Weenn looked less than confident.

"I don't know." Ranji was thinking furiously. "If we could get in touch with Squads One and Five we could bring them into the fight, but it would mean searching parallel partitions. We don't have near enough time. With Birachii's people out of the way they'll be on our headquarters before we could catch up with them." His gaze rose.

"If they can use unconventional tactics, so can we."

"What do you mean?" Weenn asked.

"Everybody has their cutter?" His companions checked their service belts for the tool, which was intended to help them in downing and shaping vegetation for defensive fortifications and shelter.

"We're going on, into the next partition. And watch yourselves. Like their squad leader said, he might've been lying."

They left their smug opponents behind. They would be restricted to the place where they had been removed from the competition, their weapons and instrumentation deactivated.

"If there are fifteen to twenty of them operating together and they know exactly where they're going, why are we wasting our time?" Tourmast struck angrily at a protruding branch. "We're going to *have* to rely on the determination of the judges."

"I'm not relying on anybody but myself," Ranji shot back.

The next partition was filled with cool, dry deciduous forest. While his companions kept puzzled watch, Ranji circled trees until he found what he wanted.

"Get out your cutters," he ordered, making three marks on the nearest trunk with his own. "Cut here, and here. Everybody pick a side."

"What's the point of building a barrier?" Weenn demanded to know even as he set to work.

"We're not making a barrier." Smoke rose from the trunk. "Just do as I say."

Working in unison, they soon had the tree felled. Ranji pocketed his cutter and started climbing. Tourmast gaped at him.

"You can't do that, Ranj. This is cheating, too."

His squad leader looked down at him. "If they're going to invalidate this Trial, it might as well be with equanimity. Are you coming or not?"

Tourmast and Weenn exchanged a glance. Then Weenn started up the slanting trunk. His companion followed.

Strange to be standing *atop* a partition wall. It was barely as wide as his boot, Ranji noted. Just wide enough to walk . . . provided you put one foot carefully in front of the other, had no fear of heights and superb balance.

Below and to his right lay the partition of deciduous forest. Behind them haze rose from the temperate desert until it was blocked by the artificial atmospheric inversion layer of the Maze. His left hand hung over wave-tossed water thick with the smell of salt: an oceanic environment. Lucky they hadn't chosen to enter that one. If he fell he wanted to make sure it was to his right. Better bruises and broken bones than immersion.

Demonstrating their unsurpassed training to the full, the three Ciilpaanians headed north, running along the crest of the narrow wall.

It all looked so easy, so simple from up here, Ranji reflected as he ran. Habitats which on the ground would have blocked or hindered their progress slipped rapidly past.

Once, they observed figures slogging through a low, boggy environment, advancing in a familiar diamond pattern. He recognized Gjiann's squad and wanted to call out to her but did not, knowing she could not hear him. Each partition was sealed for sound as well as ecology, to prevent groups in neighboring partitions from communicating with one another by the simple means of shouting over the barriers. He ran on.

The number of walls decreased as they progressed, until Ranji ordered a slowdown above a partition filled from one side to the other with a field of tall golden grain. A compact complex of monitoring instrumentation, the Kizzmati headquarters lay at its far end. They had reached the last partition, the north end of the Maze. The unit's internal lights were on, indicating that the distant Ciilpaan headquarters continued to function. A Kizzmati banner fluttered overhead.

Beyond the headquarters Ranji thought he could make out a couple of senior referees, standing in the shade and chatting idly. They did not see the three Ciilpaanians who crouched atop the wall for the simple reason that there was no reason for them to look *up*.

"The Kizzmati didn't lie," Tourmast murmured. "I don't see any defenders."

"That doesn't mean they didn't install some kind of defense." Ranji pointed.

Stretching in a sweeping curve from one wall to the other immediately in front of the headquarters instrumentation was an exquisitely camouflaged ditch. Ranji admired the workmanship. At ground level it would be quite invisible. An attacker getting this far and seeing no defenders in sight would likely rush across the last open space to touch the switch on the beacon mast and proclaim victory, only to stumble into the wonderfully well-concealed trap. The entire Kizzmati team must have set to work in an orgy of excavation the instant the Trial had begun, moving out only after it had been completed. They'd had the time to install such a complex defense only because they'd known from the beginning the shortest path through the Maze.

Though you couldn't design something whose intent was to physically injure an opponent, he suspected that anyone falling into the ditch would not find it a simple matter to climb out.

"See," Weenn was saying as he pointed. "It goes all the way from one wall to the other, and it's too wide to jump. Cozzinza's squad could have made it all this way only to be trapped or stopped at the last minute."

Ranji was nodding to himself as he studied the layout. "No trees in this partition; only grains. Nothing to build a bridge with. No wonder their squad leader was so confident. They were sure they had an unstoppable offense and an impregnable defense."

Weenn shook his head slowly. "No way we could have won with normal tactics."

"So we'll use abnormal ones."

Tourmast was frowning. "Not only is there nothing to build a bridge with here, there're no trees to climb, either. How do we get down?"

"Quickly." Ranji squinted south through Maze haze. Having long since overwhelmed Birachii's squad, the Kizzmatis were doubtless moving fast toward the Ciilpaani headquarters.

The internal walls of the Maze were perfectly smooth, perfectly vertical. An insect could not find a purchase on that slick surface.

Ranji rose from his crouch to regard his companions. "Weenn, cross around. I'm going to have the two of you drop me."

"I dunno, Ranji." Tourmast was estimating the height of the drop. "It won't us any good if you break both legs."

"It won't do us any good to squat up here wondering, either." Turning, he knelt and gripped the edge of the wall as best he could with both hands, then lowered himself over the edge.

His companions lay down on their stomachs and pressed their thighs and knees against the opposite side of the wall. Each took one of Ranji's wrists in their hands and lowered him another half body length toward the waving, beckoning grain below. It was at that moment that one of the referees spotted them. Ranji decided that the look on his face was worth everything it had taken to get to this point, even if he and his friends were eventually disqualified.

Shutting his eyes, he ran through a series of relaxation exercises. When he was through there was nothing more to be done but to do it. "Okay," he whispered brusquely. The restraining pressure on his wrists vanished.

It seemed a million minutes to the ground. He flexed his knees as he struck, but the impact was still considerable. The shock ran from his feet all the way up to his neck and he crumpled onto his right side.

When he tried to stand, the shooting pain that blasted through his left leg brought him back to the ground. Whether it was broken or simply badly twisted he didn't know. He crawled for a while, then managed to straighten by using the unyielding wall as a brace against his back. Limping severely, pain dulling his vision, he stumbled toward the Kizzmati headquarters beacon.

His friends had dropped him behind the defensive ditch, so the only thing that was stopping him from flipping the switch on the beacon was the pain that threatened to overwhelm his senses. He knew Tourmast and Weenn must be cheering him on, though he couldn't hear them. They were above the inversion layer.

Having stopped at the Maze entrance, the two senior referees stared openmouthed at the advancing limping figure. Ranji could hear people running toward the site, though the pain made it impossible for him to identify individual shapes. There were a few cheers, but mostly the air was dense with stunned silence.

He felt himself weaving and swaying and fought to stay erect and keep moving through the pain. It was entirely up to him, he knew. Neither Weenn nor Tourmast could take such a fall.

He wondered how close the Kizzmatis were to his own head-quarters as he threw himself forward to slam an open palm against the beacon switch. He was very careful to hit it the first time because he sensed through fading thoughts that he would not be able to mus-ter enough strength or control for a second try.

As it turned out, they beat the Kizzmatis by less than four min-utes.

3

To say that the outcome of that particular Finals Trial was controversial was to say that the monsters were somewhat incorrect in their opposition to the tenets of civilized society. Debate roiled the general population as well as the Trials committee for days thereafter.

In the end it was decided that since the rules barred only physical violence from the competition, everything else must be allowed. And since the Kizzmatis had been the first to utilize what the committee referred to euphemistically as "unorthodox tactics," they could hardly object to the Ciilpaanians responding in similar fashion.

Ranji's group was declared winner.

The decision produced no animosity among the losers. There was no shame in finishing second in a worldwide contest, and after all, their ultimate aim, the advance of civilization and the conversion or defeat of the monsters, remained the same. The Kizzmati group leader went out of his way to congratulate Ranji on his inspired leadership.

"We were lucky," Ranji told him. "Extremely lucky. I could just as easily have crippled myself."

"In the end we underestimated you," the Kizzmati replied. "We were convinced we had devised a plan that could not fail. I now believe that plans of that nature are inevitably doomed to failure."

They sat together in a young persons' eating establishment, sharing strategies and stories as though both groups had won, which indeed they had.

"Wouldn't you have been confident? We had overwhelming firepower, a map of the Maze, and a solid defensive scheme."

"I sure would." Ranji was gracious in victory.

The Kizzmati leader sipped from a cup. "The one thing we didn't count on was an opponent capable of thinking more perverted than ours." He grinned and they all laughed softly together.

Except for the ever somber Weenn. "I wonder what fighting the monsters will be like?"

"It doesn't matter." The last Trial over, Ranji was brimming with confidence and self-esteem. "We will defeat them no matter what stratagems they may choose to employ."

"They win a lot of battles." The Kizzmati second-in-command gazed into his drink. "It's said that in one-on-one combat they can't be beaten."

"They've never met anything like us," Tourmast shot back. "Our great Kouuad says that we're as good as them, maybe better, and he should know. He fought them for years."

"I'm sure we'll get the chance to find out," Ranji murmured.

"Myself, I can't wait." Tourmast made a melodramatic show of raising his cup. Comrades together now, Kizzmati and Ciilpaani toasted their future.

The future arrived sooner than they expected, immediately following their official graduation the following year to warrior rank, and in a manner that surprised them all.

Those who had achieved high scores expected to be promoted to officer status and given command of fighting units. Instead, the top hundred achievers were combined into a unique fast-attack group, to be utilized in special situations. Disappointment was minimal, as it meant that childhood friends would stay together instead of being spread across the cosmos.

Despite all his training, despite years of anticipation, Ranji was surprised to discover how upset he was at the prospect of leaving Cossuut.

They were a year older. Faster, stronger, smarter, he and his friends were confident of their ability to handle anything the monsters could send against them. They were all impatient to test their skills in real combat.

Their destination was a planet called Koba, a lightly populated world where recently settled monsters had established a foothold against the forces of civilization. In such conditions a small, irresistible force could hopefully achieve results all out of proportion to its size.

They had real weapons now, explosive and energy both. No more training pistols. No more simulations and partitions and mazes. No more toys. Ranji had been appointed second-in-command after the Kizzmati veteran Soratii-eev, perhaps because of the difference in their ages. Ranji did not feel in the least slighted. Soratii was a clever and accomplished commander, and it would be an honor to serve under him.

If the new soldiers were intimidated by anything, it was the confidence far more senior soldiers placed in their prospects.

As they prepared for emergence from Underspace and the subsequent rapid drop to Koba's contested surface, Ranji found he was surprisingly calm. Regardless of what they might face on the surface below he had unlimited confidence in his colleagues, no matter whether they hailed from Ciilpaan, Kizzmat, or elsewhere on Cossuut. Together they constituted a cohesive fighting unit the likes of which civilization had never seen before.

Furthermore, they were motivated by something few others possessed: a desire, a need, for revenge.

Ranji wasn't thinking of that as the Underspace emergence warning sounded. He was thinking of his parents; of his younger brother Saguio who was now undergoing the same testing Ranji had passed in such accomplished fashion. Of his little sister Cynsa, and of his birth parents. Others might fight to protect their friends, to defend the cause of civilization, but he would fight so that he could return to those he loved.

Koba was a blessedly cool world distinguished by rolling grassy plains and high, heavily treed plateaus. Though diverse in content, the local ecosystem was unspectacular, dominated by the dense evergreen forests of the plateaus. Animal life tended to frequent the green canopy or burrow underground. Large predators were unknown, possibly due to the absence of ground cover in the form of bushes and high grasses in which prey animals could hide and thrive. There was no native intelligent species.

A hundred years before, the enemy had placed a number of scientific installations on Koba. They'd held it ever since. Large-scale colonization had commenced only recently. It was the kind of expansion civilized beings had to contest. The enemy had resisted, thus far successfully, expanding their local production of domestic food animals and grains. They had also begun to exploit Koba's mineral deposits. The place was in danger of becoming a significant contributor to the war effort. Not a particularly rich world, but one whose resources were definitely worth denying to the spreading forces of evil.

Major forces could not be spared to attack Koba, but it was decided that one or two quick surgical strikes might render the enemy's position there less than tenable. While substantial, planetary defenses were widely dispersed. It would take time to bring them to bear on an assault.

This was confirmed by the fact that Ranji's group was able to make the drop to the surface without incident and with all their equipment intact. Nor were they forced to deal with immediate opposition. Perhaps the locals were confused by the size of the invasion, on the face of it far too small to present any real threat. They would be even more unsettled by the movements of Ranji's group, which in a radical departure from traditional strategy had been empowered to operate independent of the rest of the landing force.

The new, high-performance air-repulsion skids the attackers brought for surface travel were virtually noiseless. Their minimal heat signature allowed the strike force to advance rapidly under cover of night. While other groups engaged local defenses, Ranji's simply raced out over the flat plains, bypassing enemy positions on several occasions.

They were heading for the high country, their target the communications and information center for the most heavily populated portion of the planet. Despite the speed of their advance there was some question as to whether they would even get into position to attack. Within a day of their touchdown, enemy opposition had stiffened to the point of wiping out several assault groups, and Command was forced to consider calling a quick retreat off-world. Fortunately, enough senior officers demurred. But if they expected to remain on Koba, they would have to show some progress.

Ranji's group continued to avoid detection by the enemy. In that respect they had already proved their worth.

The communications complex was located on the outskirts of the major population center, which itself was strung out along the edge of one of the numerous high plateaus which dominated Koban topography. The plateau sloped down to the plains. It was from there that Ranji's group intended to make their final push.

Instead of landing and attacking atop the plateau as the enemy would expect, Soratii and his advisors had decided to cross the plain below and work their way up a shallow canyon, following a cascading river system. Only when they had begun to ascend was their presence finally detected and the alarm passed to the city's defenders.

Ranji's group threw back one counterattack after another as they continued to move upslope, traveling in twos and threes to further confuse an already badly rattled enemy. They advanced on both sides of the white-water cataract, whose noise and constant motion further served to mask their approach. Light camouflage armor blocked individual heat signatures, so that the defenders were forced to try and pinpoint each oncoming soldier visually.

Fighting became fragmented as the terrain grew steeper and more difficult, with squads unable to effectively support one another. As geology was neutral in any conflict, the enemy was forced to deal with the same problem. This led to a chaotic battlefield situation, especially at night. Ranji's people throve in the resulting confusion.

Flashes of light from energy weapons and continual explosions filled his senses as he ascended. They soon found themselves in among the large trees and dense tracts of forest which clung to the upper slopes, rendering fighting even more difficult. Thanks to the presence of running water they were able to travel lighter than usual. Even in an era of advanced instrumentation and sophisticated weaponry, the absence of clean water could still be more debilitating to troops on the move than heavy explosives.

Ranji was thankful for the presence of the dense vegetation, which screened them from aerial surveillance. With luck and camouflage suits, they would be on top of the communications complex before the enemy knew what hit them. If they could destroy that it would not only panic the local population, it would put a considerable crimp in the enemy's efforts to coordinate a planetary defense. An intense firefight broke out off to his immediate left, on the far side of the river. They were close enough to the rim of the plateau now to see the first of many communications antennae protruding into the night sky, though the structures from which they sprouted were still concealed by slope and trees. Closed-beam communicators on both sides were frenetic with shouted orders and reports.

Ignoring the difficulties of his compatriots on the other side of the cascade, Ranji led his own group onward.

They had just crested the rim when they ran into the enemy

squad, advancing cautiously through deepening twilight. The defenders were in the process of crossing the river, intent on joining what they perceived to be the major engagement taking place just below.

Ranji waited until the enemy troops were halfway across before giving the order for his people to open fire from the cover of rocks and trees. That their presence was still unsuspected was confirmed by the surprise among the defenders as they were attacked. Those caught out in midstream had nowhere to run, though from Ranji's standpoint too many escaped. Most went down, either on the rocks or in the water itself. Limp and lifeless, one body after another was lifted by the current and carried downstream. The survivors scattered back into the forest.

It offered Ranji his first opportunity to examine the monsters at close range.

Only a few of the corpses were wearing armor or camouflage, further proof that the assault had caught the defenders of the communications complex unaware. Given its strategic importance, Ranji was surprised. Overconfidence, or simply a lack of adequate preparation? Clearly they hadn't expected any of the invaders to come this far this fast.

Tourmast knelt and rolled one of the bodies over. Only the upper half was armored. A gaping hole showed darkly in the lower portion of the abdomen. Though Ranji had studied innumerable images of the monsters, it was still something of a shock to view one close up.

Just as in the tridimensional imagery he'd been exposed to as a student, the similarities were impressive. There was little enough to differentiate him from the body on the ground. Physically, that is, he reminded himself. Mentally and morally the gulf between himself and the creature that lay dead in the dirt was vast.

"We don't want to linger here," he muttered uncomfortably. "Let's keep moving." Tourmast grunted and rose as Ranji checked in with the rest of his group via communicator.

The squads on the other side of the river had been hurt, but had quickly beaten back the counterattack and regrouped. They were moving upslope again and were not far from Ranji's present advanced position. The single enemy slider which had come a-hunting with heavy weapons had been shot down. As they had hoped, the majority of the enemy's ordnance was occupied farther south, engaging larger elements of the invasion. Their opposition was lightly armed.

They expected to encounter heavier resistance as they spread out and raced toward the target, and were pleasantly surprised to find little in the way of opposition. Brushing that aside, they entered the complex and methodically took it apart. The communications personnel had fled just ahead of them. After every piece of instrumentation had been melted or otherwise dismantled, the buildings themselves were reduced to ashes. Ranji regarded his group's handiwork proudly. It would be a long, long time before anyone dispatched so much as a friendly greeting from this location.

They departed just as enemy reinforcements began to arrive from the nearby city, leaving them to contemplate the total destruction of the communications complex as well as the absence of its perpetrators, who were already retreating rapidly under cover of night.

Halfway down, the slope leveled off enough for them to use their skids. Now it would be difficult if not impossible for the enemy to catch them, Ranji thought with satisfaction. Rather than being tired, he found that he was eager to embark on the next operation. His colleagues and friends shared his feelings.

The following morning the enemy did its best to cut them off. Maybe they expected the ravagers of the communications complex to be exhausted from the previous night's activities. Ranji's group smashed through them, not even deigning to take up a defensive posture and wait for assistance.

An enemy female slung her slider alongside, firing as she did so. He evaded, whirled, and came back atop her. As he shot her at close range it occurred to him that she was rather pretty, for a monster. There was, however, nothing to love in the brief glimpse he had of her distorted, unnaturally gaunt face. Trailing smoke and flame, her craft slammed into the dry plain below.

A heavier attack came later that evening. This time large aircraft were involved. We really upset them, Ranji mused as he glanced backward and smiled. The enemy was furiously engaged in demolishing the decoy vehicles his group had left behind for just such a purpose.

By the next morning the numerous skids and their triumphant operators were streaking unopposed across rolling plains, well beyond range of attack.

Their initial mission had been a complete success. In addition, the group had sustained minimal casualties, remarkable considering the riskiness of the operation and the fact that monsters had been prominent in the defense of the complex.

Ranji took time to visit the wounded. All were in good spirits, not in the least depressed by their injuries. Among the special assault group's personnel, only two had been lost. All of the injured had been successfully evacuated and were intact enough to be medically restored. It was an unprecedented accomplishment.

The destruction of the facility had seriously complicated the Kobans' defense. Non-Cossuutian Ashregan and Crigolit forces which had been pushed back used the resultant confusion for a breathing spell, and in two instances were actually able to resume their advance.

Though Ranji and his friends were anxious to return to combat, they were informed by their superiors that they were too valuable to risk so soon in another similar operation. Instead, to their considerable disappointment, they were ordered off-world.

"You've earned your reward," a senior officer informed him as they chatted on board the transport ship. It hovered safely in Underspace, in orbit around Koba's single moon.

"But fighting on Koba continues," Ranji protested. "We can help. We can . . ."

"You did what you were brought here to do," the officer informed him brusquely. Then she added, more gently, "I myself do not know why you were evacuated. I personally think your mere presence below would be a considerable asset to our efforts. Everyone knows of your group's accomplishments. But it is not for me to question. My orders were to see your people taken safely off-planet. Command is not always generous with explanations."

"What now?" Disappointed but resigned, Ranji leaned back in the lounge and crossed his legs.

"I believe you are to be singularly honored," the officer informed him.

"How can anyone be honored for one operation?" Tourmast fingered the skintight attached to his forehead, where he'd been grazed by an enemy energy bolt. Skin and bone were healing nicely, Ranji noticed. "Especially when the battle has yet to be won."

"It is not for me to say." As the officer spoke she idly caressed the knuckles of her left hand.

"And when is this 'singular honor' to be bestowed?" Tourmast muttered.

"Soon after your return home, I believe." Noting their reaction, she added, "I see that you have not yet been informed. Allow me the privilege. I am informed that the Teachers intend to commend you personally."

Weenn spoke up from nearby. "Ah. That will be real joy for Kouuad."

"No." The officer looked at him. "Not your teacher. *The* Teachers."

Ranji tried to prepare himself mentally as the transport sped through Underspace toward Cossuut. His emotions were mixed. While he was delighted at the prospect of seeing his family again, as a soldier he regretted leaving Koba unsecured. He had not expected his initial combat experience to be so . . . episodic. Perhaps next time they would be allowed to stay and fight until the world being contested had been won for civilization.

There were worse fates, though, than being plucked from the field of battle to suffer exaltation and honor.

Not only was the Cossuutian media saturated with the news of their accomplishments, their arrival was recorded for rebroadcast throughout the civilized worlds. The military made a great show of it, presenting the heroes of Koba to the public one by one in the capital city's largest outdoor amphitheater. The ceremony seemed to go on forever, and the heroic fighters soon found themselves dreadfully bored.

Officialdom saved the leaders of the attack, the group officers, for last, developing the presentation as efficiently as if they'd been orchestrating a piece of music. Soratii, Ranji, Tourmast, and the others dutifully took their respective turns at the podium.

What most impressed Ranji when his turn came was not the surging crowd, the plethora of recording devices, or even the knowledge that his parents and siblings were in the front row of the audience. It was his sudden proximity to two of the Teachers.

Warmth and affection poured from them to envelop not only those on the brightly decorated stage but all who were fortunate enough to be in their immediate vicinity. As had those who'd pre-

ceded him, Ranji approached and extended a hand. The four manipulative digits at the end of one tentacle opened like a flower, then
closed with the silky softness of shy petals around his closed fist. A
warm rush of admiration and thanks filled his mind.

How wonderful it was, he thought, to have achieved his life's
dream. To be honored for doing what he would gladly have done in
anonymity. To be alive, and healthy, and assisting the advance of
civilization. The Amplitur's digits withdrew. Mentally and emotionally elated, Ranji pivoted smartly and returned to his place on the
dais.

One-who-Surrounds was feeling much wellness. The local weather
was amenable, and the excitement and reverence their visit had generated among the Ashregan was gratifying to behold.

Though they did not know it, the proceedings honoring the special fighters was another graduation ceremony of sorts. It signified
the official success of the Project, in which the Amplitur had invested
a substantial amount of time and effort. It was a great day for the
Purpose.

Though the weather was pleasant, One-who-Surrounds was still
less than optimally comfortable. The Ashregan preferred drier worlds
than the Amplitur, and it was something of a sacrifice for One-who-
Surrounds and its companion to remain exposed to the desiccating
air for such a long period. But could they have done any less to honor
the fruits of the Project?

It had been a long time aborning, and had involved the most
intense efforts of the Amplitur and their Ashregan allies. To see those
hopes so powerfully fulfilled, and ahead of schedule, was more than
sufficient justification for the somewhat uncomfortable visit. When
one served the Purpose with one's whole being, one could not fuss
at inconsequentials such as temperature and humidity.

It was touching to observe the pleasure their mere presence induced in their allies. One-who-Surrounds was curious to see how the
special fighters would react, but it was no different for them. There
was the same receptivity, the same calm acceptance and mutual admiration one would find among any ordinary Ashregan.

Except that this group was not ordinary. They had proven that already, on Koba, succeeding beyond the wildest hopes of the Project's supervisors. The fighting abilities and unique characteristics which they had been bred for would be passed on to succeeding generations, to the betterment of the Purpose. Another carefully chosen field test or two and the survivors would be retired with honors, encouraged to produce as many offspring as possible. They would want to continue fighting, of course, since that was what they had been trained to do, but in the end all would accept their retirement gracefully. The Amplitur would suggest that they do so.

They did not mention any of this to the individuals they honored. It would be impolitic to refer to members of an allied species as breeding stock, just as it would have been counterproductive to inform them that certain of the specialized characteristics they would pass on to their offspring were not natural in origin but rather the results of unsurpassed Amplitur efforts at nanobioengineering.

Even as One-who-Surrounds congratulated the heroes of Koba, efforts continued to refine and expand the scope of the work which had produced them. Success could always be improved upon. The scientists of the obstructionist Weave did not rest in their efforts to thwart the Purpose. Those who promulgated its tenets could do no less.

One-who-Surrounds looked forward to the results of the next test, in which the special fighters would be asked to confront fully operational Human forces. If they could defeat not merely Massood or Chirinaldo but Human soldiers in direct combat, then the triumph of the Project would be assured. The effect on Weave morale would be devastating.

Turning to face the audience, One-who-Surrounds raised both tentacles, spreading all eight manipulative digits wide in a gesture of greeting and unity. A wave of genuine warmth and appreciation flowed out to wash over those in the front rows. The bulbous eyes, each on the end of its short stalk, swiveled independently to survey the native crowd as it cheered softly.

Following the ceremony's conclusion, One-who-Surrounds was relieved to retire to a room in which the humidity had been raised to meet Amplitur requirements. The itching which had begun to torment its mottled orange skin began to fade. It was no longer necessary to use drops to keep sensitive eyes moist.

Green-goes-Softly settled into a hammocklike lounge nearby. The large, dark blotch on its dorsal side indicated that the other Amplitur had recently budded, giving birth to a new individual.

"I thought it went well."

"Wellness aplenty," One-who-Surrounds concurred. "They honor their heroes."

"As well they should after what they accomplished on Koba." Green-goes-Softly rolled slightly, into a more comfortable position, straddling the lounge for maximum support. "I sensed in the favored ones no indication of deviation or genetic degeneration."

"Nor did I." Disdaining the other empty lounge, One-who-Surrounds settled into a shallow pool of warm, scented water. "All the reports have been accurate."

"I wish we could have gone to Koba to monitor them in person."

"You know why we did not. Personal danger aside, our presence would have been a burden on the regular Ashregan troops, much less the progeny of the Project. In active combat against Human beings our presence is a hindrance." Its skin rippled, showing iridescent silver highlights.

"They defeated Humans on their own ground," Green-goes-Softly murmured. "It is a wonderful thing. According to the reports I have seen, the Humans were much surprised."

"As well they should have been." One-who-Surrounds waxed philosophical. "In such small ways does the mental disintegration of an enemy begin. Not only were the fighters successful in their military objectives, they were happy in their work. The Purpose could ask for nothing more."

Green-goes-Softly gestured with a tentacle. "For all their Ashregan upbringing they fight as well as any Humans. The nanobioengineers have done their work exceedingly well. Their alterations have taken perfectly. The overriding desire of the special fighters, like that of their less well-endowed fellow Ashregan, is but to serve the Purpose."

"Yes. It means that the end of the Weave can be envisioned."

Green-goes-Softly knew that the end One-who-Surrounds spoke of might lie several hundred years in the future, but the Amplitur took a longer view of things than most species. Their patience extended well beyond individual lifetimes. It allowed them to wait for new special fighters to enter the fray, and for the genetic alterations which had been performed on those already serving the cause to be passed on to other fighters as yet unconceived.

"It is still a risky business." Scented water sloshed gently around the bulk of One-who-Surrounds.

"I know, but thus far there is only success to show for it. With luck and skill, the Project will continue to prosper."

"There are still those among the brethren who think it unwise, even dangerous."

Green-goes-Softly mentally envisioned a shrug. "One must take risks in war. Our ancestors took many as with far simpler resources they spread the Purpose across the cosmos. We, too, must be bold. Our ancestors never had to confront a sociobiological aberration as extreme as Humankind. New difficulties call for new ways of thinking, new countermeasures. The continued success of the Project will assuage the doubters."

"I concur. I feel wellness about it." One-who-Surrounds retracted its eyestalks, luxuriating in the warm water, pleased to be again in dark, damp surroundings instead of the dry bright light favored by so many of their allies.

4

A morose and dejected Fifth-of-Medicine squatted beneath the towering tree. Warm rain trickled down his dirty green scales to nurture the mud below as he sat contemplating his unnatural fate.

Truly he should not have been there, was not supposed to be in a combat area. The Hivistahm were not fighters. With proper training, some of them could be counted on to serve as support personnel. That was more than could be said for the too-civilized Wais or Motar.

Actual fighting, a barbarity most races had difficulty contemplating, was left to those species in whom the requisite primitive genes had been retained: Massood and, increasingly, Humans. The relentless, horrible, wonderful, utterly unpredictable Humans.

But there were only so many Massood, so many Humans. Other races had to back them up by providing necessary logistical support. That task fell to such as the Bir'rimor, the Lepar, the O'o'yan . . . and the Hivistahm.

A fine medical technician skilled in multiple species repair, Fifth-of-Medicine had been assigned to what for a Hivistahm constituted a forward battle position: emergency physiotech on a rear battle-control sled. He did not expect to be exposed to combat, much less to experience it. But that was precisely what had happened when the combined Ashregan-Crigolit force had surprised the attack group.

Like everyone else he had heard the rumors that the enemy had begun experimenting with new and untraditional strategies, and like everyone else he had dismissed them out of hand. The events of the morning had transformed him instantly from skeptic to true believer. Perhaps if there had been more Humans in the sector the attack might have been beaten off. But they were widely scattered across the surface of contested Eirrosad, and there had been few on his command vessel or its escorting sliders.

After taking several direct hits, the badly crippled transport sled had turned to flee, scraping the jungle canopy as it did so. As it pivoted on its repulsion axis an internal explosion had sent it slamming into a giant forest emergent. It skewed wildly before finally recovering to shudder on its way, shimmying on its stabilizers.

But not before the impact had pitched half a dozen crewmembers through a gaping hole in its side and into the foliage below.

Only two of the six had survived the fall, the otherwise fatal plunge cushioned for them by fortuitously placed branches and leaves. The others had not been so lucky.

By some miracle he had landed in the top of a densely foliated tree, the reedlike upper branches slowing his descent before bending to deposit him, one level at a time, onto similar growths below, until he was finally dumped, bruised but otherwise undamaged, into a puddle of soft mud.

The same mud which had saved his life made fighting on Eirrosad's surface an untenable proposition. Combat was largely restricted to encounters between Weave sliders and enemy floaters, which could dart and hide among the trees and vines. Only the foolish or suicidal would think of trying to conduct a battle on the mushy, planetwide morass which passed for ground. So the surface was left to the specialized native fauna best equipped to cope with it.

And to the unfortunate such as himself. Truly.

He was stuck in the middle of the hostile wilderness the ever irreverent Humans had dubbed the Sludgel: part swamp, part jungle, mostly muck. Without communicator, weapon, or armor. All he had to help him survive was his green physiotech uniform with its attendant equipment, and his wits. He placed little confidence in either. Even his footgear worked against him: high-laced sandals instead of bog boots. He was grudgingly grateful for the overhead vegetation which kept a little of the rain off his scaly scalp.

At least, he thought, the ambient temperature amenable is, and the natives not a worry are. Poor and backward, they lived in transitory jungle villages raised above the ooze on cleverly interwoven stilts, marveling at the incomprehensible forces which contested for control of their world. The Eirrosadians were the second truly tripedal intelligence ever discovered, which made them rather more interesting from a scientific than strategic point of view. By the same token, civilized morality demanded that despite their backwardness they should not be abandoned to the manipulative mercies of the

Amplitur and their allies. None could say but that in a thousand
years or so they might contribute significantly to the war effort.

He adjusted his eyeshades, which had defied all the laws of physics by clinging to his face despite his violent ejection from the sled
and subsequent fall. Their presence contributed significantly to what
little comfort remained to him. Reflecting his emotional state, his
skin had lost its bright green shininess and turned a dull olive hue.
At least it would make him hard for the enemy to spot if they decided to make a visual search of the canopy for survivors.

Beneath the shades, double eyelids blinked at his depressing surroundings. The absence of the bright sunshine so favored by the
Hivistahm contributed to his emotional funk. Silently he damned the
clouds which blocked out the sun, the rain they gave birth to, and
the circumstances which had deposited him in this place.

He considered his situation, quite aware as he did so that it would
not improve upon reflection. They were an unknown but surely considerable distance from the nearest forward Weave outpost, which as
near as he could estimate lay to the south of their present position.
He hadn't devoted much attention to such matters on board the sled,
since there was no need for him to be aware of them. Now he was
paying for his indifference.

It was going to be a long walk.

They would have to experiment with local foodstuffs, but water
obviously wouldn't be a problem. Taste was something else again.

That would likely not be a problem for his fellow survivor, whom
he regarded distastefully. Not satisfied with placing him in this ridiculous position, the fates had decided to heap irony atop discomfort
by giving him for companionship on the arduous trek to come not
another of his own kind, not a Massood or Human to protect him,
not even an attentive O'o'yan or sardonic S'van.

No. He was going to have to travel with a Lepar. With a representative of the Weave's slowest-thinking, dullest species. It did not
boost his spirits to know that the amphibious Lepar was far better
equipped than he to survive an extended sojourn in the Eirrosadian
ecozone.

His name was Itepu, and he seemed agreeable enough despite his
innate handicaps. He'd been a low-level maintenance assistant aboard
the command sled. As was characteristic of his kind, his work had
been repetitious and often dirty.

Standing there in his simple uniform of shorts and vest, his slick tail switching reflexively, webbed hind feet buried in mud, he did not look half as uncomfortable as Fifth-of-Medicine felt. Though half his tools were missing, the Lepar's service belt still held equipment that might prove useful during the long march ahead.

His left arm dangled by his side. Badly sprained in the fall, it was the first thing Fifth-of-Medicine had tended to when they'd stumbled into each other while searching for fellow unfortunates.

The medic regarded the Lepar's coccygeal appendage. Imagine an intelligent race that still retained a tail! Tiny black eyes and an enormously wide mouth contributed to an overweening impression of bland stupidity. Yet the Lepar were not stupid. Merely unclever. And as devoted to the defeat of the Purpose as far more intelligent species, Fifth-of-Medicine reminded himself.

Itepu slogged over to the medic's tree, ignoring the rain which ran in rivulets down his green-brown, slightly slimy skin. "Where we go, and when, friend Hivistahm?"

"How know should I?" A disconsolate Fifth-of-Medicine adjusted his translator as he gestured in a vaguely southward direction with a long, delicate, claw-tipped finger.

The Lepar stood silently for a while, listening to the rain and fiddling with his own speaker and earplug while waiting for the higher-ranking Hivistahm to move. "We should go soon," he said finally. "Enemy in this area."

"I do not think so." Fifth-of-medicine slid off the root on which he'd been brooding, wincing as his legs sank ankle-deep into the fetid, clinging muck. "The battle over is and we have not any shooting for some time heard."

"Rain makes hearing hard."

The physiotech restrained himself. Simply because the Lepar were slow did not mean they were always wrong.

"You are probably correct. We should this area leave."

Better to die out here, he thought, than to be taken alive. Captives were sometimes turned over to the Amplitur for mental "adjustment." A portion of the mind wiped out here, another small section replaced there, and a prisoner was transformed without its consent into a useful agent for the Purpose. He shuddered as he slogged off southward.

A thin film of water covered the boggy surface, magnifying the deceptively solid appearance of the soil beneath. The polite Itepu matched his pace to that of his considerably slower companion.

By evening they had covered more ground than the medic dared hope. As they sat beneath a sheltering leaf the size of a small vehicle eating a peculiar purplish fruit the Lepar had picked, Fifth-of-Medicine felt a little better about their situation. They were in good health and thus far untroubled by the local fauna. He allowed himself to imagine that they might actually have a chance of reaching the outpost.

As near as he could remember, that blessed destination lay on the western shore of a wide, meandering river which ran roughly north-south. If they could make it that far, they could build some kind of raft to carry them the rest of the way downstream to safety. He swatted at something tiny, orange, and persistent. If the local arthropodan life didn't suck all the blood out of them first, he told himself.

He could envision himself among family again, both close and extended. He even managed to meditate for a while, the Lepar observing him silently as he sat cross-legged in the mud, eyes tightly shut, his back to the imaginary contemplation circle. Warm, bright sunshine and hot, dry sand filled his stabilizing thoughts, relaxing him, restoring mental balance.

After a while Itepu turned away and began digging in the mud for things to eat.

By morning the rain had gentled to an occasional light drizzle, and Fifth-of-Medicine's scales began to dry out. His misery quotient fell perceptibly. By midday he was feeling well enough to stride through the undergrowth with some confidence.

They had survived, and would doubtless be feted as heroes upon their return. Even Massood and Humans would have to acknowledge their achievement. Among such hopeful musings Fifth-of-Medicine found time to admire the profusion of chromatically hued jungle flowers.

"Do you like your work?"

"What?" The medic glanced sideways at his lugubrious companion. They were making camp for the evening.

Shiny black eyes looked back at him. "Your work. Do you like doing it?"

As the Lepar were not famed for initiating conversation, Fifth-of-Medicine was somewhat startled by the question. It took him a moment to formulate a reply.

"Truly. I am at what I do very good and hope someday to be a third- or even a second-of-medicine called." To his own surprise he found himself adding, "What about you?"

"I don't think about it much." Itepu yawned, his wide mouth seeming to split his face in half. The dark gullet gaped. "I just do what I was trained to do."

Fifth-of-Medicine was building a bower of leaves and broken twigs. "Sometimes I think it is better that way. Hard it is to see others suffering and not be always able to help. Like the others who out of the sled were thrown but did not survive the explosion or fall. Nothing for them could I do. Truly."

"You did what you could. Tell me: If any enemy was hurt here, would you try to help it?"

It was surprising enough for a Lepar to initiate a conversation. For one to venture a philosophical query bordered on the shocking.

"Truly I do not know. That is something *I* have not thought about. It would on the specific circumstances depend."

When Itepu digested this without replying, Fifth-of-Medicine felt oddly cheated. It was still on his mind when he rose to wash his eyes the next morning.

By then he was more than merely confident. He was convinced they were going to make it back. Even the weather cooperated, as the rains remained light. So relaxed had he become that he did not jump up from his resting place in panic when a clammy hand unexpectedly clutched at his shoulder.

Itepu was bending over him, making small circular motions with his other hand. It took Fifth-of-Medicine a moment to recognize the movement as the Lepar gesture for silence. Puzzled but for the moment compliant, the physiotech rose and followed his crouching companion into the trees.

The amphibian halted behind a wall-like buttressing root and gestured. Following the pointing finger, the medic nearly let out an involuntary hiss.

Not far enough away sat a single Human, perhaps one of those who'd manned an escort slider. No doubt he'd been shot down by the Crigolit and now found himself in straits similar to their own. Fifth-of-Medicine's spirits rose. If the creature was armed, he and Itepu would be able to travel the rest of the way back to the base in the company of serious protection. In circumstances such as theirs it was better to have the companionship of one Human than three or four Massood. Humans adapted much better to the heat and humidity of Eirrosad.

As he started to rise and wave, the Lepar grabbed him and dragged him down. "I know what you are thinking." Itepu's face was uncomfortably close to his own. "Not Human."

All four of Fifth-of-Medicine's eyelids blinked impatiently. "What are you saying? Of course it Human is."

"Not."

"Look at it. At the lanky form, at the proportions. Human it perfectly is."

Itepu rose slowly to peer over the crest of the root. "Wait and watch."

Confused and resentful of being handed an order by a lowly Lepar, Fifth-of-Medicine complied, but with considerable reluctance.

After a while the creature rose to methodically survey the surrounding jungle. The medic's eyes widened as he hastily ducked back down behind the root.

"Truly correct you were," he whispered tautly. "Ashregan it is! With Human proportions, but Ashregan." There was no mistaking, he thought uneasily, those bony ridges over the ears or the wide eye sockets. It was surely Ashregan, despite its height and build.

"A giant among Ashregan," Itepu agreed.

The medic's long tongue commenced to vibrate nervously inside his mouth. "By the Circle! It one of the mutant Ashregan fighters may be that so much havoc on Koba wrought. They were spoken of as tall, fast-moving, and much stronger than is of their kind typical. It is supposed they by the Amplitur from normal Ashregan stock bioengineered have been."

The longer they cautiously observed the creature, the more certain Fifth-of-Medicine grew that this indeed was one of the half-mythical altered Ashregan warriors. It was taller even than most Humans. In retrospect it was not so surprising that he should have misidentified it. After all, the Ashregan bore the same kind of superficial external resemblance to Humans as Hivistahm did to the smaller but distinctly different O'o'yan.

He discussed his observations with Itepu, wishing as he did so that the Lepar was one of his own kind or even a sardonic but brilliant S'van. He could do with a little humor just now.

"How peculiar it is," he found himself murmuring. "It looks Ashregan but moves like a Human."

"Amplitur bioengineering." Itepu was absolutely convinced of the explanation. "They seek to breed Ashregan who will be the equal of Human fighters, so they graft Human characteristics onto them."

Like the isolated incident it was, sudden realization burst in the Lepar's slow but persistent brain. A thick black tongue emerged to clean his left eye as he spoke.

"Do you know what this means? Only two specimens of such as this one were found on Koba, both severely damaged. Here is an example that is not only intact, but alive. If we could capture it and take it back with us . . ."

Fifth-of-Medicine was sure his companion could see the bulging orbs behind the Hivistahm eyeshades.

"Are you truly truly mad? Do you not realize what the creature could do? The Ashregan fighters are. Hivistahm and Lepar are not."

"But this is important." The Lepar's insistence was marked by childlike directness and simplicity. "It would be useful to Weave specialists who are trying to understand what happened on Koba."

Fifth-of-Medicine clicked the claws on his right hand decisively together. "If we near it go, it kill us will. Truly. I refuse absolutely to have anything to do with such a crazy idea."

Itepu stared back at him. Surely he will not try anything on his own, the medic thought. Normally a Lepar would display about as much initiative as a vegetable drying in the sun.

His companion took more time than usual to formulate a reply. "If the Amplitur have been able to give the Ashregan Human fighting abilities in so short a time, it is important that the military council know all about it. It is our responsibility to . . ."

"Truly in this matter we no responsibility have." Fifth-of-Medicine was decisive. "I a fifth-level medical technician and physician am. You a maintenance worker are. Let the Massood and Humans specimens capture. Our responsibility is to our way to the river make, our return to the nearest outpost effect, so that those tasks we may resume."

Ignoring his companion's protestations, Itepu continued to sneak glances over the root. "I think it is wounded. The chance to find one alone and in such circumstances may not happen again soon."

While every instinct screamed at him to run, to get away from that place, Fifth-of-Medicine was unable to completely submerge his curiosity.

"Are you sure it hurt is?"

"Come see how it limps," Itepu whispered down at him.

The physiotech rose alongside his companion. "Even if the injury substantial is, if the creature has been given Human combat abilities, it still more dangerous is than the two of us combined. An ordinary Ashregan would be more dangerous than the two of us combined." Like any healthy, normal Hivistahm he found himself quivering at the very idea of taking part in actual fighting.

"There are no Humans and no Massood here to help us," Itepu pointed out. "We must do this on our own or the opportunity will be lost."

"Then let it be lost."

"I will try to do something alone if I must."

Better quickly to die, Fifth-of-Medicine thought, than to be trapped in this place by himself.

"What do you suggest?" he heard a voice asking. Astonishingly, it was his own. "Charging the creature? We have no weapons."

"It does not seem to have any, either."

"Here, let me again look." Fifth-of-Medicine was not about to take the Lepar's word for it. Though they could see equally well below and above water, the Lepar sometimes suffered from short-sightedness. He flipped his protective eyeshades up onto his low fore-head, where they automatically tightened in place.

The Ashregan had resumed its seat and was consuming some kind of local fruit. Stare as he might, Fifth-of-Medicine could not see so much as a crude club. The creature's clothes were badly torn, reveal-ing blackened splotches on the exposed scaleless skin. So in addition to an injured leg, it was suffering from burns and exhaustion. It wore no body armor at all. Perhaps it was not even a warrior but some kind of frontline technician. Though all Ashregan were trained in fighting techniques, not all were soldiers.

It is not as if we contemplate capturing a Molitar, he told himself. Nor even, he added wryly, a Human. He reconsidered his compan-ion's suggestion. If they could do this thing, the merit they would acquire would be substantial. His musings in the meditation circle would be honored.

The alternative was unpleasant. If they tried to capture it and failed, the Ashregan might well kill them both. He fumbled at his medic's belt and removed a small plasticine cylinder.

Itepu watched quietly. "What are you doing?"

"Trying myself to prepare. Be quiet," the Hivistahm hissed. Tilting back his head, he put the cylinder to his mouth and swallowed two of the pills it ejected. "Field tranquilizers. My reactions will not be affected." He clicked the claws of his left hand together. "But I will physical conflict be able to contemplate with greater equanimity. I may even actual violent contact be able to experience without vomiting."

"The Lepar are no more warlike than the Hivistahm," his companion reminded him.

"If that is meant to encourage me, a dismal failure it is. What do you want to do? I know nothing about fighting."

Itepu's tiny black eyes half closed. "We could wait until it sleeps and then sneak up and hit it in the head."

"Brilliant. If we hit it too hard it dies, and if we do not hit it hard enough it leaps up and dismembers us."

The Lepar considered, straining. "There are two of us. If the first blow is not enough, the second one could hit it again."

Typically complex Lepar cogitation, Fifth-of-Medicine mused. He tried to force himself to think like a warrior, ignoring the slight trembling in his limbs and the rising queasiness in his gut. The tranquilizers were helping.

"There are several deep, water-cut holes." He turned and pointed back toward the tree among whose root structure they had spent the previous night. "If one of us injured pretended to be, he could the creature intrigue and lure this way. We could the hole camouflage: put branches and leaves over it. The one injured pretending to be could carefully avoid the trap but the pursuing creature in would fall."

"That is a good idea." There was admiration in the Lepar's voice. "I would not have thought of it."

Of course you wouldn't, Fifth-of-Medicine mused sympathetically, but that not your fault is. "You will toward the trap the Ashregan lure. I will nearby wait . . ." He started to say "with a club" but knew he could never wield a blunt instrument with harmful intent and so finished, ". . . to make sure everything properly goes."

His companion regarded him solemnly. "We are not runners."
He displayed a webbed hind foot. It was bare, the Lepar having discarded his extraneous sandals long ago. "We are swift in the water,
but not on land. The Hivistahm," he added, with sufficient emphasis
to startle the medic, "are famed for their sprinting abilities."

How odd, Fifth-of-Medicine thought, that I had not that considered before my mouth opening. Itepu was staring at him pointedly.

"I cannot that imagine doing. Truly. We will have to something
else think of." His teeth gnashed lightly, indicative of his distress.
"To deliberately induce an Ashregan to chase me; no. I could not
such a thing do."

"It would be a brief chase," Itepu argued ingenuously. "Over a
modest distance a healthy Hivistahm should be able to keep ahead of
an injured Ashregan. They have short legs."

"Not this mutant," the medic reminded him. "It legs like a Human has."

"You only have to cover a little ground. I will . . . I will hide in
the bushes between here and the hole and if the creature is getting
too close to you I will hit it with a rock." Itepu's tumescent expression brightened at the unexpected realization. "This is good! It com-
bines my idea and yours."

"Unless the creature catches me anyway and you miss with the
rock." Fifth-of-Medicine was much subdued. On the whole, he would
rather have been meditating.

"I do not see how we can do this without taking some risk.
Remember, the creature has an injured leg. Surely it cannot run very
fast."

"Truly, that is so." The medic felt a little more optimistic. "It
might not even try to chase me."

"You should not be in much danger." The Lepar was stolidly
remorseless.

"How will I its attention attract?"

Itepu considered. "Throw something at it. With luck that will
make it mad."

"With luck?" The Hivistahm were not as skilled in the art as the
S'van, but they could still muster sarcasm when the occasion demanded it. "That an offensive action would be." His stomach roiled
at the very thought. "I do not know if I can . . ."

"Then throw nearby. If you are not actually trying to hit it, there is no offense in the action."

"Truly," he had to admit. He flipped his eyeshades back into place. "First we have a hole to choose and camouflage."

The Lepar's wide mouth clapped together twice. "I will take care of that. I am good at manual labor."

And I will watch, Fifth-of-Medicine thought. I am good at that.

By late that afternoon Itepu had demonstrated surprising skill in masking the trap they'd chosen. It was steep-sided and deep enough to keep even a tall Ashregan from climbing out.

That the easy part was, he reminded himself.

He'd had most of the day to ponder what they planned to try and had almost convinced himself they could bring it off. After all, it wasn't as if he was going to have to fight. Just attract the creature's attention, and run. Except for Humans and Massood, the Hivistahm were about the best runners in the Weave, especially over a short distance.

They approached the creature's resting place quietly. Itepu murmured something intended to be reassuring in his own language, then sank out of sight back into the forest, leaving Fifth-of-Medicine on his own. He hoped the Lepar located a particularly large rock.

Am I actually this doing? he asked himself silently as he advanced. I, Fifth-of-Medicine, sophisticated technician and member of respected circles, stalking a soldier of the Purpose? He was awash in fear and revulsion.

The Ashregan had an injured leg, he kept reminding himself.

He'd adjusted his translator to handle the creature's own language, having determined that throwing words could be as provocative as throwing stones. It would not work perfectly, but it should function well enough for him to make himself understood. Not that he intended to engage the enemy in an extended conversation.

What he had not counted on was its imposing size as he drew close. It was the biggest Ashregan he'd ever seen. Truly the Amplitur had bred notable Human characteristics into it. His task suddenly seemed more daunting, his companion Itepu much farther away.

They had invested too much effort and he had come too far for him to back away now, he told himself nervously. Nor could he envision himself confessing his inadequacies to a Lepar. Not that he feared being accused of cowardice. Cowardice was a primitive concept invalid among civilized peoples. Fortunately he found himself possessed by a kind of paralysis of determination.

The tranquilizers helped.

It was almost as if someone else were picking the small round stone out of the muck, as though another being was straightening and throwing it in the Ashregan's direction, supporting its unimpressive trajectory with inane insults in an alien tongue.

The creature reacted with shocking speed and unnaturally fast reflexes, rising and whirling in one motion. Though its proportions were mutant, the face that confronted Fifth-of-Medicine was wide-eyed and wholly Ashregan.

Feeling numbly foolish, he continued to stand where he'd risen, exposed and vulnerable, staring back at the enemy. To break the paralysis he jumped up and down several times and twitched obscenely, though it was unlikely the Ashregan was knowledgeable enough to interpret the gestures.

The stone, the words, the gestures or a combination thereof had an effect, however. Like some great primeval forest spirit, the mutant Ashregan crouched momentarily.

When it rose anew a horrified Fifth-of-Medicine saw the long spear which the creature had until now kept concealed in the underbrush.

The weapon was even taller than its maker, as thick around as the medic's wrist, straight and lethal-looking. Its tip of sharpened stone looked quite capable of slicing through iridescent green scales, flesh, and organs.

With an inarticulate cry, Fifth-of-Medicine put all carefully considered plans aside as he turned and ran.

5

He could hear the Ashregan crashing through the brush behind him. It was making less noise than he'd hoped, slipping through the brush and vines and across the spongy surface with entirely too much ease for so large a creature. Nor were they the sounds he imagined would be produced by something massive traveling on a damaged leg.

Expecting to see nothing so soon, he glanced back over his shoulder and was aghast to note that the Ashregan was not only in sight but already closing. It was not limping.

What had happened to its injury, he wondered frantically?

It occurred to him suddenly that maybe there had never been any wound. Perhaps it had been feigning injury all along, just in case it should encounter Weave troops. So perfect had been its ruse that it had deceived even those it had not seen.

Long, powerful, heavy-boned legs carried it easily from log to log as it methodically ate up the distance between them with strides the shorter Hivistahm could not hope to match. The ominous spear hung from its fist, parallel to the ground. Fifth-of-Medicine was sure it was already within throwing distance.

He could feel the stone-tipped, heavy piece of jungle timber slamming into his back, piercing vital organs, emerging from his sternum with sufficient force still unspent to pin him like a specimen bug against the nearest tree. He tried to accelerate, his three-toed sandaled feet hardly touching the ground as he flew through the woods.

No matter how fast he ran or how radically he swerved, the creature continued to close the distance between them.

He knew then with absolute certainty that they were not going to trap the Ashregan in their carefully concealed pit because it was going to overtake him long before they reached the place. He imagined he could feel the creature's breath on the back of his neck. His eyes wildly scanned the vegetation he ripped through. Where was Itepu with his poised rock? Still somewhere ahead, too far ahead.

Another glance backward filled his eyes with that horrible flat face, the parted mouth with its squarish cutting teeth, the projecting bony ridges over the ears, the throwback patch of fur atop the slightly flattened skull. And the eyes, those round burning eyes, gazing un-blinkingly back into his own.

It's toying with me, he realized suddenly. It knows it can bring me down at any time.

Emitting a hiss of absolute and complete hysteria, knowing that he would never reach the pit in time, too terrified to lament the accomplishments and merit that would never be his, he ran on.

There was a crash behind him. In focusing its attention on its prey had the mutant slipped on the perpetually damp ground? Had it tripped over an especially well-concealed liana? Fifth-of-Medicine didn't turn to look, didn't stop until his heart threatened to bang its way out through his heaving chest.

He blinked. There was nothing behind him.

Was it still playing with its quarry, sneaking through the brush nearby, silently amused at his inchoate terror? To the best of his knowledge that was not a characteristic of the Ashregan. It had all but run him down. Why pause to prolong the game? Humans were occasionally reputed to do such things, but not Ashregan.

It was against his better judgment, but then he'd been acting against his better judgment all day, he reminded himself. He started retracing his path, trying to keep to the denser vegetation, working his way slowly and carefully back the way he'd come.

Eventually he came to something which caused him to suck in his breath with a soft but perceptible hiss.

The Ashregan stood close by the trap. A portion of the branch-and-leaf camouflage had been contemptuously kicked aside to reveal the pit beneath. Blood streamed from the side of the mutant's skull.

Itepu lay on his back at the edge of the hole, the tip of the Ashregan's spear dimpling his belly. The medic recalled the crash he'd heard in the midst of his panicky flight.

The Lepar. Itepu must have leaped from concealment to strike the pursuing Ashregan. Only, the poor amphibian hadn't struck hard enough. The mutant must have been staggered, but instead of going down he'd chased the clumsy Lepar to this point. Itepu had tried to lead the Ashregan into the pit, to succeed where Fifth-of-Medicine had failed.

He ducked down as the enemy soldier suddenly looked around, scanning the surrounding trees intently. Wondering what had happened to its original quarry, no doubt. Trying to decide if any more Weave fools lurked in the tepid jungle.

It turned away and began querying Itepu via its own battered battlefield translator. The sounds of the Lepar language filtered back to the cowering physiotech. Fifth-of-Medicine winced as the Ashregan emphasized its inquiry by prodding the prone Lepar with its spear. Each time the unfortunate maintenance worker refused to reply, the spearpoint probed a little deeper.

Why doesn't he answer? the medic wondered. The Lepar's defiance would only get him killed more slowly.

They'd tried, he told himself, and failed. It struck him that the Ashregan's preoccupation with Itepu offered him a chance to slip away quietly. Could he do that? It was the eminently sensible thing to do, of course. Logical, if not civilized. Given time, he was sure he could rationalize his actions.

He hesitated, hiding deep in the undergrowth, his insides churning. The alternative to logic was a likely death. It was known that certain Hivistahm had succeeded in executing offensive gestures under extreme circumstances. Was he capable of such an action? Of overriding a lifetime's conditioning? To, of all things, help a *Lepar*?

The tranquilizers were still active in his system, helping to dampen dangerous thoughts. This is the result of the Lepar's misguided cogitation, he reminded himself. *He* had wanted to do the sensible thing, to avoid the mutant and continue on to the river and the nearest outpost. He was responsible only for his own safety. And there were greater responsibilities. To his meditation circle. To the war effort. A dead physiotech was of no use to the Weave.

It was the Lepar who had insisted on this ill-conceived effort. Therefore it was only right that the Lepar should pay for its failure. He owed it nothing. A last look, he decided, and then he would be gone.

Peering through the vegetation, he saw that the creature was now wholly occupied with its interrogation of Itepu. It no longer showed interest in its surroundings. That was good. He let the leaves he'd parted fall silently back into place.

He didn't recall when he began to move. Nor did he remember striking the towering Ashregan behind its knees—most likely because both his eyelids were tightly shut at the moment of impact. The Hivistahm were light of build, and his greatest fear was that he wouldn't have sufficient mass to carry out his intent.

His concern was not misplaced. Intent as it was on its questioning of Itepu, the mutant did not start to react until Fifth-of-Medicine was upon him. As it began to turn, the medic struck as hard as he could. The startled Ashregan dropped the spear and flailed its arms in an attempt to maintain its balance. The startled look on its face showed that it could not believe it had been surprised, much less by an inoffensive Hivistahm.

The soil at the edge of the pit was no less slippery and unstable than the rest of Eirrosad's surface. For a horrible moment the creature appeared to regain its equilibrium. Then it dropped out of sight in a great crash of crunching leaves and twigs, emitting furious emanations as it fell. It struck bottom with a spongy *thud*.

Fifth-of-Medicine slumped to his haunches, breathing hard, tongue dangling to one side as he struggled to slow his heart rate. Angry noises continued to bubble from the depths of the trap. When the trembling stopped he rose and moved to help Itepu to his feet. Save for a minor cut where the spear had prodded, the Lepar was unhurt.

"You saved my life."

"Crazy it was. I am of commitment worthy. You must turn me in for observation upon our return. I insist on it!"

Ignoring him, Itepu cautiously approached the lip of the pit and peered in.

The Ashregan was on its feet, uttering curses as it inspected its surroundings. Fifth-of-Medicine did not approach the trap. He knew what the Ashregan looked like.

Itepu backed away from the edge. "Well, we have done it."

"Do not remind me. I prefer not to think on it."

"Now that we have captured the creature, we must think of a way to take it with us."

"I a better idea have." The medic was still breathing hard. "Let's leave it here. We can some food and water provide and mark the spot in our minds. Others come and recover it can."

"No, we can't do that." Itepu was inexorable. "Given time it may find a way to escape. We must take it with us or everything we have done may go to waste." It glanced in the direction of the trap. "We know for certain now that it is Ashregan. A Human would not have bothered to ask questions, but would have killed an enemy instantly."

Reluctantly Fifth-of-Medicine joined his companion at the edge of the pit as they considered what to do with their prisoner.

Once, it backed into a far corner and unexpectedly took a running leap at them, powerful hands reaching for the physiotech's legs. Fifth-of-Medicine took a startled hop backward. He needn't have bothered. Though it could jump impossibly high for so massive a creature, its fingers still fell far short of the trap's rim.

Next it tried to climb out, expending in its frantic efforts more sheer energy than the medic believed a single being could muster. The damp, soft earth crumbled under its fingers and beneath its feet. Several times it ascended nearly a body length, only to tumble back to the bottom as the treacherous soil gave way beneath scrabbling hands and feet.

Though astonishing in their scope, its physical resources were finite. It tried, failed, and fell exhausted one last time into the shallow puddle of water which had collected at the bottom of the pit. Quiescent at last it lay there, breathing hard and glaring murderously up at them.

Fifth-of-Medicine's teeth clicked softly. "We here have to leave it. How can we such a killer restrain? If we bring it out it surely kill us will, and if we down after go it will kill us there. We cannot incapacitate it without near it going."

"That may not be true," Itepu replied slowly.

The Hivistahm's eyelids closed halfway. "Explain yourself."

Itepu gestured at the physiotech's service belt. "You have medicines designed to make the injured feel better. Do not some of them also put you to sleep?"

"Truly. But the emergency vials I at all times on my person carry are calibrated for treating Massood and Human fighters, and to a lesser extent Hivistahm, Lepar, and whatever other species I am at the time serving with. To an enemy treat requires the resources of a field hospital."

"I have heard that Human and Ashregan physiology are very similar."

"Truly they are, but whether they identical enough are for pharmaceuticals designed for one to affect another is a far more complex matter. I am only a fifth-of-medicine, a field medic. I am not in such matters competent."

"This creature has been given Human physical and fighting characteristics," Itepu pointed out. "If anything, it should be more receptive than others of its kind to serums designed for treating Humans. Would it not be worth trying?"

"Still remains the main problem," Fifth-of-Medicine insisted. "How to get near enough to an adequate dosage inject."

"Must it be injected? The creature is tough, but it still needs to eat."

Fifth-of-Medicine considered. "Would it not suspicious of food from us be?"

"Probably, but hunger should eventually overcome suspicion. It must realize that if we wanted it dead we could throw rocks down on it, or leave it here. Nor does it know that you are a medic with access to sedatives."

He made the dose strong. Very strong. After all, the worst that could happen was that it would kill the creature, thus sparing them the difficulty of somehow hauling it back with them. He was able to concoct the dose without qualms because it was not his *intent* to kill but to tranquilize. The possibility of a fatal accident weighed only peripherally on his conscience.

As expected, the Ashregan at first refused all offers of fruit and meat. But two days of clawing futilely at the walls of its prison left it ravenous, and it finally devoured the proffered food, exhibiting an extraordinary appetite as well as atrocious table manners. It not only finished what they had provided but asked for more, after which it sat down in the slimy puddle and regarded them with a baleful expression on its flat, ugly face.

An hour later its eyes closed as its head fell over on one shoulder.

"We can use vines braced around a tree to drag it out," Itepu suggested, "and to bind it. I think the two of us working together can manage the load."

"One of us will have to go down to secure it." The medic was studying the motionless alien form. "What if it deceiving is?"

"I will find out."

It took the Lepar a few moments to locate a rock of suitable size. As Fifth-of-Medicine looked on, Itepu carefully positioned himself on the other side of the pit and let it drop. It was large enough to start a trickle of blood from the Ashregan's scalp but not to crack bone. The mutant's eyelids did not even twitch.

"Truly unconscious it is." Fifth-of-Medicine was satisfied. "Let us make sure we bind it beyond possibility of escape."

A variable-focus surgical cutter allowed them to sever and gather very thick vines. After wrapping the heavy alien in a green cocoon, arms secured behind its back, they strained to haul it out of the hole, working quickly lest it awaken before they were finished. Since they did not have the inclination, much less the strength, to carry their prisoner, they left its lower limbs relatively free, binding each ankle to opposite ends of a short, stout tree limb which severely restricted each leg's range of motion while still allowing the creature enough leeway so that it could stumble forward.

When it regained consciousness it was more than a little surprised at the condition in which it found itself. After trying its bonds and finding them unbreakable, it looked accusingly at Fifth-of-Medicine. Its translator was in bad shape, but still functioning.

"You drugged me," it said accusingly. "I didn't suspect. What are a Hivistahm and Lepar doing out in this jungle with drugs?"

"I a medical technician am," Fifth-of-Medicine found himself replying. Even bound and helpless, the Ashregan still cut an intimidating figure.

It emitted an untranslatable grunt. "That never occurred to me. I should have noted your uniform type when I was chasing you. It serves me right. Well, now that you have me, what do you intend to do with me?"

"Take you back with us." The physiotech retreated several steps as the Ashregan struggled to its feet. The limb secured to its ankles reduced its stride considerably, its mobility completely. Enmeshed in its cocoon of vines, it towered over its captors.

Itepu clutched the prisoner's spear. The Ashregan grinned contemptuously. "You don't expect me to believe you'd use that."

The Lepar's reply was admirably firm. "I have hit you twice with rocks. I might surprise you again."

"You might at that. You Lepar are difficult to understand. Some day you'll be useful participants in the Purpose."

"Not while any of us lives," Itepu assured him.

"Nor any Hivistahm." Fifth-of-Medicine was not about to be exceeded in defiance by a Lepar. "You are back with us coming. You a physical anomaly are. Ashregan you appear, yet with Human characteristics."

"I *am* Ashregan," the captive replied proudly. "You hold the Unifer Ranji-aar of Purposeful Cossuut." He strained at his bonds. "And if I can free myself I will destroy you both, as I destroy all enemies of the Purpose."

"Yes, we know." Fifth-of-Medicine's confidence increased in proportion to the Ashregan's inability to loosen its bindings. "It is clear that altered you have been. Doubtless responsible the Amplitur are."

The soldier glared narrowly at his captor. "The Amplitur do not do such things. Such tales are only Weave propaganda. The Amplitur . . ."

"Spare us the lecture on the wonderfulness of the Amplitur. I have eyes, and I a trained medical specialist am. You both Ashregan and Human traits possess. There is here something very peculiar going on. We are taking you back so that better minds than mine can what the truth is find out."

"They'll find no more than you." The mutant expectorated. "You've taken a captive; that's all." It turned sharply to Itepu, who flinched slightly, black eyes blinking, but held his ground. "You I should've killed when I had the chance."

The Lepar's expression did not change. "But you did not."

"No. You were on the ground and helpless, and I had questions to ask. I should have been faster, like a berserker Human."

"I am glad you were not." Itepu stepped boldly forward and poked the bound Ashregan with the spear. "Now move. That way."

The prisoner gazed a moment longer at the amphibian, then pivoted to start off in the indicated direction. His captors followed. Amazement at their accomplishments thus far caused them to walk proud.

Despite Fifth-of-Medicine's fears, they were not attacked. Nothing leaped out at them from the undergrowth, nothing materialized to impede their progress. Having delivered himself of several proclamations, the Ashregan had turned surprisingly docile. Fifth-of-Medicine and Itepu did not relax, staying as alert as when they'd first trapped the soldier. For surely this creature's companions would be searching for him.

They reached the river without incident. The prisoner sat quietly while his captors, making good use of Fifth-of-Medicine's surgical instruments and Itepu's remaining tools, fashioned a crude raft. If they needed any further proof that the creature was Ashregan, its continued docility as they worked with logs and vines confirmed it. A Human would have jumped into the river despite the likelihood of drowning, or struck out with its restrained legs, or at least inflicted on them a constant stream of invective. That was the way of Humans. It was not the manner of Ashregans.

Instead, he continued to lecture them endlessly on the true way of the Purpose, until the medic was ready to put aside the value of their prisoner and strike him dead with the spear.

"We have everything you could say already heard," he finally informed the mutant exasperatedly. "Despite what you believe, there is civilization outside the Purpose. Truly."

"Civilized peoples do not slaughter the helpless civilian populations of undefended worlds," the Ashregan shot back.

Fifth-of-Medicine glanced up curiously from where he was working on the raft. "What are you talking about?"

"My parents. My entire family and all its friends and relations were wiped out by Humans and Massood."

"Truly now, I cannot imagine to what you refer."

"The massacre of Houcilat, of course. I can't believe you never heard of it, no matter how thorough is Weave control of your information media. Houcilat was my world of origin."

Fifth-of-Medicine reflected as he worked. "Houcilat, Houcilat. Truly, yes. That was a world colonized by both Ashregan and, I believe, Bir'rimor. It contested was, and taken back by the Weave some time ago. I am at recent history fairly competent. Do you anything of what he speaks recall, Itepu?"

The Lepar looked up from where it was working waist-deep in water. "We do not have good memories. But the name strikes me."

"The fighting was lengthy but modest in scope, and the world was back for the Weave won. But there no massacre of inhabitants was. Truly." Fifth-of-Medicine fastened two logs together, eyeing his handiwork with satisfaction. Misapplication of his extensive medical training such construction might be, but there were none present to proffer objections.

"All inhabitants were allowed under Weave supervision to remain, or to other Ashregan worlds repatriated were."

Ranji's brows drew together. "Weave propaganda. Everyone on Houcilat was slaughtered. Including my natural parents."

The medic drew a thick liana tight. "Killed they may have been. I am sure some civilian casualties there were. But a massacre there was not."

"All my parents' friends, all my relatives and their relatives, were killed. Do the Hivistahm describe such atrocities in languid phrases?"

Fifth-of-Medicine glanced behind him. "Even that may be truth, but I tell you that there was no slaughter. That is not the way of the Weave. You have been lied to."

"The Amplitur . . ." Ranji started to remind his captors that the Amplitur never lied. Even they would have to admit to that. But as he thought back it struck him that no Amplitur, either in person or on recording, had ever spoken directly about Houcilat. The story of the massacre of Houcilat had been told to him by his parents and teachers, who were Ashregan. It might be interesting some day to put the question to an Amplitur and observe the response.

No! Absurd, inconceivable, a thing he could not countenance. Why should he for an instant question parents or instructors because of what a Purposeless, enemy Hivistahm chose to say on the bank of an unnamed river on a primitive, contested world?

"*You're* the ones who've been lied to," he responded confidently. "There *was* a massacre."

"That possible is," admitted Fifth-of-Medicine readily. "Truly I was not there. But tell me this, Ashregan Unifer: What would be the purpose of such slaughter? What would it gain the Weave?"

"It need have no purpose if Humans were involved."

"Even Humans more restrained are. There are of isolated barbaric incidents some rumors, but nothing on the scale to which you refer. Nor are Humans alone to fight allowed. Massood or others are always present, and would have such a terrible thing confirmed."

"Are you so sure? It would be to the Weave's benefit to conceal such an incident. Because you do not have the Purpose, you are always fighting and arguing among yourselves. Knowledge of such an outrage could cause trouble among you."

"You very plausibly argue." Fifth-of-Medicine secured a vine, snugging two cross-limbs tightly together. "Though I do not believe you, I allow as how you might be correct. Will you not grant me the same privilege? Anything is possible which cannot disproved be."

Ranji went silent as his captors worked. Silence offered time to think, which, as his teachers had sometimes pointed out, could be dangerous. Why would they lie to him, especially about something as important to him and his friends as the destruction of Houcilat? The Hivistahm had seemed genuinely surprised by his disclosure, and equally convinced no such massacre had occurred. Yes, the Weave government could have covered it up, but was such a thing really possible in this time of rapid interworld and interspecies communication?

"My friends will drive you off this world," he declared for lack of anything more convincing to say. "And massacre or not, the Weave remains responsible for the death of my parents."

"I am for that most sorry," the physiotech told him. "Even when great and exalted ideals at stake are, civilians sometimes perish in their cause. But I and my companion nothing to do with that had. We were at the time of Houcilat not adults."

Ranji calmed himself. He should be looking for a chance to escape, not wasting his energy arguing with the enemy. "I didn't mean to imply that I blamed you personally. Only the misguided and misled organization that organizes your war effort. To do otherwise would not be in keeping with the higher tenets of the Purpose."

"Of course it wouldn't." Fifth-of-Medicine's claws clicked together sideways, a gesture his kind used to express sarcasm. "Your form puzzles me greatly."

"I am wholly Ashregan. If you think otherwise then you're wasting mind time."

"Truly you must pictures of Humans have seen. I cannot believe you have never upon the physical similarities remarked."

"I'm aware of the superficial resemblance. Also the differences," Ranji assured him.

"It would not be beyond the Amplitur to with an allied species genetically interfere if they believed their goals they could enhance." If this was a development the Weave was aware of but keeping secret from the general populace, he thought, then a quick strike at the world where the Amplitur were carrying out their activities might stop it cold.

It shocked him to realize that he had just promulgated a possible rationale for precisely the kind of massacre their prisoner insisted had taken place at Houcilat. But surely the S'van, the Hivistahm would not permit such a thing.

Surely.

"That's nonsense." The prisoner shifted against his bonds. "The Ashregan are a physically diverse species. Just because some of us are taller and stronger than the rest doesn't mean we're the products of some bizarre, not to mention unethical, genetic manipulation."

"It is not for me to determine. You will by better minds than mine be analyzed and studied." Seeing the look on the Ashregan's face he added, "I doubt you will to vivisection be subjected. Do you think truly that we are the barbarians the Amplitur make us out to be?"

"They don't call you barbarians," Ranji told him.

Sharp teeth clicked in the medic's narrow snout. "Not directly, no. But they suggest it. Your Amplitur masters at suggestion very good are."

"They're not our 'masters.' Within the Purpose all species are equal."

"Have you not Amplitur suggestions been subjected to?"

"I've had mind contact with a couple, yes." He said it proudly. "I feel only elevated and honored for the experience."

"Of course. They would 'suggest' that you feel that way."

"I *did* feel that way," Ranji shot back, more loudly than he intended.

Fifth-of-Medicine was not in the mood to discuss the inefficacies of circular logic. Together he and Itepu shoved the finished raft all the way into the water. It drifted motionless next to the muddy shore, reassuringly stable.

"Let's go," he told the prisoner. "Do not anything foolish try. You could perhaps into the river dump us, but my friend is as at home in the water as on land and you can be sure he would expend his energies on rescuing me, not you. You could not escape."

Ranji shuffled forward, the restraining log heavy against his ankles. "Just because I'm a warrior doesn't mean you have to belabor the obvious."

6

As Fifth-of-Medicine had anticipated, their unexpected appearance at the outermost defensive perimeter of the nearest Weave outpost touched off quite a celebration among the station's astonished personnel. Tired and dirty but otherwise intact, they were escorted from the outpost to Weave military headquarters. Not only had they survived the devastating attack on the Weave's northeastern front, they had made their way back on foot through hostile terrain, without weapons. And they had brought a prisoner out with them.

It was the type of exploit expected of Humans or Massood, not Hivistahm and Lepar.

Though concerned about his mental state, Fifth-of-Medicine's colleagues accorded him a place of honor the first time he joined a meditation circle, and his accumulation of merit was duly and ceremoniously noted. As for Itepu, the accolades he received were offered quietly: an occasional congratulatory word, a casual admiring touch. He did not bathe in them: he was anxious to get back to work.

The initial eagerness of the base's medical staff to examine the prisoner soon gave way to discouragement as they realized they were ill equipped to carry out anything like a proper study of the creature. Still, their necessarily cursory studies only confirmed what Fifth-of-Medicine had already noted, that being a confusing melange of Human and Ashregan characteristics in the same body. It was a biological puzzle the Hivistahm and O'o'yan technicians on Eirrosad did not have a large enough key to unlock.

It was decided to send the captive out on the next supply shuttle. A Human would have reacted violently to the news that he was to be shipped so far from his friends, but their prisoner was not Human. As an Ashregan soldier trained in the Purpose he acquiesced calmly to the decision, making only one small and rather quaint request.

Though Command thought it baffling, they graciously consented to its fulfillment.

So while Ranji found himself speeding through Underspace toward an unknown destination far from Eirrosad and even farther from his beloved Cossuut, he did not travel alone. More than a few were bemused as to why the single demand he made was for the company of a particular Lepar.

Headquarters psychologist Third-of-Mind thought he had an explanation. "Here is an Ashregan prisoner, of mind probing probably afraid. He knows of the Lepar reputation for simplicity, and knows personally this particular individual. He will try the Lepar to employ to check the veracity of what is to him told by others."

The base commander was Massood. It was his task to try and win a world for the Weave—a world of suffocating humidity and cloying rain, two meteorological traits he was not particularly fond of. He was not much interested in the physiological aberrations or mental workings of one Ashregan prisoner, now blissfully removed from his jurisdiction.

He dismissed the psychologist without comment.

On the ship racing away from Eirrosad's sun, however, there was more time for curiosity. Everyone was conscious of the regard in which muttering specialists held the unique passenger, who communicated his personal requests through the eccentric medium of a Lepar maintenance worker. They marveled at its size during its occasional escorted walks through unsensitive portions of the ship. It was far and away the largest Ashregan any of them had ever seen.

The S'van captain was somewhat disappointed in their destination. True, there were large and competent scientific facilities on Omaphil, but it was a Yula world. He would much rather have taken their prisoner to one inhabited by his own kind.

The option was not available to him. The military counselors had been quite specific. The Yula settled planet of Omaphil was the nearest fully developed Weave world to Eirrosad, and for reasons unknowable it might at some time in the near future be desirable to return the captive to that contested globe. He stroked his beard reflexively. It might be all right. Yula was a cosmopolitan place. There would be S'van present to keep an eye on developments, even if they were not directly involved in the examination process itself.

There was no reason for him to concern himself with the prisoner specifically except that the S'van made it a point to concern themselves with everything. Not that they were overly curious. Merely paranoid.

Yulans in fact comprised a substantial part of the crew, together with the usual complement of Hivistahm, O'o'yan, Lepar, and S'van officers. There was also a squad of Massood, who had been suborned from Eirrosad specifically to keep watch on the captive. As the Ashregan proved to be a model prisoner, they were able to pass their duty time in comfort.

They were accompanied by a trio of Human soldiers whose resemblance to the captive provoked a good deal of whispered comment among the crew. The Ashregan displayed no inclination to seek their company, however, instead preferring the companionship of the Lepar who had accompanied him on board. That pleased the more imaginative among the crew, who found the Ashregan's proximity to look-alike Human soldiers inexplicably unnerving.

Not that the prisoner's preference for the Lepar's company was any less puzzling. To the average Lepar, a couple of sentences constituted an extended conversation. What did the Ashregan find to talk about with his amphibious attendant? The crew amused themselves inventing outrageous explanations.

With his three legs and three arms, his unusual tripodal posture, three yellow eyes centered on the flat front end of the triangular skull, mottled yellow-and-brown fur which bulged from beneath the skirt of his light-duty uniform, Teoth looked a lot like an overstuffed child's doll. Though he was no taller than the average Hivistahm, all that fur made him appear far more massive.

It was real fur, thick and dense as a S'van's beard though far softer and infinitely better groomed. It covered Teoth's entire body, including the head and limbs, and its complex pattern of spots defined his identity.

While not one of the more populous or important races, the Yula had been part of the Weave for hundreds of years, believed fully in the cause, and contributed what they could to the resistance against the Amplitur. They were fully civilized, which meant that they did not participate in any actual fighting but instead gave aid and support to those who did, like the Humans and Massood. Which explained their presence aboard the transport vessel.

The Yula inhabited, not surprisingly, three worlds, of which Omaphil was the most prominent. Its economy was dominated by agriculture and light industry, of which only a portion was dedicated to the war effort. Despite their sensitive galactic location, the Yula enjoyed the deceptively peaceful existence common to most worlds of both the Weave and the Purpose. Actual fighting was something that took place elsewhere, on lightly populated planets, between the primitive species of the Weave and those unfortunates who had been adjusted for the purpose by the Amplitur.

It was for this reason that Teoth was concerned that conveyance of this special captive warrior to peaceful Omaphil did not seem to greatly trouble his fellows. Despite repeated and earnest attempts to discuss the matter with them, they chose to go about their tasks unconcerned.

He found more sympathy among the perpetually brooding, always somber Hivistahm. Two in particular, Eighth-of-Records and Sixth-of-Technics, provided a willing audience for his polemics. They shared his fear of the prisoner and what it represented.

They usually met in the zero-g bubble, trying to choose times when it was not too crowded. While others bounced off the soft, padded walls or drifted through the ever-changing central maze or engaged in various null-g games, the three conspirators kept out of the way and to themselves.

Teoth's motives were simple: he did not want to see some crazed Ashregan fighting machine imported into his world. While most would insist that a single hostile alien could not pose much of a threat, Teoth would have violently disagreed. In that respect his attitude was more Hivistahm than Yula. Certainly that contributed to a unanimity of opinion among the three.

Because of his position, Eighth-of-Records knew as much about their passenger as anyone aboard. Sixth-of-Technics and Teoth had caught glimpses of it during its occasional escorted walks through the ship. Those brief encounters were terrifying enough.

Eighth-of-Records was declaiming softly. "They say that a new kind of mutant Ashregan fighter it is an example of, bioengineered by the Amplitur the Humans to counteract."

"I wonder how successful it has been," murmured Sixth-of-Technics.

"Truly I do not know." His companion's teeth clicked. "It a secret is. There are rumors, though. As tough as Humans it is said they are."

"Why my world? That is what I want to know." Teoth fiddled with his translator, wanting to make certain everything he said was clearly comprehensible to his Hivistahm companions. "Why not one of the Massood planets? Or better yet, the Human world, where it could be well and truly isolated. Were it to get loose there it could not wreak havoc on a civilized society."

"You know why," said Sixth-of-Technics. "Because Omaphil the nearest fully developed Weave world to Eirrosad is."

"Council is anxious." The other Hivistahm's inner, transparent set of eyelids were shut against the bubble's glare. "They do not what to make of it know."

"Well I know what to make of it." Teoth was emphatic. "I believe that all the worst rumors are accurate, that this creature is the latest example of the Ampliturs' immoral experiments in bioengineering."

"There must be more," insisted Sixth-of-Technics. "The Amplitur would not just a single such creature release."

Teoth gestured significantly. "Surely you have heard about what happened on Koba."

"Truly." Eighth-of-Records shuddered. "Can you imagine what might happen if it were to aboard this ship get loose?"

"I am less concerned with what happens aboard this ship than I am about my cherished homeworld." Seeing that he was starting to rotate, Teoth reached out with two of his three hands to steady himself against the padded wall.

"If that were to happen, how many cubs would it kill before it could finally be destroyed? How many homes would it ravage? The 'specialists' admit they know little about it, about its ultimate abilities or potential. Why subject a peaceful place like Omaphil to their dangerous experiments?" He focused all three eyes on his companions.

"The Yula have always been willing participants in the workings of the Weave. So why should they be singled out for additional risk?"

"They are not singled out being." Sixth-of-Technics felt compelled to restate the obvious. "The Ashregan is being there taken for reasons of time and urgency, and proximity to Eirrosad."

"I am not mollified by the explanations." Teoth's tone grew less peremptory. "My people are not as mature as yours, or certain others. They would not deal as well with the knowledge that this creature had been brought into their midst."

"Sure I am that the intention is to keep its presence on Omaphil a secret." Sixth-of-Technics hissed softly.

"The Yula believe in openness." Teoth's fur bristled. "I simply do not agree with any of this, any of it at all. Is this but the first of many such impositions to be made upon my world? Does the Weave military council intend to bring all such mutants to Omaphil for study? What if they should begin to breed in captivity? If one is as rumored capable of great horrors, what might many do?

"We are not fighters. The Yula are civilized. We would be helpless in the face of such an onslaught. Massood would have to be brought in to control the problem, or even worse"—and his distress was palpable even to the Hivistahm—"Humans."

"Truly I would not on my homeworld wish this being loose," agreed Eighth-of-Records.

"Let them take the scientists to Eirrosad if they wish to study it." Teoth's legs drifted lazily.

Sixth-of-Technics clicked claws together. "What do you think should be done?"

"I am not sure." Three eyes blinked. "I am only a simple technician like yourself. But I do know that this matter is too important to be left to the likes of self-serving scientists."

A group of gamboling S'van came near, and the trio went silent until they had passed. "Are you something uncivilized preparing to propose?"

"I would not think of it that way," Teoth argued. "I am only saying that those who are closer to the people should take it upon themselves to carefully monitor the situation."

The two xenologists regarded the prisoner thoughtfully. Its occasional volubility notwithstanding, it remained as much of an enigma as when they had first encountered it.

Half the pair was S'van. He was typically short and squat. A dense black beard practically obscured his face. More thick, wiry hair was visible where his wrists and ankles emerged from his clothing. His eyebrows threatened to obscure his vision.

His Massood associate towered over him, her uniform of ship-duty vest and shorts snug against close-cropped silvery fur, gray cat eyes alert to the captive's every move, black-tufted ears flicked alertly forward. Her muzzle and whiskers were in constant motion. As she worked she picked at her short, sharp teeth, a type of grooming as natural to the Massood as breathing.

"I don't understand it." The S'van spoke in a soft, reassuring tone much like the recordings Ranji was familiar with. It was as tranquil a voice as a Vandir's. Certainly his interrogator was anything but physically intimidating. Hardly a being to be afraid of, Ranji told himself. The S'van's manner was at all times cordial and civilized.

The Massood female was much more physically impressive. Taller than Ranji but not as strong, her attention was concentrated on the compact device she carried. Probably recording everything he did or said, he decided. Not that he minded. He had nothing to hide and could do nothing to prevent it in any event.

He paid close attention as the finely tuned translator they had given him interpreted their conversation.

"His responses are typically Ashregan," the S'van was saying. "Even to the trick questions I composed."

"That is my opinion also." The Massood gazed at the silent prisoner. "Mentally and emotionally he is completely Ashregan. Physically he is unique. You have seen the preliminary medical report?"

The S'van bobbed his head. "Internally he's as Human as your average soldier from Earth. The differences between Humans and Ashregan are modest, but distinct. In this one they're absent except for the notable exceptions of the skull and fingers. He displays the familiar Ashregan bony ridges over recessed ears, the same expanded eye sockets, flattened nose, and the longer fingers with the extra knuckle on each." He gazed at the pocket readout screen that rested alight on his lap.

"Of course we're not supposed to concern ourselves with physiology. That's for others to delve into. We're supposed to be working on his mind, not his guts."

"What do you intend to do with my mind?" Ranji inquired politely. "Do you think this will do any good?"

"There!" The S'van xenologist was pleased. "That's the most Humanlike response he's given yet. No Ashregan would volunteer such a sarcastic remark in the course of an interrogation."

"I was not being sarcastic." Ranji leaned back in his chair. "You don't understand my people at all. We may look a lot like your Humans but our thought processes are completely different . . . thank the Purpose! Your obtuseness on this matter is wearying."

The S'van was not easily baited. "Oh, I don't know. I think the psychological data base we've managed to construct from interviews conducted with thousands of your kind down through the centuries has resulted in a pretty accurate profile of Ashregan thought processes." He chuckled and stroked his tangled steel-wool beard. Among Weave races the S'van were reputed to have the most highly developed sense of humor, together with, perversely, the otherwise utterly barbaric Humans.

"There should be a Human xenologist present," said the Massood, hastening to add, "I intend no suggestion of incompetence, D'oud."

"That's all right, though I'm not sure I agree with you. I don't know that a Human xenologist would bring any more insight to this process."

"What are you going to do with me?" Ranji asked them. "Different interrogators give me different answers."

D'oud belched. His Massood companion looked pained. "You are being taken to a Weave world for study. You confuse us. We are convinced that you are some type of mutant, though whether natural or induced it's premature to guess. That will be for the specialists to determine.

"We tend to think that many of your Humanlike physical characteristics are the result of Amplitur interference, of an attempt on their part to develop more effective warriors. Bioengineering on a large scale is standard Amplitur modus. We know from Koba that you are not an isolated example and that there are others of your physical type."

"I don't have any Human properties." Ranji controlled his anger. "I'm entirely Ashregan."

"So you have repeatedly insisted." The S'van's eyes glittered. "I'm sure you're telling the truth as you believe it. The reality will eventually emerge only from unprejudiced analysis."

The Massood's upper lip curled by way of emphasis. "Your type is taller, stronger, faster, and according to the reports more aggressive than the average Ashregan. In short, Humanlike. How the Amplitur have managed this we do not know, but they can pick apart DNA as easily as I would dismember a small food animal."

"The Amplitur have done nothing to me. I am Ashregan and only Ashregan. Analyze all you wish. You'll find nothing to support your ridiculous suppositions."

The S'van sighed as he flipped off his readout and rose. Clearly the interview was at an end. It was Ranji's turn to smile.

"I'll be happy to talk with you whenever you like. There's always the chance of winning an enemy to the Purpose."

The two xenologists departed. "We need much more in the way of in-depth study facilities," the S'van was saying as he exited Ranji's cubicle. "These cursory interviews do not—" the door slid silently shut behind them, cutting him off in mid-declaration.

Shortly thereafter it reopened to admit a familiar bulbous, guileless face. A student of alien expression would have noted immediately that the smile with which Ranji greeted this new arrival was quite different from the one he had so recently bestowed on his interrogators.

"Purposeful greetings to you, Itepu."

"Warm water and light currents." The Lepar had acquired the habit of bringing Ranji's meals to him personally. It gave them more time to talk. Itepu enjoyed their conversations, so long as the Ashregan kept them simple. There was much to learn from him, and Itepu liked to learn.

Ranji swung his legs off his bed and bent to inspect the meal. As usual, the foodstuffs were unfamiliar but edible. The ship's automatic providers knew what to prepare. The Weave had been taking its share of prisoners for hundreds of years. The workings of Ashregan physiology were neither mysterious nor complicated. The meals might not delight him, but they would keep him alive.

His captors were treating him well, even to providing him with

Ashregan eating utensils. He made use of them as the ever inscrutable Itepu looked on silently.

Their deceptive friendliness did not fool him. Everything they did was for the sole aim of securing the cooperation of a valuable specimen, nothing more. If they harbored any illusions about turning him to their way of thinking they were in for an extended period of disappointment. He dug into the meal enthusiastically, knowing he would need his energy for the arguments to come. A prisoner he might be, but that did not mean he could no longer serve the Purpose.

"How did the session go?" Itepu leaned back slightly, using his strong tail to balance himself.

Ranji poked something pink and fleshy into his mouth. Useless to wonder about drugs. He had to eat and drink in order to survive, and if they wanted to medicate him they could do so at any time without having to resort to subterfuge.

"I think they went away frustrated." He chewed as he spoke. "I also think they're a little afraid of me. That's good. They should be afraid of me." He picked up a lump of baked grains and glanced across at the Lepar. "You're afraid of me, too, aren't you?"

"Of course I am. Like any civilized race we find the very notion of combat unsettling and those species who engage in it quite terrifying."

Ranji tore a chunk off the brown loaf and waved it at his visitor. "But you're not as afraid of me as you would be of a Human."

"The Humans are our allies. I am not afraid of Humans."

Ranji swallowed. "In addition to fighting, I'm trained to observe. My interrogators learn from me, I learn from them. I think you're lying." Itepu said nothing.

"My visitors keep telling me how many Human characteristics I have, how they've been 'bioengineered' into my friends and me by the Teachers to enable us to fight more like Humans. I see how they react when they speak of such things, and it doesn't matter whether they're S'van, Hivistahm, O'o'yan, or Massood. It's been very enlightening.

"I know from my training and studies that Ashregan and Humans look a lot alike. It would be foolish of me to try and deny that I look more like Humans than most of my kind. But that doesn't make me Human, or mean that my genes have been tampered with.

It means only that I'm a taller, stronger, more dangerous than usual Ashregan. I don't understand why your scientists keep trying to make something very simple into something much more complicated."

"I would not know," replied Itepu quietly. "Such matters are beyond my comprehension."

"Yes. The Lepar are a simple, straightforward people. That's why we don't understand why you cannot see the benefits of joining with the Purpose. Despite what is said for public consumption, you are looked down upon within the Weave. That would not be the case within the Purpose, where all species are treated as equals. You would be one with the Crigolit and the Ashregan and the Amplitur Teachers."

"It is true that we are simple." Itepu spoke slowly and carefully. "But we are intelligent enough to be realists. No matter what you say, all species are not created equal. Since we realize and accept this, it does not trouble us. From that realization stems our contented independence, which we will never trade for some obscure alien ideal."

Ranji sighed and pushed the remnants of his meal aside. "More skewed thinking. If we are allowed more time together, I hope to reveal the truth to you."

Itepu gestured with one thick-fingered hand. "I am touched by your concern for my welfare."

Stymied by his inability to convince, Ranji reached for the container of fortified liquid. The contents were pleasantly tart.

"I like you, Itepu. I like you and your fellow Lepar a great deal. I think that in some ways you represent the best of the Weave, though you remain as misguided as any. There's an innocence about you, an honesty, that's absent from your sophisticated allies."

"I like you, too, Ranji-aar. I am glad that I was permitted to accompany you. It must be a terrible thing to know that one is so far from one's companions, alone among aliens." A slight quiver ran through the amphibian, culminating in a sharp twitch of his tail. "I know that I could not long stand it."

"That's because you're not a fighter. Don't condemn yourself for lack of abilities you were not born with. Each of us has a different role to play in this temporary existence."

"In the current that meets itself." Tiny black eyes regarded him from the middle of an unintentionally comical face. "Are you so sure you know what your role is?"

"No question about it." Ranji settled back on the bed. "To fight for the Purpose. To make my family and friends proud of me."

"As I am sure they are." Itepu straightened, holding his tail off the floor. He smelled of the scummy water in which he and his companions spent their off-duty hours. "It must be a wonderful thing to be so certain of everything, to know always what to do, what is right and what is wrong. Sadly, the Lepar are a stupid folk. The universe confuses us. We have difficulty choosing from among infinite possibilities. If only the cosmos were a simpler place. Then we could be more confident, more like the S'van, or the Ashregan, or the Amplitur."

"The Teachers?" Ranji blinked, surprised.

"Yes. The Lepar think there is much to admire in the Amplitur. It is their attitude that troubles us. Their attitude, and their intentions."

"It doesn't have to be like that," said Ranji earnestly. "You could change."

Itepu touched a wall plate and the door slid aside. "I think we would rather see the Amplitur change." He paused in the gap.

"I hope no harm will come to you, Ranji-aar of the Ashregan. I hope you will live out a long and contented life among your own kind. There is much about you that intrigues me. Much that I, simple representative of a simple people, can never hope to understand." The door closed behind him.

7

The authorities went to considerable trouble to keep his arrival a secret. He was the only passenger on the shuttle which transferred him from the Underspace transport to the surface of Yula. There he was promptly hustled into a small, self-powered air-repulsion vehicle. It was a lot like an attack floater save for civilian appointments such as darkened windows and comfortable seats.

He and his escort sped through a city of modest size and alien architecture. Soon they were traveling through rolling green hills dotted with small agricultural establishments. Fields were lush with crops: green, yellow, brown, and purple. Clearly Yula was a comfortable, prosperous world. Civilized. Peaceful. Its young people did not run mazes or simulate warfare.

Ranji felt sorry for them.

The fluffy, fast-moving clouds scudding past overhead were painful reminders of home. A few raindrops hit the vehicle's shieldfield and evaporated. He wondered how his parents were doing, how long it would be before they learned of his disappearance in battle. He tried not to think of what their reaction would be. Saguio would handle it best of all, he thought. Cynsa was too young to understand. All of them would take comfort in the knowledge that he had sacrificed himself fully for the Purpose.

Except that he had not sacrificed himself fully. He was still alive. As long as he could still think clearly he knew he would not willingly go on living just to satisfy the misguided curiosity of Weave scientists. He would find a way to resist, somehow. For the honor of his parents. For Kouuad, and for doomed Houcilat he was fated never to see.

There might yet be opportunities to serve the Purpose.

His captors were taking no chances. They had honored him with an escort of not one but two Humans—both males. A lone Wais

driver sat in solitary splendor in the forward compartment, separated
from the prisoner by a transparent shield. The two males flanked
Ranji, their sullen, narrow faces focused straight ahead. If anything,
they looked bored. Ranji was impressed, but far from awed.

As evidence of the respect in which his captors held him, he was
compelled to travel with his wrists securely bound behind his back.
It was uncomfortable and he said so, but in this one regard, at least,
his captors seemed prepared to act in an uncivilized manner.

He used the travel time to study his escort. They were the first
Humans he'd seen in the flesh whom he was not engaged in trying
to kill. One was quite large, taller and more massive than himself. Its
right ear was plugged with a tiny metallic button from which
very faint musical sounds emerged. Whether that had anything to do
with the way he moved in his seat, occasionally flicking his fingers
against each other in the manner of a nervous Hivistahm, Ranji could
not be sure. Certainly it was linked to the universal translator he
also wore.

The Human on his right looked no less competent for being
smaller and slimmer. His skin was extremely dark, especially in contrast to that of his colleague. Ranji knew that color variance among
the species could be extreme, whereas the Ashregan were all the same
golden sepia hue. The man spent most of the time staring out the
window at the rapidly changing countryside.

They climbed into slightly more rugged terrain. Fields gave way
to orchards and groves of wild trees. A range of snow-capped mountains materialized in the distance. So far he had seen more Yulans on
the ship than on this world.

No vehicles overtook them, nor did they pass any. Only a few
shot past, traveling in the other direction. Perhaps they were travers-
ing some kind of restricted route, Ranji mused.

Since everyone had been equipped with translators, he found
himself wondering at the presence of the Wais. Not that their contribution to the Weave was restricted to translating. They could do
other things almost as well. But he would have expected a Yula or
O'o'yan driver. Possibly the ornate ornithorp was also a scientist,
assigned to observe the specimen as it was conveyed to its eventual
destination. He amused himself with the knowledge that the Wais
probably found traveling in the company of two armed Humans far
more unsettling than he did.

The very image of isolated elegance, it never once turned to look back at its fellow passengers. Ranji considered lurching forward should it do so, bulging his eyes and baring his teeth. Very likely it would keel over in a dead faint.

As for trying to imbue the Humans with knowledge of the Purpose, he knew instinctively that would be a waste of time. Uncivilized and barbaric as they were, it wouldn't be surprising for them to react with violence to an attempt at simple conversation. So he sat quietly, held his peace, and studied the world outside.

They began to slow, and he leaned forward slightly for a better look. Some kind of attenuated freight transport was traveling north-to-south perpendicular to their path, forcing their pilot to come to a complete halt while they waited for the longer, slower machine to pass. The dark-hued Human shifted irritably in his seat, a disgusted expression on his face. His larger companion continued to twitch to the strains of unheard music. Beneath them, the vehicle's repulsion unit idled softly.

Ranji erupted from his seat, spinning to his right, the fingers of his left hand striking the door-release mechanism in the combination he'd memorized when he'd first been shoved into the vehicle. As he landed hard on the darker Human's lap he brought both legs up and over to grip him tightly around the neck. Twisting, he used powerful calf and thigh muscles to thrust his captor's upper body explosively forward. The man's skull slammed into the transparent barrier that separated the front and rear compartments. Blood splattered as Ranji released the dazed guard and tumbled out backward through the open door.

"Get him!" the injured man moaned as Ranji felt the bigger Human's fingers fumbling at his ankles.

Instead of dashing for the nearest trees, Ranji spun and kicked the startled smaller man directly beneath his chin. Weapon half-drawn, he collapsed in the doorway, effectively blocking his larger companion from pursuing. The big Human blurted a stentorian oath and turned to the door on his side of the vehicle, ripping the music device from his ear and fumbling for his gun. Clearly the prisoner was either going to sprint into the nearby orchard or else stand and try to fight with his feet as he'd just demonstrated he was quite capable of doing.

Instead, as soon as the big man emerged and started to come

around the rear of the vehicle toward him, Ranji jumped back *in*. Kicking the dark Human out, Ranji deftly manipulated the door controls with the toe of his boot, shutting and locking first one door and then the other. He was now alone in the secured rear compartment with the deceived guard gesticulating angrily through the window.

Furious, the Human rushed to the front of the vehicle and yelled at the Wais to open one of the front doors. Unfortunately for him, the sudden outburst of raw violence had shocked the ornithorp into a quasicataleptic state. It sat staring straight ahead, feathers quivering, utterly unresponsive. The more the Human ranted and raved, the deeper its paralysis became. Just as Ranji had hoped.

He could not count on the condition persisting, however. Hands still bound behind him, he began hunting for a way of accessing the driver's compartment. His obvious intent only added to the Wais's terror.

His search revealed a small compartment built into the back of the front section. It contained small, finely machined instruments of alien design and unknown purpose. There were also a number of thin transparent cards on whose surface fine etching was visible.

The excluded Human continued to pound on the window while bellowing untranslatable imprecations.

Ranji turned and carefully removed the cards from the shallow compartment. His back to the barrier, he tried one after another in the slot obviously designed to receive them, hoping one would lower the transparency that separated him from the driver's section. A soft beep accompanied each insertion, but the barrier did not fall.

The slick plastic band that tightly encircled his wrists, however, metamorphosed into a handful of foam beads.

Relieved and surprised to have regained the use of his hands, he ignored the rampaging Human as he tried the rest of the cards. The last in the pile turned out to be the one he was searching for.

The barrier vanished into the floor. In no particular hurry, Ranji pocketed the card as he climbed into the empty seat next to the Wais. It continued to stare straight ahead, resolutely ignoring him. The big Human was now frantic.

From the moment he'd been placed inside, Ranji had taken careful note of how the Wais operated the vehicle. After re-raising the barrier, he removed the control disk from the ornithorp's paralyzed fingers, pulling it across on its flexible stalk until it was in front of his seat. The disk was cleverly designed to accommodate a variety of manipulative digits.

The lengthy freight vehicle which had instigated their delay had long since vanished southward. Experimentally resting his palm atop the unit, Ranji moved one finger slightly, as he'd seen the Wais do. The floater drifted forward, the agitated Human having to run to keep up as he pounded on the glass. Once he aimed his weapon through the transparency, but Ranji didn't flinch. He was relying on his importance as a specimen to preserve him from hostile fire.

Sure enough, the Human backed off. But he didn't give up. Instead he grabbed the dangling rear door and pulled himself in. Once safely back inside the vehicle he straightened on the seat and carefully aimed his weapon at the card slot Ranji had utilized to gain entrance to the driver's compartment.

Ranji's fingers convulsed on the disk. As the rear door slammed shut, a front one opened. After pounding the disk against the front part of the compartment until several buttons and switches had been dislodged, he calmly jumped from the rapidly accelerating vehicle, landing hard on the ground outside and rolling to his feet.

The look on the Human's face as the vehicle sped away with him locked securely in the back was worth the pain in Ranji's shoulder.

The man was going to have to shoot his way into the front seat (assuming his attempt shorted out the barrier's controls instead of freezing them) and try to turn the vehicle around or, more likely, call for assistance on its communications system. It was now traveling too fast for him to consider duplicating Ranji's leap. Hopefully the control disk had been damaged too badly to function. In that event the vehicle would not slow down for quite a while. By then Ranji planned to be deep in the nearby woods.

He trotted back to where the Human he'd kicked lay on his back, groaning softly. Ranji bent and struck the man just hard enough on the side of his neck. The moaning stopped, but not his breathing. Killing him would be against the tenets of the Purpose and would in any event do him no good.

The man's pockets were full of personal effects which Ranji ignored. There was a military chronometer, which he took, along with another set of the ubiquitous etched cards. A small sealed square contained solid pieces of dark, sweet food. There was also an incongruously ordinary spool of fine plastic thread. Sadly, when he'd been kicked the man had dropped his weapon on the floor of the floater's rear compartment.

Straightening, he surveyed his surroundings. He couldn't count on pursuit delaying too long, especially if the surviving guard managed to break into the driver's compartment and gain control without crashing the vehicle. Ranji headed for the thick stand of trees off to his right, using long strides to try and leave as little in the way of a track as possible.

The orchard quickly gave way to dense, uncultivated woods. The terrain grew rougher as flat land was replaced by steep hills cut by gullies and rivulets. Some were dry, others cuddled running streams which nourished thick entwined vegetation. There was plenty of good cover. He smiled as he ran, pretending he was back in the Maze.

Wild fruit was a natural food source which he planned to sample at the first opportunity. Like the majority of intelligent species, the Yula were warm-blooded. Hopefully he would be able to eat some of the same food which nourished them.

His intentions went no further than the next morning. He could not flee this planet, could not escape to Cossuut or any other friendly world. From now on his contribution to the war effort would consist of denying himself to his captors. Beyond that, given time and thought, he might also be able to do a little more, if only by disrupting the local peace and tranquillity. He wondered how long the secret of his escape could be kept from the local populace.

Teoth received the news from Eighth-of-Records, who because of his job had access to information routinely denied the rest of the crew. Together with Sixth-of-Technics they had a conference of their own, during which all of his worst fears were confirmed.

"The creature escaped from the vehicle in which it was being transported to the study site," the Hivistahm was saying. "As of the latest information I was able to acquire, despite mounting efforts to recapture it, it still running free was in the countryside."

"I am not surprised." Teoth scuffed at the deck with his fore-center leg. "I almost expected something like this to happen."

Sixth-of-Technics blinked at his friend. "Truly you do not upset at the news seem."

Three eyes turned to the slightly smaller of the two Hivistahm.

"Why should one be disappointed when one's hopes are about to be fulfilled?"

The nighttime temperature on this part of Omaphil was moderate. Despite nerves and lack of facilities, Ranji was able to manage several hours' sleep.

Upon awakening, he scoured the nearby trees for a selection of fruit. Tentatively peeling and eating as efficiently as he could, he filled his belly and then settled down to wait. The queasiness that resulted was due as much to tension as to anything he'd eaten. Only when he was confident that the food he had consumed was going to stay down did he allow himself to drink from the nearby brook.

Morning had brought a number of animals to the water's edge to quench their thirst. Most were clad in green and blue fur that seemed too thick for so mild a climate. They ignored him, accepting him as one of their own as he washed fruit pulp and seeds from his face and hands. Thus refreshed, he took his bearings by the sun and set off deeper into the forest, his eventual goal being the high western mountains he'd seen from the vehicle.

They would be frantically searching the length of the road, he knew, but since he'd waited until the floater was out of sight before starting off, they wouldn't know which way he'd gone. Nor were his captors likely to have ready access to tracking specialists on a peaceful, civilized world like Omaphil. It would take time to bring in trained individuals and specialized equipment to hunt him down.

He couldn't count on any of that, though. He had to assume they were already on his trail. The thought did not discourage him. On the contrary, the more resources they had to divert to tracking him down, the greater was his contribution to the advance of civilization.

As the day wore on he found himself gaining in strength and determination as he moved along, keeping to the trees that protected him from aerial discovery as well as helping to mask his heat signature. The longer it took for them to locate him, the deeper into the mountains he could go and the more difficult it would be for them to eventually dig him out. If he could find a cave system, he might be able to stay hidden for years.

By the third day he had begun to gain some real altitude. Continued progress now involved climbing as well as simple hiking. Silently he thanked the Yula settlers who had kept to population centers and left this portion of Omaphil, at least, in its wild, undeveloped state.

Descending a steep but shallow gorge brought him to the base of a roaring cataract. Where the foaming waters were sharply bent westward by an unyielding wall of granite he found a mass of storm-tossed driftwood that provided him with a fine-grained, water-polished club.

A subsequent search through a pile of splintered rock produced several sharp triangular chips. His patient efforts to secure one to the end of the club with fibers drawn from a local plant eventually resulted in a serviceable if primitive weapon. He swung it in short, experimental arcs, exulting in the *swoosh* it made as it swept air aside. Now the means for defending himself extended beyond mere bare hands.

Hoping to find material from which to fashion a sling, he pocketed some of the hard round pebbles from the bottom of the stream as he followed it for a while before striking off again into the brush.

On the fifth day he killed a grazing herbivore. It was nearly his size, and skinning it with the crude tools at hand was a messy and time-consuming process. He persevered, however, and when he was through he had acquired an outer garment which not only would shed rain but disguise his smell. If he dropped to all fours and imitated the animal's gait, it might be enough to fool a casual observer into believing they were seeing anything but a renegade Ashregan.

He had now acquired weapons and camouflage that, although simple, were a great advance over nothing at all. With luck, his pursuers would not imagine him capable of such inventiveness.

He was beginning to think he could roam the wild, heavily vegetated mountains forever when he was nearly surprised by the Tracker.

Though there had to be many of them on his trail, this one was alone. No doubt they had spread out to cover as much of the countryside as possible. The procedure struck him as eminently sensible. Anyone finding evidence of his presence could immediately call for assistance.

Unless he spotted them first.

The bipedal figure was still some distance away, too far for him

to make out the species without a scope. Probably Massood, he
thought. Their height, sharp vision, and long stride made them notable Trackers.

Not that it mattered. From now on he would move at night,
when his pursuers were likely to be sleeping, and hide himself during
the day. Either he would outpace them or they would pass him by.
He began searching for his first hiding place.

In this manner he successfully passed the first week, then a second. No doubt those local authorities whom the Weave had seen fit
to entrust with a minimum of information about his escape were
frantic by now, wondering where in their civilized midst the dangerous escaped warrior might choose to materialize. Better yet, they
might think he'd fallen over a cliff or perished of hunger and scale
down the pursuit.

He was feeling very good about his situation as he worked his
way through a night-shrouded grove of tall, oddly bent trees and
stumbled over the dozing form of the Tracker.

Because of the camouflage blanket, the low mound had looked
like any other clump of earth. Only when he started across did it
yield spongily beneath his feet and emit a startled yelp. A blast of
heat lit up the night and singed his ear as a weapon went off wildly
under him.

The blunt side of his club was less urbane, but more effective.

There were no more shots. The struggling figure beneath the
blanket went limp. Ranji staggered backward a couple of steps and
sat down heavily, gulping air. Everything had happened so fast that
he was only now beginning to sequence the events in retrospect.
Gingerly he touched the left side of his head. He could still feel the
heat of the bolt's passing. A finger length more to the right and it
would have gone through his eye. If not for his extensive training
and superb reflexes, he'd be sprawled out on the ground right now
instead of sitting up considering his assailant.

His instinct was to flee. Instead, he forced himself to approach
the motionless shape under the blanket. If it was dead, its companions
would soon learn of its fate by reason of its noncommunicativeness.
Regardless, it might be carrying much he could use.

After pocketing the surprisingly small gun, he dragged the blanket off the unconscious form and began to fold it neatly. The Tracker's pack lay near its feet. It was encouragingly full and would ride

easily on his back. That done, he knelt and felt along the furless legs—
clearly not Massood—until he came to the service belt. Undoing the
secure-tight he slipped it around his own waist and was gratified to
find that though he had to place it on the last possible setting,
it fit.

Continuing to probe the body in hope of finding something else
useful, he was mildly interested to discover that the Tracker was
female and mammalian, very much like an Ashregan in consistency
and shape. His interest was wholly dispassionate. The notion that
anyone would find contact with a barbaric, half-mad, crazed Human
in any way stimulating made him shudder. Not to mention the fact
that the individual in question had just tried its best to melt his skull.

It moaned softly then, proof that his reflexive blow with the club
hadn't been fatal. When he reached the head his fingers encountered
the thick wetness flowing from the scalp. The figure moaned again,
louder this time.

He considered how to proceed. The thought of killing another
Human did not bother him—he'd done plenty of that on Koba—but
the less damage he inflicted during his period of freedom, the easier
it would go on him if he eventually was recaptured. Neither side had
much sympathy for prisoners who killed while escaping.

A check of the service belt turned up the expected communications module. With the aid of the translator that had remained in
place in his ear and around his neck during his flight, he might be
able to monitor the other Trackers' positions as they spoke to one
another. That would be more than a little useful.

Ought to be on my way, he mused. Still, if he lingered until the
Tracker regained consciousness, he might be able to acquire valuable
information about the size, disposition, and strength of his pursuit as
well as the countryside in which he found himself. He was not Amplitur and could not mind-probe, but there were other methods of
interrogation—following which he could always render her unconscious again.

Occupying himself with a cursory search of the pack's contents
in the feeble light of the single small moon, he settled down to wait.

He dozed off more than once during the night, awakening each
time with a start at the cry or movement of some nocturnal creature.
His concerns were unfounded. The Tracker had not moved.

As soon as darkness began to give way to morning, he rose and

walked to the nearest stream. Using the Tracker's collapsible puri-
fying cup he scooped water from the surface and returned, putting it
to her lips until she began to cough. Pouring the rest over her face,
he settled back and watched, gun in hand.

She rolled over and blinked without straightening. When she saw
him, she woke up very quickly. Her gaze dropped to his waist, where
her service belt rode snugly, then to his feet, where he had placed
her pack.

He must have made quite a picture, he mused, clad as he was
in her equipment, his Ashregan duty suit, and the rapidly ripening
animal skin. Before speaking, he double-checked his translator set-
tings.

"Sorry I had to hit you so hard, but keep in mind that you were
the one doing the hunting. I stumbled over you in the dark and you
shot at me, so I reacted as necessary. You might've killed me."

"Didn't want to." She had a pleasant voice, he thought, but then
there was little difference between the Human and Ashregan larynx.
"Supposed to bring you in intact. For study." Now she sat up and
felt gingerly of the lump on her head where his club had connected.
"You surprised me, too. Might've killed *me*."

He made an Ashregan gesture of negativity. "Didn't want to.
Keep you alive. For study."

She looked at him sideways, then smiled hesitantly. As it wasn't
a maximum Human smile, with the concomitant obscene baring of
teeth, he was able to observe it without flinching.

He saw the lean muscles start to tense beneath her clothing and
leisurely raised the muzzle of the little heat pistol. "Please don't.
Unnecessary killing distresses those of us who believe in the Purpose." She relaxed.

"Better. My name is Ranji-aar, though you probably know that
already, along with much else about me. As I find imbalance in the
universe personally displeasing, you will be good enough to supply
me with your name."

She hesitated, then shrugged. If he wanted to, she knew he could
make life uncomfortable for her.

"Trondheim. Heida Trondheim. You move fast. You've been
giving us a hell of a time."

"Independence is a great motivator."

She turned to face him, straightening her legs as she rose, leaning against a tree for support. "Enjoy it while you can. We're closing in on you. This country is swarming with Trackers. Any time now they're going to start missing me." She studied him with interest. "You must be pretty special. I'm told that when news of your escape reached local Command, the authorities went a little nuts."

"Delighted to hear it. As for your friends closing in on me, they've been closing in on me for days. They just can't seem to catch me."

Her gaze narrowed. "You don't talk or act like your average Ashregan. Don't look much like one, either."

He bristled. There it was again, this elementary emphasis on his appearance. "I'm not average," he growled.

Again her fingers felt of her forehead. "You sure don't hit average." She tensed again and for the first time he saw fear in her eyes. "Are you going to kill me?"

"Not unless you make it necessary for me to do so. I would rather ask you some questions."

"Don't expect me to answer freely."

"You don't have to answer freely." He gestured with the gun. "Feel free to answer under duress." From her service belt he removed a small device the size of his middle finger. It was fashioned of dull gray metal and sported a miniature grid at one end, a single button at the other. "What does this do?"

Her lips drew into a tight line as she crossed her arms.

"Very well. I suppose the only way to find out is to try it." Pointing the grid end at her, he placed his thumb over the button.

Alarmed, she ducked and raised both hands defensively. Only after he'd reattached the device to the belt did she resignedly explain.

"It contains a powerful binary narcoleptic gas that activates on contact. Designed for close-quarter capture. It's not harmful."

"I can infer that from your reaction," he replied dryly.

Again that hesitancy. "I swear you keep joking with me. The Ashregan don't joke."

"Some of us do."

She sat up again, dusting her shoulder off. "I studied the pictures they gave us, but they don't begin to suggest how close to Human your appearance is."

"All Humans and Ashregan look alike," he replied with the tired air of one who was heartily sick of the subject.

She shook her head. "Not this much. For one thing you're much too tall, taller than most Human males."

"I have many friends who are considerably shorter, and others who are taller still. There is considerable physical variation in both our species."

"It's more than that."

Her intense gaze was making him uncomfortable. If one disregarded the flattened skull, protruding ears, and tiny eye sockets, she was almost attractive. Her legs made those of the average Ashregan female look stunted, though her fingers were far shorter. He was glad of the intensifying daylight, which tended to emphasize the differences between them.

"We were told that you were one of a group of specialized Ashregan who've been genetically altered by the Amplitur. Seeing you in the flesh, I can believe it."

"I am the Ashregan Unifer Ranji-aar," he reminded her stiffly. "Your philosophical and physical enemy. Nothing more than that. Do not think to compose an appeal to any imaginary 'Human' characteristics you think I possess. You will only be disappointed."

"Well, you talk like an Ashregan, and you act like an Ashregan, but . . ." She was still dubious. "No wonder Research and Development wants to look at you so badly."

"I am not flattered."

"This is going to ruin me," she muttered. "I'll be laughed out of my unit."

"Your personal social difficulties are of no concern to me." He rose and she shrank back against the tree. "I don't think you can track me without this." He held up the seeker visor he'd found in her pack and slowly slipped it over his face, the headband tightening automatically. Adjustment of its internal controls would provide him with greatly enhanced vision and a plethora of information on his surroundings.

"With this on, I think your colleagues will have a harder time 'closing in' on me." He turned away from her to pick up the backpack.

"Then you're really not going to kill me." She was still hesitant.

"I've already told you: those who believe in the Purpose—"

"Yeah, yeah. Some of your allies take a less exalted attitude on the battlefield."

He took a step toward her. "I'm afraid I'm going to have to render you unconscious again. Just to preserve my lead. Nothing personal."

She sighed. "If you must. I hope you trip over a rock and break both legs. Nothing personal."

He smiled. "I must tell you that your appearance borders on the attractive."

Her gaze narrowed. "Don't go getting any funny ideas. We're different species."

"Ah," he said, gratified. "Then you don't think we're that much alike after all." Holstering the heat gun, he hefted his club.

8

Under normal circumstances he wouldn't have been trapped so easily, but his unnatural attraction to the Human female had made him careless. The result was that he fell victim to a relatively clumsy ambush.

By the time he realized what was happening it was too late. Fur bristling, triple eyes staring, the Yula stepped out from behind the boulder in front of him while the Hivistahm—Hivistahm!—rose from behind the fallen log off to his right. Each held a stinger focused on different parts of his body. He didn't recognize the weapons type . . . not that it mattered.

He was furious with himself. A moment ago he'd been preparing to set off into the real mountains, better equipped to remain at large than he'd been since his initial escape. Now all was lost. Not to Human or Massood Trackers, but because of a native and a Hivistahm, noncombatants both.

The Hivistahm he thought he could outmaneuver, but he knew nothing of Yula reaction time. The triped spoke through a translator.

"Put your right hand atop your head and drop the club you hold to the ground, then put your left hand atop your right. Do it quickly, please!"

As soon as Ranji had complied the Hivistahm bounded forward and, trembling slightly, removed the heat pistol from the service belt and retreated.

"Good." The tiny black eyes never wavered. "Please keep your hands where they are so that I may note the position of your manipulative digits at all times."

Out of the corner of an eye Ranji saw that the Hivistahm was still trembling, and he wondered how the highly civilized, inoffensive creature had been talked into participating in the ambush.

The Human rose and brushed at the back of her suit. "It's about time relief got here, though I was expecting one of my own kind. Not that I'm complaining, mind." She started toward him.

"Stop there, please."

Halting, she gaped at the Yula. It had remained motionless while confronting the prisoner, but under that Human stare it quivered ever so slightly. Ranji noted the reaction.

"What is this?" she murmured. "I'm one of the designated Trackers. You two have done well and will be suitably commended. I'll see to that myself. But you're not trained soldiers. I am. I'm not trying to steal your thunder. I'll hold the gun while you take my stuff off him. Then we'll call for a sled to lift us all out of here." She took another step.

The Yula retreated an equal distance and flicked the muzzle of its weapon in her direction. "Stay where you are, Human. Do not make me tell you again. Your presence here complicates matters and I am trying to decide how to proceed."

Hands atop his head, Ranji watched and waited silently for an opening.

"You want to take it back alive, to keep it here on Omaphil for observation and study," the Yula was saying.

"Of course." The woman continued to stare at the triped.

"I cannot let you do that." Its fluffed-up fur made the native look twice as big as it actually was. "The thing has to die."

"What are you talking about?" Trondheim's gaze was focused on the stinger. "Don't you realize what an impressive accomplishment this is for one of your species, how you'll be feted when the word gets out that you and a Hivistahm captured an escaped Ashregan warrior?"

"We do not want to do anything 'impressive,'" the Yula told her.

"Truly feted we do not wish to be," added the Hivistahm.

With the rocking, jerky motion of its kind, the Yula took a double step toward Ranji. "The thing needs to die. It is a dangerous mutation, an aberration that could wreak havoc on Omaphil were it to escape from captivity. As it already has. So much for vaunted government safeguards." He gestured with the pistol.

"Look at it! Twisted and distorted by the addition of Human fighting characteristics. Can one imagine anything so grotesque? It will be better off dead."

"How did you know that I had escaped?" Ranji asked curiously.

The Yula did something with its tiny mouth which might have been the equivalent of a smile. "I have well-informed friends."

"Then your friends should've told you that its fate is not for you to decide." Trondheim glanced in Ranji's direction. "There's a sled on its way here now. How are you going to explain their dead specimen to them when they arrive?"

"We did not think of that." The Hivistahm scanned the sky uneasily. "Truly we did not think of that."

"Be quiet!" Teoth snapped. "The female attempts to preserve the monster's life with the aid of a fabrication." He aimed the pistol. "This will only take an instant and then we will be away from this place."

"As a Human soldier of the Weave I am *ordering* you to turn your weapons and this prisoner over to me!" Trondheim took a step toward the triped, eyes glittering. "Or are you going to shoot me, too?"

"You may kill me after, but that does not matter." Teoth was calm, anesthetized by the prospect of incipient martyrdom. "My life is not important. I gladly die to preserve my world from this creature. If word of its presence was made known there would be panic. The Weave had no right to bring it here. Omaphil is peaceful and civilized. I shall insure that it so remains." It looked back at Ranji.

"Do not attempt to convince me otherwise. I was on the ship with it. I watched, and I know."

"Word won't get out," Trondheim told him.

Teoth made a gargling sound deep in his throat. "It has already escaped custody once."

"It won't happen again." She spoke slowly and deliberately.

For the first time, the Yula seemed to hesitate. "Can you guarantee that? Can you assure it beyond doubt? I think not. Its presence here says not. Better it should die."

Trondheim advanced another step and extended a hand. She was quite close to the native now, Ranji noted. "I'm afraid I can't allow that. If you're going to shoot it, then you're going to have to kill me, too. Now *give me that pistol.*"

The use of the Human command tone shook Ranji slightly. Unsurprisingly, it rattled the Yula even more. As soon as the weapon's muzzle had drifted sufficiently toward the woman, Ranji moved.

The sandy gravel he kicked up struck the Yula in the face. It uttered a high-pitched squeak, dropped the gun, and clawed at its eyes with the instinctive reaction of a nonfighter. Ranji pivoted and leaped to within arm's length of the Hivistahm. Bug-eyed, it fired wildly as Trondheim dove for cover. Neatly severed by the stinger, a large branch tumbled from a nearby tree.

As he landed Ranji brought his closed fist around in a sweeping arc to strike the Hivistahm in the left eye. Fragile occipital bones crunched and blood squirted. The much smaller, reptilian creature gave a slight shudder and collapsed onto its haunches, then onto its side.

Brushing grit from sensitive eyes, the Yula bent its fore-center leg and reached to recover its weapon. As it did so Ranji spied a fist-sized stone, snatched it up, aimed and threw all in one motion. A Human or Massood might have been able to dodge, but the Yula was not nearly so quick. The rock struck it above the middle eye, denting fur and bone both. It exhaled reverberantly and fell backward.

Panting hard, he stood wondering at the psychosis which would drive a Yula and Hivistahm to such a confrontation. Before he could come up with any answers, something heavy hit him in the ribs. Much more massive than a Yula or Hivistahm, it sent him sprawling.

Trondheim rolled off him and scrambled for the pistol still clutched in the motionless Hivistahm's fingers. Ignoring the pain in his side, Ranji flung himself in pursuit, landing on the back of her thighs. She twisted and pain shot through his whole body as her elbow connected with his nose.

Wrenching the pistol from the unconscious alien, she whirled and fired, aiming to wound, not kill. Ranji froze, waiting for the bolt from the stinger to take effect. Nothing happened. Frowning, she sighted carefully along the barrel and fired again.

An unsmiling Ranji climbed to his feet and charged.

It all made perfect sense. The Yula had been very much in command, just as it had been quite mad. Not being possessed by a similarly extreme form of insanity, the Hivistahm had agreed to provide backup ... but could not bring itself to handle a loaded weapon capable of killing another intelligent being. The stinger it had carried was not charged. It didn't really need to be, since their quarry wouldn't know otherwise.

He did now.

Trondheim threw the useless weapon at him and made a dive for the Yula's gun. She would have beaten a normal Ashregan to it, but not Ranji. It was his turn to hit her hard in the ribs. She wheezed painfully and tried to use the elbow again, but this time he was ready for it and the blow caught him harmlessly on the shoulder. As it did so he brought the edge of his palm down against the side of her neck and she went limp.

Panting hard, he rose slowly and picked up the Yula's stinger, not taking his eyes off her as he did so. Next he walked back to the Hivistahm and recovered her heat pistol. Only then did he allow himself to relax a little. He took his time rearranging the backpack and service belt, sorting through the pack's contents as he waited for her partial paralysis to wear off.

Finally she sat up, rubbing her neck and staring at him. "You're very good." The admission came grudgingly. "More than just quick. A lot more. Better than any Ashregan I ever heard about."

"Thank you." He straightened his translator, which had been knocked askew but not broken during the fight.

"Not only don't you fight like any Ashregan, you don't even feel like an Ashregan."

"And how many Ashregan have you felt? Not that I understand what you're saying."

"Your bones, your muscles. They're too dense. It's one of the traits that makes Humans so tough. Our bones aren't hollow like those of most other intelligent species and we have more muscle fibers, so we're stronger and heavier. Strength and mass aren't Ashregan characteristics. You felt like a Human, not an Ashregan."

"I reiterate: How many Ashregan have you felt?"

She didn't look away. "I'm only repeating what I learned in training."

"Weave intelligence is far from perfect." Try as he might he couldn't just brush her observations aside, not least because the Hivistahm and Lepar who had captured him on Eirrosad had made much of similar observations.

"So you're what the Amplitur have been up to. It makes sense. Genetically you're their nearest allies to us, so you'd be the easiest to imbue with Human characteristics. Be a helluva lot harder with an Acaria or Korath. Doesn't it make you think?"

"About what? I think only of the Purpose."

"Well, think about this for a change. If the squids keep screwing with your racial DNA, how long before you become more bastardized Human than honest Ashregan?"

"That is not possible," he insisted. But the notion upset him.

"Isn't it? The squids play with DNA the way a kid does with building blocks. How do you know what they are and aren't capable of? *We've* never underestimated them. Why should you? Look at yourself: Human size, muscles, bone density, reflexes. How do you know what the hell you are? How much of you is still Ashregan?"

Ranji was silent for a long moment. "My *mind* is all Ashregan," he said finally. "So are my intentions. I have been privileged to experience mind-to-mind contact with the Teachers themselves, to receive accolades and advice from them directly. No Human could do that. Your nervous system would react violently and defensively."

Trondheim considered. "All that proves is that your nervous system is still Ashregan. Externally, except for your skull and hands, the rest of you is as Human as me or any of my cohorts."

"Appearances mean nothing." The assurance Ranji voiced so readily did not extend to his thoughts. What was he, really?

A servant of the Purpose, he reminded himself firmly. Biological coincidences notwithstanding. He indicated the badly injured Yula and Hivistahm.

"The more contact I have with representatives of the Weave, the more convinced I am of the righteousness of the cause. Your governments fight, your organizations argue, and as individuals you spend much of your time engaged in petty internecine squabbling. I want no part of that."

"You haven't been given a choice."

He eyed her derisively. "Did you notice that your so-called friends and allies feared the threat of attack from you more than from me? What kind of higher civilization is that?"

She glanced down at the unconscious Yula. "These two were extremists. Probably mentally unbalanced as well."

"But what if they were not? What if their greater fear of you was the sensible, intelligent attitude to take?"

"We're not exactly universally popular throughout the Weave. But we're respected. I have a number of non-Human friends."

"Are you so certain? Or do they just force themselves to be pleasant when in your company so as not to offend you?"

"Hey, you're the one we're discussing here. For better or worse, I *know* what I am." She sounded sad. "The Amplitur and their damn 'Purpose.' Look what they've done to your people. Not to mention the Molitar, and the Segunians, and the poor VVadir. Turned them into soldiers, fighters for the Amplitur cause, when all they want is to be left alone."

"No race wants to be 'left alone,'" Ranji told her.

"My kind does."

He hoped his response would translate. "I rest my case."

She sighed and sat down on a nearby log, careful to keep both hands where he could see them. "Doesn't it bother you that your supposed 'Teachers' might have messed with your genetic makeup without your knowledge or consent, might've been busily splicing your genes like toy cutouts while you were still in the womb?"

"Nothing like that took place. Nothing like that would be *allowed* to take place."

"How do you know? Because they told you so? You must know how forceful their 'suggestions' can be."

"I am Ashregan," he all but shouted. "Not the product of genetic engineering!"

"No," she murmured almost pityingly. "Just the by-product."

"I don't need to think about it. I *know*."

She eyed him intently. "Maybe you do. Maybe you do. But I think you're either a greatly gifted liar or else you've been completely mindwashed by the squids." She rose and he tensed slightly, but she made no move toward him.

"Well, it's obvious I'm not going to convince you otherwise. Maybe this one was right." She prodded the prone Yula with a foot. "Maybe it'd be better if he had shot you." She looked back at him. "If you're going to knock me out, get on with it. I'm fed up with trying to talk to someone who's unable to speak for himself. I don't blame you; it's not your fault. But it's boring, and I'm tired."

Ranji rose and drew the little cylinder full of sleep gas from the service belt. Despite her outward show of bravado he saw her flinch expectantly. He hesitated.

"Perhaps I will allow you to remain conscious for a while yet. Every time you open your mouth you tell me something useful."

"Then you're easily sated."

"Yes," he told her, pleased with his decision, "I think that for now I'll have you accompany me. If you become too much of a burden there are always the alternatives." He looked back the way he'd come. "And if your peers are closing in on us, it would be useful to have a hostage."

"So now I'm a hostage?" Her eyebrows arched. "What makes you think I won't break your neck the first time you doze off, or shove you over the nearest cliff the next time you relax?"

"Nothing," he told her blandly. "The implied threat of your company will help to keep me alert." He smiled thinly. "Keep in mind that if you do try something like that I may not have time to gauge my response. Keep in mind also that if your theory is correct and certain of my abilities and characteristics have been bioengineered into me by the Amplitur, I may also possess abilities you know nothing about and cannot imagine."

There! he thought with satisfaction. That's got her thinking. "Did I not just defeat you?"

"Yeah, you did," she admitted, downcast. "But you surprised me in my sleep. I wasn't ready for you. And I was expecting to have to fight an Ashregan. A bigger, tougher version of an Ashregan, but an Ashregan nonetheless. You," and she gave him another of her uninterpretable looks, "you're something different."

"Remember that as we walk." He put the sleep canister back on the belt, hefted the backpack, and slid the seeker visor down over his eyes. Then he gestured with the Yula's stinger. "I think it's time we moved away from here."

She started off in the indicated direction, glancing back over a shoulder as she spoke. "You won't find anything up there. I've seen the topos. It gets rugged and steep and there's no serious climbing equipment in that pack."

"I'm not concerned. I have you to test any dangerous places for me. Since you'll be walking in front, I think I can rely on you to choose the safest path."

She stared back at him as if trying to see past the Ashregan mask, past the narrow-minded dedication, to the real individual within. Then she shrugged and turned away from him.

Later that night she said, "You're awfully young to be a Unifer. That's a command rank among your kind."

Pistol close at hand, he kept an eye on her as he ate ravenously from one of the self-heating food packs he'd found among her supplies. "Humans also advance rapidly."

"Yeah, but we're born to be warriors. We don't have to be 'suggested' into it."

Finishing the food, he carefully slipped the empty packet into a hole dug for the purpose and covered it over. "You Humans. You're as unfamiliar with the other races as you are with the Purpose. All you know is fighting and killing."

She smiled. "It's something we're good at." Of apology in her confession there was none. "We know other things, too. But when you get a reputation for something . . ." She paused a moment, then slid closer to him. "You're so damn Human-looking. Except for that face, and your fingers. A keyboardist's fingers."

He picked up the pistol. "That's close enough."

"Take it easy. I just want to see something. You've got the gun. If I make any sudden moves you can shoot me."

Slowly she reached out and gently traced the ridge of bone that ran from the back of his right cheek along the side of his face and up over his recessed ear. Her fingers withdrew, touched the flattened nose, and retreated. His skin tingled from the brief contact.

"Well, it's real, all right," she said, sitting back.

"Of course it's real. What did you expect? Plastic?"

"I don't know." She sounded somehow disappointed. "It's just that the rest of you is so Human. I half expected everything else to be fake."

"Nothing about me is fake," he told her.

When she didn't comment he opened another of the food packets and waited patiently for it to heat. Steam began to issue from the perforated lid as the container expanded, drawing moisture from the air as it cooked. The result was chewy and full of meat bits.

When he'd finished half he offered her the rest. Without hesitation she accepted and ate, scouring the packet clean.

A quick search of the area turned up a hollow filled with small branches, leaves, and other forest detritus. After hanging the backpack and service belt high in a nearby tree, he bunched the debris into a soft bed. She was clearly surprised when he offered it to her.

"This is for my comfort, not yours," he explained. "There's no way you can roll off that or even stand up without crunching dried stuff and making noise. I'm a light sleeper and I have very good hearing."

She eyed the mound of dry fluff. "Sometimes I toss in my sleep."

He gestured with the stinger. "Better train yourself fast to lie quietly."

When he awoke just before dawn the mound was empty. But she had not fled. Instead he was startled to find her curled up against him. He reached for the pistol, only to have her hand cover his. The resultant struggle was brief, and indifferent.

She was extremely close and she felt very Ashregan.

"It's all right," she whispered. "You probably can break my neck if you want to. But there were things I wanted to, had to know. I got curious, that's all. I'm only Human." She pulled away slightly.

"That doesn't explain why you're still here."

She rolled onto her back, staring at the sky. "I'm not sure I've got a better explanation. All I know is that you could've shot me, back there. You didn't."

"I've already explained that. You're useful both as a source of information and as a hostage." He was watching her closely. "There has to be more to it than that."

She seemed to reach some critical inner decision. "It doesn't matter. My colleagues are going to run you to ground eventually. Damn my curiosity. I didn't really want to be a Tracker. I should've gone into Research." She moved against him anew.

He sensed it was not to attack.

9

When he awoke the following morning she was sitting off to one side, deep in contemplation. The thin stick protruding from her lips gave off wisps of aromatic smoke at periodic intervals. Reflexively, his fingers felt for the pistol.

It wasn't there.

Nor were they alone any longer. Three other Humans sat off to his right. The two males were enjoying their morning meal while their female companion paid close attention to Ranji, the grid of the narco cylinder held firmly in her left hand aimed unwaveringly at his face.

Seeing that he was awake, the nearest male turned in his direction and spoke politely through a translator.

"We decided to let you sleep. After the race you've run us we figured you must be exhausted, and we want to deliver you in good condition. Don't think we'd have caught up with you yet if we'd done much sleeping ourselves."

His gaze shifted from the new arrivals to the Human Heida Trondheim. She sat parallel to him on a smooth rock, her slim form outlined against the rising sun, knees drawn halfway up to her chest.

"Sorry," she said. "I told you my friends would catch up with us."

"I thought—" he started to reply. What had he thought? What could he conceivably have been thinking?

It was simple enough. He hadn't been thinking. If he'd been thinking he would have shot her.

He'd been very tired, and she had been warm, and comforting, and understanding, and had raised intriguing issues of mutual interest, and the two of them had been very alone.

The look on his face must have been close enough to its Human equivalent for her to recognize. "You know, I thought about helping you stay free for a while. I really did." She shifted her legs around. "It must be terrible to be all alone so far from friends and family and familiar surroundings. But it would only have postponed the inevitable, and you had two loaded weapons. You might've shot at someone, and they might've shot back. I didn't want to see you killed."

"Why should you care?" He stared searchingly. "What difference does it make to you what happens to one enemy soldier?"

"Because I'm not sure you are an enemy." She sucked on the slim, silvery stick. Fragrant haze momentarily obscured her expression.

One of her male counterparts glanced at her. "What's that supposed to mean, Heida?"

"Have you looked at him? I mean, taken a really good, close look at him?"

The woman holding the gun on Ranji responded. "We all saw the images. They were pretty detailed. He's supposed to be some kind of a cross, isn't he? A mutated Ashregan?"

"Maybe," Trondheim murmured. "Or maybe something else."

"Not our business to propose answers." The man pulled a tab on his empty meal pack and watched as it turned to biodegradable powder. "We track; Research and Development pontificates."

Ranji marveled at his calmness. He could have been angry at her but he wasn't. After all, it wasn't as if she'd betrayed an intimacy. Their brief interaction had been nothing more than a scientific experiment. She'd as much as said so. They were representatives, albeit compatible representatives, of two different species. She could not "betray" him if she wanted to.

If he was angry at anyone it was at himself. For succumbing, for letting down his guard. He drew what consolation he could from the knowledge that nothing in his training had prepared him for what had transpired the previous night.

They were *very* careful with him this time. Everyone had heard the story of his escape, and they were determined not to repeat the error of his earlier escort. The sled that arrived to pluck the Trackers and their prisoner off the mountain came equipped with limb restraints and a lockable compartment hastily installed for the benefit of a single important guest. It afforded him privacy while easing the minds of his hosts.

He saw Heida Trondheim several times during the flight back

down the mountain as the sled retraced in minutes terrain it had taken him days to cross on foot, but they did not speak. He did not feel so inclined and she appeared uncertain and hesitant.

The sled sped through orchards and across fields of rippling grains. Eventually it approached another range of mountains, lower and less impressive than those which had given Ranji temporary shelter. The sled hovered while a barrier in one yellow-brown hillside parted. It closed behind the vehicle as it ducked inside.

He'd expected an underground base. The Weave would not be likely to place it on the surface where the import of its presence might disturb the civilized inhabitants.

The apartment they gave him was spacious, even luxurious, his quarters commensurate with the importance they attached to him. That did not make it any less a cell. There were scenic viewscreens on which he could call up custom landscapes, but no windows. A cursory inspection of his new home suggested strongly that he would not be escaping it any time soon.

Well, he had managed to unsettle them for a couple of weeks, he still had the tenets of the Purpose to console him, and he was alive and intact. Opportunities to create mischief might again present themselves.

He was provided with captured or synthesized Ashregan entertainment and food. It was rather more hospitality than he would have expected from Humans, but then he'd seen no Humans since his arrival. Apparently the base was staffed principally by Hivistahm, O'o'yan, S'van, and of course, Yula. One day a chelatinous, alien Turlog stopped by to gaze inscrutably, its eyes weaving lazily at the tips of extensible stalks, but no Humans came to visit him.

There were periodic interview sessions conducted by methodical Hivistahm and, once, a pair of Massood. He spoke freely about himself, refusing only those queries which he thought might have some slight military value. They did not press him on those questions he declined to answer. Not yet. This was because they were far more interested in him than in any information he carried.

The medical tests and examinations were far more intimidating, though he was never hurt or subjected to any painful stimulation. It was the unfamiliarity of the equipment and procedures, the fact that he had no idea what to expect, that he found daunting.

Once they slid him on a pallet into a machine that enclosed him like a cylindrical coffin and bathed his body in light of alternating colors and intensity. As with similar tests, he emerged physically unscathed but mentally apprehensive, and as always no unpleasant aftereffects resulted.

They took samples of his blood, of his waste and his skin, hair, and bone. He was probed and prodded, scanned and scoped, calibrated and appraised. It went on endlessly. In all that time he saw not a single Human, and why should he? They were soldiers, warriors, not scientists and research specialists. They did not study; they destroyed.

He was not especially displeased, only piqued by their absence. It would have been disconcerting, for example, for Heida Trondheim to have been among the personnel examining him. Far easier to remain dispassionate and aloof in the presence of querulous Hivistahm and S'van.

The idea of suicide did not occur to him. That was an alien concept familiar to him only from studies. Killing oneself constituted an offense against the Purpose by depriving it of an otherwise undamaged and potentially contributory intelligent mind. It was a gesture that could be conceived of only by truly alien beings. Like Humans.

He was not let in on his examiners' discussions and so had no idea if their extensive studies of him were resulting in anything useful. When not under observation he tried to relax as best he could, maintaining mental alertness and physical conditioning so that in the event his captors grew lazy or overconfident he would be ready to seize any opportunity to escape or cause trouble that might present itself. While one lived, one could still serve the Purpose.

Twice a day they took him topside, as he came to think of it, for a stroll in a secluded, fenced, parklike area, where he could exercise, bask in the sun, and smell cultivated Omaphilian flora. Though only a single guard accompanied him on his sojourns, he did not delude himself into thinking he could get more than a few steps away from the complex by climbing the vine-covered wall. They would be alert for anything so obvious; therefore, he made no moves in that direction. His captors were not stupid. The presence of only a single escort was proof in itself no others were needed.

So he spent his time learning the names of various trees and flowers, and toying with the odd-shaped pink-hued fish and multi-shelled domesticated cephalopods that swam in the garden's central pool. Once while he was topside it rained, and the evident delight he took in the unfettered natural phenomenon almost moved his Massood guard to sympathy. Almost.

Then came a day when the routine was broken. He knew it was going to be different when Humans instead of Massood arrived to escort him. As they exited the familiar elevator they turned him left instead of right.

"What's up? Where are we going?"

The big, burly dark-skinned Human on his immediate right didn't reply. He carried what appeared to be an unnecessarily large weapon. Ranji eyed it longingly, but knew that even if he could appropriate it, it would do him no good to do so. Each weapon here was attuned to its individual owner's unique electrical signature and no one else, not another guard and certainly not a prisoner, could make it fire.

"Is something the matter?" The farther they walked, the larger unpleasant thoughts loomed in his imagination. "I'm not scheduled for anything at this time of day."

"Look, buddy, I don't know nothing." The translator managed to convey the other Human's gruffness along with his words. "I'm just taking you where I'm supposed to. I don't know what happens after you get there any better than you do, understand?"

"I understand," Ranji replied, though he didn't.

They took him to a room he hadn't visited before. In addition to a small table and chairs it contained the ubiquitous wall-mounted communications screen, some medical equipment of modest complexity, couches, and potted plants. Except for the instruments it looked more like a lounge than an examination room. He thought it deceptively welcoming in appearance.

Not unlike Heida Trondheim, he thought. She sat on one of the couches and turned in his direction as soon as he entered. Instead of her camouflaged Tracker gear she wore a light rust-and-white-colored uniform. Detailed patches lined her right sleeve. He was surprised to see her but uncertain whether to be pleased.

Two other Humans looked up from the medical equipment. One was exceptionally short, almost as short as a S'van. Ranji knew it was not a member of that highly intelligent race because of the absence of the characteristic S'van hirsuteness. Both wore identical high-necked beige-and-black suits. Neither looked much like a warrior.

The room's population included a Massood of advanced maturity. She was slightly stooped, and most of her cranial and facial fur had aged to a rich silver hue. Ranji had no idea if it was due to her many years or to other circumstances, but for one of her kind she was unusually self-possessed. Her whiskers and nose hardly twitched at all as she examined the new arrival. She was surrounded by several Hivistahm and O'o'yan but, rather surprisingly, no S'van or Wais.

The two guards remained outside, flanking the open door. A farrago of round and vertical pupils stared back at him.

"Please sit down." The taller of the two Humans spoke perfect Ashregan. Startled, Ranji complied. Obstinacy would gain him nothing, and besides, rejection for its own sake burned proteins.

There followed a pause as awkward as it was brief before a mature, extremely self-possessed Hivistahm approached him.

"I am First-of-Surgery." The scaly green alien studied him with a fearlessness remarkable for one of his kind. Or perhaps, Ranji decided, it was merely scientific detachment. Whichever, he was duly impressed. "I the honor have in charge of the examination to be placed."

"Examination?" Ranji determinedly avoided looking in Heida Trondheim's direction. "What are you charged with 'examining'?"

"You. Truly it has enlightening been to observe you these past weeks."

"Sorry I can't say the same." He indicated the assemblage with a sweep of his hand and was gratified to see several of those present flinch. "Why the party? Are you going to let me go?" He smiled thinly.

"Actually, we are not quite sure what to do with you." Ranji turned toward the speaker. The shorter Human's Ashregan was not as fluent as that of his companion, but despite an atrocious accent his words were comprehensible. "You are an anomaly."

"So I've been told. I'm glad you're confused."

"Perhaps you can that help us to resolve," the Hivistahm hissed softly. "We would like you some pictures to look at."

In response to his gesture an O'o'yan handed him an oversized plastic envelope. Delicate fingers explored the interior, brought forth a rectangular tridimensional image.

"This the interior of your brain is."

Warily Ranji turned his attention to the flat sheet, conscious of the fact that everyone in the room was watching him intently. Heida Trondheim, too? He chose to affect indifference.

After careful consideration he handed it back to the surgeon. "Is there something here that's supposed to surprise me? I see an Ashregan brain. Nothing more."

"For the moment I would simply like you at all of these to look. Elucidation will follow." The Hivistahm patiently passed Ranji two more sheets. He glanced at each before returning them. They were side and front views of the first.

The fourth was different.

"This a close-up image of one small part of your brain is. Truly much reduced." The surgeon extracted still another sheet. "And this another." A slim-boned finger tapped the plastic, the finely manicured claw seeming to sink into the image. "I ask that you in particular note the minuscule white spot which has been in deep red color-enhanced."

Ranji's gaze narrowed momentarily before he once more passed the sheet back. "Glad to oblige. Anything else?" So suffused in droll solemnity was the gathering that he nearly burst out laughing. "I'm afraid that as revelations go this misses the mark. I've seen pictures of my insides before."

"I am certain that you have." First-of-Surgery hung close. "If you do not object I should like for you your attention to devote to them one more time."

Ranji sighed. If this was some kind of test, at least it was less discomfiting than others he had undergone.

"This picture here, for example." The Hivistahm removed a compact indicator from a vest pocket and used it to highlight portions of the image. "Do you see these points . . . here, here, and here?" The indicator shifted precisely as he spoke.

Ranji squinted, unimpressed. "What about them? Am I supposed to volunteer identification? They could be bits of bone, or blood vessels. You're the surgeon, not I. If you're offering me lessons on my own physiology, I don't need any."

"Truly that to be seen remains." The indicator moved anew. "These are grafting points." Wide slitted eyes gazed up at him, both eyelids drawn back. "You no comment have?"

Ranji blinked at the image, trying to make sense of what the Hivistahm was saying. What was the object of all this, anyway? Why were there so many of them in the room, and why were they all watching him so closely? What did it matter if such things were inside his head, or anywhere else in his body?

"No, I don't have any comment." He tapped the plastic. "This means nothing to me. Should it?"

"It should indeed." The surgeon removed another of the sheets. "That the right side of your skull was. This the left is. On this one you will see three additional points. Note that as to location they are to the previous three identical. It is thought that this work very early was carried out."

"Still means nothing to me." Ranji was cautiously indifferent. "Does it mean something to you?"

"Truly. It tells me that the prominent bony ridges which just beneath each of your eyes begin and over your ears and into the back of your skull run are not natural, but rather the result of prenatal osteoplasty."

Ranji started to reply, hesitated, instead said slowly, "I don't know what you're talking about."

"Permit me." First-of-Surgery strained on the toes of his sandals to reach the right side of Ranji's face. With a clawed finger he delicately traced the prominent bony line which dominated each side of the prisoner's skull.

"These are to you not natural. They are of surgery and implants the result. Your skin was similarly modified to allow for the additional unnatural projections. The same sort of modification has to your occipital orbits, ears, and fingers been done. Everything carried out was before you were born, before your bones time to set had.

"To insure that such work 'takes' without interfering with the natural process of bone maturation and fusion requires skills we do not possess. Only one species at bioengineering so clever is." He replaced the current sheet with a new one.

"See here, your hands. Again the grafting points." Ranji stared without comprehending.

"But . . . if any of what you say is true, why?"

The Hivistahm's teeth clicked softly. "To give you the appearance of an Ashregan. If one backward works to delete these points

and their projected effects, the result is a quite different skeleton."
He hesitated and took a step away from the prisoner. "Truly truly
what one has is not a mutant Ashregan, but a normal Human."

Ranji snorted derisively. "That's crazy."

First-of-Surgery slipped the pictures back into their protective
envelope. "The rest of your body—your muscular structure, density,
organ placement and function, sensitivity of sense, everything—
comfortably within Human-normal parameters sits. You grade out
high-end *Homo sapiens*, not off-the-scale Ashregan. You are as Human
as the three others in this room."

The prisoner's gaze darted reflexively to the Ashregan-fluent
woman and her squat male associate. They stared evenly back at him.

"This is more than aberrant; it's insane. No, it's more subtle than
that. You're all trying to trick me. You've got some ulterior purpose
in mind and in order to carry it through you need to confuse and
trick me. You might as well forget it. I'm not so easily fooled."

"Perhaps not," said the short Human, "but you're not stupid,
either. You scored as high in intelligence as you did in everything
else. Environmental factors aside, scanner tridis aside, can't you tell
just by looking at yourself that you're more Human than Ashregan?"
His companion took up the refrain.

"No Ashregan ever grew bones as dense as yours, or had such
median muscular strength. No Ashregan ever had your reflexes or
striking ability." The emphasis on the elements of the ruse he expected and was prepared for, but not the imploring tone in her
voice.

Still he remained perfectly composed. "I concede that I may have
been slightly altered to give me certain specific Human fighting characteristics and abilities. That conclusion's inevitable and I no longer
try to deny it." Comments in different tongues filled the room. "Nor
does it trouble me. Obviously such information needs to be withheld
from children and young adults since they are not sufficiently mature
to cope with it. Whereas as an adult I can understand what was done
and why. So what if maybe I've been physically enhanced in order
to better serve the Purpose? I see nothing sinister in that."

"Truly it no wonder is how confused you are," First-of-Surgery
said. "You still do not see."

"See what?" Ranji snapped impatiently. He'd had about enough
of this nonsense.

"That you are not an Ashregan to whom Human characteristics given have been, but a Human into whom Ashregan features have been engineered. We have your genome pattern scanned and found the alterations which will enable you to pass on these features to your offspring. They into your genes have been induced. The Amplitur the long view take.

"To the Amplitur you are a warrior only second, Ranji-aar, and breeding material first."

10

He waited until he was sure he was still in complete control of himself before responding. "If everything you claim is true, then how do you explain my parents? My memories, my homeworld? The Houcilat outrage?"

"We've been doing some research, using as a starting point some of the things you've told us." The woman's manner was far more soothing than anything Ranji would ever have associated with a Human. "You and the friends you have spoken of are indeed the survivors of a massacre of civilians."

"Ah," Ranji said.

The woman continued. "There was a colony. Not Houcilat. A world whose name is now synonymous with mindless destruction. It was utterly obliterated a number of years ago by an unsupervised, unanticipated Crigolit attack. Just the right number of years ago, in fact, to place you and your age-group companions there as fetuses.

"Whole regions were incinerated. It was the only time within modern memory that weapons of mass destruction have been utilized on a planetary surface. The Crigolit commanders who directed the attack were severely disciplined by their own superiors and by the Amplitur. Based on what we have learned from you we have come to believe that this did not prevent the Amplitur, ever pragmatic, from seeing the possibilities inherent in the situation.

"At the time it was thought that no one could have survived. The majority of bodies were incinerated, carbonized. An accurate count of the dead could not be made. Therefore it was not possible for those who came after to say whether or not any children, men, women, or—" Her voice broke for the barest instant. "—pregnant women had been taken prisoner. Considering the unprecedented scope of destruction it was presumed not. Your presence vitiates a reappraisal." She tried to go on, couldn't, and left it to her colleague to continue.

"You were *taken* by the Amplitur, not rescued," the man said curtly. "Of course you have no memory of it. The abductions were carried out prior to your birth."

"Many images of the devastation are available for scholarly study." The elderly Massood spoke for the first time. "The world in question is there for all to see, a barren testimonial to war without rules."

"My parents." Ranji was mumbling. More than his self-assurance was under assault now. The walls of himself were under attack, and he was frightened, terrified because he could feel them crumbling.

Too much. Too much to listen to at once, to try and absorb and dissect and analyze. Too much to think about. Pictures and words, stories and facts. Invention, invention! They were trying to drive him mad.

The woman was remorselessly gentle. "As soon as you were born you must have been taken from your natural mother and placed with foster Ashregan parents. The same would be true for your brother." She paused. "We suspect that the much younger sister of whom you have spoken is the result of in vitro fertilization and subsequent implantation. With sufficient medical support an Ashregan womb will support a Human fetus. Such action would contribute to familial verisimilitude. The Amplitur are careful about details."

None of it could be true, he told himself numbly. Not a word of it. Because if it were so then it meant that his real parents were dead, extinguished by the Amplitur as soon as their usefulness had come to an end. It meant that the two individuals on Cossuut he had all his life called mother and father were no more than Amplitur agents who had dedicated their lives to perpetuating a monstrous fraud on innocent children. It meant that all his hard work, everything he had devoted his life to preserving and fighting for, was no more than sham and shadow in the service of monstrous eugenics.

"Deception." He was muttering under his breath now. "Tricks and lies. You're trying to convince me I'm something I'm not."

Abruptly the eviscerating uncertainty vanished. Once again he was composed and relaxed. The fear that possibly they were right, that everything he was and had stood for all his life was a lie, simply evaporated under the cool glare of knowledge.

"If I am not Ashregan but Human," he inquired triumphantly of them all but the two Humans in particular, "how is it that I can have mind contact with the Amplitur without the Human neuro-cerebral defensive mechanism engaging? I've experienced this without any harm coming to either myself or the Teachers involved. No Human could do the same, even if they so desired."

First-of-Surgery consulted with a cluster of O'o'yan and other Hivistahm. Removing a sheet from the envelope of lies, the elderly surgeon approached the prisoner for the second time.

"Remember this picture?"

Ranji glanced haughtily at the plastic. "Maybe."

"I again call your attention to the small area in red highlighted. This a much deeper scan is than any of the others. It shows a tiny portion of the interior of the right side of your cerebral cortex."

"If you say so," he replied indifferently. "What's this one supposed to be? Another graft? Another trick?"

The Hivistahm's teeth ground against one another as he slowly explained. "The red-enhanced portion the location signifies of a minute ganglionic complex. A nodule, a collection of nerve endings and connections. It took quite a while to find and was not at first noticed. Once it was identified a great deal of our time it occupied." The sheet rustled slightly in his fingers.

"The Human brain no such formation contains."

Ranji smiled. "You see? That only proves what I've been saying all along."

The short Human scratched at an ear. "There is also no such nodule present in the Ashregan brain."

Ranji involuntarily found himself eyeing the picture again. There it was: a fuzzy blot of indeterminate size and indistinct outline. Reason enough to concede one's sanity?

First-of-Surgery handed him another picture. "Here still another view is. The magnification is greater."

The blot resolved itself into a tight cluster of cells from which tiny filaments extended in many directions. It looked like any creature one might observe through a microscope.

"And still greater magnification."

The third picture revealed the filaments and cells in detail. No biologist, he was incapable of identifying any of it. Except . . .

He pointed. "What's that?"

First-of-Surgery forced himself to lean close. "A nanoneural weld. A place where nerve endings artificially joined have been." The slit-eyed, scaly reptilian face stared up at him.

"Your body no code contains for such a complex. It was built and then in your mind installed. As one would accessorize any rare precision instrument. It in a portion of your brain reposes which Human scientists have designated as unused. I should prefer to say hitherto dormant.

"Research leads us to believe that this is the region of the Human mind which holds the key to *Homo sapiens*'s ability to resist Amplitur mind-probes and suggestions. It therefore follows logically that this unique addition to your cerebral structure was by Amplitur nanobioengineers there emplaced in order susceptible to their mental manipulation to render you. It a bridge appears to be. A neural by-pass, if you will. As artificial and unnatural as the bony ridges above your ears."

"Not only are they breeding Ashregan-looking Humans to fight for them," said the woman softly, "if they can get you and your friends to mate with Human captives or others, they can breed out of the species the neurocerebral mechanism that enables humankind to resist their mind-probes. That has to be their eventual aim."

"First-of-Surgery *told* you they take the long view," her companion huffed.

Ranji stared blankly at them. A psychosomatic throbbing started near the back of his skull, where the minuscule nodule supposedly reposed.

"I don't believe you," he finally managed to mutter hoarsely. "If this thing is for real, then it's something all my people possess. All *Ashregan* people. You're trying to make me paranoid by showing me some obscure, harmless growth or faked imagery. Well, it won't work. You're crazy if you think I'm going to be taken in by something so obvious."

"The nodule is to you unique." First-of-Surgery was quietly insistent. "It is real, it is not found in Humans, it is not found in Ashregan. Only you."

"This is a wicked thing," the elderly Massood whispered. "Barbarous. Uncivilized."

"Like war itself." The short Human scanned the roomful of allies. "Mankind is just the only species that readily accepts the fact, is all. That's why this discovery only surprises but does not shock us."

"Indubitably." The Massood's comment was a peculiar mélange of distaste and admiration.

"Lies, clever lies." Ranji glared defiantly at the two Humans. "They won't help you. Did you really think you'd be able to convince me of such a sweeping hypothesis on the basis of such paltry evidence? This," and he shook the plastic sheet violently, "is nothing!" He whirled and flung it as far as he could. It sailed through the air.

In the split second that every eye in the room turned to follow the picture's progress Ranji was out of his seat and moving. First-of-Surgery went flying as a powerful forearm brushed him aside.

With no one else standing in his way Ranji was at the door before the two guards could react. The larger of the two caught a brace of stiffened fingers square in his throat. He gagged and went down as heavily as if he'd taken a slug to the chest. His companion was trying to backpedal and aim his gun when the prisoner's spinning heel caught him across the side of the face, sending blood and teeth flying.

Ranji roared up the corridor, legs and lungs functioning smoothly in tandem. If he could just reach the surface . . . He was counting on his specimen value to preserve him from destruction, betting that the order was out to shoot only to stun.

Turning a corner brought him face-to-face with a single Wais. The ornithorp was seated behind a high metal desk in the center of a floor inlaid with speckled stone. Walls of glass revealed the underground parking area he remembered from his arrival many months earlier. Few vehicles were in evidence. More importantly, the external door was open. Beyond lay blue sky, clouds, and fringing vegetation.

Turning, the Wais started to speak, recognized him for who he was, and froze. Ranji was racing past the desk and halfway to the exit when his right leg went numb from the knee down.

He kept moving, dragging the paralyzed limb, lurching desperately forward. A glance over his shoulder showed a pair of Humans firing as they came up the corridor. He ignored them and concentrated on the egress. If he could just make it outside he might be able to appropriate a vehicle and get clear before they shut the tunnel on him. The paralysis would wear off soon enough. He tried to will himself to limp faster, to run on one good leg; to levitate.

Something shocked his left thigh and he fell forward onto the smooth stone floor. The Wais at the desk had yet to move. A pair of Hivistahm technicians hesitated in the doorway, staring blankly at his prone form, clicking their teeth at one another with soft reptilian eloquence.

Ranji began pulling himself hand over hand, struggling to get a purchase with his fingers on the slick tiles. Out of the corner of an eye a pair of legs appeared, effortlessly paralleling him. Turning to look up, he recognized the guard he'd jabbed in the throat. The man's expression as he drew back his leg was more than simply hostile.

Despite the throbbing in his legs Ranji smiled up at him. "You see, I would never contemplate doing what you're about to do, but that's because I'm not anything like you. I may be a soldier, but I'm also civilized Ashregan. Whereas you are only Human."

The guard hesitated, then slowly let his foot drop to the floor. He stood close, keeping the rifle he carried pointed at the back of the prisoner's skull. Muttering nervously to themselves, the pair of confronted Hivistahm entered in haste, scurrying across the floor to disappear down another corridor.

A resigned sigh escaped Ranji as he gazed longingly at the vacant portal. "Almost made it. I should have hit you harder."

The guard rubbed his neck. "Wouldn't have mattered. They would've caught you before you'd gone far." He glanced back the way he'd come. Other guards were moving to seal the exit and block off the far corridor. Shaky but now mobile, the Wais was frantically filling her headset unit with declamations in several languages.

Some of the scientists and research specialists from the conference room had arrived. Bunched up behind the guards, they were murmuring and pointing in Ranji's direction, worried lest their precious specimen suffer further damage.

"You know," the burly Human standing over Ranji informed him conversationally, "I want to kick you really bad. A good, hard, uncivilized shot right to the kidneys. Assuming you've got kidneys. If the brainoids are right, yours are just like mine. Waited too long, though. Too many witnesses now."

Ranji pushed himself into a seated position, leaning back on his palms. He regarded the Human as one would a particularly nasty carnivore recently collected from a hostile, uninhabited world.

"Nothing about me is anything like you."

The man looked indifferent. "Doesn't matter. If a Human had hit me like that I'd want to smack him just as badly."

"Contemplation of violence against your own kind. What an astonishing racial conceit."

"Yeah, ain't it? That's why our Weave brothers love us so much." As one of the other guards approached, the man passed him his rifle and stepped behind Ranji. Slipping both arms underneath the prisoner's, the guard heaved him to his feet. A sensation as of stabbing needles tormented outraged muscles as the Human forcibly walked Ranji in circles to rush feeling back into his legs.

"I hope they decide you are Human."

"Why?" Ranji's grunts of discomfort elicited no sympathy from the man.

"Because then maybe we'll have the chance to meet up with each other another day, when you won't have whining rats and lizards to protect you."

Able to stand on his own now, Ranji shook himself free of the other's grasp. "I look forward to it," he replied placidly.

As the guard recovered his weapon he responded to the challenge with an utterly heinous, completely lurid Human response: he grinned.

Heida Trondheim was among those who now crowded the hallway. Ranji gazed thoughtfully in her direction as the guard nudged his spine with a rifle butt. "I'd love to spend some time alone with you, friend, but your keepers are getting anxious. Let's move it. And if you try anything again, if you so much as look funny in my direction, I'll stun you right where it hurts. Assuming our equipment is similar in that respect as well."

Surrounded by wary, armed Humans and Massood, Ranji was marched back to the room from which he'd taken brief but exhilarating flight. This time they were careful to shut the door behind him.

Once back inside Trondheim came close. "It's all right. I don't blame you. You've been severely traumatized." She tried to put her hand on his shoulder but he shook her off. Hurt, she resumed her seat.

Once again he found himself surrounded by a roomful of curious gazes. "Go ahead. Show me all the pictures you want. Though if your intent is to amuse me there are simpler ways. But don't think you can ever convince me that I'm something I'm not."

The tall woman was shaking her head slowly. "You're Human. Like it or not, the evidence is overwhelming. If anything, that little outburst of yours just now confirms it. No Ashregan, no matter how altered or enhanced, could've gotten that far."

"Truly he is right." Attention shifted to First-of-Surgery. The elderly Hivistahm appeared to have handled the unpleasant episode well. "I do not think we will with words and pictures convince you," he told Ranji. "Your conditioning too ingrained is, too much a part of you. We will have to something more do."

"Go ahead," Ranji taunted him. "It won't make any difference."

Double eyelids blinked over snakelike pupils. "Truly I beg to differ."

— 11 —

He never knew how or when they slipped him the anesthetic. It might have arrived in his drink, or his food, or the air of his apartment. When he sensed the impending clutch of lugubrious drowsiness he tried to fight back, screaming imprecations and pounding the walls in a futile attempt to stay awake.

As awareness faded he found himself wondering why they suddenly felt the need to render him unconscious. Perhaps they planned to move him to another installation and, mindful of his recent outburst, were taking no chances. Considering his state of mind and demonstrated capabilities, he wouldn't have taken any chances when moving him either.

He appreciated the fact that oblivion came painlessly, but then Omaphil was a civilized place. He wondered how he would've been treated on the Human homeworld. That disagreeable thought was the last he recalled before sliding into a sleep of abyssal dimensions.

A great many individuals were gathered around viewscreens scattered throughout the installation and elsewhere on Omaphil. The Surgery itself was uncrowded. First-of-Surgery was among those present, not to perform but to advise and observe. He had been teaching for so long that he no longer felt in possession of the necessary skills required to supervise the delicate operation. But he had been associated with the study from the beginning and realized that his presence would be a comfort to the others.

Another First-of-Surgery would handle the actual mechanics in conjunction with a highly experienced O'o'yan. Together they represented the zenith of Weave medical accomplishment.

Save for a single exception, interested Humans were excluded from the Surgery itself. While it was to be performed on a Human

brain, no Human physician could have hoped to duplicate the sure-
ness of movement and delicacy of touch possessed by Hivistahm or
O'o'yan. They could only watch and envy.

Though everyone involved exuded confidence and expectation,
an undercurrent of unease still permeated the proceedings. While the
procedure had been thoroughly discussed and mapped out in advance,
everyone realized they were entering unknown territory. Weave study
of *Homo sapiens* had resulted in more than one surprise, not least to
its own kind, and while expectations could be formulated, where the
Human nervous system was involved nothing was absolute, nothing
was certain.

In addition to the Hivistahm-O'o'yan staff there were two Humans in the Surgery: the man on the operating pallet, and a huge
coppery-skinned male whose fine long-fingered hands seemed to have
been lifted from a different body. Despite possessing skills which
rendered him supreme among his people, he was present only to
observe and advise. Hands which had worked on hundreds of his
own kind would not go near this particular patient, would not in the
event of emergency manipulate the microsurgical instrumentation.
That would be left to aliens possessed of a touch finer than that of
the greatest Human surgeons who had ever lived.

A thin sheet of softly opaque, nonreflective material covered
Ranji-arr from the neck down. His forehead gleamed beneath the
superb overhead lighting. Due to the nature of the tools which were
to be used it had not been necessary to shave his skull. Invisible air
clamps locked his head in place, allowing access by hands and equipment but no involuntary movement.

The attending physicians had already performed the operation
many times on a virtual-reality simulator. Still, actual reality was
different. If you made a mistake, there was no Reset button to push.
In actual reality, patients died. So the surgical team was confident,
but not certain.

The single Human towered over the roomful of Hivistahm and
O'o'yan technicians, looking clumsy and out of place. His presence
was something of a concession, and he knew it. Privately he had
assured the two surgeons in charge that he would do his best to stay
out of their way.

"As we begin," the Human said through his translator, "I have
to remind everyone both present and looking on that we don't know

what the result of our efforts will be. We may as readily kill as cure the subject. As those of you who have been following developments already know, scanning has detected at least one cluster of contained explosively carcinogenic cells implanted within the nodule. Any attempt to remove it would likely release these cells within the brain in a region where any hasty attempt at counteraction or emergency prophylaxis would be at least as damaging to the patient as the cells themselves. A carcinogenic time bomb, if you will.

"If this mechanism were located elsewhere in the body, we might be able to deal with it, but because it is buried deep within the cerebral cortex we cannot take the chance. Therefore it has been decided to leave the nodule in place and untouched while severing the neural connections between it and the rest of the patient's nervous system with nonintrusive instrumentation. The aim is to render the growth harmless without removing or traumatizing it."

"Truly this a delicate procedure is," said First-of-Surgery senior, continuing the explanation for the benefit of onlookers. "As is any manipulation of the interior of the brain." He turned to the table. "My colleague will now begin."

The other First-of-Surgery fingered sensitive controls. The operational details had been programmed into the relevant instrumentation earlier, movements and reactions having been gathered from numerous operations carried out in virtual reality. The surgical computer would automatically compensate for any minute differences it detected between its programming and actual reality. Having installed the requisite programming and instructions, the surgeons' presence was required only in case something went wrong. Should it encounter anything unexpected in the course of the surgery, the master computer would pause the operation and ask for new instructions.

A small metal dish lowered on a gleaming automatic arm until it stopped a few centimeters above Ranji's skull. Medical scanners were active on both sides. Several small needlelike instruments projected downward from the dish.

"If we missed any neurological booby traps similar to the one we found earlier, we're likely to lose him," the tall Human muttered to no one in particular.

First-of-Surgery senior looked on intently as the sonic scalpel hummed softly for a split second. One needle shifted its position infinitesimally on the surface of the dish. Each time the needle moved and hummed a single neuron within Ranji's brain was severed.

"All that can be done has been done. Scanning was rescanned, computer-enhanced, and scanned afresh. No other 'traps' were found."

"Amplitur nanobioengineering is infernally subtle."

"Truly. But science it only is, not magic." A click of sharp teeth emphasized the point.

Monitors scattered throughout the Surgery displayed rock-steady images of the operation as it progressed. They could clearly see the ganglionic complex, the flow of blood through a nearby cerebral capillary, the neurons which connected the nodule to the rest of the patient's brain. One by one they were neatly severed with impossibly brief, precisely applied bursts of high-frequency sound, progressively isolating the nodule with the intent of rendering it as harmless as a benign tumor.

"I've heard," the tall Human murmured as his attention shifted from monitor to subject and back again, "that there are some on the staff who wouldn't be particularly distressed if during the course of the operation this patient happened to die. This Ranji-aar's no monster. He's a normal Human who had his birthright stolen from him before he was born."

"I have his genome map seen. You do not me need to convince," replied First-of-Surgery.

"Sorry." To his surprise the man found he had bitten his lower lip. He'd never done that before, but then this was no ordinary surgery. There was more than one life at stake here. All of the subject's friends were also potential candidates for cutting. Though if they failed to restore this first one . . .

He knew that if he lived to be *two* hundred he could never hope to match the supernal precision of the medical computer or the programming skill of the Hivistahm, but something within him still made his fingers twitch slightly, as if he and not binary impulses were manipulating the instruments.

First-of-Surgery interrupted his thoughts. "I know of those of whom you speak. They believe that this individual and all like it should on sight be killed. They the interbreeding and contamination fear which could to Amplitur subjugation of the Human species lead.

"They do not individual salvations consider. As physicians we differently think."

Not to mention how much you can learn from him so long as he lives, the Human surgeon mused. Though he could not condemn the Hivistahm. Not when he felt the same way.

Except for the barely audible, methodical sparking of the scalpel and the click of other instruments the Surgery was as quiet as a tomb. Above the patient nothing moved save the scalpel's angustipunctal needle.

Only when the gleaming dish rose and withdrew, its programming completed, was the air filled with general conversation in several tongues and the febrile hum of busy translators. The scanners showed the nodule clearly, isolated and no longer connected to the rest of the patient's brain. Even so, it was far too soon for shouts and hisses of triumph. Apparent success required medical confirmation.

The attending physicians crowded around the various technical stations, anxiously scanning readouts and eyeing monitors. The patient's cerebrum did not explode. No armies of ravening cells were released from the nodule to destroy his brain. Circulation, respiration, wave functions, and all relevant vital signs read normal. There was no internal bleeding. First-of-Surgery allowed himself to gnash his teeth hopefully.

To the Human physician hardly any time seemed to have elapsed since actual surgery had commenced. He left the monitor he'd been studying to rejoin First-of-Surgery.

"That should do it. When he wakes up he won't be any different from before, except that for the rest of his life he'll carry a minuscule knot of useless cells around in his brain, and any Amplitur that tries to give him 'suggestions' will be in for a big surprise. Assuming that the operation has restored his nervous system's natural defensive mechanism, of course."

"It enough is that he can no longer be subject to their mental whims," said First-of-Surgery decisively. "That the principal intent of the operation was. If the Human defense also restored is, that is a bonus to him." First-of-Surgery looked thoughtful. "I also believe the knowledge can and should from the general Weave population be withheld."

Conversing in low tones, the two physicians left the Surgery, together with the rest of the staff which had supervised the sensitive operation. Their patient remained behind. A second surgical team had entered and was busying itself with checkouts of fresh programming and different instrumentation.

The sonic scalpel had withdrawn into the ceiling. Its position above the recumbent form was now taken by different instruments riding on slightly larger supportive arms. While the nature of the initial procedure had been far more sensitive, the second was to prove messier, for the newly arrived team planned to remove the excess bone from the patient's cheeks, rebuild his ears, shorten his fingers, and restore additional bone around his unnaturally wide occipital orbits.

It was their intention to render the patient as Human externally as the first team had made him within.

It did not matter that there were no Humans among them. Hivistahm and O'o'yan physicians knew the physiology of *Homo sapiens* inside and out, having spent much of their careers repairing injured Human soldiers. Artists as much as surgeons, they were completely confident that when the protective wraps were finally removed the patient would resemble anything but a member of a hostile species.

The Human surgeon who'd been present would have preferred to have remained to see that day, but knew how unlikely it was. His presence was required in combat. Few Humans chose anymore to enter professions at which others species excelled. This made the value of those who did so that much greater. The surgeon understood the situation completely. It was both simpler and more gratifying to specialize in what a Human did best.

Killing.

12

Funny thing about mirrors. Like individual thoughts, they can't be avoided forever. After some time had passed, Heida Trondheim came to see him. She talked, and he listened. There was an exchange of inconsequentialities punctuated by long silences. Then she left.

Ranji's next visitor was a lanky Human male, slightly shorter, slightly older than himself, a little lighter in color. Not a mirror image, but close.

That's when Ranji allowed himself to cry, not much caring whether they happened to be Human or Ashregan tears. It was a strain on his surgically altered eyes, but he ignored the discomfort. The young man, puzzled, returned the room to Trondheim.

Ranji still had to use a translator to talk to her. He might look Human, might be Human, but his speech remained that of another species. She was very patient with him.

"Appearances," he mumbled. "Just appearances. Why?"

"Because you should look like what you are," she replied straightforwardly.

He tilted his head back to stare at the recovery-room ceiling. "I admit that visually the change is striking, but that doesn't mean I accept it intellectually."

"You've been more thoroughly analyzed and appraised than any single Human being in recent history. While Humans and Ashregan look a lot alike, subtle chemical and physical differences remain. The Amplitur missed some of those. They didn't alter everything. You're definitely Human. As Human as I am."

He looked back at her. "Why doesn't that possibility fill me with glee?"

Their conversation was interrupted by the opening of the single door. First-of-Surgery entered, resplendent in dress vest and shorts. Even for one so cosmopolitan it took an effort of will to enter a room occupied solely by Humans, but he concealed his unease gracefully.

Ranji was shown reams of charts and figures (which could have been faked) and dozens of three-dimensional pictures (likewise fakable). The senior Hivistahm was very persuasive, but not completely convincing. Numbers and words were feeble levers with which to try and topple a person's entire life. The brief visit of the young Human who had so closely resembled him had carried more weight than all their statistics.

Though unprepared to acquiesce, he confessed a willingness to contemplate possibilities. First-of-Surgery considered it a victory.

"My head hurts," Ranji muttered.

Three claws on the Hivistahm's right hand snicked together. "As well it might, considering the quantity of excess bone that has from both sides of your skull been removed. A portion was used your occipital orbits to restore to normal Human diameter. For the same reason your appropriately shortened fingers will ache for a while. The discomfort will pass."

The disconsolate patient fingered the thin bedsheet. "Why bother? Why go to the trouble?"

"So that you'll be comfortable among your own kind," Trondheim told him. He looked over at her.

"My kind? Which 'kind' is that? You?"

She didn't look away. "Yes. Me. It helps to explain . . . certain things."

"There more is." First-of-Surgery found a suitable seat. "The ganglionic complex the Amplitur emplaced in your cerebrum remains, but all neural connections between it and the rest of your brain severed have been. It can affect you no longer."

"I see," he said quietly. "This means that the Teachers can no longer communicate directly with me?"

"That is so. We hopeful are also that the operation has restored your Human mind's ability to against uninvited mental probes defend itself. You from now on against that enemy should secure be."

Against the enemy? Who was the enemy and who ally? he thought tiredly. It was too much for a simple soldier's mind to grasp. Soldier . . . for whom, and whom against?

Vast resources had been brought to bear to convince him of his Humanity. Did he continue to resist them from reason . . . or stubbornness and fear? Had something vital been taken from him . . . or restored? How would he know? How could he find out?

Confrontation with a Teacher would answer all his questions, but somehow he doubted any were to be found on Omaphil. Therefore he would have to arrive at conclusions by other means. Of one thing he was certain.

If everything they'd shown and told him was true, if he was Human and not Ashregan, then his whole life up to this point had been nothing more than an elaborate lie.

How much did they know, his parents? Mother and father whom he'd respected and honored from the day he'd learned how to speak. Were they no more than innocent recipients of irresistible Amplitur "suggestions"? Or was the nature of their participation more elaborate, more sinister?

He blinked, conscious of warm pressure on his forearm where Trondheim gripped him gently. "Are you all right, Ranji?" Even his own name sounded unnatural, he thought. She did not have the right accent.

First-of-Surgery had risen anxiously to stand behind his chair. "You are not again violent going to become, are you?"

"No. I'm too tired to be violent, even were I so inclined." Keeping a wary eye on his patient, the surgeon resumed his seat. Ranji directed his words to Trondheim. "While I've been listening to everything you've been telling me I've also been remembering my childhood."

"Your Ashregan parents," she murmured sympathetically. He gestured, then hesitantly added the Human equivalent; a terse nod of affirmation. The movement felt not unnatural.

"Tools of the Ashregan, willingly or otherwise." First-of-Surgery was unrelenting.

Despite his promise Ranji experienced a sudden urge to smash the surgeon's toothy snout down his throat. A perfectly natural reaction, he told himself. For a Human. The harder his mind tried to convince him that they'd been telling him nothing but lies, the more his body and emotions argued otherwise.

Trondheim was talking. "It'll be okay. Everything'll be all right."

"Will it really?" He wondered if the translator was conveying something of his fear and uncertainty along with his words. "I've been Ashregan all my life. Now you ask me on the basis of images and figures to suddenly be Human. No matter what happens I'll always be Ashregan."

Surprisingly, she smiled. "You act more Human than you know, Ranji-aar."

"I say that this thing you cannot do! Unscientific it is. Against accepted procedure it is. Truly forthrightly dangerous it is!"

"Dangerous to whom?" The gray-furred Massood towered over the Hivistahm. Though he wore the uniform of a full field commander, his recent duties had been largely administrative in nature.

The uncommon insignia of the S'van who waited patiently nearby identified him as a scientific advisor to the military with attendant special privileges and qualifications. The Hivistahm found the combination inherently contradictory. First-of-Surgery knew he could not, for example, have sanely combined soldiering and medicine.

The three sentients stood on a long wide porch that clung like an attenuated bird's nest to the sheer cliff of black basalt. The dawn did its best to mitigate against unpleasant discussion. It was near the end of the second of Omaphil's two springtimes, an uncommon seasonal arrangement that was the result of orbital peculiarities. High forest grew right to the base of the cliff, succumbing only in the distance to cultivated fields. On the horizon sunlight diverted by the towers of Oumansa sought oblivion in yellow gleamings.

A storm was massing behind the distant city, silhouetting it in black weather. Hard to believe, the S'van thought, that on a day like this the civilized inhabitants of Oumansa were a people at war. As were his companions of this bright morning, and all their relations. Out beyond the crisp, unpolluted atmosphere of Omaphil, ships and sentients wheeled and maneuvered for strategic advantage, seeking opportunities to capture and destroy. The S'van tried to work it all into a joke, but just then there was little humor in him.

A handsbreadth from a sheer dropoff an empty table awaited them. An automated server brought refreshments.

"Your opinion will be noted but it will not change anything." The field commander sipped from his peculiar drinking utensil. The Massood were noted for their dedication to the cause and for their fighting abilities. Masters of tact they were not. The S'van hastened to intervene, disdaining the use of his translator in favor of fluent Hivistahm. He could speak Massood as well.

"I'm sorry, First-of, but the commander is right. The decision has already been made, at Military Council level. Even if we wanted to, there's nothing we can do about it."

"This is not a decision for the Military Council to *make*." The surgeon was livid, which in a Hivistahm generated interesting color changes in the scales which covered the head. Teeth clicking in agitation, he settled into one of the self-adjusting chairs. Among his people brooding had been raised to the level of fine art.

Deep within the wiry mass of black beard the S'van's lips worked soothingly. "I realize that your staff here still has preliminary studies they would like to complete."

"Complete? Preliminary?" The Hivistahm ignored his drink. "We barely begun have. Conceive of it! A Human child raised as an Ashregan. To like an Ashregan think, talk, believe, but to like a Human fight. We have his Humanness restored."

"But not his Humanity," the Massood interjected.

"That will in time come to him. All the more reason here to keep him, so that help we can provide as well as study."

"Personally, I agree with you." The S'van sampled his drink.

"Then why is it not so ordered?" The Hivistahm eyed the splendiferous sunrise morosely. "Why this precipitous decision?"

The Massood put down his drinking utensil. "Admittedly it is something of a gamble. But it is one that the Council feels it must take."

"He is not properly to his new condition acclimated," the surgeon grumbled. "As you say, he has not yet had his Humanity restored. We cannot his mind rebuild as we have his body. Yet you wish us via prostheses to temporarily back his Ashregan appearance give him." Claws clicked against claws.

"If this thing the Council proposes in its finite wisdom fails, we lose not only this individual but the unique opportunity he presents."

The field commander sipped delicately. Working and living alongside Wais and Motar, he had learned manners. "I remind you that the subject's wishes must also be taken into consideration, and that he energetically supports the proposal."

"I am to the subject as sympathetic as any," huffed the Hivis-tahm, "but we must think first of the good of the Weave."

"As do my superiors. The fact that the Council's desires happen to coincide with those of the individual weaken your position con-siderably." The Massood leaned forward.

"As you know, this Ranji-aar is apparently but one of many like him who were in prebirth corrupted and coopted by the Amplitur. That he wishes to return to his people and reveal the heinous decep-tion to his friends and fellow fighters in order to foment rebellion among them is considered by the Council an enterprise of sufficient worth to make the risk worth taking."

"*If* that is truly what he has in mind," said the surgeon.

"Truth is always the first casualty of war." The Massood waxed uncommonly philosophical, and his companions eyed him in sur-prise. "I have seen the xenopsychs' analysis. At this point in time our Ranji-aar trusts no one, including himself. Therefore he must be allowed to find truth, along with himself. Otherwise he will be use-less to us as well as himself. As you say, physician, his problems cannot be cured by surgery. He must convince himself of what he is.

"If he can also do that for his friends, then the Amplitur will lose not only the fruits of their experiment but the most effective single fighting force they have yet developed. The Weave will benefit in the short as well as the long term."

First-of-Surgery closed both sets of eyelids against the intensifying light. "Unless the return to familiar surroundings his Ashregan con-ditioning reinforces. If that happens then he is to us lost forever. Truly."

The S'van clicked his short flat teeth in imitation of the Hivis-tahm. As was often the case with the subtle S'van, the surgeon was unable to tell if the burlesque was performed out of respect or amuse-ment.

"That's the risk. Of course, unless the reports I've been seeing are wrong, there seems to be risk of another kind in keeping him here."

"No, no." First-of-Surgery sounded tired. "Accurate they have been. Suicide he has threatened unless he is to his people permitted to return. If sufficiently determined he was, we could not prevent it. Most frustrating truly. As an Ashregan he would not do such a thing, which would mean we could for observation retain him. But that failure would signify. It seems that for him Human to be means success for our efforts, but that we lose him. Ironic it is."

It was the S'van's turn to philosophize. "Life consists of choosing between successive contradictions, surgeon."

"So I suppose we must let him go. But I fear to. Upon my Circle I do."

"You've done great things here, First-of. But in times of conflict pure research must give way to practical concerns." This time there was no suggestion of humor in the S'van's tone.

"Truly that I realize." The Hivistahm sucked at his drink. "But that does not mean I have to like it."

"The Human psychologists who have been consulted in the matter agree that to hold him against his will is dangerous," said the field commander.

"Human psychologists?" The surgeon sniffed. "That a contradiction in terms is. With Weave guidance they have barely begun to learn how their own bizarre behavior to quantify. Seek not enlightenment from them." As no Humans were present the surgeon felt he could speak freely.

An upper lip drew back and the field commander picked politely at his teeth. Nose and whiskers twitched reflexively. "Well, if it is a ploy on his part we will know soon enough. If not, then we may achieve a great deal. Even if he is eventually discovered and killed, he will hopefully have had enough time to sow some confusion among his fellow fighters."

"I still a bad idea think it, and will so my opinion officially register," muttered the surgeon.

"That's your privilege." The S'van smiled, aware as he did so that neither of his companions could discern it through the forest of a beard.

They were still arguing when evening commenced to darken the cliff face.

The battered uniform he'd been wearing when the lone Hivistahm and Lepar had surprised him on Eirrosad had been carefully preserved in its original state. Muddy and torn, it was returned to him in an airtight transparent container.

The prostheses which restored his Ashregan appearance clung uncomfortably to his skull and fingers. To once more look in a mirror and see himself as he'd always been was unsettling, though the attending medical personnel assured him he was coping well. Head, eyes, ears, nose, and fingers looked natural enough. Unless a scarce variety of organic solvent was applied at specific locations, the prostheses could not be removed without damage to the underlying bone. On that score, they assured him, he need not worry. Though they did not possess the skills of the Amplitur, the Hivistahm and O'o'yan surgeons were in their own right extremely competent. Ranji felt that the deception would pass.

He was instructed to say nothing to the Weave military personnel who transported him back to Eirrosad nor to the bemused strike team which had been charged with conveying him as close as possible to the spot where he'd originally been captured.

Occasionally a Human or Massood would look up from its position on board the sled to favor the enigma in their midst with a bemused stare. The single passenger would in turn ignore them, sunk deep in contemplation as he gazed intently at the treetops slipping past below.

His noncommunicativeness made the Human soldiers nervous and the Massood twitchier than usual. If their passenger was, as rumored, one of the dangerously modified Ashregan warriors of whom they had heard, why were they returning him alive to a contested zone? Visions of accidental homicide visited many thoughts, but weapons stayed in their holsters. The carefully chosen mixed-species strike team was nothing if not highly disciplined.

So he intercepted no misguided shots as they lowered him to the soggy ground, reeled in their cable and confusion, and pivoted to retreat westward before the sled could be detected and targeted by an enemy missile.

As he had seemingly so long ago, Ranji once again found himself alone among towering unfamiliar growths. Somewhere high in the canopy an arboreal creature peeped querulously, wondering if it was once more safe to emerge from its hiding place. Water dripping from broad spatulate leaves dampened him with elfin reminders of the morning's shower.

They had dropped him in a pleasant, peaceful, relatively dry spot. A good place to relax and think, except that he'd already done too much thinking recently. Better to concentrate on the arduous trek

ahead instead of wasting energy on difficult questions he had no answers to. If he lingered, he might encounter a uninformed Weave
patrol. It would be embarrassing to be captured all over again. Ori-
enting himself, he started off in an easterly direction.

The Eirrosadian fauna caused him more concern than unseen
trigger-happy Massood/Human scouts. Once, something sinuous that
crawled on eight short legs struck at him, aiming curving fangs at his
knees. They ripped his pants but did not penetrate the flesh beneath.
He flayed the repulsive creature with the beam of his pistol, and it
curled and died.

Over fallen trees, through rotting clumps of wood, around impenetrable clusters of vine-strangled bushes he climbed and waded,
until an explosive shell made smoke, ash, and decomposing rubble of
the top of a broken snag off to his right.

Throwing himself prone, he landed in spongy muck near a smaller
stump, straining to see where the fire had come from. Another shell
whined through the space previously occupied by his head, shattering
the trunk of a waist-thick bole behind him and sending it crashing
to earth in a sonorous confusion of lianas and branches.

Scrambling to his knees, he dashed to his left, pistol at the ready.
That's when the voice ordered him to halt, drop his weapon, put his
hands atop his head, and turn. He hesitated momentarily, then complied. Whoever his attackers were, they had him outgunned.

Hopefully they weren't the panicky type. He could hear them
chatting tensely among themselves as they approached, could sense
the muzzles of their weapons aimed at his spine. Only when they
were quite close did he turn slowly to reveal his face.

When they recognized him as one of their own, their astonishment was something to behold. Startled realization quickly gave way
to relief, then amazement as he identified himself.

"Your death has been an accepted fact for some time, honored
Unifer." The soldier hastened to recover Ranji's gun and return it to
him. Another offered a food packet. It contained traditionally bland,
thoroughly pureed Ashregan food, not the coarse, tough stuff Humans consumed. He dug into it gratefully, not even waiting for it to
heat.

Another member of the trio scanned the woods alertly. "This
whole sector is crawling with enemy slider patrols. They are constantly probing our forward lines. Occasionally some try to sneak

through on the ground; such ground as there is on this miserable planet."

"I saw sliders, and our own floaters," Ranji lied. "It's difficult for anyone riding above to see down into the canopy."

The third soldier agreed readily. "It's no wonder you weren't spotted, Unifer. I'm only glad that we found you before the enemy. I am sorry we shot at you, but you must understand we didn't expect to encounter anything in this area but Massood and Humans. You have been some time unaccounted for." Ranji tensed slightly until he realized that the soldier's tone was devoid of suspicion.

The one watching the forest spoke up. "Your special unit has been pulled back and reassigned to operations elsewhere, Unifer." Convinced of their safety, he turned to gaze at the young officer. "How is it you've spent all this time wandering about in this patch of jungle?"

"Lost my direction finder." Ranji grunted. "Lost about everything. Got hurt and had to hide from enemy patrols. Took time to find food, build temporary shelters . . . I've been too busy just staying alive to try working my way back." He gestured appreciatively. "I knew that if I could just keep calm and stay clear of the enemy, my own people would rescue me eventually. I am sure there will be commendations in this for all of you."

That observation distracted the questioner sufficiently to interrupt what threatened to become an ominous line of thought.

"Spent a lot of time in the hollow of a tree," he continued inventively, seeing how enthralled they were with his tale of survival. "Kept me hidden and dry, but impossible to spot from the air by friend or enemy. I needed time for my leg to heal. Hurt my face and hands, too," he added in a sudden flash of inspiration.

They all touched the backs of their right hand to his. "It is good to find you alive, Unifer."

He could feel his indoctrination, his recently acquired Humanity, beginning to crumble in the presence of Ashregan compassion. Weren't these his people? Hadn't he spent his whole life among them? What was the difference between Ashregan and *Homo sapiens* anyway? A few genes, some slight differences in stature and appearance. It was good to again be speaking in a familiar tongue, to be eating the food of his childhood, to slip easily into the casual byplay of words and gestures he'd known all his life. He'd prepared himself to cope with familiarity, but not with warmth and affection. It weakened and unsettled him.

Not unnaturally, his alarmed rescuers assumed his reactions were the result of his extended sojourn in the jungle. They hastened to help him back to friendly lines.

His nervousness faded rapidly. Everyone was overjoyed to see him. No one voiced suspicion or incertitude. His tale of injury and survival was accepted verbatim, in part because there was no reason to doubt him, in part because they wanted to believe it. When there is a need for heroes and they are so inconsiderate as not to invent themselves, others take up the task for them.

No one questioned his appearance or physical condition. Insofar as they were concerned it was a miracle he'd been found alive in *any* condition. When pressed for details of his experience, he relaxed and allowed his fecund imagination to take over.

When finally he was reunited with his own unit, the response was overwhelming and utterly accepting. If he had told them he'd spent the previous weeks on Eirrosad's major satellite collecting mineral samples they would have believed him implicitly. He received so many backhanded slaps he feared for the integrity of his prostheses.

"Such a long time!" The naked adoration in strong Birachii's eyes forced Ranji to turn away in embarrassment. "Notice of your death was posted officially over two months ago."

"It was premature" was all he could murmur.

They were walking the grounds of a forward firebase, concealed in the eternal jungle some distance from where Ranji had been found. It seemed that everyone recognized him and waved or shouted in passing, regular Ashregan and insectoid Crigolit troops as well as familiar members of his own unit. He forced himself to acknowledge each undeserved accolade, acutely conscious of how his miraculous return had lifted their morale.

It was hard to keep from staring at his friends, knowing what he knew now about their birthright. Appearances, which hitherto he had paid little attention to, now aroused in him an almost morbid fascination. Cranial ridges that did not belong, eyes that now seemed unnaturally wide, fingers lengthened by the presence of extraneous bone, unusually flattened nostrils, and the absence of external ears all struck him as both alien and familiar. There was within him taking place a crisis of perception.

His reactions were noticed, and sympathetically attributed to the understandable aftereffects of his exhausting experience.

The more time he spent among old friends and familiar surroundings, the darker grew the shadow of doubt that had once more begun to shade his thoughts. Was what he had seen and learned beyond doubt? Had every question been adequately answered? That he was being manipulated he knew for a certainty. But by whom? By which side? By the Amplitur, by the Weave . . . by both?

What was he, who was he, and where did his loyalty rationally lie? With appearances, with genes, or with friends? He had been exposed to and had been asked to accept in a very short period of time multiple revelations of mind-shattering import. This he had done. Or so he had believed. At the time.

It was easier to live the days in languid succession, to simply exist, to *be*, and not constantly torment oneself pondering the greater mysteries of existence. One thing he could not escape, however. One thing there was always before his eyes. No matter how he tried to avoid it, he could never again escape the realization that his friends looked far more like Humans onto whom a few Ashregan features had been grafted than the other way around.

When they inquired, as he knew they would, as to how he had survived for so long without supplies, he told stories of gathering edible fruits and nuts, of killing and eating small animals, of gathering rainwater in cupped leaves. He'd done everything they'd been told to do in survival training, and this had preserved him. They listened raptly, their appetite for his memories insatiable.

Had he in the course of his odyssey encountered any of the enemy? Several, he admitted. No, not Massood or Humans. Hivistahm and Lepar. Yes, their presence in a combat zone had surprised him. More than they could know. He had dealt with them as circumstances required.

It was during one such gathering that swift, pretty Cossinza-iiv came forward apologetically. "I have something important to tell you, Ranji." The others tried to shush her. "I'm sorry, but I can't keep it a secret any longer."

"Keep what a secret?" Ranji asked guardedly.

"Did you know that the big advance base to our immediate rear is tomorrow to receive the newest batch of special fighters from Cossuut?"

Ranji was openly surprised. "This is the first I've heard of it."

New recruits from home. New graduates. Had that much time passed since *his* only concern in life had been to do well in the Maze?

"When they're cleared to join us it will more than double our strength. The next time Command gives us a special assignment we'll be able to hit the enemy a lot harder than we have here or on Koba."

"That's great." Ranji mustered a minimum of enthusiasm. "That's the secret?"

"No." Cossinza was smiling. So were some of those behind her. "Your brother's with them. They jumped him a level."

Distantly Ranji heard himself expressing his pleasure at the news. So Saguio was here, on Eirrosad. Wonderful. Thus far he'd managed to beguile other Ashregan, Crigolit, even close childhood friends. But could he fool his own brother?

That Saguio was his brother was something Ranji did not doubt. They shared similar height and strength, the same desire and skills. Ranji was a little smarter, his younger sibling slightly taller. The resemblances outweighed any differences. He and Saguio had been fashioned from identical genetic stock. Whatever that was. It didn't matter to Ranji whether they shared the same natural parents or not. Saguio was and always would be his brother.

His apprehensions were overcome the next morning as soon as he caught sight of his brother stepping off the transport sled. As for Saguio, if Ranji had sported two heads it would not have lessened his pleasure at finding himself again with his elder brother.

They spent hours catching up, reminiscing, and swapping stories. If Saguio detected a certain reticence on the part of his revered sibling to discuss their parents, he chose to ignore it.

"I heard about what happened to you out there. I can't imagine what it must've been like."

Brother benign, truer words never fell from your lips. What would be his reaction, Ranji mused, when he finally learned the truth? Like everyone else, Saguio was convinced his brother was a hero. But that didn't matter, because he was only a hero among the Ashregan, and he was not of them. Nor was Saguio, nor Cossinza, nor clever Soratii-eev. Or were they?

He needed to arrive at truth: without interference from Humans, or Ashregan, or Amplitur, or anyone else. Let them skirmish over the future of worlds or the disposition of half a galaxy. The fight for his identity concerned him nonetheless.

When he judged the moment propitious to finally reveal what he'd learned to his friends, he realized they might very well kill him. Even Saguio might partake of the festivities. There were no armed Humans, no self-assured Hivistahm around to help him now. The balance of his life lay in his hands and no others. Whatever else he might think of his former captors, he had to admire the risk they'd taken in allowing him to return to his people. That suggested confidence . . . or great daring. Both were reputed to be Human characteristics.

Before he spoke, before he put his life on the line, he had to be certain beyond any doubt. Despite what he'd told his captors prior to his departure from Omaphil, that was a destination he had yet to set eyes upon.

Meanwhile he relaxed in the company of his brother, and reminiscences of simpler times. Of days when certainty had ruled his life, and the Purpose was always there for comfort. Now that hitherto exalted philosophy struck him as something less than grand.

How was he to proceed when the time came to try and convince Saguio and the others that they were not Ashregan, but mere dupes of the Amplitur? He had with him no damning pictures, no reams of statistics, no means for conducting tests on querulous companions. Only his reputation and strength of character, and he knew full well those might not be enough.

He didn't have to do it, he knew. He was safe among those who admired and respected him. On the basis of his perceived ordeal he could claim combat fatigue and put in for a noncombat position. They would love to have him as an instructor on Cossuut. He could try to forget what he'd seen, what he'd learned, and return home to live out the remainder of his life among familiar surroundings and friends. His participation one way or the other wasn't going to alter the course of a thousand-year-old conflict anyhow. Even if he was Human, he owed nothing to that dire and unfamiliar species.

There remained, however, one responsibility he could not rationalize away, could not shrug off. That was to the unborn. Unless they were treated, his friends' offspring would unknowingly inherit the traits and physical distortions intended for them by the Amplitur.

There would be no convincing a child born of such circumstances of its Humanness. Whatever his eventual fate, he did not see how he could let it happen to those for whom no choice would be allowed.

He would make a beginning with Saguio. That decision, at least, was easy to make. His brother would listen to what others would reflexively dismiss as madness. With luck he would be able to continue at least a few before they carted him away for medical treatment.

13

Ranji's friends and colleagues were not the only ones who listened with interest to his tale of solitary survival in the jungles of Eirrosad. The Amplitur devoted much attention to the exploits of their new fighters. Among them his story provoked a certain amount of contented jubilation . . . and curiosity.

Certainly his experience confirmed the viability of the genetic line they hoped to propagate. It would not do for such a feat to pass ignored. Congratulations were in order . . . as well as careful debriefing.

"The Teachers are coming!"

Ranji, Saguio, and several friends were relaxing in the field barracks when Tourmast burst in with his announcement. Until Operations decided on their next assignment there was little for them to do but exercise, try to stay active in the debilitating humidity, and wait.

Silently Ranji absorbed the declaration's import. The forthcoming confrontation induced in him neither panic nor visible unease. He was surprised only because he had not expected it to come so soon. A great calm settled over him. He would not have to go seeking the answers to some of his questions: they were about to come to him.

His future, like his self, would be defined by the reactions of the Teachers. For the first time he would be bringing something other than simple awe to the encounter. No matter what the outcome he could no longer think of them as purely altruistic custodians of universal truths. The Humans and Hivistahm and Massood had taken away his innocence and traded it for a dubious Humanity.

The Amplitur insisted they could not read minds, only venture suggestions. What if he did not respond properly? What sort of suggestions ought he to expect? He was almost too tired to care.

Ashregan and Crigolit officers hunted frantically for the dress uniforms which were important only to them. While the Amplitur were not big on ceremony, many of those races which fought alongside them felt otherwise. A formal multispecies welcoming committee was hastily assembled north of the central landing disk.

The heavily armed transport skid was setting down silently even as stragglers continued to arrive, uniforms hastily straightened, to swell the ranks of the impromptu honor guard. An air of anxious uncertainty hung about the ranked officers like stale pheromones.

None of which appeared to trouble the Teachers. There were two of them: impressive when one realized that only four were present on all of Eirrosad. None among the assembled Ashregan and Crigolit could imagine what would motivate a surprise visit on their part to the potentially dangerous vicinity of a forward support base.

Together they approached the regional commander on their four short, squat legs, advancing with ponderous grace. Tentacle tips danced snake ballet in the turgid air, describing arcs and circles pregnant with import only to another Amplitur.

As a Unifer, Ranji was among those in front. He looked on silently as the esteemed pair conferred with the regional commander and his team. Among the Teachers' escort were a pair of tall, angular Copavi. Never having seen a Copavi in person before, he focused his attention on them. They looked too fragile to manage the long, narrow-barreled weapons they carried.

Then he saw that the Teachers were making their way toward the line in which he stood. Any attempt to further divert his thoughts was reduced to an instant exercise in futility.

Alongside him friends and fellow fighters murmured expectantly. Saguio expanded with pride. His brother might be in for more excitement than he expected, Ranji mused quietly.

Abruptly there was no more time for speculation. Stumpy eyestalks tipped with black globes tilted toward him, and pupils like streaks of molten gold focused on his own. As he returned the gaze he did his best to make his mind a complete blank, intimidated despite supposedly firm resolve to the contrary. After all, these were the *Teachers.*

He felt warmth and good fellowship flowing outward from them, to envelop him in a soothing, reassuring mental blanket. How could such as these be responsible for the abominations postulated by the representatives of the Weave? They were the very essence of empathy and understanding. There was within them only goodness and light. He decided not to think; only to react.

The base commander, a portly Ashregan of incongruously sorrowful demeanor, was speaking.

"... And this is the famous Ranji-aar of Cossuut, who as you have heard only recently returned to us, having spent many months alone in the jungle behind enemy lines."

"A most remarkable episode." Instead of projecting its thoughts into the minds of its audience the second Amplitur utilized its horny mouthparts to replicate the supple sounds of the Ashregan language. The utilization of natural speech was in itself something of an honor for the one so addressed.

"You bring Wellness to us all." Eyestalks bobbed at arm's length from Ranji's face.

Simultaneously he felt the familiar tickling inside his head, indication that one or both of the Amplitur was projecting directly to him. In spite of himself he tensed, but the Teacher did not jerk away. There was none of the thrashing of tentacles and twitching of limbs that would have signified contact with the mental defense mechanism of a mature Human nervous system.

So he was not as Human as the scientists of the Weave insisted. Matter for contemplation. How much more of what they had told him on Omaphil was nonsense and propaganda? If he was fully Human, then his mental contact with a Teacher should have sent it reeling backward in shock and pain. Instead those slitted black eyes continued to weave imperceptibly on the ends of their stalks, regarding him with beatific solemnity.

The gentling contact was full of admiration for his accomplishment and joy at his safe return, as well as concern for his current health. There was in it nothing hostile, nothing threatening. Nothing to fear.

What followed then was no more than an afterthought, a casual inconsequentiality. An indifferent suggestion that Ranji's line step forward so that they might all be singled out for special praise. Ranji blinked against the sun, and in the duration of that blink he hesitated.

His brother did not, nor did any of the others. Only Ranji lingered;
deliberately, minutely, making of his hesitation a slight stumble before joining the others in their crisp advance.

The tight smile stayed frozen on his face. Because he knew that
among his companions he alone could have held his position, he
alone could have resisted the suggestion. For the briefest of in-
stants he had sensed command instead of suggestion, pull instead
of request. For such a small revelation it filled him with great confusion.

And fear. Had his pause been noted and understood for what it
was? The smoky bulbous orbs hovering before him were impenetrable, the cephalopodian face behind them unreadable.

The Amplitur gave no sign that anything was amiss or that it
suspected anything abnormal had just taken place. Sensitive tentacle
tips reached out and around to embrace him. He stood in that warm,
alien grasp, numb and smiling, until he was released. Wordlessly the
Teacher retracted its tentacles and together with its companion began
moving down the line of fighters, leaving Ranji to try and analyze
the confrontation as best he could.

For the first time he had felt that contact with the Teachers involved more than mere suggestion. There had been a definite tug, a
compulsion. Having recognized it, he'd been able to resist it, though
he had eventually complied with the actual command for fear of
being found out. His friends, he realized, had not been allowed that
choice.

How many such "suggestions" had he and his companions un-
wittingly been compelled to comply with in their lifetimes? This time
he had been able to recognize and resist. But neither had he reacted
as a Human would have. What was he? What had the Hivistahm
surgeons made of him?

He had little time to wonder, because the Amplitur retraced their
steps until they were again confronting him.

This time the insinuating, insistent probe was directed at him
alone. There was no opportunity to conceal resistance among mass
movement. He waited, fighting to conceal his unease.

It was "suggested" that he tell his story once again, so that the
Teachers as well as his fellow fighters might benefit from his experiences. Under other circumstances Ranji would have demurred, but
he knew he was not being asked: he was being *told.*

Though he knew he could have refused, he complied promptly and with apparent enthusiasm, turning to face the ranks of silent soldiers. He could feel black and gold eyes on his back, studying him intently, and did his best to ignore the sensation as he once more regaled his companions with his carefully composed sequence of elaborate lies.

Occasionally one Teacher or the other would silently suggest that he elaborate on this or that particular point. Ranji complied readily with the mental coaching that passed unnoticed by his audience.

When he'd concluded the tale he was offered the greatest honor of all. Had not the Amplitur for thousands of years carried the burden of the Purpose figuratively upon their backs? The Teacher nearest him knelt, beckoning to him with both mind and tentacle. Given no choice in the matter, a reluctant Ranji stepped forward and settled himself atop the Amplitur, straddling the smooth, fleshy back. The Teacher thoughtfully steadied its passenger with a tentacle, then stood.

One of the tall Copavi approached and activated an instrument to record the image for distribution purposes. See! the picture would say. The accomplishments of this brave Ashregan have raised him even above the Amplitur themselves. Figuratively, of course. A sardonic Ranji had no doubt that the image would be widely displayed.

As he quietly held the unaccustomed position Ranji noticed that he could easily have slipped a knife into the base of the fleshy skull, penetrating the brain and forever shutting off the flow of gentle but irresistible suggestions. The violence of the notion unnerved him. The very concept would have been anathema to an Ashregan . . . but not to a Human.

When the Copavi finished its work, a shaken Ranji was allowed to slip off the slick, spineless back and resume his place in line. The Teachers formally addressed the entire gathering, praising them for their dedication and bravery, exhorting their dedication to the Purpose. Ranji listened as intently as the others, but drew no comfort from the compliments. It was as if something unwelcome and vaguely diseased were squirming unimpeded through his thoughts, rearranging them to suit its own specific notions of right, wrong, and reality.

A parasite, he thought, only becomes a parasite when one is made

aware of its presence. There were on many worlds bloodsucking creatures which released anticoagulants that allowed blood to flow painlessly and unbeknownst to the host animal. The Amplitur, he now
saw, did something similar with thoughts, causing commands to be
perceived as suggestions, orders to be seen as polite requests. The
realization made him feel unclean.

As the nearest member of the pair stared at him he again felt the
mental contact, the suggestion that by way of concluding the ceremony he offer a few inspiring words to his fellow fighters. Anger
momentarily overcame common sense.

"I'm sorry, but I'd rather not." Even as the words left his mouth
he found himself regretting them.

The Amplitur's weaving tentacle froze. Protuberant black eyes
tilted further in his direction. The suggestion was repeated, this time
with compelling force.

Damn all ignorance! Ranji thought furiously. He deliberately ignored the unmistakable command. Though the Teacher was three
times his mass, in a close-quarter fight it would be no match for his
Humanized bones and muscles.

Unable to restrain their curiosity, a few fellow soldiers leaned
forward just enough to stare in his direction. The continued silence
was making them uncomfortable.

The second Amplitur approached and reiterated the suggestion.
In the grip of projected compulsion Ranji should have enthusiastically stepped forward to harangue his friends. Instead he remained
stolidly immobile, his expression blank.

The Teachers conferred. Though Ranji could not read their
thoughts they broadcast their confusion through the active movement of eyestalks and tentacles. Clearly they were puzzled rather
than apprehensive.

After several minutes they turned again to face him. He readied
himself to attack or run as the situation dictated.

"You are tired," came the empathetic thought. "It explains your
hesitation. You have been through a most difficult and trying time
from which you have not yet fully recovered. We understand."

Ranji's muscles untensed. Having discussed his defiance, in the
absence of any other immediate explanation they had chosen to interpret his noncompliance with their request as the result of lingering
trauma! His immunity remained a secret.

Relief continued to flow through him as they turned to exchange final formalities with the base commander and his staff. He was angry with himself. His resistance had been foolish and unnecessary. Had they suspected anything unnatural he would have soon found himself in yet another operating theater full of Amplitur surgeons eager to explore the parameters of his enigmatic mind. Luck and circumstance had saved him, not a dubious intelligence.

He joined his companions in voice if not enthusiasm in shouting fond farewells as the Teachers reboarded their transport. The encounter had left him more confused and uncertain than ever. What sort of creatures were they, these Amplitur, who could urge others to violence against their will while simultaneously anguishing over their welfare? He had personally experienced that concern along with their exercises in mental dominance. It was a contradiction he found himself unable to resolve.

About one thing they had been quite accurate. He was extremely tired.

As the skid rose to treetop level and pivoted, the assembly began to break up, officers and troops returning to duty stations or barracks. Conversation was split evenly between the unprecedented visit and the forthcoming evening meal.

A number of Ashregan and Crigolit came over to congratulate him on the honor he'd received, intercepting him before he could make it back to his room. One Crigolit subjoiner was particularly effusive in her praise, offering by way of the ultimate compliment the opportunity to copulate. Metaphorically, of course.

Saguio was waiting for him, the naked adulation on his face painful to behold. Ranji found himself looking past his younger brother's admiring eyes, deep into the brain, in search of a peculiar neuroganglion that was not of natural origin. Suddenly he wanted to thrust his hand in, through one of the unnaturally large eye sockets, to pluck out the offending, traitorous organ.

How many other races sported similar Amplitur-induced modifications within their minds, he wondered? The Crigolit? The Mazvec? Perhaps even the intelligent Korath. The Amplitur dominated a vast number of worlds, he knew, and the more he learned the more it was made clear to him that all of them were in need of exploratory surgery.

"Wait until the family hears about this!" Saguio was rambling.

"To be so congratulated by a Teacher . . . no, *two* Teachers. That they should take the risk to come this close to a fire zone just to praise you in person . . . it's a singular honor, Ranji."

"I know." He glanced up. "Did you sense them in your mind?"

"Sure. Several times. It felt good, like it always does." He blinked uncertainly. "Why would you ask such a thing? Didn't you feel them?"

"Of course." He looked away. "They asked me to do something. They asked more than once. I refused each time."

Saguio considered. "Well, I guess they felt you weren't up to it. What did they want, anyway?"

"For me to make a concluding speech. 'Fight to the last for the Purpose!' That sort of thing."

"You couldn't manage that? For the Teachers?" Saguio eyed his brother askance. "You don't look that tired to me."

"I'm afraid that I am." Ranji found himself staring outside, at the surrounding, all-encompassing jungle. "I'm very tired. I'm more tired than you know."

A note of alarm crept into his sibling's voice. "Maybe you'd better check back in to the infirmary. You might've picked up something latent out there."

No, I didn't pick anything up, he thought. I left something. "I'll be all right. I just need to rest. The strain of having the Teachers here . . . you understand."

"I guess so." Saguio sounded doubtful but willing.

"It's almost meal time. You start on over. I'll be along in a minute." Ranji barely quashed an incipient Human smile.

"If you're sure . . ." His brother managed a grin. "I'll find some good seats, though after what you've been through you can probably sit anywhere you want."

Ranji watched until Saguio disappeared around the next barracks. Surprisingly, he felt the first pangs of evening hunger. Food, at least, was devoid of biological and philosophical complications. Human or Ashregan, he could still take pleasure in eating.

He had to tell Saguio soon, regardless of possible consequences. Better to have it all out at once than wait for it to slip out in confusing, contradictory bits and pieces.

Or he could end it. Just lift the service pistol from his belt, place it gently against the side of his skull, and in an instant banish all pain, all confusion, all uncertainty. No need then to agonize over who was telling the truth, over the true nature of himself.

It was the thought that perished, not the mind that conceived and discarded it. He did not fear death, but he refused to die without answers.

That much, at least, he knew about himself.

14

The three Humans sprawled languidly around the crescent-shaped table, shuttling down drinks as they watched the projections which cavorted amid the storm of colored lights that filled the relaxation center. Music caressed respective tympana as near-naked men and women flitted erotically through fragments of light sharp and distinct as metal shavings. They and their immediate surroundings danced submerged in the mists of a perfumed artificial twilight.

The Center was extensive and they were not alone. Representatives of other Weave species sought similar solace in the febrile evening. Massood and Wais, S'van and Hivistahm and more eagerly availed themselves of the soothing surroundings. For each, different images dwelt in the deliberately coy shapes which darted through the high-tech fog.

Not surprisingly, the perceptions of the Massood differed little from those of the Humans, though the figures that twisted and pirouetted for them in the suggestive light were taller, slimmer, and completely covered in fine gray fur. The Wais saw elegant movement devoid of heavy sexual overtones, while the contemplative Hivistahm willingly allowed themselves to be blinded by deceptive iridescence. Whatever the S'van observed amused them greatly, but then there was very little which did not. Being bright and intelligent but woefully deficient in imagination, the O'o'yan saw not much of anything. Within the confines of the Center, not merely beauty but virtually everything was in the eye of the beholder.

Most of the time the three visiting Humans preferred to eye the projections instead of each other. Though Sergeant Selinsing was moderately attractive, her fellow noncoms Carson and Moreno wouldn't have dreamed of undressing her with their active imaginations the way they did the figures in the projections. She was, after all, very much one of the group. Besides which she outranked them.

Carson manipulated a switch on the table. Instantly the projection he'd selected was sitting there beside him, inviting him with her eyes and more. He knew he could reach out and touch it, experiencing a tactile fabrication guaranteed to please. Like all such liaisons, however, it would prove as transitory as the contents of his credit line, and about as satisfying. With a sigh he nudged a control and watched as the apparition, like so many previous loves, returned to the wizard regions which had spawned it.

Moreno was next to rejoin reality. To the silent amusement of her companions, Selinsing lingered longest among the projections. She blinked as the last one vanished.

"That one was new to the files." She was mildly apologetic. "Mutant slavo-equine. Very interesting."

"Spare me." Moreno slugged down recombinant liquor. Smallest of the three, spare of word and feature, he had the doe sadness of a saint and the moves of a pit viper. His tiny black eyes scanned the rolling, uneven levels of the Center.

"I'm sick of this. Look at that odious pair over there." His head bobbed.

Like a bear emerging from hibernation, Carson swiveled in his seat. Selinsing tilted her head to one side.

The two Wais were deep in conversation, the hypnotic movement of arms, fingers, head, and neck supplementing verbal communication. In attire they were impeccable, in gesture flawless. Moreno wanted to puke.

"They squat on their feathery butts and never get within a hundred kilometers of any actual fighting, but if we happened to ask about joining the Weave they would immediately vote against us."

Carson belched, a rolling benthonic exhalation. "Who gives a shit about their stupid Weave, anyway?" He sucked at his tankard. "Screw 'em."

"We do all the fighting and they won't even let us vote in their organization," Moreno muttered bitterly.

"I don't mind that." Selinsing was incongruously petite. "What I don't like is sitting here while their stupid Military Council decides strategy. They've always been overcautious."

"Just so." Moreno straightened in his chair. "The only way we're ever going to get off this stinking, sweaty dungball of a world is to kick the living *mierda* out of the enemy, and we can't do that while we're getting blitzed in here."

"Can't do it out there, either," Carson reminded him. "Orders. You know what the Council says. Patience."

"Yeah, patience," said Moreno morosely. "And the Massood go along with 'em. Damn shrew-faces."

"They've always gone along with the Council." Selinsing drew imaginary lines on the tabletop. "That's why this war's been going on for so long. Not that they're cowards. Just overcareful. They've been listening to the S'van and Wais for too long. Not to mention the Turlog."

"I heard that two of the crabs were on Eirrosad, dictating tactics." Moreno glowered at a distant pair of necking S'van. Their eruptive beards intertwined indistinguishably.

"It would not surprise me," said Selinsing. "Orders are that no unit can advance more than two kilometers for fear of being flanked."

"Flanked *mierda*." Moreno's disgusted gaze abandoned the S'van. "War's been going on here long enough for everybody to know everyone else's position. We know pretty well where the enemy headquarters for this region is situated. We ought to smash right in there, take it out, *verdad?*, and not stop until we reach their planetary HQ. That'd put *fin* to the Purpose on this piece of dirt. Then maybe they'd post us somewhere decent."

"I agree," said Selinsing, "but Command doesn't."

Carson leaned back in his chair. "Why don't you two quit yer bitching? We're stuck here and there ain't a damn thing we can do about it because our own officers spend all their time diplomatically disagreeing with Massood and S'van tactical drivel. They've got less guts than the squids."

"As a matter of fact," Selinsing murmured softly, "it is said that the Amplitur actually have two sets of guts."

"Then they're probably real happy with the current state of affairs." Carson sought wisdom in the depths of his impressive tankard. "Me, I personally don't think they want to beat us. Just keep things stalemated until they can outlive us."

Moreno rested his forearms on the table. The music of many-species music ricocheted off surrounding walls. "I say somebody's got to do something to change the present state of affairs. Somebody's got to do it *now*."

"What did you have in mind?" Eyes half-closed, the relaxed Selinsing contemplated invisible amours.

"Our position is pretty isolated, the farthest advanced of any fire-base. The ideal place from which to strike. An end could be put to the business of Eirrosad . . . if somebody had the guts to do it." Eyes narrowed, he appraised his colleagues. "Preferably several somebodies."

"You mean hit 'em with just our own squads?" Carson shifted in his seat. "Wouldn't be enough firepower to be sure of success. Anyway we'd be ordered back too soon for it to do any good."

"Not if we started out with incontrovertible orders in the first place," Moreno ventured conspiratorially.

Carson blinked at him. "Must be too many lights in here. I ain't followin' you."

Moreno put a hand on his friend's arm. "What if the word came down from Command level to carry out just such an attack?"

Selinsing uttered something unmistakably derisive in the language of her ancestors. "At least you have chosen the proper venue for wishful thinking."

"Yeah, dream on," Carson grunted.

"You know Colonel Chin?" Moreno inquired of his companions.

When they drew close together Carson's thick eyebrows resembled a pair of caterpillars engaged in unspeakable activities. "Sure. Everybody knows Chin. But Chin ain't in command of our position. Wang-lee is."

"That's so. But right now Wang-lee is busy conferencing with the major minds back at Katulla Nexus, hashing strategy with the crabs and the S'van. That leaves Chin in charge until she gets back." He leaned forward eagerly. "I happen to know Chin's as tired of waiting on the Council as the rest of us."

"I have never heard him say anything along those lines." Selinsing was being cautious.

"You wouldn't expect him to blurt it out in public, now would you?" Moreno smiled like a man in possession of a considerable secret.

Carson's eyes widened. "You've talked to him! About *this*?" He whistled softly. "One wrong word scrapes the wrong nerve and you'll find yourself back at Supply Central, busted in rank and cataloging foodstuffs for the duration."

"Anything would be better than squatting in the middle of this jungle, waiting to go mad."

"You are joking," said Selinsing slowly. "Though if someone like Chin were to give the orders . . ."

"Give orders, hell." Carson turned to stare intently at Moreno. "If Chin feels the same way about these delays as the rest of us, could be he might consider doing more than just issuing orders. Like maybe leading an assault himself."

Suddenly aware he might have gone too far too fast, Moreno adopted a cautioning tone. "Slow down, my friends. I've only suspicions. I don't know Colonel Chin's feelings exactly. It's only been mentioned on a couple of occasions, and casually at that. Chin never got specific. He's a funny kind of guy, even for an officer."

"Nothing wrong with his rep. I know he's got what it takes upstairs." Carson rapped his belly. "Question is, does he have it here?"

"If we hit the enemy with our full strength," Selinsing was murmuring, "not just our three squads but everything on the base, we could roll right over them and strike for their planetary headquarters. *Ja*; maybe even get ourselves a couple of squids. Vacuum them right out of the forest."

"That's the wipe!" Carson drained his tankard, glanced hopefully at Moreno. "How about it, Juan? You think Chin might go for it?"

"Not in so many words," the shorter man replied carefully. "Chin's as focused on his career as any officer. He'd have to feel he was covered in case of a screwup."

"Certain ambiguities might creep into official communications, rendering ultimate comprehension a matter of individual interpretation." Both men looked at Selinsing, who smiled like a petite wolverine. Communications was her subspeciality.

"There is a certain officer in Base Operations," she explained unctuously. "He is Massood. If these hypothetical orders happened to be received in Massood, difficulties in translation might have to be resolved as best as possible by whichever personnel happened to be present at the time."

"Like you?" Carson wore a grin of a different sort.

She smiled ever so slightly. Escaping rainbows stained her jet-black crewcut. "It is not inconceivable. It would of course also be incumbent upon me to see that matters of ambivalence were conveyed personally to the acting base commandant so that he could propose a determination based on available evidence and expert opinion."

"You again." Carson's admiration knew no bounds.

Having intended only to submit the first draft of a casual notion, Moreno was somewhat taken aback by the speed with which his companions had proceeded to polish it.

"Slow down. We're all half-drunk."

"Not me," Carson insisted cheerfully. "I'm four-fifths, at least."

"What if Chin doesn't take to the idea in the spirit with which it's offered?"

Selinsing shrugged. "Then I can be held responsible for a poor translation from the Massood, remember? I'm willing to take that much of the risk. If he so chooses, all he can fault us for personally is an excess of enthusiasm."

Carson's chair hummed as it retreated from the table. He rose, weaving only slightly. As he stepped out of the Human cone of influence, the shape in the shadows changed from that of a tall, voluptuous woman to a short and to the sergeant's eyes utterly repulsive female S'van.

"Let's do it now." His eyes blazed. "Let's do it *quick*. I'm sick of sitting on my ass blowing kisses at shadows. I want to *kill* something."

That was Carson for you, his friends knew. Just a regular guy. Whispering excitedly among themselves the noncoms exited the club, oblivious as always to the expressions of disgust and relief which crossed the faces of their non-Human allies and fellow patrons as the three primates departed.

Chin's apartment was located deep within the forward firebase's central accommodations complex. Given the option, on Eirrosad as elsewhere, high-ranking officers usually elected to sacrifice sweeping views in favor of claustrophobic safety. As befitted the base's second-in-command, Chin rated not one but three rooms: a sleeping cubby, private hygienic facilities, and a meeting and strategy room. Native vegetation had been planted atop the complex, which in combination with sophisticated methods of camouflage allowed the base to blend into the surrounding jungle.

It was quite late and typically dark outside when the three noncoms ventured from their quarters. Overhead, the camouflage aerogel shimmered like frozen smoke, concealing movement, mass, and heat from possible detection. Beneath its distorting imagery hundreds of soldiers and support personnel sheltered.

The stone-faced, uninhibited Chin greeted them in a pair of briefs. He disliked climate control as much as official ceremony and in the privacy of his own quarters disdained the use of both. Formally attired, his nocturnal visitors were soon sweating profusely.

Physically Chin was anything but impressive. He was shorter than any of them, Selinsing included. Like her, his features were small, verging on the delicate. The Malay returned Chin's stare boldly. There was about as much fat on him as on an egret, which he superficially resembled. Despite that he looked older than he was.

Yet this was a man who had spent his entire adult life fighting in the service of the Weave. The mere fact of his continued survival was all the testimonial he needed. The numerous scars which covered his body, scars which even Hivistahm medical science had been unable to eliminate completely, underlined his accomplishments as rakishly as they clothed his muscles. Small he was, but nothing to trifle with.

In his expectant presence Carson and Selinsing wavered. In the confines of a commandant's quarters at two o'clock in the morning, intentions nurtured by boredom and booze tended to lose immediacy. As the one who had originally conceived it, a hesitant Moreno was therefore left to give birth to the proposition.

"Colonel, sir, my colleagues and I, well . . . we've been talking."

"So I presumed when you requested a meeting at this unconscionable hour." Chin's words were like the rest of him: short, clipped, to the point.

Moreno was not intimidated. Chin was widely respected as a soldier's officer. "It's something that's been bothering us for a long time, something we've talked about a lot. It's not anything we can take care of without help. Command-level help."

"Your help, sir," Selinsing chipped in. "And your discretion."

"Really." Eyebrows ephemeral as a late-night regret rose slightly. "It's good to know that one's opinion is respected by one's troops. Excuse me a moment." The near-naked officer rose to check the door, then his viewscreen, before resuming his smile and his seat. "Cool out tonight. Metrolg predicts rain."

"When doesn't it rain on this stinking planet?" Carson muttered rhetorically.

"When indeed. Tell me now: with what do you need my help?"

"Something of vital importance, sir," Moreno told him.

"Allow me the privilege of making my own evaluation," Chin murmured. "It may differ from yours."

"I don't think it will, sir." Moreno glanced at his friends for support, then smiled tightly back at the commandant. "None of us do."

When the word came down from Colonel Chin's Tactics Group that something big was in the offing, the Massood were willing, if a shade puzzled. It struck several of their officers that they had not been consulted on procedure. Informed that the success of the exercise hinged upon surprise and unpredictability, they had to confess that it had indeed caught them completely unprepared, and might logically therefore have the same effect upon the enemy. Debate, they were informed, would only slow them down. It was time to *act*, not discuss.

When informed of the nature of the forthcoming operation, the Human officers and noncoms expressed unqualified enthusiasm. Though most of them were as tired of sitting around as the trio which had confronted Chin, none had heretofore manifested their feelings in half so overt a fashion. One or two of the younger officers did find themselves pausing to wonder at the abruptness of it all, but their curiosity was drowned in the rush of preparations which followed the handing down of orders.

Among the support personnel, Hivistahm and O'o'yan, Wais and Yula and the rest, there were only the usual misgivings. As the representatives of the noncombat species lived in a perpetual state of apprehension anyway, it mattered little to them whether Human and Massood forces were coming or going. They performed their assigned tasks with silent efficiency while doing their best to keep their attention averted from the bloodthirsty grimaces and exclamations of those sentients who were preparing to die on their behalf.

Some who were hobbyistically inclined to philosophical consideration of matters strategic wondered why this particular moment had been chosen for a massive attack and could find no reason. It did not trouble them overly. It was in the nature of Humans to do the unpredictable. They had been doing it with regularity and to great effect ever since they had been recruited into the effort. No Hivis-tahm, no Lepar was about to second-guess them.

Imagine mounting an all-out assault on the enemy when there was no obvious justification for doing so! Clearly a stroke of purest brilliance. The support teams threw themselves energetically into the last-minute, frantic preparations.

F'tath was not a high-ranking officer, but he *was* S'van. Even as he joked and hurried to carry out his own duties, he found himself questioning the press of activity. Not the actual orders; they at least were in line with historical Human-Massood strategy. What con-cerned him was the narrow chain of command down which they had been passed. For example, as pertained to his own department, there hadn't even been time beforehand to discuss projected lines of supply, an omission which to him smacked of the blatantly neglectful.

He promptly made it his announced intention to bring the over-sight to the attention of his superiors at Sector Command as soon as he finished supervising requisite preparations for the battle group's departure, this being about as close to actual combat as a civilized S'van could come. So hectic was the press of work, however, that he could not seem to find sufficient time to properly formulate the ques-tions he badly wanted to ask.

Which was very much the intention of those who had drawn up the departure schedules.

By the time F'tath and those few others to whom similar thoughts had occurred were allotted a break, dozens of heavily armed sleds and sliders were rising above the forest canopy and streaming away eastward, the start of the assault undeterred by the morning rain. At which point it seemed foolish even to a S'van to question an opera-tion already under way. So F'tath and others of like mind carried their concerns with them to bed.

No reserves were held back. Every slider, sled, and soldier on the base was thrown into the all-out attack. Humans and Massood rolled over the first couple of enemy positions before the startled defenders realized what had hit them. Crigolit and Ashregan were prepared to beat back surgical thrusts by small groups of fast-moving troops, not the kind of ravening firepower which the attackers now brought to bear. That was how it had gone on Eirrosad: probe and flee, strike and retreat. Hurt your enemy as much as possible and then fall back to heavily fortified bases deep in the jungle.

The Crigolit and Ashregan had no idea how to react to the sudden shift in tactics. Not that their assailants gave them time for prolonged contemplation.

The Massood in particular were elated at the speed with which the first couple of enemy positions were overrun. Casualties were light, boldness and determination having proven themselves the equal of twice the firepower. They complimented their Human allies even as they redoubled their own gracefully lethal efforts.

Certain Human noncommissioned officers felt themselves vindicated. The first enemy bases had been taken with greater ease than anyone could have hoped for. Not only Human senses had been dulled by the long war of attrition on Eirrosad. Crigolit and Ashregan reaction times were likewise well below the usual, to their detriment. It was a damn good thing, Carson told his colleagues, that they had decided to move first.

Conferencing with his subordinates, Chin hit upon a strategy of racing past instead of engaging the remaining three enemy firebases to strike at enemy Sector Headquarters itself. Barely enough time was allotted for the squad supervisors to bellow their agreement, let alone voice any objections.

If they could not merely take out but capture that critical installation it would place them in position to flank and put pressure on the enemy's planetary HQ. A victory of that magnitude might not end the war for Eirrosad, but it would unequivocally upset the status quo. Dispersement of this possible conclusion induced tired soldiers to redouble their efforts.

Where resistance was weak or even nonexistent slider riders and sled troops raced ahead, bypassing bewildered enemy emplacements and floater forces, leaving them with nothing to shoot at but vacant forest and empty air. Though increasingly spread out, the combined Human-Massood battle group persisted in its wild, mad advance, shoving aside or smashing everything in its path.

Floaters were blasted out of the sky before they could assume adequate defensive positions, or were shot down from behind as they tried to retreat. Enemy stores and structures were demolished on the ground as the sled teams strafed and bombed them in passing.

Stealing a modicum of time, the commandant of one of the remaining enemy firebases did manage to mount something of a counterattack. Sliders and floaters and sleds filled the air with explosive projectiles and needle beams, cohabiting in technologically advanced mayhem as they darted through and around tree-covered Sludgel while driving the unfortunate native fauna half-crazy.

The Humans excelled at such random, individual combat, cutting up and isolating enemy forces into smaller and smaller groups, until there was nothing left to fight back. Outmatched, Crigolit and Ashregan units had no hope of halting the assault.

Ineffective as it was, when the first enemy counterattack came F'tath fully expected Command to give the order to hold and consolidate their substantial gains. When no such directive was forthcoming he sought clarification beyond his immediate command level, only to be informed that Colonel Chin and his staff were far too busy plotting the next stage of the advance to grant an audience to a lower-level supply officer. Though he responded with the usual S'van humor, it was not the response F'tath had hoped for.

In a combat situation, even S'van had learned the value of deferring to Human judgment, but something about this particular campaign left F'tath feeling more than a little uneasy. Though bold and clever on the battlefield, Humans were not perfect, not immune to the occasional tactical mistake. He tried to share his concerns with others, but they were either numbed by the incivility of it all or else too busy to listen to him. In point of fact he was usually too busy to listen to himself.

But there was always time for worrying.

15

So swift, brutal, and effective had the Weave assault been that both forward firebases had been lost by the time Ranji's group received word to mobilize. Saguio had been lounging close enough to unit communications to overhear the first reports.

"They came in so fast, with utter recklessness," he said breathlessly. "Our people didn't have a chance. Northwest Base managed to put together a counterattack but Command Central doesn't expect it to stop them." Outside the barracks, members of different species were running or scuttling about frantically. Sirens wailed and vehicles sped across the grounds with criminal disregard for equally frantic pedestrians. The base's inhabitants were hastily trying to bring order out of chaos.

Crigolit barely paused long enough to exchange greetings via antenna touch, while Segunians tripped over everything including their own gangly limbs in their fervid attempts to reach their stations.

Ranji paid little attention as his brother harangued fellow members of the team from Cossuut. The Humans and Massood, it appeared, had attacked in overwhelming numbers, concentrating a tremendous amount of firepower on a small front. They had pushed past or broken through successive defensive layers and were apparently striking directly for Sector Headquarters itself, with little in their path to slow or stop them. The battle front, which had been relatively stable for many years, had been completely shattered.

Skids landed outside the barracks, fully stocked and readied for combat by the base's Acarian equipment handlers. A dazed Ranji felt himself swept along as the transport rose and sped northward, skimming the treetops in its haste to reach their assigned position.

The Cossuut unit was supposed to be utilized only for special purposes, but in the face of Sector Integrity's collapse every available fighter had been conscripted for defense. As the craft began to de-

scend toward the line which had been established outside one of the
three surviving firebases, Ranji was forced to seriously consider the
likelihood that he might soon be called upon to strike at Human
beings with something more damaging than sharp queries.

Could he give the order to fire on his own kind? If they were
indeed his own kind, he reminded himself. In the frenzy of confusion
and preparation that engulfed him he was no longer certain of anything, except that prospects for a long and comfortable retirement
had recently been drastically reduced. Death at least would resolve
all uncertainties and put an end to his private sufferings.

Once more the peculiar calm which his troops mistook for quiet
confidence settled over him. Then someone was shaking him by the
arm.

"Did you hear, Ranji?" Saguio regarded his brother with concern. "Change of plans. Command's leaving all the firebases to fend
for themselves. We're being committed directly to the defense of
Sector Headquarters." His eyes glittered expectantly. "We're going
to be right in the front of the fighting. No more sneaking around in
the middle of the night."

"I heard. Get into your armor. Tell Tourmast and Weenn to pass
the word. We're liable to come under fire before we arrive."

Saguio frowned slightly. "Headquarters hasn't come under attack
yet. Body armor can get hot. There's plenty of time."

"Where Humans are involved there's never enough time. Just
ask the survivors of the two forward firebases . . . if there are any.
Move it!"

Startled, Saguio rushed to comply.

Ranji followed deliberately. War of a different kind was raging
within him, unsupportable claims doing battle with reluctant truths,
emotion locked in earnest combat with reason.

Abruptly the grandiose futility of it all struck hard. A thousand
years of unending conflict, not over survival or culture but an idea.
The more tenuous the concept, he mused, the greater the ferocity
with which it was contested. It seemed a wasteful repository for a
gift as precious as intelligence.

But if there was nothing to do battle over, what place did someone like himself who had been trained to fight from birth have in
civilized society, be it Ashregan or Human? He began to think of
himself as an intellectual as well as emotional foundling. Did such

thoughts trouble his friends from home? Had they ever worried any Humans, and if so, how had those mysterious creatures dealt with it? He wondered if he would ever know.

Certainly they were a most unique and peculiar species, and what was he if not peculiar enough to be one of them?

The cataract of concern dulled his mind as he slipped into his own field armor, a task he'd drilled at often enough to perform without thinking.

"They're doing *what?*" Field Marshal Granville gaped at his Massood counterpart only long enough for the import of the other's words to sink in before the two of them started toward Communications. Granville was a mature, stocky, slightly overweight man, but over the short distance he had no trouble keeping up with the long-legged alien.

Additional confirmation of the initial reports was mirrored in the expressions of the communications personnel on duty, irrespective of species.

"There is no longer any question of what has happened." The Massood district commander's whiskers were twitching violently. "On-site verification arrived just before I left to inform you. I felt it would be more believable coming from me than via courier or over the system, and I am sure that like myself you desire to waste as little time as possible in dealing with the consequences of these actions."

"Gratefulness for that, Shatenka," wheezed the field marshal in passable Massood. The two sector commanders hurried to the nearest console, causing the Hivistahm technician seated there to fumble nervously at his translator in the presence of so much feral rank.

"Are you in contact with the base in question?" Granville inquired bluntly. The Hivistahm replied in the affirmative. "Then put me through."

"Truly I should like to, honored Commander, but I cannot," the Hivistahm replied sorrowfully.

"Why not?" Granville's tenebrous Human tone made the noncombative Hivistahm shake slightly.

"Because there is truly no one there. All responses from programs are. Apparently everyone in the attack participating is, even to including support personnel."

"This is madness." Commander Shatenka added something in colloquial Massood which none of the tangent translators near him succeeded in picking up.

The two commanders moved to another console and confronted a Human officer. "Who's in charge out there?"

Names scrolled down the screen in front of the woman like damned souls plunging hellward. "A Colonel Nehemiah Chin, sir."

"I have remembrance of that name." Shatenka's upper lip curled emphatically. "A good officer. It makes no sense."

"All say it makes no sense," Granville growled. "Who sent him orders requesting an all-out assault in his sector? It leaves us damn exposed back here."

"I have already called for a full defensive mobilization," Shatenka assured him.

"I know, I know. That's hardly the point."

A Hivistahm analyst looked up from her console, wary of the Human commander's temper. "Honored sirs, first reports indicate that the forces in question already taken have two major hostile positions and are directly for the enemy Regional Command center striking."

"You're right. Someone is mad." Granville glanced up at his tall counterpart and lowered his voice. "What's your considered opinion, Shatenka. Can Chin bring this off?"

The Massood considered, digging energetically at a back molar. His whiskers subsided. "The forces in question are composed largely of your own kind. However, since you ask my thoughts, I should say it depends on how much firepower they can ultimately bring to bear when they finally reach their target. If by then the enemy has not profoundly reduced them in strength and they do not pause their attack long enough to give the Ashregan time to muster reserves from other regions, then I should think it possible. Just."

Granville angrily fingered his translator. "If this attack fails, or even stalls, they'll find themselves trapped between large-scale enemy regional defenses and those they've bypassed or failed to wipe out on the way in. In which event we could lose the entire battle group."

"Your thinking mirrors my own. They have advanced too far too fast. Now they have no choice but to press the assault."

"Maybe not. If we can reach individual squad leaders, we can countermand their orders. If enough of the group turns together, they ought to be able to fight their way back." Granville plotted a path toward fieldcom.

Shatenka followed. "Communications at this range will be bad."

"I know. I wish R&D could find a way to defend a communications relay satellite against knockdown for longer than a couple of days. We'll just have to do the best we can."

Somehow he was not surprised when the O'o'yan technician informed them that he could not make contact with a single element of the rogue Weave force.

"The problem is at the receiving end, Great Marshal. It matters not which frequency I employ. There is no acknowledgment."

"It fits."

"What fits, my friend?" Shatenka inquired anxiously.

"Chin's acting on his own, without orders."

The Massood growled softly, his small triangular ears flattening against his skull. "That is a very serious assumption."

"Grounded, I think, in more than coincidence."

"Perhaps. But irrelevant should the venture succeed."

"Truly, as our Hivi friends would say. He's been very clever." There was grudging admiration in the field marshal's voice. "He'll emerge from this either a damned hero, or just damned."

"We cannot reinforce them," Shatenka pointed out.

"I know. The extent of their advance places us in enough danger as it is. I only hope that our opponents are so dazed and confused by Chin's attack that none of them take the time to realize how exposed it's rendered us back here.

"In the meantime, until the situation resolves itself we'll back him every way we can and pray his people bring this off. We can forward certain classes of supplies by unpiloted sled. I'll see to that. You deal with any questions from Central."

"I would far rather be on the battlefield." The Massood sniffed pointedly.

"Your thoughts," muttered Granville acerbically, "mirror my own." He turned back to the O'o'yan tech. "Keep trying to make contact. If you reach anyone—Human, Massood, Lepar, regardless of rank or position—I want to know about it. If I'm not here, find me. If I'm asleep, wake me. If I'm in the can, beat on the door."

The O'o'yan inclined its narrow, delicate head. "Understood, Great Marshal."

———

Any early feelings of uncertainty among the members of the attacking force about their chosen course of action vanished as enemy resistance collapsed under the fury of the Human-Massood assault. There was barely enough time to savor each triumph before orders arrived directing the next attack on the enemy's position. Certainly there was no time to formulate questions, which was the intent of Chin and his collaborators from the beginning.

The attack gave no sign of faltering. The soldiers of Chin's battle group were in superb condition, and even seemed to gain strength with each objective attained. Though the initial advantage of surprise had been expended, the battle group continued to forge ahead on skill and dedication alone.

The counterattack gave some members of Chin's staff pause, especially when he insisted on sending shock teams and scouts on ahead to probe the enemy's SHQ defenses in spite of the fact that the enemy now had to be aware of their intentions. But since Chin's predictions had been coming true with edifying regularity, pause did not give way to objection. Not that a few concerns would have swayed the colonel in any event. There were too many others on the staff who fully supported his strategy.

While Chin's reaction to his accomplishments thus far was less than boisterous, some of his personnel were less restrained. Three noncommissioned officers in particular made no attempt to hide their feelings. Though exhausted, they had no intention of requesting a break, neither for themselves nor their troops. Not with the perimeter of the enemy's Sector Headquarters already under attack from outlying scouts striking from superfast sliders.

Take that objective, they knew, and the poofs back at Regional would have no choice but to back them with fresh troops. They would have gained too much to risk giving back. Enemy influence across the entire southern quarter of the Eirrosadian landmass would be broken.

Things were going so well that Chin had decided to send several squads racing around behind the enemy HQ in order to be in position to interdict any attempts at reinforcement. In an earlier era such strategy might have been carried out with aircraft, but with the advent hundreds of years before of compact computer-guided missiles and energy beams capable of knocking anything out of the sky, control of the air had become irrelevant to modern warfare. Among the clouds there was no place to hide.

Increasingly tired but increasingly confident, Chin's group continued to advance.

Even in moments of direst distress it was in the nature of the Amplitur to remain calm, a characteristic which their allies found endlessly reassuring. Since the universe had evolved gradually, they were fond of pointing out, it similarly stood to reason that there was no need to concede emotion to haste. It required an extraordinary series of debilitating circumstances to reduce an Amplitur to agitation.

While distinctly nonplussing, the current situation failed to qualify.

"It would seem," commented High-manyfold-Leaving, "that our position here has changed rapidly from dangerous to precarious."

"That is unarguably so." Place-bereft-Inward favored the speaker with one eye while the other swiveled independently on its stalk to study the slowly shifting topographical image that floated in the air between them. "An exceptional effort will have to be made if we are to stave off serious damage to local expectations."

They would have liked to have conferenced with their colleagues at Planetary Headquarters, but the press of battle and Weave interference techniques had rendered that impossible. It was only by chance that they, the only other pair of Amplitur on Eirrosad, happened to be at the Southern Sector HQ when the Weave had launched its blistering and utterly unexpected attack. Both were acutely conscious of the demands their allies had subsequently placed upon them and determined to resolve the situation to the best of their abilities.

Unfortunately, the attacking Humans and Massood were disinclined to cooperate.

Though reluctant to expose themselves to the exigencies of a combat situation, the Amplitur had no intention of concentrating their efforts on securing their safety through personal flight. Such an action would have had a devastating effect on the morale of their allies. If they were cautious it stemmed from understanding of an underlying reality: there were not that many Amplitur in the universe and their survival was vital to the advancement of the Purpose. They did not run, but, rather, guarded themselves well.

The Ashregan and Crigolit officers who joined them in the chamber were neither calm nor composed. It might even be said that they had passed beyond agitation to panic.

"What are we to do?" The Ashregan spoke without offering so much as a polite greeting or casual honorific. The Amplitur understood and said nothing. Most other species had not yet begun to come to grips with the vagaries of their endocrine systems.

Besides, desperate circumstances did not permit time for civilized verities.

One of the Crigolit scuttled forward and employed its forelimbs to unfold a collapsing readout. "We have concocted a plan." Chitinous digits traced glowing lines on the screen. "First we concentrate our forces much as the enemy expects."

High-manyfold-Leaving commented dryly. "I do not see the reinforcement of tactical redundancy as extricating us from our present situation."

The attempt at sarcasm caught the Crigolit unprepared, but it continued anyway. "The intent is to lull the enemy into false expectations of quick victory."

"Given our present circumstances it will not be necessary to lull them," the Amplitur murmured.

A sound akin to rusty whistling and air escaping underwater emerged from behind the Crigolit's mouthparts. "I elucidate further, honored Teachers. Here," and his digits moved, "we place the special squadron from Cossuut. Fortuitously they are among us. Only when the enemy finally attacks in full strength do we exert our utmost to hold them back, as the special Ashregan fighters stab into them from behind.

"Under ordinary battle conditions this would seem a futile tactic, but even Humans must grow tired from continuous fighting. They are spread out and their lines of communication and supply grow longer as they advance. In such a situation a small, irresistible force operating behind their lines might wreak considerable havoc."

The two Amplitur consulted, leaving the representatives of their allied races to mill about in awkward silence. It was Place-bereft-Inward who finally replied.

"There is considerable risk. If the fighters from Cossuut do not have an impact then we will have reduced our defensive capabilities and gained nothing in return."

"Then we should concentrate our forces here," chirped one of the assembled Crigolit officers.

"Neither shall we do that." High-manyfold-Leaving gestured absently with a tentacle. "It is our intention to put up only minimal resistance and abandon this place to our voracious enemy."

Many of those among the assembled had thought themselves beyond shock. They were wrong.

"Honored Teachers, I ask you to reconsider," pleaded the ranking Ashregan. "The distance to Planetary Headquarters' perimeter and the safety it would provide is more than five days' travel by fast skid. During that time we would not be able to use many of our heavy weapons and could not maintain an adequate defensive formation. Fast-moving pursuit could take us apart a little at a time."

"We can defend this installation!" The ranking officer's adjutant was as insistent as she was outraged. "Whether the Cossuut group is otherwise employed or not. Let the Humans and Massood come. They are effective in the jungle, but can they dig a determined defense out of this mountain? Tired and worn as they must be, I think not."

"Our greatest weakness since Humans have allied themselves with the Weave has been our repeated underestimation of their abilities, in tandem with an unpredictability which verges on madness." Place-bereft-Inward relied on logic to convince, though it would have been easier simply to "suggest" the decided course of action to those present.

"As you so bravely state we might well be able to defend our position here. However, after careful consideration of all relevant factors we postulate an equal chance of failure. Even odds are no odds at all.

"If we utilize our full strength to defend, and lose, then this entire region falls under the control of the enemies of the Purpose. Gathering Weave strength here would threaten our very hold on this world, rendering the security of Planetary Headquarters itself untenable."

"Does not retreat allow the enemy to achieve the same goal at little cost?" The bold female Ashregan was unrepentant. "I fail to see virtue in flight."

"I shall elucidate." The Amplitur extended two of the four digits on the end of its right tentacle and impacted the drifting topograph. It froze. Colors appeared on its surface as High-manyfold-Leaving manipulated heavy air.

"We will put up minimal resistance before abandoning this installation, but neither do we propose complete retreat."

"I don't understand," said the ranking Ashregan.

"The female is half-right. The enemy will be tired, but that does not mean they will be weak. We note that Humans have repeatedly demonstrated uncommon endurance under stress. It is almost as if they revel in personal suffering, as though pain and discomfort are required before they can reach great heights. According to a captured Human psychologist this 'ennobling *angst*,' as he called it, is endemic to the species and a requirement for its survival and advancement. Insane as it sounds it is nonetheless very real. We must try to comprehend it if we are to formulate successful strategies for defeating them."

"Your pardon and understanding, honored Teacher," said the Ashregan commander, "but I fail to see how this impacts on our present situation."

Place-bereft-Inward took up the explanation. "This strange thesis holds that the more difficult the situation, the harder Humans fight. It is when everything is going their way that they are apparently at their most vulnerable. In order to make use of this knowledge we must for now accept this reversal of reason without trying to understand it.

"The Humans are superb fighters, but they are not superbeings, and they have their own unique weaknesses. It is through our comprehension and utilization of these vulnerabilities that they shall be defeated, not by any attempt to impose our system of values upon them."

In the silence that ensued the two Amplitur perceived that their attempt to spread enlightenment had produced only bewilderment. "I shall be specific." Place-bereft-Inward's words were accompanied by a mental suggestion of badly needed reassurance. "The majority of our people will pull out, but not to retreat. Some will race toward

Planetary Headquarters, giving the arriving enemy the impression that all are attempting to flee in that direction. It will seem the natural thing for us to do. Meanwhile the bulk of our forces will head not for the perceived safety of the headquarters perimeter but for the dense hilly jungle to the southwest."

"That places us farther from potential safety or reinforcement than anywhere else," one of the elder Crigolit was unable to forbear from pointing out.

"Precisely," the Amplitur replied with cool confidence. "It is the last thing the enemy would expect of us. From a strategic standpoint it is an almost Human move. New problems require equally new and radical solutions.

"After the enemy has wrested this installation from the modest force which will remain to 'defend' it, and after they have begun their pursuit of the group which will be sent fleeing northwestward, but before they can consolidate their new conquest, we will counterattack. Not in an attempt to retake our position here, which would concentrate our forces dangerously, but all up and down along their line of assault. This time the element of surprise shall be ours."

"Your pardon, honored Teacher," said the obstreperous female Ashregan officer, "but this strikes me as strategy based on hope as much as knowledge. The Humans excel at the kind of fragmented combat you propose."

"That is so." Both Amplitur agreed readily. "But you forget the Cossuut unit. Surprise and support from the rest of our forces should enable them to make a much greater impact than they would be able to if attacking on their own. Remember also that our assailants are not all Humans. According to the reports there are Massood and noncombative species in the attacking force as well. If these can be thrown into confusion or panic, it will greatly complicate the Humans' ability to fight, since they have come too far to quickly evacuate support personnel."

"And our fighters will be fresh and rested," High-manyfold-Leaving pointed out. "That counts for much."

While there was some continuing discussion both Amplitur impatiently suggested that their allies put any remaining objections aside in the interests of speed, concurring that insufficient time remained for the luxury of independent debate. So it was not surprising when the assembled officers declared in a body, "We accept the plan of the Teachers."

"We feel wellness at your decision." The Amplitur replied simultaneously, gratified by the unanimous acceptance of the foregone conclusion.

— 16 —

Hidden deep within difficult, highly vegetated terrain, the forces which had withdrawn in hasty but orderly fashion from the interior of the mountain fortress were barely able to monitor the Weave attack when it finally arrived. Those limited Ashregan, Crigolit, and allied troops who had been left behind to mount a semblance of a defense fought long and hard before they were overwhelmed by the ferocity of the assault, bravely sacrificing themselves in the cause of the Purpose. The Amplitur could not have hoped for better results.

Holding alertly at their assigned position, Ranji's group was aware of what was taking place only though infrequent and cautious internal communications. They were too far away to hear the rumbling explosions which issued with pernicious regularity from the interior of the tabletop mountain as its conquerors obliterated stores, equipment, and defenders with equal glee.

Soon squads of attackers were regrouping atop the jungle-clad butte. Espying fleeing enemy, small teams shot off in pursuit, intent upon running down and destroying every potential survivor before they could reach the distant safety of their planetary headquarters.

Ranji considered the Ashregan, Crigolit, and others who had accepted death in the service of a feint. It frightened him to know that there was a time when he might have done so with equal enthusiasm.

Now all he saw was the extinction of brave individuals whose deaths in no way enriched the universe. There was something inherently obscene in the notion of dying for a strategic advantage. For example, from what he had seen Humans who would readily sacrifice themselves in defense of their world or even a friend were much less likely to do so to preserve an abstraction.

Like the Purpose, he told himself.

He was finding it increasingly difficult to believe in much of anything.

The Amplitur, of course, did not readily sacrifice themselves for the cause. Though it was ostensibly because of their limited numbers, Ranji more and more had come to think of this as a convenient rationalization. The notion stuck in his conviction and would not be moved.

For reasons unknown, swept up in events he could not control in that uneasy time and place, he found himself thinking frequently of the Lepar.

Then the word was passed that it was time to strike, and his only thoughts were for survival.

Seemingly from behind every tree and rocky pinnacle the squads of Ashregan and Crigolit slammed into the conquerors of the mountain, most of whom were for the first time in several days just starting to relax. Their timing could not have been better had prognostication been other than a prehistoric fancy.

Innumerable firefights erupted in the terrain between the mountain and south-flowing rivers, consuming frantic members of varying species with inchoate impartiality. Humans and Massood frantically rushed to gather wits and weapons with which to defend themselves.

So furiously did they strike back that in places the counterattack was stopped cold, the attackers annihilated despite the advantage of surprise. Elsewhere it was Humans and Massood who were devastated, unable to mount an adequate defense or flee to safety.

Ranji fought to defend himself and, surreptitiously, his brother. It troubled him that he, likely Human himself, was compelled by circumstance to kill other Humans. Letting the natural killing reflex take over allowed him to ignore his initial inhibitions. This surprised him when it should not have. After all, Humans had been exterminating each other without compunction for thousands of years.

Saguio, Soratii-eev, Birachii, and the others charged into combat armored with the blissful balm of ignorance, unaware they had been called upon to slaughter their own kind, a task they executed with unalloyed vigor.

As for Ranji, under the pretext of essaying strategy he strove to avoid as much actual combat as possible. Cognizant of his recent experiences, those operating under his command considered his reticence prudent. He did manage to fire his weapon frequently, with an inaccuracy those who happened to be momentarily caught in his sights found laudable. Innocent succulents and trees suffered the consequences of his anguish.

Spread out over a huge section of swampy terrain, the conflagration would have struck an onlooker as natural rather than artificial in origin, as if some immense blaze had suddenly erupted in the heart of the tabletop mountain and spread to the surrounding forest. Indistinguishable as to source, plumes of smoke rose from burning vegetation, from burning machines, from burning bodies.

Amid heat and smoke and dense vegetation it was difficult for Ranji to tell Crigolit from Ashregan, Ashregan from Massood, Humans from his friends. Only differing armor and equipment types offered ready means for identification. One had to think fast and shoot faster if one expected to survive. He sought solace in delay and tried not to think.

By keeping his personal floater as close as possible to the ground he managed to avoid the bulk of aerial combat. It was while working his way slowly through a grove of massive, heavily buttressed trees that he came upon the two corpses.

They were Human, one of each gender. Great blackened gaps showed in their light field armor where energy weapons had struck home. Their own rifles lay nearby, punctuation marks bestriding lost lives. The right side of the man's skull was missing. Though cauterization was extensive Ranji could still see part of the brain, drying in the air like a wrinkled gray melon. The man lay crumpled on his side, his companion on her back. Her skin was pale, and he was very glad she did not much remind him of the woman he had known on Omaphil.

This close to the mountain the soil was more than firm enough to support his floater. He landed in hopes of learning what he could.

Close inspection of the corpses told him little he did not already know. He bent over the man. If he peered hard enough into the gaping cranial cavity, would he be able to see a small bundle of nerves, the nodule that Hivistahm and Human surgeons had assured him was alien to every unaltered Human mind? Since he sensed he would not his examination was cursory at best.

Rising, he resumed his seat on the floater and sent it forward, angling slowly through the grove. Every channel of his communicator was alive with orders and exchanges. Around him the jungle boomed and hissed like a gigantic reptile caught in the throes of violent death. He did not look back.

There was nothing he could do. If he tried to surrender to the opposition under battlefield conditions he would likely be shot on sight. The bulky, securely attached cephaloprostheses which had restored his Ashregan appearance could not be removed without the aid of a fully equipped surgery.

Thoughts of surrender passed quickly. That was not why he had returned to his friends.

He cruised slowly through environs become unnatural. Repeated clarion calls over his communicator heralded successive triumphs for the Purpose. Dull instinct dragged him along while his field equipment kept him alive, armor-shell protecting epidermal shell concealing . . . what?

Hammered at multiple points along their line of advance, the fatigued attackers were gradually cut into smaller and smaller groups. Expectations of glory gave way to concern for survival. Without orders, without direction, they began to retreat, fleeing back toward the meandering river they had so exultantly crossed the day before. Supplies from Granville and Starenka's joint command did not even have the chance to arrive before the retreat began, and could not in any event have prevented the disaster.

The faithful of the Purpose took many prisoners that day. When it became clear that the assault had been turned, the Amplitur sent a powerful combined battlegroup in pursuit of the survivors. Many of Ranji's friends participated.

They swept beyond the rivers and overran the forward Weave firebase from which the attack had been mounted, taking control of its minimally manned weapons systems and natural defenses and bringing a great swath of previously Weave-controlled territory under Amplitur control. The opportunities for rescue of those surviving Humans and Massood who had been scattered throughout the endless jungle were reduced from modest to nil. Indeed, Granville was forced to request reinforcements simply to hold his own position.

Carson, Moreno, and Selinsing did not even have the consolation of knowing that their deaths had contributed to a gallant failure. It was an ignominious rout. Caught between impenetrable canopy and a fast-moving Crigolit floater, Selinsing's slider disintegrated under a hail of enemy fire. Carson was shot down over the main river, while

Moreno died trying to escape the captured fortress, which was rapidly turned into a sandstone tomb by counterattacking Ashregan and their backups.

Many who were not killed fighting went down in the jungle on disabled vehicles, like so many exhausted birds unable to complete an especially difficult migration. Some were rescued by daring out-fliers who ignored Granville's orders to stand clear. Others were caught and slain or captured by the pursuing enemy.

Colonel Nehemiah Chin might have escaped to face court-martial. Instead he chose to use the concentrated firepower of his command sled to cover the retreat of less heavily armed regular troops. Those who escaped might live again to fight another day, whereas his military career was already finished.

The great gamble had not paid off. Having acquired a debt he knew he could not pay, he saw no reason to return.

It was most ironic because everything he and his coconspirators had hoped for had come to pass. They simply had not credited the enemy with the wherewithal to mount an effective response, an oversight which he spent much of the time remaining to him regretting.

Death brought peace to Colonel Chin, but not contentment.

For the Weave forces on Eirrosad the debacle was total. Plans for pressing the enemy on other fronts were abandoned as reinforcements were hurriedly rushed to defend what remained of Granville's shrunken sector. Overall strategy suffered a severe and embarrassing retrenchment. Chin's Catastrophe, as it came to be known, forced Weave tacticians to abandon an optimistic status quo in favor of a policy of anxious defense. Meanwhile, the dead commander's dour superiors reaped a harvest of recriminations.

It was as serious a battlefield defeat as Weave forces had suffered in some time. The effects were felt beyond Eirrosad, reverberating throughout the chain of command all the way up to the Grand Military Council itself.

As for the Amplitur, they did not throw up their tentacles in triumph and husk hosannas to the Purpose. It was not in their nature to celebrate death, even that of those who would destroy them. Revelry was left to the Crigolit and Ashregan, the Molitar and Mazvec. The Amplitur would celebrate only when the Purpose was fulfilled, be it a hundred years in the future, a thousand, an eon.

That did not mean they did not find gratification in the accomplishment.

For their brilliant tactical maneuver High-manyfold-Leaving and Place-bereft-Inward received quiet praise and new assignments. Of rest there would be none. There would be plenty of time for the Amplitur to rest once the Purpose had been fulfilled. Until that far distant day there was still too much for them to do and too few of them to do it.

The news from Eirrosad had depressed everyone at Weave Command on Omaphil. Conversation and spirits alike were muted. Even the normally jocose S'van were subdued.

Two Humans, a pair of Massood, and three S'van clustered in a high-ceilinged chamber afire with images of suns and ships. Rising and descending on invisible supports, they studied and analyzed the three-dimensional representation of their particular quadrant of the galaxy, not so much reading the map as voyaging through it.

One of the S'van waved the small wandlike device he carried. Representations of starships swirled and repositioned themselves according to his directions. In the enclosed chamber his translator boomed.

"We've already overextended ourselves in our attempt to take Eirrosad. It weakens our inner spatial defenses and exposes us along this entire line. I say it's time to consider pulling back. A strategic retrenchment does not a retreat make."

"We cannot," argued a Massood floating high above him. "If we give up Eirrosad, it will make it extremely hard to advance into the next important enemy sector . . . here." Her wand stirred galactic soup.

"That's true. Our next big thrust will be made much easier . . . *if* we can hold Eirrosad," another of the S'van said pointedly.

"Would you concede the Amplitur the same sort of advantage we seek for ourselves?" she riposted. "There are no other habitable worlds in its immediate vicinity."

"It's premature to speak of concessions." One of the Human officers descended to the same level as the S'van. "Our situation on Eirrosad's been damaged but not devastated. We may not be in a position to mount any attacks for a while, but I think we can hold on to what we have."

"I don't doubt that." The S'van put both hands behind his back, thrusting his thick beard forward. "My concern is that by continuing to support forces on Eirrosad we weaken ourselves elsewhere. It's well known that Humans dislike looking over their shoulders, lest they see something that displeases them. In warfare ignorance is not bliss; it's lethal stupidity."

"Look," said the other Human sharply, "I'll grant that you guys are brilliant tacticians, but you're as cautious as any of the species who don't carry guns. If it wasn't for us and the Massood, you wouldn't advance anywhere. You'd just sit around on your hairy butts waiting for the Amplitur to hit you at their leisure."

As Human and S'van glared at each other from perspectives that differed as much as their respective heights, one of the Massood hastened to change the subject.

"On a related matter, it seems clear that the decision to return the altered Human-Ashregan to his friends was a mistake."

"We can't be certain of that yet." The Human who replied sounded slightly defensive.

The more belligerent of the two S'van grinned. "Ignorance in this case is embarrassing."

The senior S'van had yet to say anything. It was a marvel to him that individual members of the contentious species of the Weave could cooperate long enough to have a discussion, much less fight an interstellar war. If the Amplitur could but see how truly fragile was the structure of the Weave, how fractious and argumentative its members, they would surely press their millennia-old assault even harder.

"That incident is history," the S'van commented. "Not every experiment produces the results one hopes for. Time spent on recriminations is divisive and wasteful."

"We don't know what the subject's present condition is. Just because he hasn't contacted us yet doesn't mean he's never going to." It was the Human's turn to be defensive.

"It's perfectly understandable that you stretch reason out of compassion for one of your own. Had S'van been the subjects of genetic manipulation by the Amplitur we would be equally concerned."

As was typical of his kind, the Human refused to be swayed by

mere logic. "We don't know for certain that his Ashregan conditioning has reasserted itself. We don't know for a fact that the work our
people did with him here on Omaphil was unsuccessful." He hesitated. "Majority opinion holds that he's probably dead, because he
was returned to the region where our recent losses occurred. Prior
to our reversal of fortunes there, enemy casualties are known to have
been heavy. It's reasonable to assume he was among them. Until then
he may very well have been trying to decondition his colleagues,
which was his avowed intention in returning."

"Probably we will never know," said the other Massood.

"Truly I would like to."

Everyone looked up as a new figure drifted in to join them. Access to the map chamber while conferencing was in progress was
supposedly forbidden, but First-of-Surgery had been granted clear-
ances usually denied even to senior officers.

The darkling enclosure was alien to him, so very different from
his normal brightly lit surroundings. Furthermore, it was occupied
by intimidating Humans and Massood. He instinctively stood close
to the S'van.

"I know you." The younger Human officer frowned slightly in
remembrance. "You oversaw the whole experiment."

"As you truly remember, you may also recall that I most stren-
uously argued against the unfortunate subject Ranji-aar to his friends
returning, but was by the military overruled." He met and held the
Human's stare, something none but a Turlog could manage for long.

"At the time we felt we had no choice," said the other Human.

First-of-Surgery eyed him frostily. "Of course you a choice
had. You could to myself and other specialists have listened. But your
actions were, from what I have seen and studied, of military thinking
typical. You around you gather experts and analysts. Not to their
opinions listen to, but to an intellectual blanket create to from criti-
cism shield yourselves. Behind this barrier you carry on as before,
deluded that you of the help you have acquired made use. Now you
have for this shortsightedness on Eirrosad paid the price."

"Now just a minute," said the other Human. "Are you suggesting that the return of this individual to his former friends and associates had something to do with our recent defeat on that world?"

"I suggest nothing. I infer nothing. It is only that when the unexpected itself repeats, is piqued my interest in relational hypotheses."

"It has been determined that the Eirrosad disaster was the fault of a single renegade Human colonel who deliberately excluded from his decision-making process all tactical advice except that which arose from a select inner circle." The other Human spoke with assurance.

"An all too common fault." The Human turned sharply on the S'van who'd made the comment, but could discern nothing in the way of expression behind an all-obscuring black beard.

"It distresses me to bad news bring atop bad news." First-of-Surgery clicked his teeth softly. "Facts have an awkward way of lives of their own assuming."

"Go ahead," the nearest Human grumbled. "We've heard little else these past few days. A little more won't make any difference." The surgeon's translator rendered the primate's guttural barkings into barbaric but comprehensible Hivistahm. This maceration of his elegant language did not irritate him. As a physician he had a better understanding than most of Human cultural failings.

"Please my inadequate words excuse, but it has my experience been that visuals time as well as confusion save."

Removing a control wand not unlike those in the possession of his military colleagues, he adjusted it while waving at the empty space between them. Several star systems were rudely swept aside, to be replaced by the floating image of a Human skull. As he spoke, sections exploded and expanded to reveal hidden secrets.

"You all are or should by now be conversant with the recent studies which were conducted on this world on one of the genetically altered Humans who were preborn abducted by the Amplitur. It was my privilege in charge of those studies to be." The wand moved.

"Before the individual in question was at his request returned to Eirrosad an operation was carried out in which the Amplitur-induced alteration to his brain was surgically isolated from the rest of his nervous system, thereby negating its influence." Slitted pupils monitored Humans and Massood for reaction.

"I remind you that my staff and I considered this individual's release and return premature."

"That's old news, not bad news," commented the nearest Human.

"Truly." The surgeon's tone was sharp. "Under natural conditions Human neural tissue rarely regenerates. Modern Hivistahm and O'o'yan technology enables us such regrowth artificially to induce, thereby rendering the Human physiologic condition known historically as 'paralysis' a medical anachronism.

"Prior to the conclusion of surgery on the individual in question the Amplitur-induced neural nodule within his brain was biopsied. A computer projection on recent analysis based a potential capacity for self-regeneration of this organ suggests." As he spoke, animated neurons reasserted themselves within the immensely magnified image rotating before them.

"This is a prognostication only," observed the male Massood. "The fact that such growth can occur does not mean that it will, or that the Amplitur organ will successfully reconnect itself to the appropriate portions of the individual's brain."

"Such rapid cellular growth could even be carcinogenic," pointed out one of the S'van in uncharacteristically humorless fashion.

"That is not an impossible scenario," First-of-Surgery admitted. "In that event the individual might die before the condition could be detected and treated. Conversely, if successful regrowth and reconnection were to occur, he might despite all our arduous work with him here, under the sway of the Amplitur again find himself. Or the clash of what he knows with what he feels might well unbalance him mentally."

"Then all our work here was for naught," said another S'van.

"Not true. We learned much of importance." With a wave of the surgeon's wand the magnified bits of Human brain and neural tissue vanished. "We are certain in the future others modified by the Amplitur to encounter. Perhaps by then we will have how permanently to inhibit the Amplitur organ from regenerating discovered." To the ensuing silence he added a note of hope.

"As has pointed out been, this a prognostication only is." Double eyelids blinked. "Such regrowth may not take place, or if it does neural reconnection may not recur, nor may there be any harm to the individual. This but one of many possible physiologic scenarios is."

"You assign the worst case a high priority, though, or you wouldn't have interrupted this conference to tell us about it."

First-of-Surgery regarded the scaleless warrior Human. An ineffable sadness colored his laconic response. "Truly."

The other Human nodded slowly as he spoke. "What we really need to do is find the world where the Amplitur are doing the actual modifications on Human infants and embryos and blow the goddamned place all the way back to the First Cause."

First-of-Surgery shivered slightly at the Human's unbridled ferocity. If not for the need to recruit species capable of combating the advance of the Amplitur, he might not have been above consideration of a little genetic engineering himself. Though from the beginning he had concealed his feelings well, the whole business had unnerved him more than he would have cared to admit.

One thing his studies had led him to ponder was if a "civilized Human" might not be a contradiction in terms, a biological impossibility. He was glad he would not be around to find out, for even the most optimistic scenario had the war against the Amplitur continuing far beyond the end of his projected lifespan.

Even so, his sleep was troubled.

17

As was traditional, victory celebrations were kept to a minimum. However, Military Command decided that its triumphant but exhausted soldiers deserved not merely a rest, but that greatest of all rewards for those who serve in combat: a visit home.

Had Ranji been given the option he would have chosen to stay on Eirrosad. His genuine hesitancy was, however, interpreted as modesty, and together with his friends he was shipped back to peaceful Cossuut. His subtle hints that he be allowed to remain behind were swamped in the flush of congratulations. Realizing that excessive demurral on his part would only eventually attract unwanted attention, he had no choice but to accept the enforced vacation.

As a Unifer much attention was focused on him. Whenever possible he tried to have his subordinates answer the innumerable questions that were put to the group, with the result that he became more than ever an object of curiosity and interest. In seeking obscurity he found only fame, or at least fame as it was known within the homogenized ethical orbit presided over by the Amplitur.

Though the cephalopodians had no need of such intangibles themselves, they recognized the importance of maintaining good morale among allied races and did their best, when circumstances were appropriate, to encourage it. Public feting of the victorious was useful. Modest adulation was not discouraged. As for the Amplitur themselves, they ascribed glory to an abstract rather than to individuals.

Saguio proudly appointed himself guardian of his brother's solitude, shielding him from the queries and attentions of the curious. *I wonder if he would be so zealous in my defense,* Ranji mused in the privacy of his apartment, *if he knew how hard I fought recently to avoid combat.* But he was glad of the privacy.

His self-imposed isolation during the voyage back to Cossuut was interpreted as introspection and suitably respected. After a while even the most persistent left him in peace, allowing Saguio to relax his vigil.

Ranji used the time to try and prepare himself for the inevitable forthcoming confrontations. Despite his best efforts, however, he was unprepared for the storm of emotions that tore through him when he was greeted at the shuttle disembarkation point by his joyful parents. He was able to maintain control only by lavishing his attention on his little sister, Cynsa, of whose genetic makeup he was relatively certain. As certain as he could be of his own, he reminded himself.

"Good to have you home, firstborn." As a sign of paternal Ashregan affection his father was rubbing Ranji between the shoulder blades.

"Yes, son. We worried, and missed."

Both his mother's warmth and his father's radiant pride struck Ranji as so genuine that for a moment he nearly forgot everything that had happened to him in the previous months. Once more solid reality dissolved into an unsettling speculative mist. Once again his identity fled the realm of verifiable knowledge for distant, uncertain biological shores.

He found he could not look long in his parents' direction. Not while the great question remained unresolved. Were they innocents or collaborators, empathetic dupes or cold-blooded agents of the Amplitur? How much of what they did and said was of their own volition and how much at the prompting of Amplitur "suggestion"? Was their "love" for him and his siblings anything other than the consequence of careful calculation? Would he ever know?

Modern technology could pinpoint the location and dimensions of black holes and quasars, antimatter accretions and Underspace . . . but where was love? How did he find it? By intuition, research, simple triangulation, what?

Cynsa's hugs and laughter provoked no such introspective agonies. At the heart-wrenchingly familiar family compound he played with her incessantly, luxuriating in her innocence and ignorance. She didn't care who or what she was, only that her beloved elder brother was home for a while.

But she was growing, developing the same acute reflexes and lanky form as her brothers. Ranji knew that her innocence could not be preserved indefinitely, any more than had his own.

He'd been home more than a month when the authorities asked
him to speak at the commencement exercises for the next group of
graduating fighters. It was impossible for him to refuse.

Now he looked out across a sea of young Ashregan faces. Twice
as many as in his original group bore the telltale marks of Amplitur
genetic manipulation. He wanted to cry out to them, to hold each
and every one close while explicating the appalling details of alien
duplicity. Their upturned gazes were focused on him, eager and expectant. The Amplitur had stolen their birthright and crippled their
capacity for independent thought. To stand there on the podium and
look down at them was almost more than he could bear.

As his silence persisted murmurs arose from the other speakers
and dignitaries seated behind him. *His trauma*, those in the know
explained knowledgeably. *It will pass.*

He forced his lips to move and sensed sounds emerging from his
throat, but it was as if another person was speaking. He, Ranji-aar,
was completely detached. The cool, robotic presentation garnered
more approval from the captive audience than it deserved. Any who
found it disappointing were too polite to voice their opinions.

Only recently he had been as young as those now raptly and
unquestioningly listening to him. He could pity, but not condemn.
The great lie of their condition was not of their choice.

He had returned to seek truth and dispel lies. Now he saw that
this was neither the time nor place to try and depose something half
so elusive. They would surely lock him up or worse, seek the advice
of an Amplitur "specialist." In the confusion that would invariably
result, he would be quietly disappeared.

Though the knowledge he carried threatened to choke him,
somehow he made it to the end of his speech, reciting the prepared
text as mechanically as any artificial diaphragm. The prophylactic
distance between himself and his audience vanished when he was
asked to answer a few questions.

Had he been blind he still could have told the pure Ashregan in
the audience from the modified Humans by the nature and emphasis
of their queries. His perception had been altered by experience and
revelation. Never again would he mistake an Ashregan for a Human
or vice versa. He had become irrevocably attuned to the differences.

He was careful to reply as an Ashregan, muting the Humanity

he had acquired on Omaphil. The audience hall would be a bad place in which to arouse suspicions. It was not without some relief that he allowed himself to slip back into the familiar mannerisms of his child-hood, to be nothing more than a young warrior, even a young hero, surrounded by friends and relations.

Afterward it was impossible to forget the many faces that came up to congratulate or greet him personally, impossible not to see beyond shining eyes and obscenely swollen cheek ridges to the bas-tardized DNA beyond. Buried within those coils, at least, was the real truth.

Raised as Ashregan, they would be sent to slay Humans. Re-turned to Humanity, they would exert twice the effort to kill the Ashregan who had betrayed them before they were born. That, too, was truth, one he didn't much care for. Even at his young age he had learned that it was not in the nature of truth to be likable.

Only the fact that confusion nearly outweighed his anger enabled him to keep his emotions in check. While he was certain he could no longer be what he had been, neither did he yet know if he was truly capable of being what he was. Whether out in public or at home with his family he was careful of what he said and how he acted lest it occur to someone that he might be acting "Human."

As it mounted, the fury he felt only served to further confirm his Humanity.

New graduates not only replaced his battlegroup's few losses but nearly doubled it in strength. He and his fellow Unifers received this statistic and more during a meeting with senior Ashregan officials. In vain he searched the assembled for the revered figure of his teacher Kouuad. That was an individual he would very much like to have questioned. How much did *he* know? How ignorant had the vener-able, fatherly Kouuad been of his students' biological history?

Perhaps, Ranji thought, he was not present precisely because he was privy to such knowledge.

Soratii-eev nudged him. They were being addressed by an officer of considerable reputation and rank.

"You have rested long enough. The Purpose needs again what only you can give.

"Your sorties on Eirrosad and Koba have been but preliminaries for what is to come, tests in which you and your troops have succeeded admirably. Having accomplished all that was hoped for you, it is time for you to lead a historic assault against the enemies of reason." Ranji and his friends shuffled expectantly in their seats.

"What's our target this time?" asked Cossinza-iiv from the corner.

The speaker yielded the podium to another officer. "Eirrosad and Koba are disputed worlds. It is in such places that the forces of the Purpose and those of the Weave have contested for supremacy for the past hundred years." He paused for emphasis. "Thanks to your recent accomplishments the decision has been made at the highest levels to carry the attack directly to the enemy in a manner not attempted for some time."

Producing a wand, he used it to generate the image of an alien star system, complete to moons and asteroid belt. An occasional comet sped through the three-dimensional construction to vanish in odd corners of the room. The attentive listeners ignored such cosmic distractions.

Sharpening focus, the speaker drew their attention to the fourth world out from the slightly pale sun. It exhibited the familiar single large landmass haloed by clouds and ocean.

"This is Ulaluable." Since his translator was not programmed to react to proper names the officer had to pronounce it slowly for his audience. "Not a large world nor one particularly rich in natural resources, though it has its share. It occupies an important position beyond what the Weave would refer to as its frontline, if such archaisms had any meaning in space." As he manipulated the wand controls illuminated portions of the projection punctuated his speech.

"It possesses fewer than the usual complement of islands, a benign climate, many highlands, and modest mountain ranges. There are highly productive farmlands. Since it was first settled Ulaluable has been a significant contributor to the enemy resistance. Naturally it is well defended." Pinpoints of light sprang to life on the planetary surface.

Birachii squinted at the projection. "Mighty extensive troop distribution for a contested world. Where are our forces concentrated? In the opposite hemisphere?"

The officer caused the globe projection to rotate a hundred and eighty degrees. The scattering of indicator lights on the other side of the landmass was not significantly different from what they had already observed.

"Ulaluable is not a contested world." Only after the resultant buzz of startled conversation began to fade did he add, "It is in fact a highly developed, thoroughly civilized world, long ago settled and largely colonized by Wais, though there is also a substantial minority Hivistahm population."

"Which means there's no way we can carry out a landing there." Cossinza gestured at the rotating globe. "The defenses of a settled world would cut us to bits as soon as we touched down."

The officer turned to her. "Though Ulaluable is highly developed, its largely agricultural nature and intermittent mountainous topography offer unpopulated expanses where a determined landing force might successfully establish itself before the planetary defenses could muster a reaction. Certainly the population does not expect an attack."

"With good reason," Soratii noted. "Who makes up the defending garrison?"

"It is largely Massood, with the usual Hivistahm technical support teams. There are some Humans present but according to the best available intelligence their numbers are small." The speaker regarded his audience earnestly.

"Much time has been devoted to the gathering of requisite intelligence. There are many reasons besides its topography why Ulaluable lends itself to unexpected attack. Most of its major power facilities lie exposed in the foothills and mountains. Several important communications centers have been constructed nearby. If these could be overrun before the defenders could bring reinforcements to bear, it would give an invading force not only a tactical advantage but considerable leverage in any subsequent negotiations.

"One reason why something like this has not previously been attempted is because the usual Ashregan-Crigolit–led strike force could not advance from objective to objective quickly enough to make it viable. The enemy's confidence springs from identical knowledge. Your special teams have demonstrated the ability to attack with speed. With your people in the vanguard our tacticians believe a successful invasion of Ulaluable can be carried out. The local Wais population is of course incapable of offering any resistance." He hesitated.

"I do not think I need speak of the effect such a defeat would have on Weave morale."

The initial speaker regarded them solemnly. "If more of your kind were available we would consider attacking an even more important enemy world. Ulaluable was chosen specifically because of its perceived vulnerabilities. We value you all greatly and have no intention of sacrificing you on behalf of a gesture.

"Because of the unique nature of this expedition participation is not compulsory. No opprobrium will attach to any who choose demurral." Silence greeted his words. Wishing badly to say a great deal, Ranji could only keep still. The elder officer gestured approvingly. "I believed and hoped that would be your response."

His slightly junior colleague surveyed his expectant audience. "You will have the best backup available. Experienced Ashregan, Crigolit, and Mazvec troops drawn from other theaters of conflict will fully support your strikes. We are depending on you to provide speed and decisiveness, not overwhelming firepower.

"If it appears that despite all our careful planning the gambit is doomed to failure, you will be brought out immediately, irrespective of risk to evacuating personnel."

"Even if it means losing a ship," added the senior officer. "The High Command holds your troops in that much regard."

"We don't think you will fail." Certainly, Ranji thought, both speakers *sounded* confident. "If we did, this venture would not have reached the planning stage, much less advanced this far beyond it."

Like his companions, the proposal left Ranji somewhat dazed. It was so unexpected because it was utterly unlike the strategy of patient attrition the Amplitur had favored for a thousand years. They were adapting to new circumstances with a speed that left him breathless. How the Weave would react to such tactics remained to be seen.

He and his kind, he knew, were to constitute the centerpiece of such innovations.

The senior officer broke the ensuing silence. "Not incidentally, you are all being promoted. Every one of you, every member of your respective groups. Such honor is not unprecedented, but it is unusual. The High Command takes pride in you and your accomplishments." He sought out a particular individual.

"You, Ranji-aar, are hereby raised to Field Unifer."

Cossinza gasped softly. Soratii sat motionless. If he was upset at being jumped in rank he did not show it. Ranji didn't think it would bother him. Since the days of the trials they had become good friends, respectful of each other's abilities and opinions.

To be given command was the last thing he wanted, yet to refuse the honor was unthinkable. Doing so would expose him to relentless scrutiny. From now on it would be impossible for him to hang back and hide on the battlefield. Not only would he be unable to avoid the killing, he would be forced to direct it.

At least, he told himself, as commanding officer he would better be able to insure Saguio's safety. Aware that everyone was expecting some sort of response from him he said, "When are we to depart?"

"Preparations require another five days," the officer told him. "That should give everyone ample time to prepare, and to spend more time with mates and offspring. Rest, delight, and immerse yourselves in the Purpose."

The meeting was at an end.

"You will take care of yourself."

His father stood alongside him in the back of the family compound as together they contemplated the sunset. Ranji wanted to scream questions and accusations. Instead he stood silently, trying to sort the emotions that gnawed at his insides.

"And you will look after your brother."

Ranji heard himself replying. "Yes, Father."

Grainfields stretched from the rear of the residential square to a bilious orange horizon. This time of year they lay fallow, their unrelenting flatness interrupted only by the stark silhouette of an isolated, twisted kekuna tree.

As the dorsal arc of Cossuut's sun sank out of sight, the two turned to walk back to the house. "You know, Ranji, you've been acting rather strange since you've been home."

"Have I?" Clods of recently turned earth gave him something to focus on. Some he kicked to bits, others he spared. As he would soon be expected to do with friends in battle.

"Your mother and I don't understand. Are you sure you're all right?"

His father's concern proved nothing one way or the other, Ranji knew. Once again he was made aware of the damning ignorance that

jailed his spirit. Mind-dupe or calculating agent? A glance at the old
man proved unenlightening as ever.

"I'm sorry if I strike you as unnaturally introspective, Father.
You should know that combat tends to dull the senses."

"No; there's something else."

Halting, Ranji forced a narrow Ashregan smile. "I'll take care of
myself, and Saguio as well. Rest assured on that." There at least was
a promise he could make with assurance.

It wouldn't do to leave his father questioning. The old man might
seek answers from local officials or, worse, from the Amplitur stationed on Cossuut. Embarrassing queries might find their way back
to him, even on distant Ulaluable. He knew that only continued
caution would preserve his secret.

Leave-taking gave him no difficulty until it came time to say
good-bye to his sister. That guileless innocent cried as she hugged
him close. He could feel the growing strength in her, strength the
Amplitur intended to put to dreadful misuse, and somewhat to his
surprise he found that he was crying, too. The outpouring of emotion
must have eased his father's concerns, because the old man made his
farewells quickly, propounding no more unanswerable questions.

Sensing that it was for the last time, Ranji looked back as the
transport vehicle carried him and Saguio away from the house, away
from the grainfields in which he'd played as a youth, away from the
residential complex and the only home he'd ever known.

Because in that final moment he had to make a decision in order
to keep his sanity, he'd decided that his parents were innocent, as
captive of Amplitur machination as he and his brother. He reached
that conclusion on the basis of more than twenty years of love and
affection, understanding and nurturance. His mother and father *had*
to be ignorant of the biological truth because every Ashregan lived
in fear of the terrible, dreaded Human beings. Surely no amount of
Amplitur suggestion could have so thoroughly overcome that deep-
seated terror for such an extended period of time. Yes, surely they
were dupes, tools of the Amplitur, as innocent in their own way as
his baby sister. They had to be because he wanted it to be so.

How would they look at him if the truth were to be revealed?

The transport accelerated, plunging into the onrushing night.

———

The speech of the three Wais administrators was so rapid, convoluted, and inflected that it was almost impossible for the translators the non-Wais wore to render it comprehensible. Despite their agitated discursion, the trio of ornithorps retained their composure. To have exhibited exasperation in the presence of other species would have been, well, unrefined.

"What reason can you have to call us here, away from our daily work?" The Wais who spoke sported a fringed neckpiece of breathtaking elegance which served not only as a testament to her importance but was ravishingly beautiful in its own right. The feathers which protruded from her flowing attire were of exquisite color and expertly groomed, as were those of her two male companions.

The instant his translator finished, the S'van replied. "Evidence has recently come to light which suggests that the enemy is planning something extraordinary."

"Of what concern, pray tell, might Amplitur military intrigues be to us?" Concerned that in her haste to reach the meeting on time it might have slipped a finger-length too low, the administrator gently fluffed her neckpiece.

The S'van withheld the comments which automatically came to mind when one found oneself dealing with the Wais. "We have word that they are planning to mount an attack on one of the primary Weave worlds."

Though they found the news as upsetting as would any civilized member of the Weave, none of the Wais reacted visibly. To have done so in front of aliens would have been considered unbearably gauche.

"That is difficult to believe," said one of the male Wais finally.

"Though controversy continues, the evidence seems irrefutable."

"Which unfortunate world is to be the target of this outrage?"

"That we haven't been able to determine ... yet." The S'van wished for a platform. He didn't like looking up at the Wais. Having to tilt his head back raised his beard off his chest and exposed the sensitive skin beneath. "Thanks to our informants we have been able to reduce the list of candidates to three. Tuo'olengg, Kinar, and ... Ulaluable."

Very little could induce a Wais's neck feathers to spike and pupils to widen, but the S'van's announcement managed that accomplishment.

"How can this be?" So upset was the remaining male ornithorp that he nearly committed the unpardonable sin of misinflecting the interrogative. "Surely the Amplitur know from experience that an attack on any developed world would be soon surrounded and annihilated."

"You'd think so." The S'van readily agreed. "That's why we've gone to such lengths to confirm the information we've received. If all these enemy preparations are simply in support of a feint, it's far and away the most elaborate one they've ever propagated. We can't take that chance. As the current Administrating Triumvirate of Ulaluable do *you* want us to take that chance?"

The polyphonic Wais reply was as unanimous as it was harmonious.

"That's what we thought your reaction would be." The S'van looked satisfied. "The Grand Council has determined to implement exceptional security measures on all three worlds. If the Amplitur's purpose in this was to force us to reallocate scarce resources, then they've already accomplished what they set out to do. You'll be given everything this quadrant's Command can spare."

"What would possess the Amplitur to embark on an adventure with no chance of success?" the female member of the triumvirate sang bemusedly.

"Obviously they think better of their chances." The husky voice of the Massood officer who'd accompanied the S'van was a sharp contrast to the mellifluous tones of the Wais. "Perhaps you have heard about the new fighters they have been using? The ones who hurt us so badly on Eirrosad?"

"We have heard. While the Wais are noncombatants, we are not indifferent to the progress of the great conflict."

A half-hidden figure behind the Massood stepped forward. "If the Amplitur choose Ulaluable as their target, you'll have to be a damn sight less indifferent."

Though not nearly as tall as the Massood, the Human officer towered over the S'van and Wais. Stocky and powerfully built, he sported a heavy mustache and long sideburns which curled toward his chin. Even as they went to great lengths to conceal their distaste for the primitive cosmetic affectation, the Wais instinctively drew back from the massive primate.

"This would be a lot easier if we knew which of the three worlds they were going to hit, but we don't, so the same defensive resources have to be allocated to each. Ulaluable gets no more than Kinar or Tuo'olengg. I promise that we'll do our best for you, but I'm afraid you're going to have to issue a general alert. Besides the need to brief you, the governors of Ulaluable, that was our purpose in calling this meeting. I hope there won't be any panic."

The slightly taller male replied condescendingly. "The Wais do not 'panic,' sir."

"No," muttered the Massood under his breath. "They just freeze at the smell of a weapon."

The female glared. "We will do our part. All necessary measures will be taken . . . insofar as a wholly civilized people can respond to such a threat, of course. As a chosen representative of the populace I assure you that you will have our full cooperation. We may not be able to 'kill,' but we can do much else in our own defense."

The S'van hastened to try and lower his allies' emotional temperature. "We know the Wais do not fight. Remember, I'm S'van. We do not fight, either." The administrator seemed mollified.

"The Council will appreciate any assistance you can render to the defending forces. Additional personnel are already on their way. Massood and . . . Humans."

Feathered heads dipped together, chittering softly. Again it was left to the senior female to speak. "You must be aware that Human combat troops have never been stationed on Ulaluable, or for that matter any of the Wais worlds. It is not part of the Covenant of Agreement."

Out of the corner of an eye the S'van saw the muscular Human stiffen slightly. However, he said nothing, exhibiting a self-control not normally associated with his kind. He was a ranking officer, the S'van reminded himself, and intelligent enough to know that in such circumstances it was better to let a S'van do the talking.

"All Human personnel will be assigned to and billeted at important industrial and communications facilities. Cities and unnecessary contact with the general population will be avoided."

"Suits us fine," the Human could not resist muttering.

The male Wais who spoke affected not to hear the comment. "We are of course grateful for the assistance of all our friends and allies. It seems we are to have no choice in the matter anyway."

"On the contrary," said the S'van. "If you so desire, these additional defensive forces allocated to Ulaluable can instead be divided among the other threatened worlds."

"That will not be necessary," the female hastily assured him. "You must understand that while you concern yourselves with matters military, it is left to us to deal with the delicate social fabric of our society."

"I do understand." The S'van smiled behind his beard. Of all the Weave races, only the S'van utilized the smile more than Humans. "It is my hope that Ulaluable is not the target of the Amplitur."

The three ornithorps whistled agreement in unison, each musical exhalation pitched slightly differently from that of its neighbor. "We are obliged for your concern," the female said, "and realize that extraordinary circumstances call for extraordinary measures. We gratefully accept the temporary stationing of additional Massood and Human soldiers in our soil."

"Temporary," chorused her male associates.

The Human officer continued to observe and listen in silence. He'd served as liaison to the "civilized" Weave races too long to allow their reactions to the presence of his kind to upset him. Save for the Massood and occasionally the S'van, the thanks Humans received for putting their lives on the line in defense of other species was indifferent at best. He sighed resignedly. The Wais could not help the way they were. At such times the Human lot could be a difficult one.

They would provide ample material aid, but that was all. Once, he had seen a Wais, fortified with medication, through a tremendous effort of will actually lift and fire a small handgun before collapsing in a nauseated faint. It was an experience not likely oft to be repeated, even if Ulaluable was attacked. The defense of their world was up to him and his kind . . . and the Massood, of course. No getting around it. That was the way the pulsar spun, he told himself.

Silently he wished for the meeting to end. Someone had to serve as a liaison to the Wais, and he had been compelled to accept the role. That didn't mean he had to like it. Like the majority of his kind he had been trained as a soldier. Direct action suited him, diplomacy made him itch. He longed for reassignment to a combat unit. Even the sympathetic S'van was starting to get on his nerves.

Idly he fingered his service belt. Like his boots, the material of which it was fashioned was incredibly light, tough, attractive, and of

Wais design and manufacture. That was what the Weave was about, he mused. Each species contributed according to its talents and abilities. Wais designed, Lepar carried, Hivistahm engineered, S'van held together, O'o'yan maintained, and so forth. Turlog thought, Humans and Massood slew.

He comforted himself in the knowledge that the specialty nature seemed to have assigned his kind was at least easy to understand.

18

The grim expression Ranji wore whenever he was compelled to leave his cabin discouraged even close friends from trying to talk to him, and helped to preserve his solitude during the long Underspace journey out from Cossuut. Everyone knew that as Field Unifer great responsibilities devolved upon him. It was therefore only natural to assume that his attitude was a reflection of the serious inner contemplation that preceded battle. He was left alone.

His isolation suited Ranji just fine. Had his companions known the real reason for his solemnity they would have been shocked and dismayed. Not only was he not deeply engrossed in preparing battlefield strategy; he was wholly absorbed in trying to find a means of avoiding combat altogether.

There were too many times when he wondered why he was bothering to try. He was one man, one individual caught up in a millennia-old galactic conflagration that involved billions of intelligent beings. Events of prodigious import were in motion, and like litter on a wave he found himself helplessly swept up and washed along, to be pounded against whatever shore fate had in store for him. Not for the first time he found himself thinking that perhaps the best thing he could do was simply try to preserve his own life and live it out as comfortably and unobtrusively as possible.

Only, he was repeatedly hammered by uneasy dreams, and visions of his sister slicing Human throats at the behest of shadowy, tentacular forms. Thoughts were not as easily avoided as friends.

What could he do? They were about to attack a developed Weave world largely populated by the ultracivilized, innocuous race known as the Wais. As the mere appearance of enemy troops was likely to paralyze the population, they would have to be defended by Massood and Humans. How could he, as Field Unifer, avoid participating in battle and giving orders if not directly having a hand in the deaths of many of his own kind? Desperately seeking a means of avoidance, he found only bleak and inner despair.

Time was running out. The invasion force was less than five days from the target. Preparations for touchdown had already begun. He might yet be spared contemplated agonies, he knew, for their landing shuttle might well be blown out of Ulaluable's sky by orbiting or land-based defenses, thus sparing him the need to make life-threatening decisions. His attitude toward such a quick and exonerating death had grown dangerously ambivalent.

Perhaps worst of all, the truth gnawed at him like an insect struggling to escape its cocoon. He had returned to his people to give them knowledge, only to find himself unable to speak. The futility of his circumstances tormented him far worse than any prospect of dying.

His colleagues saw the inner struggle mirrored in his expression and misinterpreted its origin to his benefit.

He considered feigning mental collapse, seeking surcease in an inveigled disgrace. But that would not preserve his brother, nor prevent his sister from being trained to follow after. There was simply no way to extend his solitude to those he loved. He would have to find another way.

As attack preparations around him intensified, he redirected himself to the problem with ferocious application.

It wasn't until the day before the fleet was to phase out of Underspace that he remembered the kindly Lepar, Itepu. Remembered his compassion and understanding. His had been a simpler view of the cosmos, basic and uncomplicated. In such simplifications were certain virtues. He pondered those memories, trying to recall everything he and the Lepar had discussed during his half-forgotten journey from Eirrosad to Omaphil.

When the word came for all soldiers to don field armor and equipment, he was much eased in mind. He knew now what he was going to have to do. If it ended in death, then at least he would be spared the future tribulation of thinking.

Those under his immediate command relaxed when they saw their Unifer stride purposefully into the landing shuttle. Clearly the depth and extent of his hermetic contemplation during the voyage out from Cossuut had amply prepared him for the forthcoming conflict. It boosted their morale accordingly.

"Look at him." The recent graduate nudged his companion as they watched Ranji board the command sled. "Utterly self-possessed. He's ready."

"I hear he's always like that." The young woman tracked the Unifer's progress admiringly. "You heard the story of how he handled himself on Eirrosad?"

The man was checking the charge level on his stinger. "Never panicked, kept his head when everybody else was losing theirs. I'm glad we're in his group."

"By the Purpose," said a much shorter Ashregan from nearby, "I'm just glad he is on our shuttle!"

They examined each other's armor locks and visors, exchanged and rechecked weapons. Once the shuttle touched down on the Ulaluablian surface they would be thrust outside and into a combat situation, where such checks would have to be performed, if at all, under arduous and possibly lethal conditions. Better to make certain seals were tight and weapons powered up *now*.

It must have been something to see: a dozen immense starships suddenly and simultaneously materializing from Underspace just above the cloud layer of Ulaluable's blue-green globe. There was nothing present to witness the sight, however, except the alert sensors of the automatic orbiting planetary-defense system, which responded anon.

As ships dropped shuttles in the fashion of fecund invertebrates, on-board weaponry had some success in dealing with the cluster of orbiting hellaciousness. One ship was destroyed by a self-guiding orbital mine, both erupting in a flaming plume of metal, gas, and organic components. Seared vacuum momentarily blinded every instrument in the vicinity. Five other vessels were badly damaged by high-power, mirror-aligned particle beams.

The rest unloaded their deadly cargo with admirable speed and dispatch. Metaloceramic crescents dove into the clouds and made their way to the waiting surface, where their contents spread out and sought cover with slick alacrity.

Not every shuttle made it to ground. Some were obliterated by surface-based weapons. Others ran afoul of scrambling high-speed aircraft. But by the time the surviving starships retired to the protective astrophysical anonymity of Underspace, the greater portion of the battlegroup had successfully disembarked and dispersed. Now if Ulaluable's defenders chose to use heavy weapons on the invaders they would be putting at risk sensitive portions of the very world they were supposed to be protecting.

Ordinarily destruction or damage to half an attacking force's ships would be sufficient to bring an invasion to a halt, but not this time. There was too much at stake for the Amplitur to recall their ground forces, which after all had made it down largely intact. The components of the engagement had shifted surfaceward. Time to see what the Ashregan-led battlegroup could do.

Ranji's shuttle landed hard in a grassy glade surrounded by extremely thin, tall trees, rattling both soldiers and equipment. The attenuated woods provided some cover from patrolling aircraft, as did the soot-colored clouds from which a light rain was falling. As troops rushed to disembark, the shuttle's crew stayed at the equipment which projected half a dozen ghost shuttles overhead, their purpose being to bemuse and distract enemy sensors.

Ranji commanded slightly less than a thousand regular and modified Ashregan soldiers riding skids and floaters. They deployed themselves with gratifying speed, erecting camouflage and establishing a perimeter while engineers excavated a hole deep enough to conceal the shuttle. Maintained and defended by its own crew, it would serve as a field base, a point of reference, and, if need be, a means of final retreat.

Their target was the control station of the principal power-distribution grid for the entire northern third of the planetary landmass. Like any other unavoidably unsightly industrial complex on a Wais world, it had been sited as far as practicable from the nearest population center.

An intricate network of dams in the nearby mountains stored water for irrigation and hydropower. It would have been a simple matter to target them for destruction by land-based missiles, but that would require their replacement by the eventual victors. A much more sensible course of action involved the incapacitation or better yet, the capture of the complex that stored and distributed the power thus generated.

If Ranji's group could capture the complex they would control the supply of energy for half the population of Ulaluable. Nor could the defenders blast them out without destroying the critical components of their own power grid. A successful assault on the center would weaken local communications, industry, and transportation significantly.

The Wais were little better prepared psychologically to deal with an attack than if they had not been warned at all. True to the claims of their chosen administrators, they did not panic: they merely shut themselves away in their homes and waited for defenders or assailants to triumph. In the sparsely populated regions where the invaders landed, it was more difficult to pretend nothing so uncivilized was taking place. Some citizens fled, others barricaded themselves in their places of work, and a small portion went catatonic.

Of all the Weave races, the Wais were perhaps the least well equipped to deal with the awkward reality of contentious violence. The very thought of their exquisitely coiffed garden world being subjected to onerous combat was enough to induce severe trauma in the more sensitive of them. It was left to Ulaluable's Hivistahm inhabitants to maintain the abandoned planetary infrastructure and assist the defenders in the movement of troops and supplies.

The second group of invaders made swift progress toward the capital city's communications center until they came up against a small but well-entrenched cluster of determined Massood. As the defenders were in possession of advanced surface-to-air weaponry, the attackers' skids and floaters were unable to detour to their target.

Thus bogged down, the invaders were forced to take up secure positions of their own, which gave the besieged Massood time to call in reinforcements from the city. This included a flying squad of Humans, who threw themselves against the Ashregan with utter disregard for their own safety, making life miserable for the Unifers in charge of the attack by reducing their careful timetables to chaos.

In spite of the fact that the majority of actual combat was restricted to obscure or outlying areas, there were casualties among the civilian population . . . from heart failure, shock, and cerebral hemorrhage. Wais physicians (those who were not themselves paralyzed by circumstance) were kept busy tending to their own kind.

Soratii's team successfully wrested control of Ulaluable's northernmost shuttleport from its defenders. If they could hold the place, it would allow for faster and safer resupply from orbit. As their first important conquest, the achievement cheered every member of the invading forces.

Ranji's group received the news as they were skimming in attack formation toward their designated target, their skids and floaters tearing along just above the ground at maximum combat speed. Since their attention was concentrated on sensors and weapons systems, their cheers were silent ones.

Once more those close to him took his silence and otiose expression for quiet determination and resolve. It would have shaken their confidence not only in their Unifer but in themselves had they been able to see the pain and uncertainty that raged within him.

Tormented by unceasing doubt and confusion, Ranji left necessary decisions to subordinates like Weenn and Tourmast. In the absence of direction from above the group's flexible command structure allowed them to skillfully guide the battlegroup through rugged mountains toward its target. Ranji's continued silence as they neared the high, narrow valley which had been selected as a staging area for the actual attack began to concern them, but they said nothing. By now their Unifer was famed for his moodiness.

Underground lines fed power from dozens of different sources to the main distribution center, which lay on a fertile plain between the nearest conurbation and the mountains. It was decided to attack late at night. Despite a thousand years of military development, ordinary darkness still offered soldiers a certain amount of cover which strategists and planners were pleased to take advantage of at every opportunity. The absence of notable geological features in the vicinity of the target rendered a stealthy approach impossible anyway.

Ranji found himself hoping that the majority of the complex's defenders were Massood. From what he knew of the psychological makeup of the Wais, actual operations were probably being run by local Hivistahm.

Any formal defenses were probably of recent installation, since, like any other civilized Weave world, Ulaluable would have been ill prepared for a serious assault. In that respect resistance might be less well organized than it had been on Koba or Eirrosad. The downside was that they had to continue to advance, since they as yet controlled little territory and therefore had precious few places to retreat to.

He didn't doubt that the complex's defenders were prepared to extend greetings to any uninvited visitors. Since sheer cliffs and steep gorges offered some protection even from modern weapons, they would anticipate as assault from that vicinity rather than the open plains of the south, though they would doubtless be alert to an attack

from any direction. Local geology allowed little leeway for subtle
strategies.

The outcome would be determined by whose fighters were the
more skilled, the more determined, and by what sort of weaponry
the defenders had managed to put in place.

Whoever they were, boldness was not their hallmark. When Soratii's squads first sortied from the foothills they met intense fire and
promptly withdrew. Had Ranji been in charge of the complex's defense he would have followed up with immediate pursuit and counterattack, if only to test his attackers' strength and resolve. Those
inside the distribution grid's perimeter did no such thing. In classical
fashion they chose to sit behind their screens and sensors and weapons and wait for the next hostile move.

Probably not many Humans, then, he decided, feeling a little
better about the situation. He smiled relievedly, suddenly realized
what he was doing, and glanced around the interior of the command
skid to see if anyone had noticed the unnatural, un-Ashregan expression. No one had. Everyone was concentrating on work or conversation. In the future he would have to be more careful. Assuming he
had one. And if he did, what would it be as?

If naught else the long journey outward from Cossuut had given
him ample time to think. He had arrived on Ulaluable with a vague
notion of what he wanted to do. All that was lacking now was a
means for carrying it out without getting himself or any of his friends
killed while integrating his intentions into the little matter of the
battle he was expected to direct. Surely a simple enough task.

The practical knowledge he'd acquired on Koba, Eirrosad, and
even Omaphil enabled him to probe the enemy's defenses with few
casualties. Though hastily installed, they were substantial and deadly.
Soratii's people encountered and reported the presence of photic
charges, heat- and shape-seeking missiles, and intelligent explosives,
in addition to an aurora dome which would instantly short out the
components of any approaching vehicle, not to mention microwav-
ing its inhabitants. The complex was going to be difficult to approach,
much less capture.

In the attackers' favor was the fact that on a civilized world such
installations were not constructed with an eye toward defense. Most
of the distribution complex was located aboveground, buildings and
facilities arranged in an aesthetically tasteful but exposed star pattern

with typically lush Wais gardens burgeoning between. The defenders would also be hampered by the need to keep the grid functioning while simultaneously fighting off any assailants.

Ranji knew that in order to have any impact he would have to move fast. As Ulaluable's defensive command identified the invaders' targets, they would proceed to rush reinforcements to those areas. He had no intention of being stuck in the mountains for a long siege. Whatever he finally decided to do would be executed with speed.

Exhilarating, this independence of mind, he mused. Exhilarating, and addictive.

Occasional missile exchanges produced a lot of noise and flame but no serious damage to either side, as antimissile weaponry obliterated projectiles in midflight. Beam projectors were held in reserve, since the use of such advanced devices simultaneously exposed their positions to enemy sensors and return fire.

The extended, cautious firefight that occupied the daylight hours witnessed much sound and fury but nothing in the way of advance or retreat. The Massood and Hivistahm defenders soon realized that their attackers wished to capture and not destroy the distribution complex, and were able to conduct their defense accordingly.

The slightly sloping plain that halted at the base of the mountains was sliced by several mostly dry gullies, watercourses designed by nature to drain the foothills in the rainy season. An intent Ranji had begun studying them through magnifiers from the moment of his group's arrival. Now he left his position near the front of the command skid and moved to stand next to his adjutant, Birachii.

"I'll need a floater." He poked at the luminescent, hovering representation of what in ancient times would have been called the battlefield, his finger tracing one particular topographical feature until it came to rest among several pinpoints of blue light. "It looks like this one squad's made some real progress. I'm going to check out their status."

"Your pardon, Ranji?" Birachii eyed him uncertainly.

"I said, I'm going out. To have a look around."

The sub-Unifer hesitated. "I ask excusal for making exception, Ranji, but you're the group commander. If you'll just tell me what you want, there are many on board or outside who are much more expendable than yourself and who'd be glad to go in your stead."

"Thanks, Birach, but I have to do this myself. See, I'm not just going out to survey the terrain. I have it in mind to reconnoiter an idea." He turned. "Jhindah-ier will be in charge until I get back." Birachii didn't try to hide his surprise. Though a perfectly competent officer, Jhindah-ier was a member of the pure Ashregan contingent and not one of the modified.

"It's bad procedure." Ranji found his friend's concern touching. "And not in keeping with the teachings of the Purpose."

"Birach, ever since we were children we've been noted and promoted for doing the unexpected. I'm just taking another step along the same old trail. Don't worry. I just want to confer with the squad leader. I have every intention of returning to supervise the rest of the attack. Now stop mooning at me like a lovesick youngster and requisition that floater."

19

Intelligent shells dueled in the airspace between the mountains and the distribution complex, darting and feinting, occasionally annihilating each other in spectacular bursts of high explosive. Others released enervating gases, which were as quickly rendered harmless by receptor-seeking neutralizing bonders. Rapid-mutating biological agents had not as yet been utilized, since they had an awkward habit of infecting those who employed them as readily as they did those they were intended to incapacitate.

Set afire by explosives, much of the flora proximate to the combat zone blazed hellishly around Ranji as his floater shot down the canyon he'd chosen. The coniferous forest which coated the rugged mountain slopes had been turned into a crackling, snapping inferno. He ignored the conflagration. The lightweight field armor he wore kept him cool and comfortable while supplying him with fresh, filtered air.

Just ahead a giant tree exploded from the heat, showering him with flaming splinters. The floater rocked slightly but stayed on course as he continued to descend, hugging the bottom of the canyon tight enough for the air-repulsion vehicle to send droplets flying from the debris-laden rivulet that coursed muddily below.

Then he was out of the foothills, screaming through the steep-sided gully. Smoke from burning plains grass and scrub formed dense red-brown clouds which settled in the gully, choking off forward vision and forcing him to rely on instruments.

Informed of his intentions, the scouting squad was waiting for him, hunkered down on both sides of the narrow, soot-filled stream. As he neared the shapes that materialized out of the gloom, he carefully brought the floater to a halt. Gravel crunched beneath the craft's landing struts as it settled to the ground.

Something scrabbled through the muck under his boots. Looking

down, he saw a dark green multilegged shape desperately scrambling
for the perceived safety of shallow water. Some kind of local reptile
or amphibian. For a single pure instant unsullied by war or confusion
or self-damnation the universe stopped. In it nothing moved, nothing
existed save for him and the single poor mud-dwelling creature beneath his feet whose misfortune it was to have found itself caught up
in the maelstrom of a higher confrontation. He thought of Itepu.

With the toe of his boot he gently boosted it over the last obstacle
in its path and watched until it had found obscurity beneath the
water's soot-laden surface.

His instruments indicated three troop skids and half a dozen escorting floaters strung out in line down the winding canyon. That
was the best the gully would permit. If it narrowed any further, they
would have to begin advancing vehicles in single file. The Ashregan
squad leader had properly concerned herself more with avoiding enemy detection than concentrating firepower.

She was understandably surprised that battlegroup commander
Ranji-aar, the Field Unifer, would expose his valuable person to such
conditions.

"Greetings, honored Unifer." She was short and petite even for
an unmodified Ashregan, but there was strength in her greeting and
in what he could see of her face through the protective visor. "Do
you wish to take personal command of the squad?"

"Not at this time, officer." He peered impatiently past her. Regular troops were staring in his direction, unable to restrain their curiosity. Among the modified who were present he recognized the
Sub-Unifers Tourmast and Weenn from the Eirrosad campaign. He'd
be able to work with them. "You have under your command a young
sub-officer named Saguio-aar?"

The thick smoke rendered formalities extraneous. She responded
with a thin Ashregan smile. "Your brother's on the second transport
skid, sir. If you would like him brought forward, I can . . ."

"No. Just making sure of my information. What I would like is
for you to resume your advance, officer."

She eyed him evenly. "We're very exposed here, sir. The situation could become . . . active."

He met her stare without blinking. "As you may have heard,
Unifer, I'm not exactly a desk soldier. I expect things to get active.

As a matter of fact, I'm kind of counting on it. Someone has to strike first."

"Yes, *sir.*"

"I'll let you know if I have any suggestions. In the meantime this is still your squad. I await your actions."

She turned and snapped orders to a subordinate, who cocked his head once to the side in the Ashregan gesture of acknowledgment and began relaying directions via the communicator hung around his neck.

An instant later troops were scrambling to activate floaters as the three skids rose into the smoke-filled air. Ranji turned his own vehicle over to another soldier, opting instead to join the squad commander on board her craft.

The group resumed its cautious advance down the winding channel, sensors wide open and feeling for anything that might smack of enemy defenses. Instruments showed small rapids ahead, and air-repulsion units thrummed a little harder as one vehicle after another surmounted the cataract, bouncing slightly at the bottom.

There was clearer air ahead, and a revelation which Ranji had suspected from the careful study of available maps but which could only be confirmed by on-site observation. The gully did indeed negotiate a course all the way from the mountains to the foothills through the distribution complex itself.

"Camouflage up!" snapped the Squad Unifer. Combined with the drifting haze from the many fires, the diffusion units would help to conceal their presence.

They were close enough to see Weave attack sleds rising from within the enemy compound and accelerating northward. Much nearer still, tall, slim pylons quivered with energy, their presence marking the boundary of the aurora dome. They pulsed like firebrands on the skid's sensor screens.

Unaffected by such artificial constraints, the gully marched on, wending its way into the heart of the distribution complex. In the rainy season it probably ran full, Ranji decided, an impressive torrent filling the cut currently occupied only by a dirty trickle.

The complex had been designed to facilitate specific functions, he knew, of which defense against an extraplanetary assault was not one. Its hastily installed aurora dome would have been set up to stop an attack by skids and floaters. Air-repulsion vehicles. That traveled *above*ground.

The technology of modern warfare had become so complicated that sometimes the simplest things were overlooked in the rush to defend against the highly advanced.

If they went in single file on minimum power, it was just possible they might be able to avoid the center's defenses. There would be some downward leakage from the dome, but unless he was completely mistaken about its style of construction their field armor should be able to slough off its effects.

That was essentially what the squad commander proposed. Having long since worked out the details and come to the identical conclusion, Ranji let her ramble on until the time came to bestow his blessings on the plan, which he did without hesitation. After all, their initial aim was the same: to slip safely inside the enemy's defensive perimeter. It was only afterward that their objectives would diverge.

Her subordinates expressed quiet enthusiasm for the plan. Visions of triumph and rapid promotion filled the minds of those gathered in the command skid.

"If we can do this," one of them murmured, "we can change the whole thrust of battle."

Truer than you can know, Ranji thought approvingly.

Of course, the stratagem which had gradually been gathering strength inside him ever since they'd left Underspace might be doomed to failure. His attempt to implement his intentions might well result in the death of Saguio and all their friends in addition to himself. He wouldn't live long enough to shoulder the responsibility of failure.

But he'd waited and stalled and delayed long enough. It was time to act. Consequences would remain forever unforeseen unless he forced the issue. With a little luck he might be the only one to die. He could hardly dare countenance the possibility that he might succeed.

They were working out the line of approach when he vouchsafed an objection. "I hate to point this out—" The Sub-Unifers and their commander looked up at him. "—but there're too many of us." He stirred the hovering projection with a finger. "No way will we be able to slip three transport skids and half a dozen floaters inside unobserved."

The squad leader glanced at her second-in-command, then back at Ranji. "What do you suggest?"

"The success of this little sortie rides on surprise, not numbers. I think we should go in with the most compact, toughest unit we can condense out of your squad. Nothing against the other troops, but to me that means every soldier who hails from Cossuut. They've had the same training, they know what each other is likely to do in a given situation. We'll have less firepower but better control over it.

"Furthermore, those of us who hail from Cossuut have Human stature if not facial features. If we're spotted inside, the defenders may hesitate before challenging us, a delay of judgment which could prove crucial to our success. Our moving at night can only contribute to their confusion."

"Those who don't participate in the initial attack can be held back as reinforcements or in the event cover is needed for any eventual retreat." She waited for him to finish.

"I want you to take every non-Cossuutian soldier with you on two of the skids and four of the floaters, assume a position halfway back up the gully, and wait."

"Yes, sir," she said uncertainly. "Wait for what, sir?"

Ranji did not hesitate. "Developments."

The squad commander was tapping her nose with a forefinger. "What you say about surprise versus firepower makes sense, sir, but there are no more than twenty or thirty soldiers from Cossuut in my unit. I'm afraid that if you go in with so few you'll achieve surprise but little else." Assertive murmurs rose from her non-Cossuutian subordinates. By their silence Ranji saw that Tourmast and Weenn sided with him.

He hadn't convinced the others, though. If the argument continued and the squad commander remained obstinate, sooner or later someone would think to pass the proposal on to field headquarters. He knew what kind of response that would produce. It would mean the end of everything he'd planned. Nor could he hope to wait for another chance that might not come. He *had* to convince her.

Staring straight into the female Ashregan's eyes, he tried to will her to his way of thinking. "I understand your concerns but if we don't try this, we'll have wasted a unique opportunity. Either we do it my way or we don't do it at all." He leaned as close as courtesy would allow, trying to utilize his overbearing height. "Surely you see that it has to be done my way?"

She started to reply, caught herself, and blinked. "Yes, of course you are right. It has to be that way. I'm sorry. I just did not see it at first." Her tone was perfectly level as she addressed her bewildered subordinates. "The Field Unifer is right. His is the best way." As Ranji straightened she turned back to him.

"We will position ourselves as you suggest and wait for further orders."

"Good." Though pleased, Ranji was a bit startled at the speed with which she acquiesced. "With fewer troops we can get in and back out that much faster."

"Yes, sir," she murmured agreeably. "Whatever you say, sir."

Thick smoke and the onset of a dismal evening combined to conceal the bustle of activity in the gully as soldiers responded to the new orders, changing craft according to whispered directions. When all was done, the two floaters and single transport skid in the forefront of the column held only special troops from Cossuut.

"You're sure you know what to do?" Ranji and the Ashregan squad commander stood up to their ankles in gully mud, enveloped in near total darkness. All suit and vehicle lights had been turned off lest someone inside the Weave compound spot them moving about.

"Yes, honored Unifer. I am to assume a defensive position and wait for developments."

"Don't forget it." If she thought his emphasis redundant, she chose not to point it out.

With Tourmast and Weenn at his side he watched as the two heavily laden skids and their escorting floaters made their way back up the canyon. They were soon swallowed by the smoke-filled night.

"You sure won her over fast," Tourmast commented.

Ranji gazed in the wake of the last floater. "Not really. My way *is* the best way."

"Is it?"

He frowned and turned to his friend. "You don't believe in my plan?"

Tourmast essayed the kind of thin Ashregan grin he'd grown up with. "I have my doubts." He glanced at Weenn. "But we believe in you, Ranji. Because of what you accomplished back home. Because of Koba, and Eirrosad."

Ranji was more shaken than he cared to admit. He'd have to proceed carefully. If he lost the confidence of such as these, it would be they and not the Ashregan squad leader who would bring his unjustifiable tactics to the notice of higher command.

Of course, if it got to that point, it would mean that everything he'd planned and hoped for had failed anyway, and what happened to him would no longer matter. And he knew that if he tried to intimidate Tourmast the way he had the Ashregan, that tough Cossuutian noncom would simply laugh at him. From here on everything had to go smoothly, he knew. There would be no time for involved explanations and no second chances.

Tourmast was right. The squad commander had given in with surprising ease. It was something to think about . . . later.

Saguio ventured an encouraging sign as Ranji and the two noncoms climbed aboard the remaining skid. Ranji found himself wondering what his brother would look like without his genetically engineered cranial ridges and unnaturally expansive eye sockets, with protruding nose and ears and shortened fingers. If everything went according to plan, he might soon have the chance to find out. He kept his expression carefully neutral.

"We will wait until midnight local time," he told his subordinates.

When there was no more time left he gathered his friends and fellow soldiers close around him. Communicators carried his words to those mounted on the pair of flanking floaters outside.

"You should all have been briefed by now. Since they have a lower profile the two floaters will try the gap first, keeping as close to the ground as possible. If they make it through undetected and without damage or injury to those aboard, the rest of us will follow on the skid.

"If the radiation from the aurora dome doesn't fry us through our armor or incapacitate our vehicles, the plan is to keep moving down the gully until it passes close to a structure. At that point those on the floaters will abandon their vehicles and attempt to force an entrance. As we will by then be inside the defensive perimeter the likelihood is strong that individual buildings will not be guarded.

"If entry is successful the rest of us will follow in twos and threes.

The one thing we don't want is to bunch up in a large group which could easily attract attention."

A soldier in back gestured for attention. "Your pardon, Unifer, but leaving our vehicles behind means going in without heavy weapons.

"That's right, but remember: if at all possible, we want to capture this facility, not destroy it. We'll be a lot less conspicuous without them and once we're inside it would only inhibit our maneuverability anyway. If things get too tight, we can always return to the gully and bring them on line." He let his gaze rove over his expectant audience.

"I want every one of you to take the attitude that we're out to avoid a fight." Bemused muttering rose from the group. "No shooting, no killing unless in self-defense. If we can just keep our calm we may be able to stroll into sensitive areas and quietly take over."

"That's not how we did it on Eirrosad." This time the objection came from the center of the group. Ranji didn't waste time trying to identify the speaker.

"This isn't Eirrosad," he reminded them quietly. "It's a civilized world, with much worth preserving. Our goals should include the concept of minimal destruction. Any idiot can fire at anything that moves. It takes a true soldier to know when to pick his shots."

"It's unnatural," said someone else.

The irony of his reply was not lost on Ranji. "You know, you're starting to sound exactly like a bunch of Humans."

No one had a rejoinder for that, the ultimate insult.

"What happens if we do manage to make it inside?" Weenn said into the ensuing silence. "There'll be illumination. Under lights we look a lot less Human."

"So does our armor," Ranji admitted. "We won't fool anyone who gets close into thinking we're Human, but our shapes are Human enough that at a distance or on first glance they may very well hesitate, and he who hesitates is lost."

Tourmast's gaze narrowed. "That's a Human expression, Ranj."

"Consider the applicability and not the source." Ranji stared at his subordinate and friend, focusing on the facial ridges that no longer looked natural. From experience he knew that they could be removed, but first he had to excise doubt and ignorance, and keep those around him alive long enough to perform the necessary preparatory intellectual and emotional surgery. His revelations would be of little use to the dead.

"This is crazy," Weenn was muttering. "Precisely the sort of thing one would expect from you, Ranji-aar. It also just might work."

"If you pull this off," Tourmast was saying, "you'll be the biggest hero since Sivwon-ouw of Hantarie."

"I'm not interested in herodom. I'm just trying to accomplish the maximum gain with the minimum risk to life." Ranji turned and considered the smoky view forward. "If our latest information is correct, the installation is currently being operated principally by Hivistahm, with Massood and S'van assistance and Massood defenders. There will also be the usual scattering of other species. Doubtless some Human soldiers will be present."

"It doesn't matter if they're all Humans in there," said someone behind him. "We'll handle them, Unifer!"

How much more than your safety I am now charged with none of you can imagine. He checked his chronometer.

"Very well then. It's not time yet. Ready yourselves, and those of you on guns and sensors keep alert. All the enemy has to do to ruin our plans radically is overfly this gully and take one look down."

Between the smoke, fumes, and moonless night, the darkness when they finally began to move was stygian. Fitfull bursts of light flared occasionally overhead as intelligent shells and missiles expunged one another with joyful determination. Energy beams probed vaporous reaches, singeing atmosphere and soil, seeking enemies. Ranji was a gratified witness to the ballet of destruction: it would make the work of the defenders' detection systems more difficult.

Oblivious to the petty discord of contumacious sentients, a storm blew in from the east. Wind and driving rain stirred the swirling clouds of smoke, putting out fires and driving exposed soldiers on both sides to shelter. Thunder and lightning would serve to further confuse sensitive detectors on both sides. Ranji knew they had to move quickly now. If the gully down which they were traveling filled with runoff from the foothills, his entire plan of action would have to be abandoned. Neither skid nor floaters were designed to operate underwater, much less their occupants.

Everyone held their breath as the first floater eased beneath the lightly glowing wall of the aurora dome. A generating pylon just to the left of the gully gleamed on the pilot's screen, its lethal outline clear and sharp despite the torrential downpour.

Moments later the second floater followed, powered down to the point where its landing skids dragged in gully-bottom mud. Once on the other side of the charged aerogel dome its pilot pivoted the craft to signify that they had made the transition safely.

The much bulkier, less maneuverable transport skid rose and moved slowly forward, its air-repulsion units functioning at the minimum level necessary to lift it off the surface. Ranji found his attention flicking between the bank of sensors that would scream for attention if the aurora dome began to affect the craft's instrumentation and a rearward-facing detector. At any moment he feared that a wall of water might come rushing down the gully, forcing them upward into dangerous prominence.

But the water level remained unchanged beneath the advancing skid, and the sensors slept on.

Once safely inside the defensive perimeter the three craft regrouped lest even their weak emissions be picked up by the complex's defenders. Tight-beam communicators were not employed. Instead, Weenn passed instructions to the floater pilots by climbing out onto the dripping nose of the transport skid and yelling at them through the rain. Ranji smiled to himself. So much for advanced technology. Its unavoidable drawback was that no matter how clever in design, as soon as you employed it to disturb or otherwise make use of the usable electromagnetic spectrum, some other equally sophisticated device somewhere else could sense its operation. Not so two people chatting back and forth.

Still advancing on minimum power, the three vehicles drove deep into the heart of the energy-distribution complex, following the winding path of the gully. Once everyone tensed as a large freight skid thrummed past just ahead of them, gravid with cargo. As it was not a military vehicle it possessed no sensing equipment of its own, and the crew was intent only on their assigned destination, not the familiar, unremarkable terrain they were crossing. No one looked outside and down, and so the huddled intruders were not seen.

Where the gully made a sharp bend to the west it widened slightly, leaving a steep bank on one side and a shallow muddy beach on the other. There they disembarked from their cumbersome vehicles, Tourmast in particular bemoaning the need to leave behind the heavy weapons that were mounted on the skid. All internal power was shut down as the troops assembled outside in the rain and muck.

"Remember," their Unifer admonished them, his visor flipped up to expose his face to the rain and darkness, "from here on you have to try and look like Humans, walk like Humans, think like Humans." Nervous laughter rose from people as yet unaware that they were being instructed to act like themselves. The mounting irony threatened to overwhelm Ranji.

"What happens if we're challenged?"

He squinted at Weenn through the pounding rain. "We're a battle squad on our way to take up newly assigned positions. Nobody shoots, nobody even makes a hostile grimace unless I give the word. I'll handle any confrontations. I can speak Human pretty good, without the aid of a translator."

Tourmast was close by his side. Very close. "I didn't know you could talk Human, Ranj." The downpour muffled his words. "When did you pick that up?"

"What did you think I've been doing all the time I haven't been talking to anybody? There's a lot you don't know about me, Tourm. Maze me if there isn't a lot you don't know about yourself." He headed off into the rain, leaving his friend and subordinate to gaze after him thoughtfully.

Scouts from the floaters scrambled up the crumbling north wall of the gully, momentarily vanished, then returned to indicate that the grounds surrounding the nearest large structure were occupied only by decorative plants, walkways, and fountains arranged according to typical Wais design. Advancing at the run in double file, the rest of the squad followed. Exterior lights from the building and other nearby structures scarcely illuminated the line of dim bipedal shapes that splashed forward through dark rain and expanding puddles.

With a very few exceptions a door is recognizable anywhere civilization has taken hold. As expected, no guard lingered in the downpour outside the one they soon confronted. A small amber glowlight shed minimal illumination on the solid landing below. While the rest of the squad hugged the shadows, Ranji tried the door pull. It opened easily.

The light inside was much brighter than he would have preferred, but there was little to be gained by trying another structure. They were in a relay or switching station of some kind. Around them massive machinery hummed with purpose, oblivious to the conflict that raged outside as loads were shifted and power shipped to urban centers far to the south. Illumination came from lightstrips laid into ceiling, walls, and floor. Those in the floor were color-coded.

Muttering an order to Tourmast, he waited nervously until everyone was inside out of the storm. As Weenn shut the exterior door behind the last soldier a pair of Massood appeared in the corridor just ahead. One was intent on a recorder pad while her companion recited readings from a panel of telltales. He grunted something, started to move on to the next in series, and froze as his eyes met Ranji's. One long-fingered hand instinctively reached for the sidearm secured at his waist.

"Don't do that!" Ranji's Massood was erratic, and he hastened to adjust the translator built into his field visor as he approached the pair. "We're here to talk, not fight." Glancing back at his troops, he added in a terse whisper, "Try to look relaxed and indifferent."

The Massood's cat eyes widened slightly as the figure in field armor slowly came forward. The female stood motionless, still clutching the recorder pad. Ranji felt his companions' eyes on his back, heard their confused whispers as they wondered what their Unifer was up to. But they were mindful of his orders, and kept their weapons lowered.

He stopped an arm's length away from the towering, lanky, gray-furred figure. Vertical pupils expanded and contracted. Both short, pointed ears were cocked sharply forward. Whiskers twitched violently. The Massood was clearly confused.

"We're not hostile," Ranji assured it.

The technician swayed slightly. "But you are Ashregan," it declared with certainty.

"That doesn't matter. I'm telling you the truth."

He expected further argument, wondering how he was going to persuade them before someone in his squad came forward, gun at the ready, to see what was going on.

Instead, the Massood's twitching eased and it relaxed visibly. "I believe you."

"Yes," added his companion with utterly unexpected alacrity, "we believe you."

Desperation must make a man convincing, he told himself, bemused but much relieved. "Why don't you go and inform your superiors of our arrival? Tell them there's a squad of armed altered Ashregan down here ready to surrender. We'll await your return."

"That is a good idea." The two technicians turned and departed. Ranji waited until they were safely on their way before rejoining his companions.

Their unease was palpable. "What's going on?" Tourmast wasn't the only one who crowded close, demanding an answer. Saguio's anxious face was visible behind his visor. "Why'd you let them leave like that?"

"What did you tell them? They didn't look worried," Weenn asked.

During the walk back Ranji had composed a response. "I told them that we were a special floating unit disguised to look like Ashregan."

"And they *believed* that?" Tourmast was more than doubtful.

"You saw what happened, didn't you?" said Saguio. "They just walked away quietly. No fear, no panic. Just like we were allies."

The Sub-Unifer wasn't convinced but couldn't think of anything else to say. Nothing he could envision nor anything in his training had prepared him for the scenario he'd just witnessed. "What now?" he muttered.

"We go forward, of course." Ranji turned and beckoned casually. Several soldiers exchanged glances, but all followed.

They had nearly traversed the length of the switching station when Weenn, advancing on the right, called for a halt. Tension took hold of the squad as they sensed movement in front of them.

"Something here doesn't make sense." Tourmast gripped his weapon, waiting for the sensors in his hood and visor to interpret what he couldn't see with his own eyes.

"Everything makes sense," Ranji assured him quietly.

"There they are!" A startled soldier shouted as she started to raise her rifle. Ranji rushed out in front of her, raising his voice.

"No shooting, I said!" In the stunned faces of those who gaped at him there was much confusion and in several cases, the first inklings of painful suspicion. Saguio could be counted among the latter.

By the time anyone thought of wresting command it was too

late; they were completely surrounded by armed Massood. Engulfed in an unprecedented and inexplicable calm, intruders and defenders regarded one another nervously.

"Stranger and stranger." Tourmast regarded his friend and superior closely. "Why haven't they fired on us?"

Feeling more vulnerable than he ever had, and with good reason, Ranji addressed his troops. "Turn over your weapons." He glanced in Tourmast's direction. "They haven't fired because I've informed them that we're surrendering."

"We're doing *what*?" Weenn blurted.

"Surrendering." His eyes roved over the squad, trying to seek out the one unsteady weapon that could reduce his plans to chaos. "This is an order. You are to comply . . . now. If the thought troubles any of you note that we're thoroughly outnumbered."

Someone mumbled loudly. "Traitor!"

Flinching, Ranji tried but failed to identify the speaker. "I'm no traitor, as you'll see. I know exactly what I'm doing and everything will be explained to you so that you understand."

"What's there to understand?" A resigned Tourmast deactivated his rifle and slowly placed it on the floor. "It looks pretty straightforward to me." His tone left no illusions about what he was feeling.

Ranji walked over to him. "I know what you're thinking, Tourm, but you're operating under a significant number of mistaken assumptions."

Tourmast didn't meet his gaze. "Is that so? What sort of 'mistaken assumptions'? That you're someone any of us should continue to pay attention to, for example?" Around them disgruntled, angry Cossuutians were laying down their arms under watchful Massood eyes.

Ranji held his temper. "For starters, how about the fact that you're not Ashregan, but Human."

Tourmast's expression twisted unpleasantly. "My first thought was that you're a traitor and a coward, but I see now that's not fair. You're only crazy."

"It would shock you to know how many times I wished it were that simple." He backed up and raised his voice. "All of you, listen to me! We're not Ashregan who've been modified to look and fight like Humans. We're Humans who've been raised to believe that we're Ashregan. I'm sure that at one time or another you've all noticed and remarked on the similarities, from our reaction times and muscular density to our physical stature and enthusiasm for combat."

"What nonsense is this?" The brief speech had done nothing to convince Tourmast of his friend's thesis. Or his sanity. "It's all been explained to us from childhood. Such characteristics are the gifts of the Teachers, given to us so that we may better defend the Purpose."

"Rather than given us gifts they've stolen our birthright," Ranji shot back. "We *are* Human. No Ashregan can be 'modified' to do what we've done. All our lives are lies. Yours, mine, my brother's." Utterly baffled, Saguio gaped at his mad sibling. "All of us.

"Once we were all wholly Human children, or at least Human embryos. We were abducted, stolen from our parents, and without consent surgically and genetically altered solely to serve the Amplitur's needs. They placed us with Ashregan families, gave us Ashregan histories, had us raised to believe we were Ashregan. They've trained us to fight as Ashregan warriors, and when they're satisfied with our performances, we'll be withdrawn from combat." He paused for emphasis. "For breeding. So that we'll pass on the traits they've inserted in us to our unknowing offspring."

"You forget one thing," said a soldier as she reluctantly divested herself of her weapons. "I myself have felt the Teachers in my mind. Most of us have. If we were Human something in us would resist such Teacher contact. This is a fact that is widely known."

"True," Ranji replied, "but what's not widely known is that the Amplitur have inserted into each of our brains a special neural nexus of their own design." He tapped his forehead. "Here. Through means no one as yet properly understands it negates the mechanism in the Human nervous system which responds defensively to attempted Amplitur probing. It renders us susceptible to their mental 'suggestions.' " The Massood soldiers, he noticed, were paying as much attention to him as his fellow Cossuutians.

"Why should we believe you?" Without really understanding why, Weenn found himself wavering. "Why should we believe anything you say?"

"Because I've seen the nexus inside my own skull." He swallowed. "Many of you have heard the story of my miraculous survival on Eirrosad. It's all falsehood. I did not spend months wandering alone in the jungle. Instead, I was captured and taken to a world called Omaphil, where Hivistahm surgeons severed the connections between the Amplitur nexus and the rest of my brain. As a freed, restored Human on Eirrosad I saw how Amplitur probes were used to manipulate the rest of you. I saw because self-determination had been restored to me, if not the biological defenses common to all natural-born Human beings.

"It nauseated me, and it made me angry. I determined to bring the truth to as many of my fellow abductees as possible. Until we were sent here I had no idea how to do that because I knew that as soon as I started trying to explain you'd think me insane and have me turned over to the psychologists. They, in turn, would call in the Amplitur. And that would likely be the end of me as a free-thinking, independent-minded individual.

"I understand what you're going through right now, what you're thinking. I understand because I fought the idea as hard as you're fighting it this minute."

"They did something to you, all right," Weenn murmured sadly. "Affected your mind somehow. Messed up your thoughts."

Ranji was nodding grimly. "I know words alone won't be enough to convince you, because they weren't enough to convince me. You're going to have to see the scanner images and the rest of the proof for yourselves."

Under the watchful gray cat eyes of a group of wary and very puzzled Massood, the disarmed Cossuutians were led from the switching station. Outside, the rain had eased. A cluster of Hivistahm and Massood hovered at the edge of the gully where Ranji's people had abandoned their vehicles.

"Images can be faked," someone in the group muttered.

Ranji was ready for every objection because not long ago he'd voiced them himself. "True, but close-quarter surgery cannot. I don't expect any of you to believe or understand until one of you undergoes the same operation I did while the rest look on. You can't deny the evidence inside your own heads."

Tourmast strode disconsolate but thoughtful across the damp walkway. "So someone has to volunteer themselves for the operating table. The enemy's operating table."

"You're going to have to stop thinking of Humans as the enemy. The enemy is us, we are them. I know it's going to take a tremendous readjustment on everyone's part."

"Our Unifer," Weenn muttered. "Master of understatement."

"I know how hard this is." Ranji implored his friends. "You're going to have to throw out everything you think you know, think you feel. But it can be done. It'll be easier for you than it was for me because you have me to help you. I had only Hivistahm and Humans."

They entered a large angular building fronted with sheets of bronzed translucence that glittered in the walkway lightstrips.

"This operation," Tourmast persisted. "Is it risky?"

"So I was told. I won't lie to you. Dangerous or not, everyone will have to undergo it sooner or later."

"What about this?" A female soldier had removed her now unnecessary hood and visor. She ran gloved fingers along her cranial ridge.

"More Amplitur handiwork," Ranji told her. "Along with the diameter of our eye sockets, the length of our fingers, and the other physical differences. Under the right instruments the proof is clearly visible, and it can all be corrected." He touched the calcareous mass above his recessed right ear. "This is a prosthesis. I've already seen myself as a Human. Great revelations sometimes spring from small sources."

"No Hivistahm or Human's operating on me," someone in the middle of the column muttered. Angry whispers indicated he was not alone in his determination.

"I'll do it," a voice announced unexpectedly.

Ranji looked into the crowd, to find his brother meeting his gaze.

"As far as I know, Ranj, you've never lied to me." Saguio surveyed his fellow fighters, many of them childhood friends. "If Ranjiaar says this is the truth, then I believe him."

"Sagui, it doesn't have to be you. We can . . ."

"What's the matter, Unifer?" A belligerent young woman pushed her way toward him. "Afraid to have your own flesh and blood go down on the table?"

"Yeah," said someone else accusingly. "Don't you want him made more 'Human'?"

"Don't you see?" Saguio importuned his brother. "It has to be me. If I don't have the operation, neither will anyone else."

Intending to reply, Ranji found himself choking on his objections. His brother was right, of course. Saguio had always been smarter than his older sibling had given him credit for.

Tourmast put a comradely arm around his superior's shoulders. "We'll all be watching closely when the Hivistahm cut your brother open, Ranj. It would be well for them to find something. Because if they don't, no matter where they imprison us or how they treat us or what they do to us, one of us somehow, sometime, will find you and kill you." He gave Ranji's shoulder a suggestive squeeze before removing his hand.

The response was steely cold. "If nothing is found you won't have to worry about finding and killing me, Tourm. Because I'll have attended to that particular detail myself." The Sub-Unifer grunted under his breath. There was nothing more to be said. They quite understood one another.

The dialogue was unnecessary, Ranji knew. The Hivistahm surgeons would find an Amplitur-induced nexus inside his brother's skull, just as they had within his own. They had to. Otherwise it would mean that he truly had been lied to, had somehow been thoroughly and disastrously fooled.

He refused to consider it. Another attempt to so drastically rotate his perceptions and rewrite his sense of self would put an end to him as efficiently as could Tourmast.

The column turned left at the end of the corridor. A gaping double door beckoned, and they were herded into a high-ceilinged chamber packed with instrumentation.

The Massood officer who'd taken them in charge vanished, to reappear moments later in the company of a harried-looking Human who struggled to mine sleep from his eyes. His brushy crown of red hair jolted memories Ranji thought long buried.

"What the hell is this?"

Ranji walked up to him. He was taller than the man, though not the armed Massood who stood nearby.

"My name, sir, is Ranji-aar. Despite that I am not Ashregan but Human, like you. So are my companions."

"You don't say." Having cleared his eyes, the man began rubbing his chin. "Part of you looks Human, part Ashregan. We've heard about your kind."

"The result of Amplitur bioengineering performed on Human infants and embryos," Ranji explained.

"Sounds like antimat to me. What do you expect me to do with you?" Nearby, the Massood officer's nose wrinkled in the presence of so many strange smells.

"Get in touch with your Military Council. Contact the central medical facilities on the Yula world of Omaphil, and if he's still there, ask for a certain Hivistahm First-of-Surgery. I was there not long ago. They'll tell you all about me." Exhausted beyond measure, Ranji sank to the floor on shaky legs. "In fact, they'll be more than a little relieved to hear that you've spoken with me."

The Human exchanged a glance with the Massood, who curled an upper lip by way of response. "Assuming I go to the trouble of making such contact, what am I supposed to say?"

"Tell First-of-Surgery to come with as many skilled surgeons as the Weave can spare. Tell him there's work for them here."

The Human's gaze narrowed. "At the moment we're being hard pressed by the rest of your friends. As you undoubtedly know, the local population is worse than useless in the face of armed invasion. That leaves it up to us temporary immigrants to try and save their world for them. Right now that's all that concerns me. This is no place for a medical convocation. Yet you expect me to requisition the use of deep-space relay time on behalf of some half-Ashregan freak, because he wants to see a doctor?"

Ranji looked up tiredly. "If you don't, I can guarantee that the remainder of your military career will be spent tending sanitation facilities on the airless moon of Earth."

The Massood leaned forward and whispered in broken Human. "Consider: Though armed they have committed no violence. After successfully breaching our defenses without raising any alarm they surrendered peacefully when they could have caused a great deal of damage. While I also view the creature's words with the greatest suspicion, it cannot be denied that there may be more to this than self-delusion."

Silently the Human officer pondered the tall armored enigma that called itself Ranji-aar. "How'd you get inside the dome, anyway?"

"I'll explain everything . . . as soon as you get in touch with your superiors and verify what I've told you."

Another pause, whereupon the man reluctantly turned and shouted something in guttural Human. There was movement in the corridor outside. The Massood leaned forward politely, whiskers twitching, lower lip curled slightly downward to expose sharp teeth.

"We are complying with your suggestions. You must understand that it will take some time to make contact and receive a response. Until then you and your troops will be held under guard and appropriately treated."

Ranji nodded tiredly, free at last to employ whatever Human gestures he wished. "Thank you. I have one additional request. I ask that you isolate me from my companions."

The Massood officer said nothing, but the fine erectile fur on his muzzle stiffened slightly.

20

It was strange to sit by himself in the room they had given him and wish for the defeat of Birachii and other old friends. If they overran the distribution complex and "rescued" Ranji and the other captives, even Saguio's determination to support his brother might falter. Certainly there would be no reunion with First-of-Surgery, no revealing, liberating operations for his companions. He would be shipped off-world at first opportunity, an object of anger and pity for the curious Amplitur to prod and probe.

But deprived of its Commander's strategic skills, the attack faltered. Birachii and Cossinza's squads failed to dislodge the installation's defenders. Even as they lamented the loss of the brave assault team led by their friend and Unifer, they fell back to the protection of the foothills and requested instructions from Regional Command.

Two weeks later a column of heavily armed and armored attack sleds arrived at the distribution complex, having fought off sporadic enemy attacks all the way from Usilayy, Ulaluable's capital city. The Massood and Human officers in charge of defending the installation were surprised to learn that the convoy had made the dangerous run not to bring reinforcements but solely to escort the tiny clutch of prisoners back to the capital.

The pressure of coordinating the center's defense didn't allow much time for casual conversation. Now it was too late. But the Human officer who'd confronted Ranji on that rainy, confusing night many days earlier did manage to be present when he and his companions were being loaded aboard the armed sleds.

"Look, I don't know who or what you are or how much of your story is true," he told his former prisoner, "but if you are Human under all that extraneous calcification, how did you come to look like this?"

Ranji glanced back at him. "I told you. The Amplitur."

The man nodded sagely. "Wouldn't put anything past the squids. But this . . ." His voice trailed off. "Will you do me a favor? We don't know each other and you certainly don't owe me anything, but when you get to wherever it is you're going, and your situation is finally resolved, will you let me know what the results are? As one curious primate to another?"

"I'll try." They parted with a handshake. The wholly Human gesture at last felt easy and natural to Ranji. The unconvinced among Ranji's fellow soldiers did not hesitate to curse the exchange.

In contrast to its arrival, the convoy's run back to Usilayy was uneventful. Having decided to concentrate their firepower on specific targets, the invading Crigolit and Ashregan had few personnel to spare for disruptive sorties of dubious military value. Had they known that Ranji and his companions were traveling with the convoy, its progress would have been considerably reduced. But as far as Ashregan command was concerned, they'd perished bravely while trying to infiltrate an enemy installation. Notification of that conclusion was already on its way to friends and relations.

Never having had the opportunity to examine Humans at close range, Ranji's companions were forced to admit the extraordinary similarities between themselves and their guards, while the Humans in the convoy regarded their prisoners with equal dubiety and puzzlement. Anyone who continued to insist that captors and captives were not somehow related was asking a lot of the principle of convergent evolution.

Everyone knew, however, that physical appearance was not what mattered when evaluating potential enemies or allies. What was important was what individuals believed and how they thought, and in that respect the gulf between was still wide. With the possible exception of their enigmatic leader, the clutch of captives remained wholly Ashregan in attitude and outlook.

Usilayy betrayed no sign of the war that raged around distant strategic centers and military targets. The city simmered beneath a serene autumnal sun, genial and bustling, ablaze with late-season flowers and trees that dripped coppery-colored leaves into neatly domesticated streams and dancing fountains. Within its protected and manicured confines the notion of war seemed a far-off, abstract obscenity.

Wais officials left disposition of the special prisoners to grim-faced Massood and Humans, studiously avoiding allies and enemies alike.

Despite the knowledge that he'd done remarkably well in safely delivering twenty-five of his companions to the Weave, Ranji couldn't help but lament the absence of good friends like Soratii and Cossinza. Their deliverance would have to await additional progress. With luck the invasion would fail and they would be captured before they could be evacuated.

If not, at least Tourmast and Weenn and the rest could be shown the truth. Afterward they could somehow be returned home or to their units, there to further spread the knowledge of what the Amplitur had done to them. They'd have no other choice, any more than had Ranji.

It would all have to be done with the greatest stealth and care lest the Amplitur learn what was happening. Ranji would not put it past the Teachers to sorrowfully and with great regret put an end to an unsuccessful experiment by having the several thousand participants still under their control quietly terminated.

It was proposed that the captives observe the operation via special monitors set up for that purpose, but despite the fact that no actual cutting was involved, Tourmast and the others would have none of that. Unanimously, they insisted on being present in person. Otherwise they would believe nothing.

In appropriate garb they crowded into the operating theater. It was spacious, spotless, and elegant, as befitted a Wais-built facility. Visible instruments mirrored in design the multitude of flowers that carpeted the grounds outside. In aspect it was far more reassuring than intimidating.

Ranji was with his brother in Preop. Their respective situations notwithstanding, it was Saguio who did most of the comforting.

"Relax, Ranj. If what you've been saying is true, then I've nothing to worry about."

"It's still a complex operation." Ranji gazed down at his brother. "Even if they are just severing neurons and not excising the nodule itself."

"Hey, you went through it, and look at you: no crazier than usual." Saguio grinned tightly. "Not that I'm not ready to get it over with."

"I'll be there every minute. So will the whole squad."

"Yeah, great." Fear momentarily shadowed the younger man's face. He forced it aside. "Don't let 'em cut anything I might want to use later."

An O'o'yan arrived to administer a glass of water containing an oral anesthetic. Five minutes later two of the short, reptilian meditechs were guiding the cushioned operating pallet and its comatose cargo into the Surgery.

Conversation died among the onlookers as Saguio's pallet arrived and was locked in position. The O'o'yan immobilized his head with air clamps, then stepped back. Several Massood guarded the doorways.

A pair of Hivistahm assumed operators' positions at the surgical station. They were accompanied by a Human surgical programmer, the most competent on Ulaluable. After scrutinizing them dubiously, Ranji walked over and put a hand on the top of the console.

"Wait a minute. Where's First-of-Surgery?"

The nearer of the two Hivistahm blinked up at him. "I Second-of-Surgery am, chief physician on Ulaluable. The First-of-Surgery to whom you refer unable to come is. Distance and time prohibitive are."

An anxious Ranji looked over at his recumbent, anesthetized brother. Lying there motionless he looked even younger than he was. "None of you have ever been involved in an operation like this. I expected someone experienced."

The other Hivistahm replied stiffly. "I assure you that there is no need our competency to question. The appropriate programming instructions were transmitted and thrice checked before into the computer being entered. Remember that it in control of the actual procedure is. We are present only to check and monitor."

Still Ranji hesitated. "That programming was designed for my skull, my brain. Not Saguio's."

"The instrumentation is designed variations into account to take. Truly calm yourself. If uncertainty arises, we are here to adjudicate."

Tourmast's voice sounded from nearby. "Something wrong, Unifer?"

He could insist they wait until First-of-Surgery came in person from Omaphil. That risked unnerving his fellow Cossuutians even more than they already were. He wavered, staring at the helpless form of his brother.

"Call if off," he said finally, walking around the console. "I don't care how carefully you recorded the necessary instructions, I'm not going to allow . . ." Something stung him in the middle of the back and he whirled. One of the Massood guards was standing there, pointing a narrow metal tube in his direction. Two long fingers were tensed on the complex triggering mechanism.

It seemed as if the Surgery was being pumped full of fog. He stumbled against the console, dimly felt it bang into his back. Through the thickening mist he heard the rising, uncertain murmuring of his fellow soldiers, and the voice of the Hivistahm in charge.

"Better it is that the patient not remain long under anesthesia. There no danger is. Your leader understandably concerned for his sibling is. He merely tranquilized has been. This way is for him and his brother both better. Everything under control is. By the Circle I, as a physician, swear it."

As the shot's effects spread like a deep massage throughout his body Ranji lost control of his lower limbs. Two Massood caught him under the arms and at the ankles. He felt himself being carried from the room. Fighting to shout, to call for help, he discovered that his larynx had been rendered as dysfunctional as his legs.

A face appeared before his eyes, its outlines swimming. Weenn gazed down at Ranji as he was carried past. The fluid expression on his friend's face was unreadable.

When he awoke he sat up in the bed so sharply that the O'o'yan attendant who happened to be checking his waste-recovery system fainted, with the result that instead of shouting imprecations and demands, Ranji found himself bending over the unconscious creature trying to stop the slight bleeding at the back of its head.

His return to consciousness, not to mention his abrupt physical reaction, had alerted monitoring hospital instrumentation. Hivistahm

and other O'o'yan came running. Those first on the scene were
greeted by the disconcerting sight of the Human warrior bending
over the bleeding attendant. The tension level rose quickly until Ranji
was able to explain. Thus reassured, they hurried to assist both
O'o'yan and patient.

Ranji apologized, and the attendant absolved him of any blame.
It was his fault, the O'o'yan explained. Though an experienced meditech, he'd never worked with Humans before. It was his responsibility to be appropriately prepared, and he ought to have anticipated
potential shocks.

"Your concern is appreciated," the attendant concluded.

"Never mind that." An impatient Ranji evaluated shoulder insignia until he located the highest-ranking Hivistahm present. "How is
my brother? Where is he?"

"He's fine." A young man stood grinning in the doorway. "Resting comfortably." As he entered Ranji saw above his heart the sym-
bol of the Human combat meditech corps . . . the traditional caduceus
with its entwined snakes spitting caustic venom. "Matter of fact, he's
in the next room."

Ranji started forward, stumbled, and allowed the tech to steady
him. Though concerned, none of the Hivistahm or O'o'yan stepped
forward to offer physical assistance. They were still subject to certain
inherent antipathies only a few of their kind had been able to overcome. They examined the nude primate with professional detachment.

"Take deep breaths," the tech advised Ranji. "Your clothes are
in the side closet."

Ranji nodded and did as he was instructed. When he felt halfway
steady on his feet he dressed. Still fumbling with the seals on his
undersuit he hurried to the next room down the hall. Two Massood
were posted there, two Humans within. At a nod from the tech they
let him pass.

Saguio was sitting up in bed, an entertainment projection dancing
in the air before him. As his brother entered he waved and touched
an unseen button. The projection vanished.

"Hi, Ranj." He smiled easily, looking relaxed and comfortable.
"You look worse than I do."

Ranji put out a hand to steady himself against the wall. "I suppose I must. How are you feeling?"

"Well. I heard what happened to you. That was a nice gesture, but apparently unnecessary. I've been up all morning. You haven't." He looked past his brother to the tech and the guards. "Could we have some privacy, please?"

The tech hesitated, then nodded. Turning, he spoke to the guards, smiled briefly back into the room before following them out into the corridor.

Ranji scanned the room. "Probably isn't any privacy. I'm sure they've had sensors on both of us ever since we got here."

"I'd be surprised if it was any other way. If the situation were reversed, we'd be doing the same. The rest of the squad was in earlier. They watched the operation. It must've been pretty convincing because they all believe you now. So do I, even though I didn't get to see anything. Tourmast said that organ showed up on the visual probe exactly as you described it. The meditechs even let them manipulate the visuals themselves." He ran a hand through his hair. "I don't feel any different."

"No," Ranji told him slowly, "you won't."

"They ran some tests on me right afterward. Stuck me in a machine they said came as close to duplicating a Teacher . . . an Amplitur mind-touch as could be done with circuits and programming. This time I was conscious of what was happening inside my head. I could feel the pushing. Never felt that before." He shifted in the bed, gazed earnestly at his brother. "Is that really what it's like? The Teachers really have been making us do what they want without us even realizing it?"

Ranji nodded slowly, luxuriating in the increasingly familiar Human gesture. "They've always referred to their pushes as 'suggestions.' I suppose that's all they are, except that nobody has the ability to turn one down. Except Humans. The operation doesn't give us back the Human neurodefense mechanism, but it does make us immune to Amplitur suggestion. Those of us who have the surgery will never have to suffer that again."

"And the rest of it, about us being abducted Human children and all, that's true then, too?" Ranji nodded solemnly.

Saguio looked pensive for a while. "It's a lot to handle all at once, Ranj. A lot."

"Sorry. It's not the kind of thing that can be ladled out in small doses."

"How long have you known? Since your disappearance on Eir-rosad, right?" Without waiting for his brother to reply he leaned back against the curving mattress. "I've been Ashregan all my life, and now a few scalpel passes later I'm Human. I wish I *did* feel differently. It might make it easier to accept." He touched his head. "The damned thing's still in there, isn't it?"

"They told me that it's too deeply embedded in the cerebrum to risk removing," Ranji explained. He touched his own skull. "I have one, too, remember. So do all our friends." He found a chair and pulled it over next to the bed. Though designed to support the backside of a Hivistahm tech, it would hold him if he watched his balance.

"There are things that have been bothering me ever since we landed on this world. I wanted to be able to share them with some-one, but I had to wait. Now I can share them with you."

Saguio blinked ingenuously. "Share away."

Ranji hesitated. "What time are they supposed to feed you?"

His brother gave him a strange look but replied readily. "I last ate about an hour ago. I don't imagine I'm due for another feeding until evening."

"Call an attendant. You have the means to do that, don't you?"

"Sure." Saguio thumbed the requisite switch. Moments later a single O'o'yan entered. Ranji addressed it without turning, keeping his eyes on his brother.

"We'd like something to eat, please."

"It is not yet scheduled."

Ranji concentrated on his request. "We really would like some-thing to eat. Now."

The O'o'yan blinked. "Certainly. Do you have a particular meal request?"

"No." Ranji was satisfied with the response. "Whatever you can bring will be fine."

"Very well." The slim little reptilian attendant left to comply.

Saguio was staring intently. At the same time he was quite aware of the presence of untiring monitors in the room.

"What was that all about?"

"Nothing," said Ranji in a slow, deliberately self-contradictory manner. "I was just feeling hungry."

"Oh, yeah. Hungry."

A silent Ranji sat across from his brother, pondering. The sensors overhead could record his words, his expressions, his movements; but they could not read his thoughts.

The experiment only confirmed the hypothesis that had been maturing in his mind ever since he'd had the disagreement with the female Ashregan Unifer in the gully outside the power distribution complex. She'd consented to his radical proposal too quickly, too easily. At the time he'd thought little of it, though it had nagged at him intermittently ever since.

Then had come the confrontation with the two Massood technicians inside the switching station. After that he'd no longer been able to bury his suspicions in the back of his mind.

And now the ready acquiescence to his request for an unscheduled meal. From an O'o'yan, for whom a deviation in scheduling was akin to altering respiration.

He was anxious to test his theory further. On a S'van, perhaps, or a Massood field officer. The effort required was something of a strain, like concentrating for a long time on small print.

According to what the Hivistahm had told him on Omaphil, the effect was electrical in nature. It had been explained to him that there were primitive creatures which could sense such impulses but could not distinguish those generated by the mind from those produced by the rest of the body, nor could they in turn affect them. They could only detect. On Earth they were known as sharks, and the organs capable of detecting and crudely analyzing impulses were called the Ampullae of Lorenzini. Coincidentally, the attitude and temperament of such creatures was said to be not unlike that of Humans themselves.

What name should he give to the related but far more sophisticated organ inside his brain? What did the Amplitur call that portion of their unique minds which could via projection induce subtle alterations in the firing of another sentient's neurons? Induce, adjust, rechannel. Suggest.

As he had suggested to the female Ashregan Sub-Unifer, the pair of Massood technicians, and now to a single O'o'yan medical attendant.

He'd examined and reexamined the period immediately after

his own operation and was positive that for some considerable while thereafter he hadn't possessed such capabilities. Therefore they took time to develop. Perhaps something within the brain took time to heal following the actual surgery. Whatever it was, it was utterly unexpected. Of that he was certain. The Hivistahm surgeons, his fellow Humans, none of them knew or suspected anything.

At present Saguio could do nothing, was completely unaware of the ability that might have unintentionally been bestowed on him as a side effect of the operation. As to whether he would develop anything like it only time would tell. Not a lot of time, either. Ranji would have to watch him very carefully. He was conscious of the fact that whatever had happened to him, to his mind, might constitute something unique, an aberration not to be repeated. Just because it had taken place in his brain as a result of the operation didn't mean it would recur whenever similar surgery was performed on a fellow modified Cossuutian. Individuals might heal, might recuperate differently, with wildly differing results.

"You all right?" Saguio was eyeing him curiously.

Ranji smiled. "Just the lingering effects of whatever it was that Massood smacked me with."

"What was it you wanted to share with me?"

"Tell you later. Right now I want to know how the others are doing."

"Ciscine-oon and Dourid-aer agreed to have the operation as soon as I came out of it and proved to everyone's satisfaction that no harm was involved. Ciscine's probably in surgery right now. The head Hivistahm told me that if all went well they hoped to perform two operations a day until they'd gone through the whole squad. They had a second team standing by to execute the follow-ups."

Ranji frowned. "Follow-ups?"

"You're the one who told me about it. Cosmetic surgery." Saguio scratched his cranial ridge with a too-long finger. "I imagine they'll be coming for me pretty soon. You too, Ranj. If I'm going to be Human, I expect I'd better look the part. Bet I make a better-looking Human than you." He reached out and put a hand on Ranji's shoulder. "You'd better prepare yourself, brother, because when they finish cutting on me there are a lot of questions I mean to ask you."

Ranji gazed back at his sibling. "Don't worry, Sagui. I'll answer every question you've got. In fact, I have answers to questions you haven't begun to formulate."

21

The battle for Ulaluable raged, with the invaders seemingly incapable of making significant headway and the defenders unable to drive them off-world. Meanwhile, the pace of operations continued at a steady two per day as one after another of Ranji's fellow soldiers submitted to the programmed manipulations of the sonic scalpel. The Hivistahm could easily have performed half a dozen of the surgeries per day, but the more dilatory pace allowed the anxious patients to receive greater individual attention during the recovery period, while simultaneously helping to assuage the lingering unease among the as yet untouched.

Having thus insured the Cossuutian prodigals against future Amplitur mental manipulation, Weave Command had no more idea what to do with them than if they had suddenly been presented with two dozen defecting griffins. Their view of Human culture and Humanness being understandably skewed, instructional materials suitable for correcting a lifetime of misconception were provided for the use of the Restorees, as they came to be called. These, combined with the Hivistahm's expert cosmetic surgery and the friendship and compassion of those Humans on the medical staff, helped to speed and ease the defectors' mental and emotional transition from Ashregan to *Homo sapiens*.

As their new Humanness began to take hold and the full import of what the Amplitur had done to them sank in, several volunteered their fighting abilities on behalf of the Weave. Such offers were not so much denied as avoided. Despite the assurances of the Hivistahm surgeons, Weave Command was still suspicious of them, Ranji knew. They could hardly be blamed. He and his friends were an unknown quantity. How unknown not even his brother suspected as yet.

The defectors were kept under close observation, ostensibly to insure their complete and successful recovery. They complied by adapting to their new circumstances with gratifying speed. Before long they were wandering freely among the rest of the Usilayy Human contingent, which was to say that they were restricted to the confines of the military compound lest their appearance on the city streets actively disconcert the natives.

The only Wais Ranji encountered were those official translators and support personnel who had survived the rigorous psychological training that allowed them to interact with combative sentients like Humans and Massood without suffering consequent mental damage. Ninety-eight percent of the population had never seen a Human being in the flesh, and their protective government wanted to keep it that way. The invasion had caused trauma enough.

Not that the Weave compound was confining. It was as lavishly landscaped and exquisitely maintained as the rest of the capital's facilities. The Wais desired to make conditions for their vitally needed if inherently unbalanced allies as comfortable as possible. Grassy hills, streams, small waterfalls, flowers, trees alive with delicate, brightly hued arboreals; all contributed to a placid tranquillity that belied the seriousness of the situation.

Ranji explored the compound with a dedication that provoked mild amusement among his comrades. Rather than being frantic for exercise, however, he was seeking a location where they could hopefully gather in comparative solitude. For mutual contemplation, as he explained to one curious soldier. In reality he was trying to find a place out of sight of prying eyes and ears where he could prepare them for developments they were as yet unaware of.

Eventually he settled on a smooth-sided hollow in a cluster of round, reddish boulders located at the northern limits of the compound. The small pond at the bottom was fringed with tall yellow reeds from which pinkish puffballs occasionally issued, fragile hallmarks of intermittent propagation. Amphibious ground-dwellers scuttled through the water or peeped from cracks in the rocks. It was a natural place to mingle, and their presence there should not provoke excessive comment.

They assembled in twos and threes, chatting among themselves, curious and by now more than a little bored. Ranji had a couple of technicians surreptitiously check the boulders and plants for concealed sensors. They found nothing. Their inspection was far from thorough, but it would have to do. He couldn't wait any longer. If he did, those who had been operated on first might start suspecting things, and in the absence of understanding that could prove danger-ous. None of his companions were blessed with his perspective.

Just in case, he restricted the initial discussions to inconsequential matters. Having established a pattern of meeting regularly in the hol-low, he was careful to divulge nothing of import for several days.

When he finally did broach his feelings they were met with the expected skepticism. Then a soldier named Howmev-eir recalled re-questing and finally demanding of a Hivistahm access to certain his-torical records. Informed initially that such recordings were unavailable to him, upon his insistence they were supplied with a dispatch which startled him.

Nor was his an isolated experience. Upon reflection, several oth-ers among the first dozen who had been operated on recalled similar incidents. They'd sought no deeper explanation beyond a belief that their former captors and new allies were simply doing their best to please them.

"They were doing more than just trying to help out new friends," Ranji explained. "Once each of you insisted, really pressed your point mentally and emotionally, none of them any longer had any choice in the matter, any more than they would have if an Amplitur had made the same requests. Or 'suggestions.' " He eyed them meaning-fully. "Yet if we make similar demands of fellow Humans it doesn't trigger their neural defense mechanism. So this new ability of ours can't be perfectly identical to that of the Amplitur. There are differ-ences."

Tourmast spoke up. "I thought it was strange when they acceded to my request to take a stroll outside the compound last week. We Humans aren't supposed to show ourselves to the natives." He grinned in spite of himself. "Makes them jumpy." Other members of the group excitedly related similar experiences, though these were far from universal. Not everyone had healed yet.

"If what you're suggesting is true, Ranji, we should be able to do pretty much as we please with our hosts."

Ranji nodded. "Except that Humans won't be affected, and if we aren't very careful we'll set off alarms. Asking the Massood for an aircraft, for example, and having them provide it to us would alert the average soldier that something was very definitely amiss. If we don't watch the number and degree of our 'suggestions,' pretty soon the consistently peculiar and contradictory will be tracked back to us. We're already on a kind of postoperative probation to see that we make good Human beings."

"I'm a good Human being." Weenn was strangling an imaginary victim. "I already want to kill every Amplitur I can get my hands on." Suddenly his belligerence vanished, replaced by solemn contemplation. "And I wouldn't mind finding my natural parents, either. If they're still alive."

"Unlikely." Ranji's tone was compassionate but unyielding. Cold reality suggested that all their natural parents were dead, having been replaced long ago by the Ashregan surrogates they all were familiar with.

"If the Amplitur learn what has happened to us, they will do their utmost to have us killed. Judging from the uneasy manner in which the sentients of the Weave regard their Human allies, I wouldn't put it past them to do the same. I have personal experience of that paranoia. As for our fellow Humans, they don't understand themselves, so I would not expect them to understand what has happened to us. Until we better comprehend the consequences and ramifications we must keep this secret, utilizing our new ability only when absolutely necessary.

"As a result of Amplitur genetic engineering and subsequent Hivistahm surgery we have become something new and different, something the Teachers did not foresee. In that regard, all their intricate intriguing has backfired on them. Instead of becoming their most effective soldiers we've been transmogrified into their worst nightmare: Humans who possess the Amplitur ability to suggest. But we are still few. We have a lot to learn about what's happened to us, and we need time. For all any of us know, the talent may fade with age. Other factors we can't imagine may affect it temporarily or permanently. In the meantime we could easily be exterminated by fearful enemies *or* friends." He let his gaze rove the faces of his intent colleagues. "We're going to have to be very careful."

"What I find interesting," said one of the technicians, "is that these neural connections have apparently grown back along entirely new paths. You'd think at least some would have regenerated according to their original Amplitur genetic programming."

"I've been thinking about that, too." Ranji paused. "It suggests to me the presence in the Human brain of some heretofore latent genetic command, as if programming was present but access to the computer denied. The Amplitur provided the necessary access in the form of the engineered neural nodule. When the connections they supplied are surgically interrupted, the brain provides latent reconnection instructions of a different order.

"I've learned that a large portion of the Human brain, our brain, is not used. Perhaps the addition of the Amplitur nexus activates some previously dormant portion not due to fully evolve for another million years or so. After all, the nodule confers no inherent abilities itself. It hasn't given us the ability to communicate as the Amplitur themselves do, mind to mind. It's only an organic electrical switch."

"That's all right," said Tourmast, indicating the technician next to him. "I don't want to know what he's thinking anyway." There was some nervous laughter.

"There might be other changes yet to come," Weenn suggested. "Anybody starts levitating, I'm first in line for instructions." He was only half joking.

"If this is all as you say," the technician murmured, "then it means that at least as far as cerebral structure is concerned, the Amplitur and not the Ashregan or Massood are Humankind's closest relatives. Maybe we should be allied with them after all and not the Weave."

That was a thought which had not occurred to Ranji or anyone else, and it froze the group in contemplative silence for several minutes. Then Tourmast spoke up.

"No. Remember what we were taught: biological verisimilitude and appearance count for nothing. They counted for nothing when we thought we were Ashregan and anxious to fight Humans, and they count for nothing now. As Humans we have to fight the Amplitur because of what they believe, and what they want to *make* us believe. Not because of physiological similarities or differences. The Lepar and the Sspari and the Hivistahm see the universe as we do. They believe in independence of thought and purpose like we do. The Amplitur don't. As a Human I have no intention of being a part of their damned 'Purpose.' Especially after learning the truth of what they've done to us." Murmurs of assent rose from those clustered close around him.

"What about the others?" someone in the group asked.

"Yeah," wondered Weenn. "You forced the truth on us, Ranji,

and we all but killed you for it because we didn't believe. How are we going to spread the news? How are we going to save the rest of our people here and back on Cossuut?"

"Continue to be cooperative, grateful, and helpful," he replied. "Be careful to make as few 'suggestions' as possible. Meanwhile I'll be talking to the authorities here. I have some ideas."

"They're not going to let us go back to Cossuut the way they let you stumble out of the jungle on Eirrosad," Tourmast insisted. "I don't see them taking that kind of risk with so many of us."

"Not to Cossuut," Ranji admitted.

Despite intense questioning, he would say no more.

He made his suggestions with great care, speaking now to a particular S'van, now to an influential Massood. His fellow Humans he avoided utterly, since they could not be similarly persuaded. He let no one help him, preferring to work alone. That way if he failed or caused an alarm to be raised, only he would be suspected.

As expected, strong objections were raised when he finally presented his proposal to Ulaluable's defense command. In support of his intentions he pointed out that only his release on Eirrosad, which at the time had been accompanied by similar reticence on the part of his captors there, had enabled him to liberate the twenty-five of his kind that the Weave now held.

There was much animated discussion, during which support for Ranji's position came from unexpected quarters. From Massood and S'van he had previously persuaded. Those who objected were puzzled by their colleagues' eager acquiescence, but to Ranji's relief their bemusement did not extend to suspicion.

It was therefore reluctantly agreed that much as Ranji had been turned loose on Eirrosad, his rehabilitated comrades would have their Ashregan appearance temporarily restored, whereupon they would be armed and set free in small groups to work their way back to various enemy units, in the hope that they could, as had Ranji, bring in by one means or another more of their kind to receive the benefits of restoring truth and humanizing surgery.

If questioned they were to explain that in the course of combat their squad had been captured and sent to the capital for internment, from whence they had managed to steal several floaters and flee.

Weave pursuit caused them to split up in the hope that it would enable at least some to escape. There was nothing in the story to provoke even an Amplitur into drawing an analogy between their flight and Ranji's earlier "escape" on Eirrosad.

Not everything transpired as hoped or planned. Some of those who went out were "saved" by pure Ashregan or Crigolit forces and could do nothing but bide their time and await reassignment. Others were more fortunate. Rescued by roving squads composed of their own kind, they used materials supplied by the Hivistahm and Humans to begin the slow, cautious process of explanation and conversion. The adamantly reluctant they were finally able to convince through demonstrations of their ability to mentally influence non-Humans such as Ashregan and Crigolit.

As the weeks wore on and the battle for Ulaluable remained stalemated, the rightness of Ranji's course of action was proven by a returning trickle of the Humanly disenfranchised under the guidance of exhausted but triumphant seers like Tourmast and Weenn. The forewarned Weave commanders of installations and regions targeted by the invaders who were thus visited immediately notified Central Command, which sent out heavily armed escorts to convey the bewildered prodigals back to the capital.

There they were promptly subjected to the corrective manipulations of the efficient Hivistahm surgical team under the direct supervision of First-of-Surgery, who had finally arrived from Omaphil, and an avalanche of irrefutable explanation from those who had already undergone and survived the liberating ordeal.

By the end of the Ulaluablian year, more than half of the nearly two thousand modified Human-Ashregan assigned to the invading force had in this fashion been quietly and successfully restored to their birthright and identity as Human beings. Working slowly and patiently and utilizing their newfound skills with discretion, Ranji and his companions had thus far managed to avoid piquing the interest of any enemy officers. They were helped by the fact that the invaders were suffering substantial losses among regular Ashregan and Crigolit as well.

Not all could be saved. More than a hundred had already perished or been evacuated as a result of the fighting. Ranji and his friends grieved for their lost relations even as they persisted in their work.

Ulaluable's defenders had finally begun to dislodge the invaders from their forward positions and to push them back toward the re-supply bases they had established and secured upon landing. Attempts by the enemy to reinforce their situation met with intermittent success, as ships attempted to phase out of Underspace, disgorge their heavily laden shuttles, and vanish into the safety of distorted physics before increasingly effective Weave orbital defenses blasted them out of reality.

It was decided to make an assault on the invaders' planetary head-quarters, located on the southern shore of a vast freshwater lake in the north-central part of the continent, in hopes of taking them by surprise and securing a decisive strategic advantage. It was a risky undertaking and one which received unqualifiedly enthusiastic support from the Wais, who continued to suffer spreading racial trau-matization as a consequence of the invasion. Like most of the Weave races they were desperate to destroy the enemy, even if it meant fighting to the last Massood and Human.

A large group of restored Humans demanded the privilege of leading the attack. At first the notion was resisted by Ulaluable's military command. Though eager, to many the restored soldiers had yet to conclusively prove the permanence of their conversions. What better way, Ranji and his friends argued, than to lead a dangerous assault against their former allies? Debate on the matter raged within the multispecies Command. Eventually it was decided in favor of the supplicants.

After all, certain members of that Command insisted through their subsequent bemusement, they had done nothing more than act favorably and responsibly on the numerous suggestions they had received.

22

It struck him as strange to be carrying Human-designed weapons, though he was familiar enough with them from years of studies on Cossuut. Just as it still seemed unnatural to be fighting alongside Humans and Massood instead of against them.

It was also sobering to be treated as no better than any of the rest of the troops in your battlegroup. Ranji and his companions were used to being considered the elite. Now they formed only one component of a much larger force whose average soldier was presumed to be the equal of their best.

On the other hand, it was a pleasant change to be able to melt into a larger mass of beings, not always to be singled out physically as different from everyone else. Some of the officers knew the full story behind the new squad that spoke fluent Ashregan, but other than finding them interesting oddities the regular troops readily accepted Ranji's people as their own. Tourmast and Weenn and the others quickly found themselves subsumed in an easy, informal camaraderie that would have been inherently excluded by the formalities of the Purpose.

There was something to being Human, they soon decided, that rendered the prospect of proximate battle more exhilarating than ever. Such feelings were enhanced by the fact that they now had much more to fight for than an elegant philosophical abstract.

Like everyone else, Saguio volunteered to participate, but this time Ranji insisted that his brother stay behind. It didn't matter if one of them perished, but it might matter very much if the knowledge Ranji had confided only to his brother vanished without being retained for future study. Saguio protested but could not fault his brother's logic. He agreed to remain in Usilayy.

Ulaluable Weave Command had consented reluctantly to the single strike. If it failed to achieve its objective immediately, all survivors were to pull out fast. Command was as yet unwilling to expose the restored Humans, most of whom were still feeling the aftereffects of cosmetic surgery, to the risks of an extended assault and possible subsequent recapture.

Physically, Ranji and his friends were indistinguishable from the other Humans in the strike force. As none of them had demonstrated any revisionist Ashregan tendencies since their restoration they had been allowed to form fighting squads of their own and maintain their internal lines of command. It was decided it was not necessary yet to integrate them into other Human units. Besides complicating internal communications, separating the newcomers from their own kind could only enforce their sense of isolation. Better for full integration to be achieved naturally instead of by directive. It was also decided that they were likely to fight with greater confidence and skill if surrounded and supported by familiar faces.

So Ranji was able to have Soratii and Weenn and the rest of his friends around him. Brusque Birachii had been saved, too, and Cossinza, she of the liquid voice and lightning reflexes.

But too many of the deceived still slaved in the service of enemy Purpose here and on distant Cossuut for any of the Restorees to rest.

Their salvation would have to proceed one step at a time, he told himself. First the diversion of the Ulaluablian invasion. Then resurrection.

Cossinza hovered nearby, chatting with those she commanded while experimenting with the novelty of the wide smile. Ranji was the target of many such, for during the past months in Usilayy the two of them had grown close. There had been other women. One in particular he remembered, from Omaphil. But Cossinza was of Cossuut and the other was not, and in Cossinza he knew there was no deception. It was good to have someone besides his brother to confide in.

But he continued to broker intimacy with caution, and did not tell her everything. Not yet. For her part she respected the hesitancy she sensed. Ranji's introspective nature was well known to her and her friends. She liked him too much to try and intrude, knowing that when he had something to confess she would be the first to hear of it.

The heavily armored transport sleds and their outriding sliders roared northward at precarious speed, sometimes barely skimming

the surface of plains, hillsides, and lakes. In four days they were beyond the range of ready reinforcements. If they were attacked before
they reached their target, Ranji knew, orders were to break off and
return. Under such circumstances there would be no time to make
insistent suggestions to the contrary.

But the skies and horizon stayed clear of all except startled local
fauna, and the tense strike group raced on toward their objective.

Because of the extreme danger involved, every Human and Massood in the group, including the sled crews, was a volunteer, of which
there had been no dearth once the proposal had been floated. The
strike force was split half and half between Humans, including Ranji
and his friends, and Massood. A few unusually bold Hivistahm techs
had contributed their services, though, of course, not for combat.
Their activity would be confined to sled maintenance and naviga-
tion.

Force tacticians hoped to slip at least ten percent of the small,
highly skilled strike team inside the enemy's defensive perimeter before they could fully mobilize to meet the attack. Hopefully these
troops would wreak sufficient havoc to turn the enemy's attention
inward, thus allowing the rest of the force to collapse the perimeter
at enough points to insure victory. At worst, they would inflict sufficient damage before pulling out to have made the assault worth-
while.

First-of-Surgery and his staff raised what objections they could,
to no avail. Risking a valuable scientific resource like the Restored
for mere military purposes struck him and his colleagues as the height
of uncivilized absurdity. On Omaphil their opinion might well have
prevailed, but Ulaluable was a world under siege, where military needs
took priority. Their Wais hosts, who under more pacific circumstances would have agreed with First-of-Surgery's position, voted
against him.

Besides which the Restored were now considered fully Human.
As such, they had Human rights and could do as they pleased. If they
wanted to participate in scientific research, they were welcome to do
so. It was not the fault or responsibility of Military Command if
what they wanted to do was fight.

Ranji was staring out one of the narrow sled windows at the
manicured landscape of Ulaluable speeding past when Cossinza sat
down next to him, folding herself into a fixed piece of support foam.

There were no chairs on board the transport. Only the foam, which adapted itself freely to a variety of physiognomies. Thus Massood could rest comfortably next to their Human counterparts, and Hivistahm alongside both.

At present they were traveling through high desert, the sleds keeping low enough to kick sand and gravel into the air, unsettling nonburrowing fauna and plants. Such disruption of their carefully nurtured natural order would have displeased the Wais, but there were none aboard to bear witness to the persistent disturbance.

"When Tourmast appeared to tell us what had happened to you and the others we'd thought long dead, I was not alone in thinking that the press of combat had driven him insane." She joined him in staring out the window. "Even after he and those who'd returned with him showed us the proof, I still doubted. It was only when he informed us that he was operating under your command that I began to believe. I've always thought you the best of us, Ranji-aar. It's an opinion I shared with many." She put a comforting hand on his shoulder. "I can't imagine what it must've been like being the first of us to be exposed to the truth."

He continued to stare at the alien landscape racing past before finally turning back to her. "Cossinza, do you feel 'Human'?" He studied her face: pale blue eyes, sharp but small nose, the wide, thin-lipped mouth and prominent cheekbones—a flower seared but not scarred by fire. Strange to look upon a woman without spacious eye sockets or cranial ridges, with a prominent nose and protruding ears. There was less, and yet there was more. Truly beauty was more than bone deep.

She removed her hand and leaned back into the foam. It flexed to accommodate her form. "Sometimes I feel like I've always been Human. It's hardest at night. In your dreams you tend to revert." Her eyes focused on the sled's curved ceiling. "You remember growing up, training, friends and family. Then when you awaken you have to force yourself not to think of them."

"I still wonder if our Ashregan parents were willing participants in the deception or innocent dupes forcibly inducted into their roles by the Amplitur. Some days I hope to find out. Other days I hope I never do." That was a singular ineffable sadness all the Restored shared.

"We have to rely on each other now." She shifted on the foam.

He nodded, glanced back at the window. "You can hate the Amplitur for what they've done to us, but at the same time you have to admire them for trying to defeat an enemy through genetics instead of on the battlefield. It would have taken hundreds of years for their interbreeding plan to have had a debilitating effect on Humankind." He shook his head at the presumption. "No Weave race, and certainly not us, has that kind of patience. Except maybe the Turlog."

"I've never seen a Turlog," said Cossinza. "From what I recall of my studies they're supposed to be pretty hideous to look upon, and antisocial besides." She sat up in the foam and utilized her translator to address a Massood sub-officer seated not far away. "You there! Have you ever seen a Turlog?"

"Only in recordings," the Massood replied pleasantly. "The species is underpopulated."

"Would you know where to find one?"

"Not on Ulaluable. You would have to go to their own world, or one of the major Weave centers."

Cossinza nodded understanding, then suggested almost playfully, "We're both pretty thirsty. How about getting us something to drink?"

The Massood hesitated, gave them an odd look, then rose and ambled off in the direction of the on-board dispenser, his light underarmor gleaming dully. Ranji remonstrated softly with his companion.

"You shouldn't do things like that, Cossinza. It's through lack of respect that dangerous secrets are revealed."

"Take it easy." She smiled across at him. "Some of us aren't as skilled at this suggesting business as you, Ranj. We need to practice."

"Practice on the enemy." He was unmollified. "Not on allies. If we use our abilities too casually, sooner or later some S'van is liable to discern a pattern. I understand that just about everything amuses them, but I don't think they'd laugh at that."

She replied evenly. "In a little while we're going to be killing, maybe be killed in return. I didn't think it would matter so much."

"Try to be more selective in the future." He was deliberately cool.

———

Gunecvod reached the dispenser and called for three containers of cold water. As the second tumbler filled he thought about what had just occurred and struggled to make sense of it. His upper lip curled, exposing sharp teeth. He did not feel certain enough to broach his thoughts to any of his companions, but neither could he simply dismiss what had happened as inexplicable and set it aside.

Unlike any others in his squad, he had many years ago spent time as a prisoner of war on the contested world of Nura. More remarkably still, in that time he had actually encountered one of the dread Amplitur. It had been inspecting the facility where he and his fellow prisoners had been interned. Pausing before him, it had inclined both eyestalks in his direction. To the day of his death he would be able to visualize those protuberant, glistening orbs hovering close to his twitching face.

Then had come the probe. He'd stood helpless before it, vaguely aware of but unable to resist the intrusion, that gentle violation of his innermost sanctity. For a while the Amplitur had explored his self, unable to read his thoughts but quite capable of interpreting his reactions. Then it had withdrawn and moved on. Other than a patina of uncleanliness which lingered for some time, Gunecvod had incurred no harm as a result of the probe. It was something he would never forget.

It was also something he had never expected to experience again.

Yet he had. Just now. There was no mistaking it. Though mildly, indefinably different, it was sufficiently unmistakable to prohibit confusion.

His first wild, mad thought was that an Amplitur had somehow succeeded in disguising itself as a Human or Massood and slipping onto the sled. Somehow that seemed a feat beyond the reach even of those masters of bioengineering.

His attention returned to the man and woman who had been among those who had suffered as puppets of the Amplitur. They were conversing among themselves, not looking in his direction. He reviewed what he had just experienced, scrutinized the relevant circumstances.

If they were thirsty why did they not fetch their own refreshment? Was there something unseen wrong with their limbs that they should make such a request of a Massood soldier? He had not wanted to comply, yet that was precisely what he was doing. And why?

Because he'd felt compelled to. Not out of friendship, or understanding, or a desire to be of assistance. Out of a brief, seemingly harmless compulsion.

He had served alongside Humans for many years and was familiar with their aspect. He could tell there was no tension in these two. They reposed utterly relaxed in their surroundings. Could they be unaware of what at their urging had just transpired? It seemed unlikely. What had the Amplitur done to them? What had they become?

Yet they and their fellow Restorees had been cleared to rejoin their kind by both Military and Science Command and further, to participate in the forthcoming assault. Against that weight of official evidence he could throw only a transitory suspicion born of unforgettable experience.

It didn't matter. There was no misreading the sensation, no mistaking what had just happened to him. The Humans had suggested and he had responded. They had *pushed*.

Could any of the other Restorees do it? He didn't know and felt it might be hazardous to try and find out. From now on he would carry with him the burden of dangerous knowledge. He would have to watch his back, his movements, his very thoughts lest one of them suspect that they had been found out. Nor could he tell any of his family or friends. They would not believe him, and his accusation would surely get back to those under suspicion. He suspected they might readily take steps to preserve their secret.

He feared the Amplitur, but he feared Humans in possession of Amplitur abilities far more.

It was all up to him, until he could either find the means to prove his theories to others or otherwise rectify the situation. He knew that he had to do one or the other. The danger was real, real in a way only one who had suffered the probing of the Amplitur could appreciate. Others might not understand. It had already been suggested on more than one occasion that his years in captivity had rendered him slightly unbalanced, fit to soldier but not to mate.

They were all wrong. His experience had left him enlightened, not damaged. Now it fell upon him to put that enlightenment to use for the goodness of his kind, for the ultimate benefit of all intelligent species. If these mutations were allowed to spread they would constitute a danger to the Weave greater even than that posed by the

Amplitur. They had to be dealt with. If not by a benighted, ignorant authority, then by one who knew.

If necessary, by soldier Gunecvod acting alone and for the good of all civilization, praise be to the Lineage!

But not now, not in this place. For now he would have to exercise patience. So what he did was gather up the three filled tumblers in his long fingers, still the convulsive twitching of his whiskers and lips, and return to the pair, a pleasant expression cemented in place. If they wanted to talk, he would talk. If they wished to exchange jokes, he would joke with them. He would bend the opportunity to his own needs, use it to learn as much about them as he could. If they tried to push him again, he would not resist. Unless something made them suspicious there would be no danger in succumbing to their suggestions, whereas if he tried to resist there might.

Command did not suspect. Had these Human-Ashregan been developed by the Amplitur so they could then be scattered throughout an ignorant Weave to wreak destruction of unknown dimensions? But they were going to attack the Amplitur's headquarters on Ulaluable. Maybe the entire invasion was nothing more than an Amplitur deception, Gunecvod mused, an elaborate tactical ruse designed solely to allow their Human puppets to "escape" and infiltrate Weave forces.

The Amplitur had infinite patience. Perhaps even their puppets were unaware of what was transpiring, were convinced that the actions they had taken thus far to return to their species were the result of their own discoveries and free will. Perhaps unsuspected mental commands had been implanted deep within their engineered minds, designed to go off next year, a hundred years, from now, when the Amplitur would make known their true and secret intentions and reassert control over their bewildered minions.

These before him might very well fight hard to dislodge Ashregan and Crigolit and Molitar from Ulaluable. And all the while equivocating Amplitur would sit safely in their ships, watching and silently applauding the success of their duplicitous efforts, sacrificing their ignorant unknowing allies in pursuit of some far more intimate, distant goal. It was a plan of great subtlety.

Thanks be to the Lineage that he, Gunecvod, had been clever and wise enough to have discerned it.

This was fortunate, because the man and woman did not, insofar as he was able to tell, try to influence him again. Yet he never doubted, never questioned what had happened, so lucid and powerful had the single experience been.

Ranji and Cossinza were glad of the Massood soldier's company. The need to deal with a representative of another allied race forced them to think of something besides incipient combat, helped to keep their minds off potential unpleasantries.

Gunecvod found them good company, though the woman was much more open and giving of herself than the man. This served to confirm what he had already suspected: that the male was the more dangerous of the pair and would require closer attention. Other Restorees came and went, their furless faces flexing like glutinous putty, their thoughts as closed to him as the feral suppuration of their distinctive endocrinology. Throughout it all he maintained an engaging and salutary attitude, seeking to add all he could to the mental file he was assembling on each and every one of them.

23

The sleds and sliders of the strike force put on maximum acceleration as they went in low and hard. Defensive electronic firecontrols barely had time to react to reports from querulous sensors, plot, aim, and fire before the sleds were racing past, already beyond range of outer defenses. The attackers needed to penetrate as far as possible before the full spectrum of the invaders' weaponry could be brought to bear.

Several near hits rocked the armored sled. Its companion off to the left was slowed by a missile, then fell out of the sky as it intersected the path of a high-energy particle beam. At the speed it was traveling it disintegrated as soon as it struck the unyielding ground, leaving behind a trail of flame, twisted metal, scorched ceramics and plastics, and pieces of its crew, democratically scattered across the gravel-laden surface.

The Massood pilot of Ranji's sled wove a path through the intensifying fire, doing her best to make use of available natural cover. It was no task for a predictable computer, not even one programmed with chaos logic. Fireballs and flaring energy beams singed the air around the agile craft, not quite making contact, not quite destroying.

The invaders had emplaced their installation well, siting major structures against a towering sandstone cliff that restricted approach from east and south. It would have been difficult to hit with aircraft or missiles, and presumptuous air-repulsion vehicles were forced to run a gauntlet of defensive weaponry and sensors located on surrounding buttes and hills. The entire setup was a tribute to typical Crigolit planning and forethought.

In contrast, all the attackers had on their side was boldness and surprise. Initially, those served them quite well.

The surviving sleds and their darting, nimble escorting sliders smashed through the next line of defenses as the startled enemy rushed to assemble its forces.

They were inside the perimeter. Ahead lay sloping sheets of sprayed polymer, fronts for structures which sliced deep into the towering cliff face. There were few windows and at ground level only entrances cut to peculiar Crigolit design. Explosives peeled aside reluctant doors as sleds slowed to land.

Troops fanned out fast, able to race for predetermined objectives thanks to intelligence supplied by the Restorees. Armed defenders began to appear, slowing the assault.

Ranji's group headed for the central communications complex. Years ago he'd assaulted a similar target, on Koba. Only then he had been fighting alongside Ashregan, not Human beings. He who so desperately sought communication and understanding seemed fated to always be disrupting it.

He had no time to remark on the irony: he was too busy trying to stay alive.

Entering through a two-story-high gap their sled's weaponry had blown in the outer wall, they soon encountered resistance. The combined Human-Massood force swept it aside. In some cases the Restorees were able to dupe armed Ashregan into surrendering by addressing them in their own tongue, without the aid of translators. In others and when there were no Massood around, Ranji's colleagues "suggested" that their opponents put down their arms. They did so, with gratifying if not always universal results.

Rushing past the outlying portions of the installation deeper into the mountain, they emerged into a vast supply staging complex. Armed but empty floaters sat in triple ranks, waiting to be fueled and crewed.

While some of the attackers began destroying the irreplaceable transport vehicles, Ranji led his own squad onward, still hoping to locate the communications nerve center. Their advance was periodically stalled by brief but intense firefights.

In order to combat the persistent but isolated and disorganized defenders, Ranji's squad fragmented for flanking purposes, coming together to engulf each pocket of resistance before spreading out again to make contact with those behind.

Weenn suddenly appeared. He was breathing hard and looked concerned. "We're having some trouble over on the other side."

"What kind of trouble?" Ranji asked him as they crouched behind a huge gray Segunian packing cone.

The sub-officer's expression twisted. "It's the Massood. One tried to shoot her squad leader and another tried to shoot himself. We got them both restrained, but barely. When we tried to find out what was going on, they both went comatose on us."

The slim, muscular shadow that was Cossinza hovered nearby, covering the two men as they conversed. "What's he talking about?" Her eyes never left the sighting predictor of her rifle.

"One case of combat madness I could allow for, but not two. They were influenced." Fighting echoed throughout the complex, explosions reverberating, weapons hissing in the enclosed spaces beneath the mountain. He rose alongside her and gazed speculatively into the depths of the staging area.

"There are Amplitur here."

Weenn nodded somberly. "The other Massood figured that out pretty quick."

"Tell our people to keep a close watch on them and on the Hivistahm sled techs. They may have to pull back and leave the rest of the fighting in here to us."

"They realize that," Weenn told him, "but they want to try and stick it out. Their understanding of the danger is balanced by their desire to kill Amplitur. None of them have ever even seen one. They look on it as a real potential coup . . . if they can bring it off without getting their brains turned inside out in the trying."

Ranji chewed his lower lip. "We can't order them out. The other squads must be making real progress for one of the Teach . . . one of the Amplitur to risk itself in combat. It wouldn't do so unless it had no choice. That means there are no back exits to this complex. It's trapped in here.

"You and Tourmast and the others with experience stick close to the Massood. If they show signs of being pushed, use your own abilities to push back. Knock 'em out if you have to. When this is over we'll have some allies with terrific headaches, but at least they'll still be alive."

Weenn looked uncertain. "Won't they suspect?"

"I don't think so. With their thoughts and intentions being jostled in so many different directions at once they won't have time to sort through the confusion. Later they'll ascribe their feelings to Amplitur manipulation under combat conditions. In any case we have no choice. We can't let the Amplitur influence our allies at will."

The sub-officer nodded understanding and hurried to rejoin his own troops.

Despite being fully restored, despite everything Ranji had learned and experienced, it was hard to set aside a lifetime of conditioning. The childhood awe in which he and his friends had held the Teachers lingered in his emotions if not his mind. It wasn't so very long ago that he had stood with pride before his parents and relations in the great hall of Kizzmat, waiting to receive honors from the Teachers themselves. So it was that he advanced uneasily knowing that one of the Amplitur was near. Cossinza was no less edgy.

Defenders and attackers advanced and retreated within the staging area, shooting and screaming imprecations and defiance, transforming the enclosed space into a fiery farrago of death and confusion in which it was difficult to tell friend from foe despite the aid of advanced technology. Occasionally confused but ever courageous, the Massood stumbled forward. It seemed to some among them that the Amplitur were not so effective now as they had been when first their influence had been felt. The evident waning of this particularly insidious threat impelled the tall warriors to greater effort. This in turn further inspired the Humans who fought alongside them.

Both the battle for control of the staging area and communications complex and the one for the minds of the relentless Massood were waged simultaneously. The small group of restored Humans monitored both. For the Amplitur, Ranji mused, confusion must be near complete.

Certainly that was the case for Sigh-moving-Fast. Though to its Ashregan escort the Teacher appeared calm and in complete control of the situation, inwardly their leader was appalled and stunned by what was sensed.

It seemed that individual Massood soldiers were responding readily to suggestion, but after moving on in search of others to push and then reaching back to check on those initially persuaded Sigh-moving-Fast was shocked to discover that their original belligerence had reasserted itself. From this irrefutable and disconcerting conclusions could be drawn.

Something or someone was countermanding his influence.

That unique mind reached out, probing the maelstrom of conflicting thought impulses that energized the room far more thoroughly than could mere primitive weaponry. The notion of a renegade Amplitur was never considered. One might as well anticipate a reversal of entropy.

The Weave had been studying the Amplitur for hundreds of years. Had they finally made their long-hoped-for scientific breakthrough and succeeded in duplicating the Amplitur ability to touch minds via physical instrumentation? If so, then Amplitur counterintelligence was in worse shape than anyone had imagined, for no inkling of any such development had recently been brought to the attention of the ever-alert servants of the Purpose.

Yet what other explanation could there be?

Crigolit and Ashregan kept watch, weapons ready to fend off any attack as they maintained a protective mobile barrier around the single Amplitur. The Teacher had joined the defense of the staging area because it was the only portion of the headquarters complex where the enemy had penetrated dangerously far. If they could drive them out, it would unbalance and possibly signal an end to the entire Weave assault. Hence the willingness, yea, even of a Teacher to expose its august person to the possibility of physical harm. Particularly in such close quarters, a little mental persuasion was worth many guns.

Sigh-moving-Fast tried without success to isolate the source of reactionary influence. To do so effectively and quickly the presence of two additional colleagues was demanded. None were presently available, as they were currently engaged in directing the installation's overall defense. Therefore, the burden of discovering the source of the unexpected interference fell squarely upon Sigh-moving-Fast.

Despite the concern of the mixed-species escort, the Teacher urged them onward, that exceptional mind relentlessly seeking, hoping by accident if not intent to encounter and confront the mystery. Substantial physical and mental differences notwithstanding, Crigolit and Ashregan responded instantly to their leader's orders, forming a seamless unit that gouged a distinctive salient out of the attackers' line, advancing and retreating as though they were all of one mind.

Sigh-moving-Fast's original shock was as nothing compared to the emotions that shook the cephalopodian quadruped when the source of countervaling influence was finally located. It emanated not from some intricate apotheosis of Weave technology but from several of the advancing Human soldiers! A greater horror could not be envisioned.

Alarmed but desperate for elucidating confrontation, the Amplitur bade its anxious escort remain behind, lest their presence induce this special quarry to retreat before vital information could be obtained. Of all the minds working to countermand Amplitur influence, one was noticeably more penetrating and persuasive than the rest, and it was on those thoughts that Sigh-moving-Fast attempted to focus.

Having been slowed by determined resistance, the Weave attack fragmented. It enabled the Teacher to advance without fear of intersecting a large body of enemy troops. By the same token its own path of retreat was far from assured. It was a situation that called for some daring. Understanding of the phenomenon was worth more than control of Ulaluable itself, and without proof even the least sanguine colleagues would be reluctant to believe. Sigh-moving-Fast could scarce credit its own senses.

Could the mind which was so effectively if crudely affecting the thinking of hostile Massood also influence Crigolit, or Ashregan? Sigh-moving-Fast had no way of knowing, but continued to advance quite conscious of how much was at stake. It was vital to the Purpose that at least one such specimen be obtained.

When the disagreeable alien consciousness seemed on the verge of merging with its own, the Amplitur gingerly extended a hesitant mental query. Sigh-moving-Fast knew that if the target was truly Human, the biped's ill-understood neurological defense mechanism might strike back at the probe with paralyzing fury. But no other way could be envisioned. Dangerous or not, this had to be attempted. Without contact there could be no enlightenment. The Teacher extended.

Touched.

Contact engendered no cataclysmic response. Ravening primate insanity did not erupt outward to overwhelm and destroy. A tense Sigh-moving-Fast was calmly elated. This Human and a few like it could mind-touch, but as a consequence of developing that capability it seemed they could no longer instinctively strike back at what they themselves had acquired. In that respect they were as neurologically defenseless as the carefully bioengineered Human-Ashregan soldiers of Cossuut.

At the light-speed of awful realization the import of unpleasant coincidence abruptly replaced the fear in Sigh-moving-Fast's mind.

At present it was no more than a preliminary supposition, but one that could not be dismissed out of hand. It was widely known that a distressingly large number of the special soldiers from Cossuut had been lost in the battle for Ulaluable. It was not impossible that some had survived death. Certain implications of this line of reasoning were most unpleasant. A specimen and answers were demanded—preferably both.

Though skills and ability of long standing were utilized, it was clear that the Human was immune to their influence, just as it was clear that it was unable to retaliate via the fearful reflex all its kind were supposed to possess. This contradiction was full of threat and promise.

Emboldened by continued consciousness, the Amplitur attempted to probe further. Surely there were limits to the depths it could push.

Ranji stiffened slightly and found himself placing his rifle on the floor. Next to him Cossinza was doing the same. Both straightened and took several steps backward.

"Ranji?" she stammered. "You feel it, too?"

"Amplitur," he muttered without hesitation. "Trying to get inside." He squeezed his eyes shut until tears started from the corners. When he opened them again he found he was able to retrace his steps and recover his weapon. With his help she was able to do likewise.

"It's like a commanding headache." She winced. "It hurts, Ranji. I can't make it go away."

"Concentrate on something else," he urged her. "Anything else. Try to push yourself the same as you'd push a Massood or Hivistahm. You have to. Because of Amplitur bioengineering our nervous systems don't have the ability to fight back. You have to resist with your mind." He twitched visibly as a particularly strong probe ventured the suggestion that he stick the muzzle of his weapon in his mouth.

If he could resist with his mind, he thought angrily, perhaps he could strike back the same way.

The Amplitur stumbled, nearly losing its balance, all four legs gone suddenly shaky as the incoming mental blast interrupted the orderly flow of electrical impulses in its brain. Two nearby Crigolit gazed horrified at the half-crumpled Teacher, but Sigh-moving-Fast hastened to inform them that all was well. Thus reassured, they chose to advance to their right, seeking the enemy.

Momentarily left to itself amid grounded vehicles and mountains of supplies, the stunned Amplitur struggled to equiponderate its equilibrium. It was not concerned by its momentary isolation; the Amplitur were quite self-contained, and used to being alone.

It was both shocked and repelled by what had happened. The specimen had struck back. Not in the blind, reflexive fashion of its kind but much as another Amplitur would have. It was a unique development, replete for Sigh-moving-Fast with a deliciously horrific fascination enhanced by the drug of unprecedence. There were no guidelines for what to do next. Procedure would perforce have to be invented from moment to moment.

Using the tentacles on either side of its mouth, the Amplitur steadied itself. Now that its awareness had been raised it would not again be so easily influenced. While briefly effective, the force of the push had been diffused due to a concomitant lack of direction. Its wielder had demonstrated power but not sensitivity, strength but not skill. Talent without experience.

Intrigued beyond caution, Sigh-moving-Fast continued to move forward, heedless of any personal danger. The Teacher kept probing, searching, trying to acquire a feel for attitudes and sensations that finally convinced it of the truth it had suspected: the projective Humans, or at least the pair it was in contact with, were indeed renegades from the Cossuut project. The weight of evidence had finally passed the point of denial.

But how? What had changed them so, what within them had been altered to such an inconceivable degree? Their Ashregan orientation and their desire to serve the Purpose had apparently been destroyed, to be replaced with a restoration of their Humanity . . . and something else. Something more. Explanations *had* to be obtained.

If control, however tenuous, could be established over such gifted individuals, much might become possible. Properly guided and directed, a Human who could push, could suggest, would be far more valuable than one simply educated to believe it was Ashregan. Slipped back in among their own kind they could wield influence enough to advance the cause of the Purpose by hundreds of years.

From the first moment of contact Sigh-moving-Fast had sensed that great possibilities were in the offing. Awareness induced in the clumsy, bulky form a permeating wellness. Resolve was strengthened.

At approximately that time a new, third mental presence impinged on Sigh-moving-Fast's consciousness: a Massood, hyper with xenocidal ferocity. What startled the Amplitur to the point at which it was necessary to pause and analyze was that the Massood's hostility was directed not toward any of the enemy but at the Humans around him, and in particular the two Humans with whom Sigh-moving-Fast was already in contact.

Astonishingly, therefore, the modified male and female were being stalked by enemy and ally alike. Why this should be so could not be imagined. Anxiously seeking answers, the Teacher had unearthed only another question.

The Amplitur had survived and prospered by bending evolution itself to their needs. Sigh-moving-Fast did not hesitate to reach out and touch the mind of the new arrival, inducing synapses to fire in a desired pattern. There was hesitation on the part of the Massood, then a resumption of movement.

While quite capable of proceeding alone, Sigh-moving-Fast was perfectly happy to make use of whatever tools might happen to proffer themselves.

Gunecvod ducked behind a towering ceramic cylinder the color of rotting teeth. Inclining his lanky six-foot-six-inch frame slightly to the right, he was able to see the two Humans where they crouched behind cover of their own. Around him the vast staging chamber was still afire with death and destruction.

Several other preoccupied Massood darted forward to the left and behind him. At the moment they and the two Humans were the only other ones in sight.

His quarry had not observed his approach. Whiskers twitched

violently as his lips drew back to expose his full complement of teeth. Now was the moment to end the threat to civilization, to protect his own kind! Raising his rifle, he took careful aim at the female, letting the automatic sight lock in on the back of her skull.

He hesitated.

Something was not right. The Humans looked alert, but not as though they were keeping watch for advancing enemy. They held their weapons casually, almost indifferently. Yet their attitudes were completely focused. It was not only unnatural and unsoldierly, based on all that Gunecvod had observed of the primates previously; it was quite inHuman.

The female staggered, clasping her head in both hands. Gunecvod growled in astonishment as her companion *laid his weapon aside* and moved to embrace her comfortingly. His fingers quivered near the trigger as he temporarily disengaged the sight lock. What was going on here?

Until he found out it might be better simply to wound, to incapacitate them. The three of them were isolated in this corner of the staging chamber. He would have time for hasty but effective interrogation. His knowledge of Human physiology would permit that.

He raised his rifle a second time. As he did so fresh thoughts rippled unbidden through his mind. Was he going mad? The threat needed to be terminated, not studied. He was in a combat situation, not a lab. He wondered at his hesitation, at the second thoughts.

He was certain the Humans were not the source of his confusion. There was no guile in their indifference. They were truly unaware of his presence, much less his resolve. Why then this sudden faltering? His thoughts were at war with his intentions, and the result was most disturbing.

Trembling with the effort it required, he stepped out from behind the cylinder and advanced slowly. His spasms and contortions were not the product of normal Massood hyperactivity. The rifle's muzzle swung through wild arcs, as if it had taken on a life of its own. Gunecvod gave every appearance of a creature fighting desperately for control of its own neuromuscular system.

Out of the corner of an eye Ranji saw the Massood approach. He turned, a startled expression slowly spreading across his face as he watched the swaying soldier aim his rifle.

As Gunecvod touched the trigger a flurry of tiny contradictions seemed to explode inside his brain, blurring his determination along with his vision. The shot went wild.

Cossinza was right behind Ranji as he dove between stacks of metal tubes. She was not quite quick enough. The second energy bolt struck her hip and was only partly dissipated by her light armor. She didn't collapse so much as sit down heavily.

He'd only wounded her, Gunecvod saw. Excellent! decreed one part of his brain. Horribly inadequate, insisted another. Grabbing his forehead as if he could somehow squeeze out the confusion that was tearing him apart, the snarling soldier fired again in the male's direction.

The shot struck nowhere near the retreating Ranji. Warily hefting his sidearm, he turned up the amplification on his translator.

"Soldier, are you out of your mind? Have you forgotten your Lineage? I'm Special Staff Officer Ranji-aar, temporarily assigned to the 84th HS battlegroup!"

"I know who you are!" the Massood's translator roared. It was loud, but not as loud as the pain in his head. He staggered but stayed erect. "I know all about you!"

Ranji was not very familiar with Massood mannerisms, but it was clear enough that this particular individual was unbalanced. Right now the sole objective must be to distract him and draw him away from the injured Cossinza.

"We're Human! We're your friends, your allies."

The Massood bared sharp teeth, resisting the pounding in his skull as he scanned his surroundings. "Not you, Ranji-aar! Not you and your mutant friends! You have to die, all of you. You are too dangerous to let live. You may have fooled everyone else, but not I, not Gunecvod! I know you for what you are, offspring of the Amplitur. I will not let you play with my mind. I defy you!" Cossinza flattened herself against the floor and covered her head as the soldier fired blindly into the stacks of supplies and equipment, his rifle crackling.

"You're crazy!" Ranji kept moving as he spoke.

Gunecvod whirled and scorched the floor where his quarry had been standing an instant earlier. Wheezing Massood laughter bubbled from his throat.

"I think not. I know what you can do because you've done it to me. The water. Remember the water!" He fired again, obliterating a stack of lubricating injectors. Alien stink stained the air.

"Even if you're not imagining things, what does it matter?" Ranji yelled from cover. "We're Human, we're your allies!"

Gunecvod turned slowly, searching. "Are you? I do not know what you are. I know only what you can do, and that cannot be allowed. Cannot! You have to die. All of you have to die."

Abruptly Ranji realized what must have happened. "Listen to me, Gunecvod of the Massood! This isn't you thinking, these aren't your thoughts. I know that there's an Amplitur close by. That's who wants us dead. *That's* why you're acting like this!"

Gunecvod stood swaying, blinking uneasily. The Human was trying to trick him. The decisions he'd reached had been arrived at well beyond the range of Amplitur influence. What *if* one of them was nearby? It didn't matter. Certainly the creature would delight in seeing one ally kill another . . . but he'd determined that these modified Humans were not allies, could not be allowed to live. If that put him on the side of the Amplitur, it was only temporary and coincidental . . . wasn't it? He reached up and pressed long fingers against the side of his skull. Kill, wound only, support . . . there was too much going on inside his brain. Cognitive space was limited, perception was limited, reality was far too open to speculation.

What was happening to him? Which of his thoughts were his, which those of the modified Human, which those of the Amplitur? They were crowding him out, these irresistibly subtle deep probers, shoving the mere proprietor of the mental field of battle aside. When they had concluded their contest and one had emerged the master of persuasion, would there by anything left of Gunecvod? Truth eluded him like a fast-moving insect.

A cross between a scream and a sob emerged from his trembling mouth. His nose twitched uncontrollably, and spittle dripped from the lower jaw.

Taking a calculated chance, Ranji slowly rose from behind the replacement landing skid he'd been using for cover.

"Look at me, Gunecvod of the Massood. I'm Human. I'm your friend. It's the Amplitur who's putting these evil thoughts in your head."

"No!" The end of the rifle gyrated. "No, I made up my mind before this! My own mind. I reached conclusions. I vowed . . . I . . ."

"There are only a few of us." Ranji stood ready to dive behind the protective skid again if the muzzle of the weapon rose any higher. "I won't deny that we can do . . . certain things. That doesn't make us any less an ally of the Massood. Are you so sure that we're dangerous to you? Are you completely convinced? Think, Gunecvod! We could be the *critical link* in the ultimate destruction of the Amplitur. In saving your own people from the Purpose. Don't throw that chance away. Who are you to make a decision of that scope?"

"Who am I?" Gunecvod blinked as he attempted to focus painful consideration on the suddenly confusing subject. "I am . . . I am . . ."

It was true. He was only a simple soldier. Not a S'van, not a Turlog. An ordinary warrior of unspectacular lineage.

Was that movement behind him? He whirled, searching wildly for bulging eyes on weaving stalks, for a large, soft body armed with questing tentacles and irresistible thoughts. Alone; he was so *alone*. With his wavering determination, with his cataclysmic thoughts.

The Human female lay nearby, half-paralyzed by his weapon. He took a wavering step toward her. "I . . . I am sorry. I do not understand, I didn't . . ."

She looked up at him, anxiety and compassion colliding in her expression. "I understand. You didn't know what you were doing. It's all right." She looked sharply to her left. "There *is* an Amplitur here."

Suddenly he was very calm. He knew, with the clarity of perfect certainty, exactly what it was he had to do. He raised the muzzle of his rifle. Behind him, a reluctant Ranji drew his sidearm and aimed.

As Cossinza screamed good soldier Gunecvod gripped the muzzle of his weapon in his teeth and, as a warm and welcoming peace took possession of him, thumbed the trigger.

She was still staring at the smoking body when Ranji knelt beside her. "I didn't mean for him to do that. I didn't mean for that to happen. When I reached out to him I was just trying to make him feel better, to ease the pain that was tormenting him and making him act this way."

He helped her find a place to sit up. "Meanwhile I was pushing him to withdraw and the Amplitur was pushing him to shoot, and in the midst of all that you hit him with a double dose of sympathy and understanding, the one thing he wasn't expecting and didn't know how to handle. The contradiction between what he started out to do and what he was feeling from you was too much for him. He couldn't take it anymore." He glanced in the corpse's direction.

"I guess he was tired of arguing with himself, of trying to decide which were his thoughts and which were being imposed from outside. So he resolved it the easy way. Damn. This wasn't what I wanted." He rose to survey their surroundings.

"You need medical attention. This far out in front I'd rather not use a communicator. Might be picked up and targeted by the other side." He eyed her speculatively. "I could carry you."

She shook her head. "Fighting's moved deeper into the mountain. Hand me my rifle." He did so and she cradled it in her lap. "You can find help a lot faster without me. I'll be all right here."

"Sure?"

She managed a wan smile. "Just don't stop for a sandwich on the way back."

He nodded, turned, and started off toward what he hoped was the center of the advancing Weave force.

24

Twenty strides and several thoughts later he rounded a corner . . . and there it was. A glistening, glutinous shape resembling a shift loader encased in amber. One eyestalk and one quadruple-digited tentacle swung lazily toward him. Horny mouthparts clacked rhythmically while iridescent blobs of color pulsed and contracted within the smooth epidermis, chromatic indicators of their progenitor's emotional state.

Once it had been an object of respect; indeed, veneration. A Teacher. Now it was as alien to him as a living creature could be. In place of the visceral hatred that veneered his spirit old memories, old teachings, old admiration threatened to overwhelm him.

He blinked, smiling to himself. Cold realization burst the narcotizing bubble of nostalgia.

You move fast, he thought, *but that won't work on me. Not now. Not anymore. I'm ready for you. My whole life has been spent preparing for this.*

Having identified Ranji as one of those unsettling modified Cossuutian Humans capable of pushing, the Amplitur followed its reflexive defensive reaction with more subtle suggestions. Why did Ranji fight so hard to deny his heritage? Why not allow the pain to be banished? Follow and return. Abandon this foolishness, the confusion that was tormenting him. Return to the peace of the Purpose. The harmonizing, calming, reassuring tranquillity of the Purpose.

Ranji felt as if someone were trying to stuff his head full of thick, cottony insulation, to muffle not only sound but thought. He swayed slightly but held his ground, neither advancing nor retreating. *Cossinza needed medical attention.* A moment ago that single thought had commanded his actions. Now it was fusing with a pastel mental bubble as inconclusive as a drunken sunset, its importance muted by unanticipated indecision. He felt he would need all the concentration he could muster, every iota of energy, simply to move his limbs of his own volition.

How had this happened, Sigh-moving-Fast wondered? Where had the great experiment failed, and whence this extraordinary and utterly unexpected biological development? Of one thing there was certainty: this remarkable individual had to be obtained for study, alive and intact. Alongside that the taking of Ulaluable faded into insignificance.

The Human appeared poised to flee. While simultaneously reaching, pushing, cajoling with its mind, the Amplitur spoke aloud, utilizing the translator positioned beneath its mouthparts. Anything to hold the biped within range.

"Stop! I know what you are, Human. You must come with me."

A hesitant Ranji slowly shook his head, a gesture the Amplitur sadly recognized as Human and not Ashregan. "My companion is injured and needs help."

"Come with me," said the Amplitur soothingly. "Medical assistance will be provided, wellness guaranteed."

"The kind of wellness you brought to the real world of my birth? No thanks." He was smiling now. Aware of what the Amplitur was trying to do, he was able to resist, brush it aside, fight it off. "You can't do anything to me or mine anymore. Your experiment is a failure. We're going to beat you, you know. Maybe not in my lifetime, maybe not in my children's, but the end is inevitable."

"All that is inevitable is the triumph of the Purpose." The Amplitur sounded tired. "Do you not realize that when they learn of your capabilities your own allies will annihilate you? Just as the single Massood intended?"

"This is all still new to us and we were lazy. That's what made the soldier suspect. It won't happen again. We'll be careful."

"Be careful as you will; such power cannot be concealed forever. I implore you: share what you have become, share your great and accidental gift, with those who best understand its import. We can teach you, show you how properly to make use of it. You and your kind can still be part of the Purpose. A vital part."

"No thanks. I don't want to be a part of anything anymore, except Humanity and eventually a family. Keep your damned Purpose. I prefer independence. I prefer Humanity. I prefer *me*."

"That is unfortunate. You and those like you are dangerous. You must be studied, appropriately supervised, and if that is not possible, contained."

"Sorry. Some of us are out of the cage you built for us, and we're not going back in. You can't stop me. If you could I'd be following you meekly back to your lines right now."

"You are wrong." The Amplitur reached into the pouch that was slung between its head and forelegs and extracted a small angular plastic shape. Ranji couldn't keep himself from staring.

"What is an Amplitur, the self-proclaimed epitome of higher civilization, doing with a *gun?*"

"I am not sure. This is quite an anomaly, is it not? But the gun is real. It feels real to me. If I am compelled to use it the effects will be real to you. So you see, you are after all my prisoner."

"You won't use that on me," Ranji observed firmly. "You're not capable of it."

The Amplitur pointed the pistol at a stack of small oblong crates and fired. The crates exploded.

"You know that my eyesight is excellent. It is equal to my resolve. You will come with me voluntarily or if need be I will destroy your limbs and drag you."

"This is very un-Teacherlike behavior," Ranji commented, trying to determine his next move.

"These are very unusual circumstances. Extensive mental discipline and training allows me to temporarily subvert those natural inhibitions which would paralyze a Hivistahm or T'returian caught in a similar situation. Externally I realize that my actions verge on the unstable, yet through the Purpose I am able to overcome this. Presently I am functioning within a self-induced psychosis.

"The actual methodology of the cerebroethical gymnastics required to accomplish this remarkable feat need not concern you. Concentrate instead on the weapon and the danger to your person, and respond appropriately to my instructions."

Ranji eyed the gun, thinking hard. "I'm not going anywhere without Cossinza."

"By the Wellness, bring her. I calculate that you possess the necessary physical attributes and the distance is not far. I promise you that she will receive immediate and expert medical attention."

Could he make it to cover? How much of the Amplitur's threat was backed by resolve and how much was bluff? Judging from the brief demonstration, the tiny gun was powerful enough to blow his legs off at the knees. Of course, the Amplitur could regenerate them later, but that didn't make the prospect any less pleasant.

In any civilized being thought must precede action. The homily was nonetheless applicable for all that it was Teacher training. Ranji put up his hands.

"All right. I'll go with you. Anything to help Cossinza."

"Now that," said the Amplitur as it gestured with the gun-wielding tentacle, "is a sensible response."

Ranji approached the Teacher. "Have any of you ever remarked on the cyclical nature of your reasoning? 'The Purpose is everything, so anything can be used to justify the Purpose.' "

"Humankind is a young race, and therefore prone to oversimplification. But I have great confidence. With proper education you will mature."

"What you call education I've learned through bitter revelation is something else. You utilize the same tortured logic to cripple semantics as you do independent thought."

"Both of you, freeze!"

Eyes on stalks and eyes in sockets looked leftward. A single Human soldier stood behind a loading ramp, his heavy cassion rifle trained in their direction. He was male, young, confused, and scared. The bad combination froze Ranji immediately.

The heavily armed youth was staring wide-eyed through his visor at the Amplitur. "I heard about the squids. I studied 'em. But I swear to Gaea I never thought I'd see one in person."

A field soldier's thought processes are necessarily straightforward. To him the relative positions and spatial relationships of gun, tentacle, and hands were all the explanation the tableaux before him required. He addressed Ranji without taking his eyes off the Amplitur.

"Are you all right, sir?"

Ranji turned slowly. "No problem."

"You there, thing. You're my prisoner. Put down your weapon." His finger was taut on the rifle's trigger, the muzzle focused unswervingly between the two eyestalks.

Sigh-moving-Fast hesitated, trying to apportion attention between the mature Human and the young warrior. Two subtentacular digits tensed on the firing mechanism of the angular pistol.

Ranji saw. Too far to jump. His stomach contracted to a small, hard ball.

"You're just in time, Tourmast," he said quickly. "It knows all about us."

Instantly the Amplitur's mental focus shifted fully from the prisoner to the newcomer, hoping to mute hostile thoughts and induce the Restoree to lay his rifle aside. If necessary it would try to push first one, then the other. At worst, if the soldier started to fire then Sigh-moving-Fast could still react rapidly enough to kill one if not both of them. A forceful probe impinged on the soldier's mind.

It brought forth a cataclysmic shriek of raw, uncontrolled energy, a concentrated eruption of fear, horror, loathing, and primitive primate hatred. The Amplitur shook violently. All four legs gave way simultaneously and it collapsed, managing to get off a single shot before blacking out. The pistol's explosive shell blew a hole in the staging chamber's distant ceiling.

Startled, the soldier had also fired once, missing badly. Now he leaned up against a fuel cell of Segunian design, his rifle dangling from one hand as he flipped up his armor visor with one hand and pressed against his forehead with the other. Sweat poured through his fingers.

Ranji had thrown himself to the floor. After checking to make sure he hadn't been hit, he rose and approached the flaccid body of the Teacher. Limp, rubbery tentacle-tips yielded control of the handgun.

Walking up to the fuel cell, he put a comforting arm around the younger man's shoulders.

"Shit." The soldier shakily set his rifle aside and cradled his head in both hands.

"Bad?" Ranji inquired solicitously.

"Going away now." The younger man took several measured deep breaths. "I heard about that, too." He nodded in the Amplitur's direction. "Not going anywhere soon, is it?"

"Not for a while, no."

"Good." He shuddered slightly at the memory of it. The sensation was slipping away like foam on a befouled tide. "Creepy, when it tries to get inside your mind like that. Feels . . . unclean. Like the most embarrassing thing that's ever happened to you blown up a thousand times bigger for everyone to see. Didn't it know something like this would happen if it tried that?"

Ranji regarded the slack, comatose alien form. "It thought you were something else."

The soldier's gaze narrowed. "Some*thing* else? And who's this Tourmast character?"

"Someone else. Why don't you take charge of our prisoner here?"

"What, me?"

"Amplitur prisoners are pretty rare. You'll probably get a promotion out of it, maybe even a commendation." Ranji looked past him. "Where's the rest of your unit? I've got an injured colleague and I'd rather not use a communicator to call for help this near to enemy hostiles."

"They should be over that way, sir." The soldier adjusted the communicator built into his visor. "Enemy's been pushed back pretty far. I think we're safe in calling in."

Ranji considered, then nodded. "I'll rely on your judgment. I'll go tell my friend help is on its way. We're back over here." He pointed, and the younger man indicated his understanding.

Lying immobile on its side, the Amplitur didn't look very frightening, the trooper reflected as he studied his prisoner. Soft and slow. One bulging, golden eye gazed vacantly in his direction. It was about the ugliest thing he'd ever seen, and since he'd joined up with the Human battleforce that was aiding the Weave he'd encountered some remarkably ugly things. Ashregan, Crigolit, Molitar, Acuria, Massood and Hivistahm, Wais and Lepar. Ally or enemy, it didn't much matter. Each was a greater paragon of ugliness than the next, and he wasn't especially enamored of the facial features of some of his drinking buddies, either.

He shifted his rifle to a more comfortable position, pleased that like the rest of his friends back home he'd chosen to take part in the great conflict. What more could a man want out of life than the opportunity to eliminate some of the ugliness from the universe?

The Amplitur sensed that its paralysis would fade, but until then it would have to suffer the feral attention of the biped as well as a certain amount of physical discomfort. Unable to move more than a few extremities, Sigh-moving-Fast shifted one eye to track the departure of the Human Restoree. There was no help to be had, no other brethren within range. It had taken but a moment for its personal status to change from that of captor to captive.

Tricked, and cleverly so. The Restoree had seen and seized a chance to make use of Sigh-moving-Fast's unfamiliarity with combat conditions. But in his haste to aid and comfort an injured companion the Human had forgotten one thing. Secrets could still be divulged, confusion spread, discord sowed.

"Listen to me." The translator croaked enticingly. "That man is no longer wholly Human. He has been changed. He is now more like me than you."

"Yeah, right." The soldier's expression was pensive.

"This is true! He has been modified. First by my kind, subsequently by something else. He can influence minds; he can push, just as can I. He is dangerous."

"You're telling me. All of us Human folk're dangerous, squid. As you're finding out. You know, I picked up a lot about your species in studies, but they never told me you had a sense of humor."

"You must believe me!" The primitive biped's indifference to logic was infuriating. "If you have studied my kind, then you know we are incapable of prevarication."

"Unless that's a lie, too. Our specialists don't completely trust everything the Weave tells 'em. One thing they're far from sure about is you. Don't know enough about you yet to be sure of anything. So they're withholding judgment." He gestured with the tip of the cassion rifle. "So am I. If you want to turn me against one of my own kind, you're gonna have to dream up something a lot less silly than that."

Sigh-moving-Fast raged impotently, but try as he might, he was unable to give the Restorees' secret away.

The Weave strike force took the headquarters complex, capturing or killing all but a few of its inhabitants. Human and then Hivistahm physicians dealt efficiently with Cossinza's injury. With the aid of an implanted neuromuscular stimulator, she was up and walking within a few days.

He'd always been able to talk to Saguio, Ranji knew, but this was different. It was wonderful to finally have someone to share with, in matters of intimacy as well as friendship. Cossinza did more than merely listen. She *understood*. Heida Trondheim had been sympathetic, but no more. What existed now between him and Cossinza went much deeper. He felt fulfilled.

With time now to relax a little and contemplate things besides combat, other Restorees were also pairing off, developing liaisons, getting to know one another. The special characteristic they shared made it natural as well as necessary.

Their secret remained inviolate. The one Amplitur who had learned the truth had made a desperate break for freedom while being escorted from the captured staging chamber to a waiting sled, only to be shot down by impulsive Human guards before the officer in charge could intervene. It perished ranting, spouting mental and verbal gibberish about unsuspected threats to the stability of civilization. The exact nature of its dying diatribe went unreported, as no recorders happened to be operating in the vicinity at the time.

Wherever they were sent, the Restorees would have to stay in contact with one another, Ranji knew. To report any changes or permutations in the Talent, as they had come to call it; to provide support and understanding for one another; to better assist other deceived and debased Cossuutians in regaining their stolen birthrights, and so they could, if and when necessary, act in concert.

It was good to be Human and have Human friends, he knew. Assuming he and his fellow Restorees *were* Human, and would not become something else. Actual determination of that was going to take time. He was certain they had much to learn.

For example, had the severed neural connections between the Amplitur nexus and the rest of his brain ceased growing? That was but one of many things that would have to be watched.

I am mine own experiment, he thought. As such he intended to monitor its progress very carefully.

Their plan and intentions exposed, the Amplitur abandoned the great project on Cossuut. Their modified fighters could no longer be trusted in battle, not when every opponent knew and could reveal to them the truth of their origins. Many died natural deaths on that unhappy world, until the end believing themselves to be Ashregan. Others perished in battle. The fortunate ones were captured.

As was only natural, following the requisite surgery the newly Restored were assigned for repatriation to a reeducation group composed of fellow Restorees.

After participation in many battles, Ranji and Cossinza and those of their friends who had survived multitudinous conflict were retired with full honors, the grateful sympathy of the Weave, and the melancholy compassion of their kind. The name of their true devastated homeworld became yet another in a long line of rallying cries and watchwords by which the soldiers of the Weave fought.

In due time offspring were born to those who had survived the ministrations of the Amplitur. They appeared in every way to be normal, healthy children.

Their parents monitored their maturation with the utmost care.

ABOUT THE AUTHOR

Born in New York City in 1946, Alan Dean Foster was raised in Los Angeles, California. After receiving a bachelor's degree in political science and a Master of Fine Arts in motion pictures from UCLA in 1968–1969, he worked for two years as a public relations copywriter in a small Studio City, California, firm.

His writing career began in 1968 when August Derleth bought a long letter of Foster's and published it as a short story in his biannual *Arkham Collector Magazine*. Sales of short fiction to other magazines followed. His first try at a novel, *The Tar-Aiym Krang*, was published by Ballantine Books in 1972.

Foster has toured extensively around the world. Besides traveling, he enjoys classical and rock music, old films, basketball, body surfing, scuba diving, and weight lifting. He has taught screenwriting, literature, and film history at UCLA and Los Angeles City College.

Currently, he lives in Arizona.